Joanna Wayne began her professional writing career in 1994. Now, more than fifty published books later, Joanna has gained a worldwide following with her cutting-edge romantic suspense and Texas family series, such as Sons of Troy Ledger and Big "D" Dads. Joanna currently resides in a small community north of Houston, Texas, with her husband. You may write Joanna at PO Box 852, Montgomery, Texas 77356, or connect with her at joannawayne.com.

Books by Joanna Wayne

Harlequin Intrigue

Big "D" Dads: The Daltons

Trumped Up Charges

Unrepentant Cowboy

Hard Ride to Dry Gulch

Midnight Rider

Showdown at Shadow Junction

Sons of Troy Ledger

Cowboy Swagger

Genuine Cowboy

AK-Cowboy

Cowboy Fever

Cowboy Conspiracy

Big "D" Dads

Son of a Gun

Live Ammo

Big Shot

Visit the Author Profile page at Harlequin.com for more titles.

Joanna Wayne
and
Linda Warren

COWBOY FEVER
&
TOMAS: COWBOY HOMECOMING

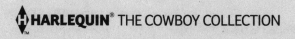

HARLEQUIN® THE COWBOY COLLECTION

Recycling programs
for this product may
not exist in your area.

ISBN-13: 978-0-373-60146-2

Cowboy Fever & Tomas: Cowboy Homecoming

Copyright © 2015 by Harlequin Books S.A.

The publisher acknowledges the copyright holder
of the individual works as follows:

Cowboy Fever
Copyright © 2011 by Jo Ann Vest

Tomas: Cowboy Homecoming
Copyright © 2012 by Linda Warren

Printed in U.S.A.

www.Harlequin.com

CONTENTS

COWBOY FEVER

Joanna Wayne

To our good friends the Mitchells.
Always nice to have you two around
to catch a movie with when I need a break
from the computer. And a hug to Wayne
for enduring my deadlines.

CHAPTER ONE

DAKOTA LEDGER WAS back in Texas and the heat was on. Sweat rolled down his back and pooled at his armpits, staining his lucky red Western shirt. The smell of livestock and manure permeated the still air. "All My Ex's Live in Texas" blared from an aging sound system. The edgy excitement of competition was electric in the stifling June air.

"Gotta love bull riding in San Antonio."

Dakota turned to the youthful cowboy who was grinning like a puppy with a new bone. "What's so special about San Antonio?" Dakota asked.

"I qualified for the competition."

"That'll do it."

Dakota didn't know the rider's real name, but even though he was relatively new to the Professional Bull Riders Association circuit, he'd already earned a nickname. "Cockroach" stemmed from the way he scurried out of the reach of a bull's kicking hooves. It was a great talent to have if you wanted to keep living with all parts working.

Cockroach rubbed his palms against his chaps. "This is my first year to compete in PBR-sanctioned events, so I'm a little nervous."

"The adrenaline will take care of that once you drop onto the bull's back."

"I'm counting on that." Cockroach adjusted his hat. "One day I hope to be the PBRA world champion, just like you were two years ago. A million-dollar purse. I could use that. Not to mention all those endorsements you have."

"Bull riding's not about the money."

"I know." Cockroach toed the dirt as if putting out a cigarette. "It's a long, hard ride from the bottom to the top, but I plan to be one of the few who make it."

"Persistence is a large part of the battle," Dakota agreed.

"And skill is the rest," Cockroach said.

"Skill, passion and luck," Dakota corrected. "You gotta love what you're doing. And you gotta stay alive to keep doing it."

Cockroach reached down and adjusted his right spur. "Have you ever been seriously hurt?"

"Never met a bull rider who hasn't. I've had cracked ribs, concussions, a broken right wrist and bruises probably on every inch of my body."

"Hey, Dakota. Looking good."

Dakota turned toward the railing that separated the paid attendees from the competitors. A group of young women were leaning over the railing, probably not a one of them over twenty years old. Not that he was all that much older at twenty-five, but he sure felt it.

Still, he tipped his hat and smiled.

"Your friend's cute, too," one of the females called.

Cockroach beamed, turned a tad red and tipped his hat to his vocal admirer.

"What's your favorite rodeo town?" Cockroach asked when he turned back to Dakota.

Dakota nudged his worn Stetson back from his forehead. It damn sure wasn't San Antonio or any other town within five hundred miles of here, but he wasn't getting into that.

"Doesn't really matter where you are. It always comes down to just you, the bull and the clock."

"Can't be the same in places like Montana. I mean look at those hot babes over there. Short shorts, halter tops, sun-streaked hair and all that luscious tanned flesh. Bet you don't get that in cold country."

"They've got hot buckle bunnies every place they've got rodeo competitions," Dakota assured him. "The names change. The flirting and seduction games remain the same."

At least that had been true for him until he'd run into a certain dark-haired beauty with class and brains after a bull got the best of him last year at Rodeo Houston. The attraction between them had struck like lightning, shooting sparks without warning. They'd had six days together before he'd had to move on to the next competition. Six torrid, exciting, fantastic days.

End of story. He hadn't been the one to write the finale. The rejection had stung a lot more than expected. His performance level had taken a drastic drop for several months after that. He could thank Viviana—along with a couple of injuries—that he didn't even make it to the championship finals last year.

Dakota turned back to the circle of dirt where he'd face tonight's battle. Letting anything interfere with your concentration was suicide for a bull rider.

Which was why he should have never come back to Texas. Even before he'd met Viviana, the odds here were stacked against him. The Ledger name was infamous in the Lone Star State and that had nothing to do with his reputation with the bulls.

Nineteen years after the fact, the brutal murder of Dakota's mother was still being written and talked about in this area of Texas. She'd been shot at home, in a ranch house less than a hundred miles from where he stood right now.

His father, Troy, had been convicted of the crime. Dakota had been six years old at the time.

Luckily, questions about his past hadn't come up today in his interviews with the local media. All they'd focused on was taking pictures and asking him about his success. He suspected that was because the competition's organizers had told them any mention of Troy Ledger was off-limits.

Cockroach got the signal to head toward the chute. He looked over to the female cheering squad and tipped his hat before swaggering toward the bucking, snorting beast that was already fighting to clear the chute.

"Remember, it's just you and the bull," Dakota shouted after him. Six seconds into the ride, the bull bucked and veered to the left. Cockroach was thrown off. Fortunately, it was his hat and not his head that got entangled with the bull's hooves. True to his nickname, the cowboy got out of the way while Jim Angle distracted the indignant animal.

Jim was one of the rodeo clown greats. It had been Jim Angle who'd saved Dakota from getting seriously injured back in Houston the night he'd met Viviana. The past attacked again, this time so strong Dakota couldn't shut the memories down.

Images of Viviana filled his head. Dark, curly hair

that fell to her slender shoulders. Full, sensual lips. Eyes a man could drown in. A touch that had set him on fire.

Damn. If he didn't clear his mind, he'd never hang on for the full eight seconds, and he needed a good showing tonight to make it to the final round in this event tomorrow. A rider couldn't rest on past laurels and the competition got tougher every year.

He'd drawn the meanest of the rough stock tonight. That was half the battle to getting a high score. The other half was up to Dakota.

He was the last rider of the evening and he worked to psyche himself up as the other contenders got their shot at racking up points. As his turn drew near, he fit the leather glove on his riding hand and one of the other riders helped him tape it in place. The resin came next, just enough to improve his grip. Then he climbed onto the chute. It was time for action.

A rush of adrenaline shot through him as he gripped his worn and trusty bull rope and felt the 1700-pound bull buck beneath him. It would be a hell of a ride. The crowd was with him. Their cheers pounded in his head, their voices an indistinguishable roar.

"Hey, Ledger. We don't like murderers around here."

Unlike the cheers, the taunt was distinct. Cutting. Jagged.

The gate clanked open and Devil's Deed charged from the chute.

In what seemed like a heartbeat, the bull went into a belly roll and Dakota went sailing through the air. His right shoulder ground into the hard earth. A kicking hoof collided with his ribs as he tried to scramble to safety.

Pain shot through him like a bullet.

Yep. He was home.

CHAPTER TWO

"STAT. AMBULANCE EN ROUTE."

Dr. Mancini looked up at the male E.R. nurse delivering the news.

"And I so needed this cup of coffee."

"I know. It's been murder in here tonight. Must be the full moon."

"More likely that I volunteered to pull Dr. Cairn's shift for her." She took a large gulp of the much-needed caffeine. "Nature of the emergency?" she asked, shifting her brain to work mode.

"Gunshot wound to the head. Critical blood loss. Vitals at life-threatening levels. "

There went her last chance of getting home on time and relieving the nanny tonight. "Any other details?"

"Caucasian male, likely early twenties, picked up in the back parking lot of a bar in the downtown area. Expected arrival…" He glanced at his watch. "Any minute."

"Alert the nurse assigned to the shock trauma center and also Dr. Evans."

"I'm on it."

She was glad Dan Evans was on duty tonight. He was one of the top neurosurgeons in Texas. "Also alert the O.R.," she called to the departing nurse.

Fatigue was forgotten as she hurried down the halls

to the trauma unit. They'd already lost one patient to-night. Hopefully, they'd save this one.

"Dr. Mancini."

She recognized the voice. Police Detective Harry Cortez, or Dirty Harry, as she'd come to think of him. Not because of his toughness—though she expected he was plenty tough—but because the front of his shirt always bore testimony to his latest meal.

"If you're here about the patient with the gunshot wound, you'll have to wait. I haven't seen him as yet."

His eyes narrowed. "You have a patient with a gun-shot wound?"

"Arriving as we speak, but don't even think about questioning him until I give you clearance. This is a hospital, not the police station."

"I'm only doing my job, just like you, Doctor. Be-sides, I'm here to talk to you about Hank Bateman."

Mention of the name filled her with disgust. "We'll have to talk later."

The squeak of a gurney's wheels came from near the E.R. entrance. She raced toward the trauma center. The slap of the detective's street shoes on the tiled floor sig-naled he was right behind her.

She was sliding her long fingers into a pair of sterile gloves when she heard the detective's voice outside the examining room.

"Who shot you? C'mon. Name the bastard. He won't come after you again. I'll see to it. Just give me the name."

She walked to the door as the patient was rolled in. She shot a stern warning look at Cortez, and he waved in surrender and backed away.

One look at the patient and her stomach rolled. She

should be desensitized by now, but the sight of bloody tissue oozing from the skull was not the kind of thing she'd ever get used to. The victim's chance of survival was next to zero. The miracle was that he had lived to make it to the hospital.

The young man coughed, and blood mixed with spittle spilled from his lips. His mouth kept moving. He was trying to say something. She leaned in close, but the gurgled murmurings were too garbled to understand.

"I'm Dr. Mancini," she said as she helped the nurse get him hooked up to the heart monitor. "I'll try to ease your pain."

"And I'm Dr. Evans," the young neurosurgeon said as he joined them.

The patient coughed again, this time choking on the blood.

"Shhh… Shell…"

She leaned in close. "Are you trying to tell me who shot you?"

Before he could nod or mumble a reply, the line on the monitor went flat.

"Either you go to the emergency room by ambulance or I drive you," Jim Angle said.

Dakota shrugged, but winced as he tried to grab a gulp of bracing air. "I don't need to see a doctor. It's just a contusion."

"You don't know that."

"I was wearing my protective vest."

"You could still have a few cracked ribs. Butch Cobb was wearing a vest in Phoenix."

All the riders knew about Butch. He'd been one of the best until a fractured rib had punctured his right lung. "A freak accident," Dakota said.

He lifted a bottle of water to his mouth. His chest protested the movement with such vengeance that he grimaced.

Naturally, Jim noticed.

"You need to be x-rayed."

"I needed to stay on that bull eight seconds."

"You don't always have to play the tough guy, Dakota."

"Who's playing? But if it makes you happy, I'll stop by the emergency room, old man, and get checked out."

"Watch who you're calling 'old man' or I'll toss you over my shoulder and haul your sorry ass to the hospital."

"How about you just collect my bull rope and glove for me?"

"Can do, and then I'm driving you to the hospital."

"Just what I need, a chauffeur in rodeo-clown makeup."

What Dakota wanted was a couple of painkillers, a six-pack and a soft bed, but he knew that Jim was right. He should get the injury checked out. If it was something serious, the faster he got it tended to, the better off he'd be.

The nearest hospital was only a ten-minute drive. He'd passed it on his way to the arena tonight. He could easily drive himself. He started unbuttoning his shirt. He had a clean one in his truck and he didn't want the hospital deciding they had to rip this one off of him.

He almost doubled over from a stab of pain as he shrugged out of the shirt. His chest felt like someone had just whacked it with a two-by-four.

"Get in," Jim said.

This time Dakota didn't argue.

CHAPTER THREE

"WE STILL NEED to talk, Dr. Mancini."

Drats. The detective was still here. She adjusted the strap on her handbag. The nagging headache that had begun at her first sight of the dying gunshot victim intensified sharply.

"Do we have to talk tonight? I was just leaving."

He nodded. "It's important."

What wasn't? "There's a small conference room at the end of the hall," she said. "But can we make this short? It's been crazy around here tonight, and I'm exhausted."

A tinge of guilt settled in her chest. She had no right to complain about exhaustion when, unlike two of the night's patients, she was alive.

Detective Cortez followed her to the conference room, which was little more than a large supply cabinet with chairs and a small round table instead of shelves. She perched on the edge of one of the chairs.

Cortez scratched the back of his head and dandruff snowed onto the collar of his dark cotton sport shirt. "We have some complications."

"Don't tell me they've postponed the Bateman trial?"

"No, but Judge Carter was relieved of the case."

"Why?"

"His wife's been diagnosed with cancer and he's taking an emergency leave from the bench."

"Won't they just appoint a new judge?"

"They have," Cortez said. "It's Judge Nelson."

"Mary Lester Nelson?"

"That's the one," Cortez said.

"You don't sound too happy about the change."

"Judge Nelson has a reputation for being soft on rotten sons of bitches like Hank Bateman. Pardon my French."

"Surely she won't let a child killer off with a slap on the wrist."

"No, she'll throw in a little community service." Sarcasm punctuated his voice. "She already decided his rights were being denied and set bail this afternoon. I'm sure Bateman is out walking the streets by now."

"Doesn't she know what happened three months ago when Judge Carter decided that the prosecution was requesting unreasonable extensions and he decided bail was in order?"

"I'm sure the prosecution made certain she knew Bateman made a run for the border."

"Not just made a run for it, he was crossing it when Border Patrol made the arrest and sent him back to jail," she said. "And still Judge Nelson released a child killer on bail. The more I learn about the justice system, the more unjust I think it is."

"At this point, Bateman is just an *alleged* child killer. His attorney is insisting he's innocent."

"But we know he isn't. He admitted that he'd been with his girlfriend's baby all evening the night the infant died."

"Yeah. Nice guy. Babysitting for the woman who's out turning tricks to buy him crack cocaine."

"I don't give a—" She threw up her hands. "This isn't

about the mother. It's about getting justice for a helpless infant. And our evidence is indisputable."

"Until a defense attorney starts whittling away at it."

"There is nothing to whittle." Her irritation was building so fast, she couldn't contain it. "There was excessive retinal hemorrhaging, and bruising on the baby's arms and stomach that was not consistent with a fall. That infant died from NAT."

"Calm down," Cortez said. "You don't have to convince me the cause of death was nonaccidental trauma delivered by a heartless bastard. I don't doubt the autopsy findings. But jurors aren't always swayed by printed reports. They react to emotion. That's why I'm counting on your testimony."

"And nothing will stop me from appearing at that trial."

"Good."

"So what is this visit really about?"

"Now that Bateman's out of jail there's a good chance he'll try to contact you himself."

"To try to frighten me into refusing to testify?"

Cortez nodded.

"It won't work, Detective, no more than his threatening notes have or last month's visit from his thug friend who showed up in the E.R. pretending to be ill."

"The trial is only nine days away. Bateman will be getting desperate. He may up the ante."

The tone of the detective's voice alarmed her. "Surely you don't think I'm in any kind of danger."

"I just think you should be careful. If you so much as see him hanging around or get a phone call from him, I want to know about it. There's a chance I could take that information to the judge and get the bail decision reversed. Having Bateman behind bars is our only assurance that he won't skip the country and hide out in some remote area of Mexico."

So it wasn't her that the detective was worried about. But she was as interested in seeing Hank Bateman behind bars as he was—permanently locked away, where he could never harm another helpless infant.

But she had other concerns, as well. "I have a seven-month-old daughter. I can't have her in danger."

"She won't be. Neither will you. I'll see to that." Cortez pulled a business card from his shirt pocket and dropped it onto the table in front of her. "Keep this with you. Call me on my cell if Bateman tries to make any type of contact with you."

She picked up the card and quickly committed the number to memory. Fortunately, that came easy for her. It was what got her through med school when she was too crushed by her mother's death to cram for finals.

They finished the conversation quickly. By the time she was ready to leave, her mind was back on the gunshot victim she hadn't been able to help.

He was young, someone's son, maybe even someone's husband or father. He'd never make it home tonight, and their lives would never be the same without him.

She'd majored in emergency medicine because she liked saving lives. More often than not, she did. But even one life needlessly lost to violence was too many.

Her car was parked about a hundred yards from the E.R. exit nearest the ambulance entrance. The back parking lot was almost deserted this time of night. An uneasy feeling skirted her senses, probably due to too much talk of Hank Bateman. She scanned the area. All was quiet.

When she reached the shiny black Acura that she'd

purchased just last week, she pulled her keys from her handbag and unlocked the door. She was about to slide in when she sensed movement to her left.

"Get in."

A man grabbed her left arm and shoved what felt like the barrel of a pistol into her side. Panic seized her, crippling her reflexes, deadening her senses. She was about to slide into the seat submissively when her survival instincts kicked in.

If she got into the car with this brute, she might never escape alive.

Her former self-defense instructor's words came back to her in fragmented pieces. *Use what you have. Cause a scene. Fight for your life.*

"Get in, bitch. Do what I say so that I don't have to use this gun."

"If it's money you want…" She slung her purse at his gun hand as she frantically fit the metal car key between her fingers, fashioning a weapon of sorts.

He shoved her. She fell forward, no longer feeling the force of the gun. She punched the man, aiming for his left eye. The metal end twisted as it buried in his eye socket.

He yelled and flailed, blindly knocking the keys from her hand. She hit the pavement running.

She was almost back to the walkway when the heel of her shoe caught on a strip of uneven pavement. Her foot came out of it and she pitched forward, her right wrist twisting beneath her as she tried to catch herself.

She heard the squeal of a car as it sped away. *Please let it be the gunman.*

But a hand touched her right shoulder. Horror

reached deep inside her and she threw back her head and screamed.

The guy backed off. "Is there a problem?"

The voice echoed through her mind. Familiar. Haunting. She started to shake. Heart hammering in her chest, she turned and looked at the man standing over her.

"I didn't mean to frighten you. I heard a yell and then spotted you running across the parking lot."

Her heart skipped erratically as she studied the man who'd come to her rescue. The same depths to the dark eyes she remembered so well. The same thick, unruly hair. Even the same worn Stetson—or one exactly like it.

He stared at her as if she were a ghost.

Her heart turned inside out.

"Dakota." It was the only word she could manage without totally falling apart.

CHAPTER FOUR

"Viviana." Dakota muttered her name and stared at the woman who'd haunted so many of his dreams. He was reeling, so stunned at seeing her that he had trouble getting his mind around what had just happened or even why he was here. His memory was jolted by a dizzying stab of pain when he reached to pick up her shoe.

"Who let the bulls out?"

Jim arrived on the scene with his usual rodeo flair, still in his trademark oversize red-and-black jersey and loose shorts. A bit of the clown makeup was still smeared around his eyes, though he'd wiped it off as best he could on the way over with his dirt-smeared bandana.

Viviana stiffened and her eyes signaled an increased anxiety level. "Who are you?"

"He's a friend of mine," Dakota said quickly. "We were driving to the E.R. entrance when we heard the commotion and I spotted you racing across the parking lot." Dakota did a second visual scan of the area. There was no sign of trouble now, yet she'd screamed hysterically when he'd knelt beside her. And a car had just burned rubber leaving the lot.

"Name's Jim Angle," Jim said.

"I'm Dr. Mancini."

Dakota steadied while she slid her foot back into her shoe. It was all he could do not to pull her into his arms and hold her tight. But too many months apart and the lingering sting of rejection made him hold back. Not to mention that it would start a barrage of questions from Jim.

"What just happened out here?" Dakota asked. "Were you attacked?"

"I was leaving work. When I got to my car, a man appeared from out of nowhere and pointed a pistol at me. He told me to get in."

"Then what?" Jim asked when she stopped talking and started looking around the parking area.

"I threw my purse at him, punched him and started running."

"You must have delivered one hell of a blow," Jim said. "Man yelped like you'd gutted him. That's actually what got our attention."

"I rammed my key into his eyeball."

Jim grinned. "A woman after my heart."

She hugged her arms around her chest and shivered in spite of the warm summer air. Her gaze turned to the parking lot. "My car is gone. It was parked next to that SUV near the ambulance entrance."

"Cars are replaceable," Dakota said. She could have been killed. If he ever got his hands on the thug…

"Did you know the yellow-bellied bastard?" Jim asked.

"I've never seen the man before, at least not that I remember. A lot of patients come through the E.R."

Dakota struggled to get his head around the emotions bucking inside him. In the best of circumstances, running into Viviana so unexpectedly would have been enough to throw him off his game.

Finally, he let his eyes meet hers. "Are you sure you're okay?"

"I am now. I think you may have frightened off the gunman, except that I guess what he really wanted was cash and my car. Now he has both."

"Then lucky I made a wrong turn and came in the ambulance entrance," Jim said.

Dakota scanned the area again. "Don't you have security around here?"

"Yes, but they can't be everywhere at once."

"They could see you to your car when you leave in the wee hours of the morning."

"I've never had any trouble before. This is normally a safe area."

"Security can't do anything now," Jim said. "Call the cops. They may be able to find the low-down thief before he clears the area."

"My phone is in my purse and I hurled that at the attacker. No doubt he took it with him."

"Most likely," Dakota agreed. "But we'll check.

"I'll take a look," Jim said.

"Where are your keys?" Dakota asked.

"I'm not sure. They may have fallen to the floor of the car, or I may have just dropped them in my panic."

Which meant the attacker could have her keys and possibly her purse with her ID. If so, he'd know where she lived.

Dakota's muscles clenched. He took his cell phone from his pocket and handed it to Viviana.

Only instead of punching in 911, she made a call to a Detective Harry Cortez. Her conversation with the man was brief and to the point. Yet, he couldn't help but wonder if her relationship with the man was business or pleasure.

By the time she finished the call, Jim had returned with her purse. "You're in luck," he said. "The purse was lying next to another parked car. Your keys were a few feet away. Guess he hotwired the vehicle."

She took the bag from him. "Good. At least he doesn't have my keys and personal information."

"What do you keep in the glove compartment?" Dakota asked.

"Usually the car registration, but I just bought this car and all of the paperwork is in my house."

"Is your detective friend coming over to investigate the situation?" Dakota asked as she returned the phone to him.

"Dirty Harry is not exactly a friend, but, yes, he's on his way. He won't be long. He just left the hospital a few minutes ago."

Dirty Harry. He must be some tough cop. But what did she mean by "not exactly a friend"? That could mean anything. A mosquito buzzed around Dakota's head. He reached up to slap it away, and his ribs screamed as if he'd leaned over a flame. He winced and struggled for a shallow breath.

"You're hurt," Viviana said.

"It's nothing."

She shook her head as if to clear it, and her dark hair danced about her slender shoulders. "If it were nothing, you wouldn't be at the hospital. What's wrong?"

"He tangled with a maniacal bull, and the bull won," Jim answered for him. "Don't happen often. This here's one of the top bull riders in the world, and he's got the buckle and the trophy to prove it."

She looked up at him, a silvery strand of moonlight glimmering in her seductive eyes. The little emotional control he still possessed cratered.

"So you're still bull riding?" she said.

"It's in my blood. And you're still tending the sick and wounded."

"Guess that's in my blood. And now you're one of the wounded again."

"Yep." He did his best to fake a nonchalance that didn't match the heated memories boiling inside him. "Guess you could say we're right back where we started."

"Not quite, Dakota."

Crazy the way his name sounded different when she said it. Softer. Warmer. A bit gut-wrenching.

Jim's brows arched and he rocked back on the heels of his boots. "Am I missing something here? Do you two know each other?"

"Old friends," Dakota said.

"Well, damn. Why didn't you say so?"

"Just hadn't gotten around to it yet."

"What type of injury did you sustain?" Viviana asked, seamlessly snapping back into her physician role.

She acted as if they were nothing more than old friends. If he were smart, he'd treat this encounter the same way.

He tried for a deep breath and managed a shallow, excruciating one. "I took the bull's back hooves to the chest. I was wearing a safety vest, so chances are I just got bruised up a bit. I'm mostly here to get Jim off my case."

"You're obviously in distress. You need X-rays and possibly an MRI. Let me use your phone again. I'll call for a wheelchair."

"I don't need a wheelchair. I ran over here and res-
cued you, didn't I?"

"Give it up, Dakota." She reached for his phone. "If
you weren't in severe pain and afraid something was
broken, dislocated or crushed, you wouldn't be at the
hospital."

"Yep, she knows you," Jim said.

While she was making the call, a small truck with a
red flashing light on the roof slowly rounded the back
of the building.

"Security," Viviana said, waving them over. "I'll handle this, but not until you're checked into the E.R."

Viviana told the men her car had been stolen but that
she'd already called the SAPD. The next thing Dakota
knew he was being rolled toward an open hospital door
and a uniformed nurse was ushering him inside. Once
behind the curtained cubicle, he answered a few questions and admitted that on a scale of one through ten,
his pain was pushing eight.

An injection of painkiller took that down quickly, but
floating in a med-induced state made it doubly hard to
keep his mind off Viviana. She could have been killed.

And she might still be in danger.

It was a piss-poor time for him to be beaten up like
this. Not only was he practically useless to Viviana, but
in mere hours, he also had another rendezvous with a
bull.

THREE HOURS LATER, Viviana stood in the hallway, poring
over Dakota's test results. There was a partial tearing
of the ligaments in the glenohumeral joint in his right
shoulder. That would need time to heal.

There was also swelling and extensive bruising

around the ribs but no serious breaks, thanks to the safety vest that he hadn't been wearing sixteen months ago when she'd first nursed him back to health. The contusions to the chest wall were making breathing and movement painful.

But what could a man expect when he made a living riding bulls?

She couldn't begin to understand his passion for danger. Couldn't make sense of his need to push his body to such physical extremes. Couldn't comprehend his willingness to put his life on the line for a rush of adrenaline and a few seconds of glory.

But, like his loner ways and his nomadic lifestyle, it was who he was. A cowboy at heart. A bull rider by choice. A man who had no desire to settle down. He'd never pretended to be anything different.

She'd accepted that months before and she wouldn't let herself start second-guessing what she knew to be true.

Betsy, the nurse who'd been assigned to Dakota, stopped at Viviana's elbow. "The cowboy in room five is gorgeous, but headstrong. He refused the offer of more pain meds, says he needs to be alert enough to drive. He's also refusing to wear the sling and says he is not about to stay overnight for observation."

"I'll talk to him."

Viviana braced herself for the emotional strain of being near Dakota and marched into room five, hugging his chart to her chest.

Dakota propped himself up a few inches with his elbows when she entered, wincing at the pain. He was going to be seriously sore for several days.

"What's the verdict?" he asked.

As she explained the findings, he maintained a poker face. He'd heard it all before, probably more times than he could count.

"You were lucky," she said. "You could have seriously fractured bones and had a completely dislocated right shoulder...if not worse."

"Luck's the name of the game."

"In here, the name of the game is survival. I think you should be admitted for observation."

"To make certain I don't get much sleep for what's left of the night and that I'll be awakened at seven for dry eggs and cold coffee?"

"So that we can manage your pain and the respiratory therapist can see you in the morning."

"I know the routine, Doc. Deep-breathing exercises to make certain I don't develop pneumonia."

"It is important."

"I know." He took a deep breath to show her he could do it.

She managed a smile. "You do seem to have that down."

"I had a great doctor once. She taught me lots of things I haven't forgotten." His eyes said what his words only hinted at.

Tension escalated in the small cubicle until her own breathing was difficult. Nothing about dealing with Dakota had ever been easy. Their relationship had been fire and ice, passion and agony, love and...

Loss. And she couldn't go through that again, especially now.

"You need to stay off the bulls for a few days to give your body time to heal. You need ice on the injured areas, several times a day, and I recommend that you keep that right arm in a sling for the next week to give it some extra support."

"Anything you say."

Would likely be ignored. Still she had to say it.

"What about your car?" Dakota asked. "Have the cops located it?"

"No, but hopefully they will soon."

"Do you have a ride to your apartment?"

"Actually, it's a town house, near the hospital."

"Do you live alone?"

Her insides knotted. "No, Dakota. I don't live alone."

"I don't see a wedding band."

"I'm not married."

"Well, at least I can offer you a ride to the town house since you stayed extra hours with me."

"You don't have a vehicle here."

"Actually, I do. Another buddy dropped off my truck and Jim gave him a lift back to the hotel."

"You shouldn't be driving."

"The hotel's only a few miles away and the pain meds have pretty much worn off. I'm in good shape— Well, at least I'm clearheaded."

"You're in pain and should be keeping your right shoulder as still as possible."

He narrowed his gaze. "I'm left-handed." He sat up, yanking the hospital gown so that he stayed completely covered. "I promise to get you home safely."

Her physical safety was not the issue. She'd be in his truck. It would smell like him and feel like him. He'd be near enough for her to hear his breathing, and his presence would roll through her in heated swells.

"It's just a ride home, Viviana. I'm not promoting anything here."

"Okay, Dakota. Sure. I'd appreciate the ride."

Her heart was pounding as she left the room. But one thing was for certain. He would not be staying for breakfast this time.

DAKOTA TURNED THE key in the ignition, and his new Ford double-cab pickup truck hummed to life. A George Strait tune blared from the radio and he reached over to lower the volume.

Viviana set a blue laptop case on the floor at her feet. "Nice wheels."

"Thanks."

"I thought you loved your old pickup."

"I did, but it had over a hundred thousand tough miles on it. It was ready to bite the dust."

She ran her hand over the dashboard. "I like this one."

"Yep. It has all the bells and whistles."

The silence grew awkward, punctuated by an awareness that all but consumed him. He'd been getting over her, or at least making a damn good stab at it. Now she was reviving the old feelings, torching the unhealed scars she'd left all over his heart.

He backed out of the parking spot. "Did the detective you called say whether or not there had been other armed carjackings in the area?"

"He said car thefts are on the rise, but that there hasn't been a carjacking in this area for a couple of years."

"Guess you never know when some thug will turn desperate."

"Apparently. Stay right when you leave the lot and then turn left at the light."

"Do you always work the late shift?" he asked once he'd made the turn.

"Normally I work from eleven at night to seven in the morning."

"Why was tonight different?"

"I was covering for a doctor friend who had tickets for a Michael Bublé concert."

"So she took your shift starting at eleven?"

"No. I'm starting a three-day break, so I wasn't on the schedule. E.R. hours run a little different from typical doctor's hours."

"Guess the graveyard shift is the bane of first-year staff doctors?"

"Not really. Having days off just suits my lifestyle better."

He understood what she meant. It gave her every evening at home with her significant other. The thought of her in another man's arms settled like lead in Dakota's stomach. Not that it surprised him. She'd never indicated she didn't want a man in her life—just not him.

"The next right," she said. "After that it's just a couple of blocks."

He did as she dictated, stopping in front of a two-story town house with a stone-and-wood fascia. A row of flowering shrubs set off a wide bay window. It was far more upscale than the small apartment she'd had as a resident back in Houston.

He wondered if she still had the same furniture. The couch where she'd given him the first massage to ease his painful muscles. His groin tightened as he remembered where that had led.

"Thanks for..."

"You need to take care of..."

They'd started talking at the exact same moment and their words became tangled.

She laughed nervously. "It was good to see you again, Dakota."

"Yeah. You, too." He leaned over, aching to kiss her, knowing it would be a big mistake.

She opened her door and slid out as if fearing he might make a move on her. He opened his truck door.

"Don't bother walking me to the door, Dakota. You're hurting, I'm exhausted and it really isn't necessary."

He watched her walk away, the finality of their brief encounter searing into his mind. She had her life all figured out and there was no place in it for him.

When she neared the house, motion lights flicked on. She looked back and waved. A few seconds later she turned the key in the lock and disappeared behind the dark wooden door.

He sat there for a few minutes, letting the memories wreak havoc with his brain before gunning the engine and starting off to his lonely hotel room.

He'd driven about four blocks when he stopped for a light and noticed Viviana's laptop case still on the floor. She might need the computer first thing in the morning, so there was nothing to do but take it back to her. Imagine her live-in's excitement to have an injured cowboy ring the bell in the wee hours of the morning.

There was movement in the shrubbery as he approached the house. He stopped and stared into the blackness. The movement evidently hadn't been enough to trigger the motion lights.

But something was in those bushes. He opened his

truck door. A man jumped from behind the bushes and started running toward the back of the house. Dakota leaped from the truck and took off after him. With the first pounding of his feet on the pavement, pain shot through him like small explosions. He struggled for breath.

He got to the back of the house just in time to see the man jump from a branch, clearing the tall privacy fence and landing with a thud on the other side. By the time Dakota shinnied up the tree, the man had disappeared.

He dropped back to the ground, his breath knifing through his lungs. Damn. Had he not been thrown with such force tonight, he could have caught the man and taken him down. But if he hadn't wound up in the hospital, he wouldn't have run into Viviana. The gunman might have forced her into the car and abducted her. If this was the man who'd stolen her car, she was clearly not a random target.

He trudged back to the truck, retrieved the computer and took the walkway back to the front door in the faint glow of moonlight. The motion light had either quit working or more likely had been sabotaged. He looked and felt like hell as he rang the bell.

A minute later, Viviana opened the door a crack and peeked out at him. "What's wrong?"

"You left your computer in the truck. I brought it back to you."

She opened the door the rest of the way, then reached up and dislodged a leaf from his hair. "You're out of breath. Where have you been?"

"Chasing a man from your yard."

"What?"

"I spotted someone at your front window when I drove up. I chased him but he got away."

"The man who stole my car." Her voice was shaky.

"That would be my guess."

Color drained from her face. She took a deep breath and released it slowly. "I didn't mean to drag you into this."

"Best I remember, I came barging into it."

"So you did. Do you mind coming in while I call the cops?"

"What will your boyfriend say about that?"

"There is no boyfriend."

So her roommate was female or platonic. More relieved than he should be, Dakota stamped the dirt from his shoes and followed Viviana inside.

Viviana carefully locked the dead bolt behind Dakota. Twice tonight, he'd appeared just in time to save her from some depraved lunatic.

But right now, even that wasn't the worst of her problems. She'd known for seven months that she had to face Dakota again eventually. She'd tried to convince herself that she'd be able to look him in the eye and explain everything without her emotions billowing out of control.

But the second she'd heard his voice tonight, those illusions had vanished.

"You need to call the cops or your friendly detective right away," Dakota said. "The man could still be in the neighborhood and if they act fast they may be able to apprehend him."

"I will, but lower your voice and come with me to the kitchen."

"Why are we whispering?"

"Someone's asleep upstairs. There's an ice pack in

the freezer." She opened a drawer, took out a dish towel and tossed it to him. "Wrap it in this and apply it to your shoulder."

"Bourbon would be better."

She opened the door to the cabinet where she kept her meager supply of liquor while she punched 911 into her cell phone. She was tempted to call Cortez again, but it was no use waking him in the middle of the night when there was little he could do at this point.

The 911 operator took her information.

"Are you certain you're not in any immediate danger?" the operator asked.

"I'm not certain, but the intruder appears to be gone."

"Stay on the line while I alert the police." The operator was back in under a minute. "An officer will be there within the next half hour. In the meantime, stay inside with your doors locked. If your situation changes and you feel you're in immediate danger, call 911 again."

"Did you stress to the police that this is likely the same man who stole my car earlier this evening?" Viviana asked.

"I made them aware of the circumstances."

"Thanks."

Which meant there was nothing to do but wait for the cops.

But at least that would give her a few minutes to clear her head and figure out how to handle Dakota.

CHAPTER FIVE

PAIN WAS KICKING in big-time. Dakota took a small bottle of aspirin from his shirt pocket and shook a few tablets into his hand.

"Meds and alcohol don't mix," Viviana cautioned.

"They do in my world." He downed them with the whiskey chaser. "Do you have a flashlight? I'd like to take a look at that bay window from the outside."

"You do realize it's almost three o'clock in the morning."

"I'd still like to check it out before a cop arrives."

"I was told to stay inside with the doors locked."

"And *you* should. So either hand me a flashlight or I'll get one out of my truck."

While Viviana opened a kitchen drawer and rummaged for a flashlight, Dakota pulled a sharp knife from the rack at the back of the kitchen counter.

"There's really nothing the man could see from out there," Viviana explained as she handed him a shiny red flashlight. "The blinds were closed. And even from the front door, all you can see through the sidelights is the foyer."

"That's good to know."

"I'd rather you not go out there, Dakota. The man has a gun and he might come back."

"I hope he does, but it's not likely."

"What makes you think that?"

"He ran both times I showed up. He's not looking to use that gun if he doesn't have to. And he's not looking for a real fight."

"How do you know so much about criminals?"

"I watch *CSI* religiously."

Once outside, the steady whir of the air conditioner dominated the still, quiet air. Dakota squeezed through the shrubs so that he was pretty much in the same spot that the trespasser had been.

Just as Viviana had said, the blinds completely blocked any view of the inside of the house. That ruled out the guy just being a voyeur. So did the fact that the screen was missing.

Dakota sprayed a beam of light over the hedge. Sure enough, the screen was tucked into one of the bushes. He moved the beam back to the window. There were marks on the wood where the guy had tried to pry the window open.

No doubt about it, the guy had come back for her. Dakota's insides bucked at the thought of what might have happened if he hadn't showed up at that exact moment.

Viviana was waiting to open the door for him when he stepped in front of it.

"Do you have an alarm system?" Dakota asked.

"Yes, and it was set. It would have gone off instantly if the man had come through the door or the window."

"Nice in theory, but professional crooks disable them all the time. I'll check it."

"So much for feeling safe in my own house. Now that I think about it, the motion detector didn't come on when you went outside."

"I know. I suspect the bulb is crushed into the lawn behind the bushes."

Before Dakota could check the alarm system, the security company called on Viviana's cell phone to say they weren't getting a signal from the house phone line.

She assured them she was fine. They promised to send a technician out to check the system the following morning, though they suspected the problem was with the phone company.

Dakota suspected it was with a cut phone line.

"What if you hadn't come back tonight, Dakota? What then?" Viviana's voice shook. "That armed thug would be in my house right now."

Dakota slipped an arm around her shoulder. "I did come back. I'm here and I'm not going anywhere."

Viviana dropped to the sofa.

Seconds later, the flashing red lights of a squad car filtered through the sidelights for a few seconds before going dark. The sirens were silent.

Viviana raced to the front door. Dakota was only a step behind her, each hurried step a bitter reminder that physically, he was no match for anyone right now.

The two uniformed police officers showed their IDs and once they'd taken seats in the cozy living room, they got down to business. Dakota let Viviana do most of the talking, though he did have to explain that he didn't get a good look at the guy he'd chased off.

Nothing in the questioning jumped out at Dakota until the younger of the cops, a guy named Greg Simmons, started asking more pointed questions.

"Is there anyone who might have a reason to target you, Dr. Mancini?"

Viviana fingered the small gold heart that dangled

from a chain around her neck. "Yes, I talked to Detective Cortez earlier tonight. I'm sure he'll follow up on that first thing in the morning, but—"

The cop interrupted. "Harry Cortez, in homicide?"

She nodded.

"How did you come to talk to him?"

"I know him from a case he's investigating."

The older cop leaned forward. "What case would that be?"

"The Compton case. I admitted Leslie Compton to the hospital the night she died of abuse. The case goes to trial in nine days. I'm one of the prosecutor's witnesses."

The cop nodded as if that explained a lot. "So you're involved in the case against Hank Bateman."

"Yes, but it wasn't Hank Bateman who stole my car. I would have recognized him. If you need to know more, I suggest you talk to Detective Cortez."

"We'll make sure he sees this report."

"I've told you everything. Wouldn't it be more useful now for you to be searching the neighborhood for the man who tried to break into my house—whoever he may be?"

"Yes, ma'am. We'll get on that. Keep your doors locked and if there's any more trouble, call 911 again. I'll see that someone's in the neighborhood for the rest of the night."

"I appreciate that."

Dakota stood and tried to wrap his mind around the new fragments of information. Viviana was to be a witness in a case against a man the cops seemed to know well. That was never a good sign.

She was massaging her right temple when she rejoined him after seeing the officers to the door. She dropped to the sofa. "We need to talk."

Her tone indicated this wouldn't be pleasant. "About the Compton case?"

"No, that's far too detailed to go into tonight. We need to talk about *us*."

As if that would be easy. "Whatever you need to say about us has waited sixteen months. Another eight hours can't hurt. So if it's all the same with you, I say we crash."

"You can't stay here. I don't even have an extra bed."

He patted the sofa cushion. "This works fine. And don't worry, I'm a light sleeper. I'll wake at the first sign of trouble. Not that I expect there to be any more tonight."

"You don't have to stay."

"I'm staying."

"Then I guess we should just crash."

She didn't sound excited about having him as an overnight guest, but she did sound relieved. He wasn't sure if it was because he was sticking around for protection or because she could put off the conversation she was obviously dreading.

She walked away but returned a few minutes later with sheets, a pillow and a fresh ice pack. The moment grew uncomfortable. Saying a friendly good-night to a woman with whom he'd shared the hottest sex of his life, albeit months before, was downright prickly.

They managed it. He watched her walk up the stairs, the gentle sway of her hips as seductive as ever.

A few hours ago, he'd had nothing on his mind but riding a bull. Now he was consumed with Viviana, and everything had become complex and tangled.

Worse, he had a feeling deep in his gut that the complications were going to get a lot worse before this was over.

DAKOTA'S FEET STRETCHED over the end of the sofa, making it impossible to get into a comfortable position. A nagging headache sat at the back of his skull. Breathing hurt. His muscles ached.

Unable to sleep, his mind juggled the night's events. It was purely coincidence that he'd arrived on the scene at the exact moment that Viviana was being attacked.

But how much of the rest of what happened was coincidence? Random attack or targeted? A determined bastard coming to finish what he'd started at the hospital?

And if Viviana had been targeted, was Hank Bateman behind it? Dakota would need to know a lot more about the Compton case before he could even make an intelligent guess.

He could call his brother Wyatt. Consulting a good homicide detective made sense, and Wyatt was one of the best. But calling him in Atlanta would open a whole new set of thorny dilemmas.

Two of Dakota's brothers lived in or near their hometown of Mustang Run. Dylan lived on Willow Creek Ranch with their father; Sean lived close by in Bandera. His brother Tyler planned to move back to the ranch as soon as he finished his stint in the army. His wife, Julie, was already there.

Dylan, Tyler and Sean had let go of the past and embraced Troy Ledger as if he were Santa Claus coming down the chimney on Christmas Eve. It worked for them.

Dakota wanted no part of it. At this late date, he wasn't about to start wallowing in the mud while pretending it was chocolate.

Dakota stretched and cringed as he sucked in the pain. He hadn't hurt this bad since…since he'd been kicked by a bull the night he'd first met Viviana. Or maybe since the night they'd said goodbye and he'd rode off into the sunset in his then-aging pickup truck.

There were all kinds of hurtin'.

He'd get over the pain in his muscles and joints soon enough, but he might as well face facts. Even if Viviana told him his presence around here wasn't wanted or needed, which he figured was the basis for the promised discussion, he'd be in no shape to ride or rack up points for the next few nights.

VIVIANA JERKED AWAKE to the sound of footfalls on the stairs. She glanced at the clock—7:00 a.m. No doubt Claire was going to the kitchen to start a pot of coffee, just as she did most mornings about this time. Only normally Viviana would be just finishing up her graveyard shift.

This morning when Claire went for the morning newspaper, she'd spy the hunky cowboy on the sofa. The officious nanny would not consider that a pleasant surprise.

Viviana untangled her feet from the sheets, jumped from the bed and grabbed her ivory-colored silk robe. She'd have to get downstairs on the double to explain— or run interference—since somehow Claire had slept right through last night's drama. As had Briana.

The sixty-something nanny was in super physical condition, but she did have a slight hearing problem. She didn't wear her aids when she slept, but she kept the baby monitor on the bedside table near her ear so that she'd hear Briana's slightest whimper.

Poking her arms through the sleeves of the robe, Viviana made a quick stop at the door to the nursery. Briana stirred and stretched her pudgy little arms over her head when the door squeaked open, but thankfully her eyes remained closed.

The smell of coffee drifted up the staircase. Dakota must have beat Claire to the brew task. Impulsively, Viviana smoothed her hair and pulled the robe tighter, looping the belt to keep the robe closed.

Her pulse quickened as she pictured Dakota in her kitchen making coffee. Barefoot. His hair rumpled. Wearing his briefs…or nothing at all. The memories of how it had once been spilled into her mind and Viviana trembled as heat suffused her body.

She paused when she reached the bottom step, and her fingers wrapped tightly around the newel cap as she eavesdropped on the conversation.

"Now who did you say you are again?"

"Dakota Ledger."

"And you're an old friend of Viviana's?"

"That's right."

Viviana hurried to the kitchen before Dakota had to answer any more questions, and before he started asking any. He was barefoot and shirtless, but fortunately wearing jeans.

"I see you two have met," Viviana said.

"Yes, and he's lucky I didn't ram a knife through him. I sure didn't expect to find a strange man in the kitchen."

"Sorry I didn't warn you," Viviana said, "but his visit was unexpected. I ran into him in the E.R. and, well, he just wasn't in any shape to go home alone. I thought he should stay here in case his pain became worse during the night."

She did not want to explain the ordeal of last night to Claire. If she tried, Claire would ask a million questions and give at least an hour's worth of advice.

Claire studied the bruises on Dakota's chest and shoulder. "Were you in an accident?"

"You could say that. I got thrown from a bull."

"Seriously?"

"Serious as a kick to the ribs."

"Hmmph."

Her skeptical tone no doubt summed up not only Claire Evers's feelings on bull riding, but also her thoughts on his having spent the night.

Viviana pulled some mugs from the cabinet over the coffeemaker. "Thanks for filling in for me last night, Claire."

"You know I don't mind staying when you need me."

"And I really appreciate that. I won't need you anymore today and you probably have things you need to do." It was the most tactful way she could think of to get rid of Claire.

"I don't have anything planned. I can stay if you need me."

"No. I can handle things."

"In that case, I'll just get my handbag and head out. I'll be back on Wednesday evening at my regular time."

"Are you the housekeeper?" Dakota asked.

"Lands, no. I'm the nanny. I've taken care of Briana since six weeks after she was born. Viviana says she doesn't trust anyone but me with her baby."

"Viviana's baby?" Dakota leaned against the counter, so stunned the words were a husky whisper.

"Yes. The doctor's daughter. Briana? Who did you think I was talking about?"

"Just checking." He stood perfectly still, staring at Viviana without saying a word until Claire was out of hearing range. "You never mentioned having a baby," he said accusingly.

"You didn't ask." She poured two mugs of coffee and handed one to him. "I guess you still take it black."

"Forget the coffee. How old is the baby?"

"Seven months."

"Seven months. Does that mean you were pregnant with another man's child when we were together?"

This was not the way Viviana had planned this encounter. Only, that was the real problem. She'd never been able to visualize exactly what she'd say or how Dakota would react. And she was starting to resent his attitude.

"I don't remember you asking or caring if I was in another relationship at the time. But I wasn't pregnant when we met, Dakota. I was pregnant when you left."

"You're not saying…"

"Yes, I'm saying you have a precious, adorable daughter—Briana. You don't have to take my word for it. You can swab her cheek and have a paternity test if that would make you feel better. But I wasn't with another man for months before I met you and I haven't been with one since."

Briana began to wail. She was a terrific baby, but she had a horrific sense of timing.

Viviana left Dakota standing in the kitchen staring into space like a zombie while she climbed the steps to the nursery to get Briana from her crib. It was past time the little darling met her bruised and battered cowboy daddy.

CHAPTER SIX

DAKOTA REELED FROM the shocking announcement. There had to be a mistake. This could not be happening to him. He had no idea how to be a father. How could he? He'd certainly never had a role model to follow.

Questions and denials stormed his mind as Viviana stepped into the kitchen balancing a smiling kid on her hip. He turned away as if that would make the whole ordeal disappear.

Viviana stopped a few feet from him. "This is Briana. Look at her, Dakota. She has your eyes, and your smile."

He turned slowly and his heart felt as if it were twisting inside him.

The child looked at him sheepishly from beneath dark lashes. "Gob a ga ga."

His insides churned. His kid, but he didn't see himself in her. He saw Viviana. Dark hair that curled close to her scalp. Cute nose, with the slightest of upturn. Rosy cheeks. But…

"She's so little."

"Not really," Viviana said. "Her growth curve is well within the average range. She's healthy and normal."

Viviana held the child out for him to take. He backed away.

"You don't have to be afraid of her, Dakota. She won't bite, though she is cutting a tooth."

"She's getting a tooth?" He sounded like a parrot, but who knew babies got teeth so soon?

"Have you ever been around babies?"

"Not that I remember." He sank to the sofa. "Why didn't you tell me I was a father before this?"

"Exactly how was I supposed to do that? Send a post card in care of a bull somewhere between the two coasts?"

"I have a cell phone."

"With a new, *unlisted* number."

He mumbled a curse under his breath. He'd changed his server and his number when some emotionally unstable buckle bunny had started calling him all hours of the day and night. Only...

"I didn't change that number until three months after I was with you."

"That's how long it took before I realized I was pregnant. I was doing my residency in emergency medicine, remember? I was working so many hours that when I was home I simply collapsed into bed. Days turned into weeks before I realized how long it had been since I'd had a period."

He did remember her long hours at the hospital. She'd been about to start a rare four-day break when he'd first met her. They'd spent every second of that time together. Then she'd gone back to her residency and worked from sunup to midnight. She'd come home exhausted. But even those two nights, she'd fallen hungrily into his arms.

And then he'd had to leave in time to make the next big bull-riding event. She'd decided that it should be a permanent goodbye. Their lives were too different. They would never make it as a couple.

He couldn't argue that. He'd never thought of himself as husband material. He was too much of a realist for that. But that didn't mean he was ready to just toss away what they had.

And now they had a daughter. The idea of it scared him to death.

"It's not as if I didn't try to reach you, Dakota, but you have no permanent address. If you do, I don't have it."

"I didn't exactly fall off the face of the earth. You could have contacted the Professional Bull Riders Association. They could have gotten word to me."

"I didn't even know there was an association, and frankly, by the time I'd tried everything else, I wasn't sure it was worth the effort."

"What is that supposed to mean?"

Briana began to squirm in her arms. Viviana pulled a padded quilt square from a basket by the sofa and spread it on the floor with one hand while she balanced the baby on her hip. She lay Briana on the quilt, then dug out a colorful rattling ball and a set of large plastic keys from the same basket and placed them on the quilt beside her.

Briana rolled over and pulled up to her hands and knees as if she were going to crawl away. Instead she started rocking back and forth and making gurgling noises.

Dakota was mesmerized by her movements, the sounds she made, her short pudgy arms and legs, the funny way she stuck her behind in the air. Yet he kept his distance.

"It means exactly what's happening right now," Viviana said, as if the conversation hadn't been interrupted.

"You're afraid to interact with Briana at all. Getting to know her might interfere with your life, might make you reconsider your priorities. And we both know you live for the competition."

"The way you live for your medical career."

That was a knee-jerk statement and totally unfair. Viviana was obviously devoted to Briana. But Viviana's comments were just as unmerited. She'd had months to mentally prepare to be a mother. He'd had a matter of minutes to adjust to being a dad.

Not that he was sure more time would have made a difference. He knew his limitations. He had nothing to offer as a father except bad genes and a killer reputation.

"What's Briana's full name?"

"Briana Marie Ledger. Marie is for my mother."

And Ledger was a curse.

"I don't need anything from you, Dakota, if that's what you're worried about. I can raise Briana on my own and I'd rather do that unless you truly want to be in her life. I won't see her hurt and rejected by a man who's a father in name only."

It wasn't a matter of wanting to be a part of Briana's life. It was that the only thing he had to offer was money. Fortunately, winning the world title two years ago assured he had plenty. "I'll support her financially. She'll never do without anything she needs. "

Viviana winced as if he'd slapped her. "Don't bother, Dakota. *I* can give her everything she needs—except you."

Viviana picked up Briana and hugged her tight. "I'll be upstairs for the rest of the morning. Just let me know when you leave so that I can lock the door behind you."

"I won't be leaving anytime soon. I have locks to

change. You need something stronger and more secure than what you have now."

"I can call a locksmith."

Shock, frustration and the fact that his arm hurt every time he moved it were eating away at his patience. "Will it kill you to just let me change the locks?"

"Suit yourself."

Viviana turned and walked away, leaving him to struggle with the fact that his life had just changed forever.

DAKOTA WAS SO sore he could barely move, but he couldn't sit still, either. And thinking about his new status as a father struck him with the kind of fear that would paralyze him if he let it.

He didn't want to leave Viviana and Briana alone until he was certain they were safe. Yet he did want to get started on those locks.

His cell phone rang. The caller ID said Jim Angle. One problem solved. He took the call.

"Morning, Jim. You're just the man I need to talk to."

"I guess you want me to come rescue you from a wicked nurse?"

"No, I'm out of the hospital."

"Ready to take on a bull?"

"That's doubtful for tonight."

"So how are you?"

"I'm a little beat-up," Dakota admitted, "but I'm making it. Nothing's broken."

"That's good news. I'll drop by your hotel room and bring you some breakfast."

"I'm not at the hotel."

"So where the hell are you?"

"I spent the night at Viviana Mancini's house, or at least what was left of the night after the hospital finally released me."

"Well, ain't you just riding the gravy train with biscuit wheels? Does that mean you're back in the saddle?"

"Far from it. It's a long story. I'll fill you in later, but right now I could use a favor."

"You got it, as long as I can still get back to the arena for tonight's show."

"That I can guarantee."

Dakota explained what he needed in the way of tools and locks from the hardware store. An hour later Jim arrived with everything on the list and some spares. Two hours later, they were done, thanks to the fact that Jim did not move with the ineptness of a guy with a bum shoulder and bruised ribs.

A few minutes after Jim left, a troubleshooter from the security company arrived to repair the system. The technician reiterated what Dakota already knew. The system had been disarmed by someone who knew exactly what he was doing.

Viviana ventured downstairs without Briana while the tech guy was there. When he left, she disappeared into her upstairs inner sanctum again.

Dakota's efforts to keep her safe were apparently not winning him any points. Not that he was expecting any, but the tension between them was getting to him.

Dakota had about decided he should just go back to the hotel and depend on the locks to keep her safe when the doorbell rang again. Before Dakota could see who'd come calling, Viviana came running down the stairs, again without Briana.

"It's Detective Cortez," she said.

"How do you know?"

"He just called on my cell phone to say he was dropping by to talk about last night." She opened the door and ushered in a man who'd never grace the cover of *GQ*.

Cortez looked to be in his late forties and was slightly overweight. His chin was dotted with yesterday's whiskers and a smear of what looked like blackberry jelly decorated the front of a wrinkled blue sport shirt.

Perspiration beaded on the detective's forehead. He pulled a handkerchief from his back pocket and dabbed at the moisture.

"I heard you made a call to 911 last night," Cortez offered, in lieu of a proper greeting.

"That goon who stole my car tried to break into my house," Viviana said.

"Did you see him?"

"No, but Dakota did."

Cortez turned toward Dakota as if just realizing he was in the room. "Are you Dakota?"

"I am."

Cortez reached into his pocket and pulled out a piece of paper. He unfolded it and handed it to Dakota. A black-and-white mug shot stared back at him.

"Is this the man you saw?"

"Is that Hank Bateman?"

"Not the best picture of him, but yeah, that's him. Do you recognize this man?"

"No. He doesn't look familiar and I'm sure I would have remembered that ghastly tattoo on his neck."

"Can you describe the man you saw outside the town house?"

"No. It was dark and he was mostly hidden by the

shrubs that border the bay window. He ran when I drove up. I chased him, but he got away."

"Did he fire at you?"

"Thankfully, no."

"Did you see a weapon?"

"No, but I was never all that close to him."

"Won't you sit down, Detective?" Viviana urged. "When you finish I have quite a few questions of my own."

"I figured you might." He took a seat in the over-stuffed chair across from the sofa.

"Can I get you some coffee?" Viviana asked.

"Already too hot for coffee. And it's not even July yet. I could use a glass of ice water, though."

"I'll be right back."

Detective Cortez crossed an ankle over the opposite knee. "You got a last name, Dakota, or is Dakota even your real first name?"

"The name's Dakota Ledger, and I don't have any reason to lie about it."

"Ledger." Cortez's mouth screwed into a frown. "I thought you looked familiar when I came in. You're that bull rider in town for the competition. I saw your picture in the newspaper yesterday."

"That would be me."

"Dakota Ledger."

He said the name again, this time as if it left a foul taste in his mouth.

"I hear your famous father's back in Mustang Run now."

"That wasn't in the newspaper."

"No, but I'm a curious man. The name rang a bell

when I read about you so I looked you up. You were what…six at the time your mother was murdered?"

"Something like that."

"How do you know Dr. Mancini?"

Clearly none of the man's business. "Am I under investigation?"

"Not that I'm aware of—at least not yet."

Viviana rejoined them with the water.

The detective gulped about half of it down. "Why don't you tell me exactly what happened last night, Dr. Mancini, and then I'll see if I can answer your questions."

She started to introduce Dakota. The detective informed her they'd already met. She went through everything again without one interruption from Cortez. Dakota figured he'd already read it all in last night's police report anyway.

"You said Hank Bateman might up the ante," Viviana said. "Showing up with a gun would certainly qualify."

"I don't put anything past him. I'm just surprised he'd let someone else do his dirty work now that he's out on bail. I'm even more surprised that he didn't make it clear that he was there to convince you not to testify. Hank is not one to beat around the bush."

"But you do think he was behind the car theft and attempted break-in?"

"It's not all adding up, but I'll find out if he's behind this. Count on that."

"I am. I have to."

The detective put both feet on the floor and leaned forward in his chair.

"Shouldn't you be getting ready to ride a bull, Ledger?"

"I'm giving the bull a break tonight."

The detective's brows arched, but he didn't comment on the statement. Instead, he turned back to Viviana.

"I've got a lineup scheduled this afternoon for a man whose convenience-store customers have been robbed three times in the last four weeks. It's the usual suspects for his area. I'd like for you to come down and see if you recognize any of the suspects A couple of them run with Bateman's old gang, so he might have hired one of them to put the fear into you."

"I just gave the nanny the day off, but I'll try to get a babysitter for Briana. Just tell me what time and where."

"They should be ready for you about two-thirty at the precinct. Here's the address." He pulled a business card from his pocket and set it next to the water. "In the meantime, keep your doors locked, and let me know if you hear from Hank. I'd love a reason to force the judge to put him behind bars again."

Cortez finished his water and stood to leave.

Dakota stood as well, the movement sending a few sharp spikes of pain along his chest wall. He had a few questions of his own.

"If a guy can handily disable an alarm system, don't you think he could hot-wire a car?"

Cortez scratched his chin. "What's your point?"

"The guy was waiting in the parking lot last night with a loaded gun. Seems unnecessary unless it was more than the car he wanted."

"Say what's on your mind, Dakota."

"The intent might have been to abduct Viviana. That would have given the gunman or even Hank the time and opportunity to frighten Viviana into refusing to testify."

"Tell you what, Ledger. You leave the detective work to me. I'll leave the bull riding to you."

"That's okay," Dakota said. "You feel free to ride a bull if you want. You could also put a tail on Hank Bateman 24/7. Then you'd know exactly what he's up to and he might lead you to the guy who took Viviana's car."

Cortez smirked and walked to the door.

Viviana walked with him. "This isn't related," she said, "but do you have an ID on the gunshot victim who died in the E.R. last night?"

"We do. His name was Kevin Lucas."

"Was he married?"

"Divorced. Thankfully, with no kids."

"Do you know who shot him?"

"No suspects yet. And no motive."

"I think he was trying to tell me something just before he died," Viviana said.

"You didn't mention that last night."

"I forgot in the chaos, and I doubt it's anything you can use. His words were garbled, and all he got out was something that sounded like *Shell*. I think he was trying to say more."

"He could have been referring to anything. But don't worry, I'll get the guy who did it, just like I'll find out who accosted you and stole your car. It just takes time."

Dakota liked that kind of confidence as long as the detective lived up to his own hype. If the detective didn't keep Bateman away from Viviana, Dakota would, even if he had to fight her to do it.

Once the detective left, Viviana walked into the kitchen. Dakota followed her. "I need to go to my hotel and get cleaned up," he said, talking to the back of her head.

"Do what you like."

"I don't want you and Briana staying here alone. You'll have to go with me."

Viviana spun around. "You're not the one making the decisions, Dakota."

Dakota's muscles flexed. He crossed the room and tugged her around to face him.

"Let go of me."

"Not until you listen to what I have to say."

"No, Dakota. You listen to me. Our only tie is Briana and you've pretty much said you want nothing to do with her."

"I never said that. She's my daughter. You're her mother. I have a stake in keeping you both safe and I intend to do just that. But right now I have to take a shower and put on some clean clothes before I start to look like Dirty Harry."

He relaxed his hold on her, but she didn't move away.

"You will never look like Cortez."

It was the first time he'd seen her smile in sixteen months. His heart melted like an ice cube in the hot Texas sun. There was no getting over Viviana.

DAKOTA'S HOTEL WAS more luxurious than Viviana had anticipated, yet the room smelled of leather, a woodsy aftershave and pure masculinity. A large, open duffel rested on the luggage rack, revealing a stack of freshly laundered Western shirts and neatly folded jeans.

She paced the spacious room, trying to ignore the ambiance and the sound of running water. To think of Dakota in the shower meant visualizing his beautiful, hard body, naked and wet. She'd never showered with a lover before she'd met Dakota. Never realized the thrill of having every inch of her hot, slick body caressed by warm, tantalizing hands.

Her pulse skyrocketed as the erotic memories took hold. For six days last year, she'd forgotten rules and inhibitions and given in to every desire Dakota had inspired. They'd picnicked naked in bed, had sex in every room of her small apartment, even the hallway. They'd snuggled in front of the fire, ruined her best set of sheets with drizzled chocolate, laughed at nothing, smiled because they simply couldn't stop.

The week had been a fantasy; she'd experienced non-stop fireworks and emotional highs that had made her as giddy as a teenager. The one thing they hadn't done was talk. She didn't know him. He knew even less about her. What she did know spelled disaster.

He thrived on excitement. She craved stability.

He lived out of his suitcase in hotel rooms, waking up in a new town every week for most of the year. He never spent too many nights in the same town. She required continuity and routine, the same town, the same house, the same bed. No risks.

The bathroom door opened and Dakota stepped out, chasing away her memories. His hair was wet and dripping onto his bare shoulders. A fluffy white towel was looped just below his waist. His bare feet were almost soundless on the thick carpet as he walked toward her, smelling of soap and looking good enough to eat.

She turned away while he retrieved his clothes from the duffel.

"No need to be embarrassed, Viviana. You've seen it all before."

"That was different."

"Right. Then you weren't acting like I had the plague."

"I'm not trying to avoid you. It's just…"

"Just what, Viviana? Because to tell you the truth, I haven't really changed all that much in sixteen months. I was just a bull-riding cowboy even then."

Her phone rang and she took the call, thankful to escape the conversation that had nowhere to go except in the tank. "Hello."

"Is this Dr. Mancini?"

"Yes. To whom am I speaking?"

"This is Melody Hollister with the D.A.'s office. I'm Nick Jefferson's assistant. We've spoken several times before in regard to the Compton case, but it's been a while."

"Yes, I remember. Please don't tell me the trial has been postponed again. I really need to get this over with."

"No, everything is set to go as scheduled one week from tomorrow. We will have a different judge presiding, however."

"Detective Cortez informed me of the change. Will it be a problem?"

"I don't anticipate anything interfering with a conviction of homicide. All we have to do is prove that Hank Bateman knew that his actions would likely result in death for Leslie Compton."

"How could he not know that shaking her senseless could be fatal? She was an infant."

"Exactly. We have a psychiatrist who will testify to his mental and emotional state. Mr. Jefferson's questions to you will basically focus on the medical condition of the child. If the defense attorney's questions stray beyond what you testified in your deposition, Mr. Jefferson will object."

"Okay."

"There is one concern."

Viviana's hand tightened on the phone. "Does it involve Hank Bateman?"

"No. It involves Karen Compton, the dead infant's mother."

Frustration hit hard. "Hank got to her, didn't he? She's decided not to testify."

"Not that we're aware of, but we're currently unable to locate her. She hasn't shown up for work in over a week and no one in her family has seen or heard from her."

"Do you think Hank's behind the disappearance?"

"It's possible," Melody said, "but unfortunately, she has a history of vanishing like this, sometimes for weeks at a time. Then when the man she's run off with stops buying her drugs, she comes home, or so say her neighbors."

"And this was the mother of that precious baby who was literally shaken to death," Viviana said. "So sad."

"Yes, and I wish it was the first case like this I've seen, but these things happen far too often in the current drug culture."

Viviana couldn't help but think of Briana. So helpless. So dependent. So precious. She was glad she'd dropped her off at Claire's this afternoon instead of having Claire come to the town house. Though she hated to admit it to Dakota, she was nervous about being in her own house unless he was there with them.

"I'll testify," she said. "Count on it. Leslie Compton was completely vulnerable and innocent. She had a right to love and life."

By the time the call was over, Dakota was dressed and ready to go, looking so like the charismatic cowboy man she'd fallen for that her heart did a nosedive.

"Bad news?" he asked.

"I'll tell you about it in the car on the way to the police precinct."

"In that case, let's get out of here." He fit a shaving kit into the duffel before zipping it and slinging the strap over his shoulder. Then he grabbed what looked like a bag of dirty clothes.

Her breath caught. "Are you moving out of the hotel?"

"For the time being. It would be a little crowded and inconvenient for you and Briana to stay here until after the trial so that means you'll have to put up with me at your place."

"The trial is not for another eight days. What about your competition?"

"It can wait." He put a hand to the small of her back and urged her toward the door. His touch was unassuming, seductive. Protective.

And here she went again. Falling hard and setting herself up for a broken heart. Would she never learn?

CHAPTER SEVEN

"You told me Dr. Mancini didn't have a boyfriend."

"She didn't. I swear. I watched her come and go from her house for a week. She was always alone. For the most part she just went to work and back home. And then all of a sudden this cowboy shows up."

"You let a friggin' cowboy interfere with the plan. What part of doing whatever it takes did you not get?"

"I get it. There's just been a slight delay, but I'll take care of it. You can count on me."

"Obviously, I can't."

"Don't talk like that. We're a team."

"I guess we'll see about that in time, won't we? And time is running out."

CHAPTER EIGHT

TROY LEDGER RINSED the lone plate under the kitchen faucet as he chewed and swallowed the last bite of his ham sandwich. It was two in the afternoon, but he'd missed lunch. He'd been hard at work since before dawn, fixing the roof on his storage barn. It was only late June, but the heat index had climbed to the mid-nineties today.

He took his glass of iced tea and walked into the family room, slowing as he passed the hearth. Without warning the familiar feeling that he was being sucked into a vacuum attacked with a near paralyzing force.

For the first few weeks after his release from prison, he had felt that way every time he walked into this room. The room where Helene had been murdered. Shot twice in the head, once in the chest. All three bullets fired at close range.

He'd found her like that, blood matted in her beautiful black hair, her eyes empty and vacant, her skin already cool to the touch. He was late coming in for lunch that day, too. If he hadn't have been, she might still be alive.

The dark memories crept from the haunted crevices of his mind and he stopped and leaned against the back of his recliner until he could steady himself.

He'd been out of prison for a year now, and he was no closer to finding Helene's killer. The beast who'd stolen his wife and the mother of his five sons was still a free man…unless he'd gone to jail for another crime. That possibility offered little consolation.

The house was an empty shell without her yet there were nights the walls seemed to vibrate with her presence. He could hear the echo of her laughter or her sweet voice singing one of the boys a lullaby. Those were the nights his arms ached to hold her and his mind conjured up images that made ragged shreds of his heart.

A weight settled on Troy's shoulders and he walked to the bookcase and studied the framed photos that his neighbor Ruthanne referred to as Helene's shrine. It wasn't. It was a tribute to the person she'd been.

He picked up the picture of Helene standing in the front yard holding Dakota in her arms. He was no more than a few months old at the time.

When she'd first realized she was pregnant, Helene had talked of nothing but how she hoped number five would be a girl. And then when she was five months along, she'd started to bleed. They'd rushed her to the hospital but it was touch-and-go for a few days as to whether she'd miscarry.

After that, all she cared about was that the baby growing inside her would be born healthy. Dakota filled that bill to perfection. He was smaller than the other four had been, but healthy and content, almost never crying. Helene had called him her miracle child, her last baby. She'd cried for hours the day he'd started kindergarten.

Still holding the picture, Troy walked to the master bedroom and then through the sliding glass doors to the courtyard garden. Helene's garden, though it was his daughter-in-law Collette who kept it in shape now.

He dropped to the ornate metal bench and watched the honeybees dart among the blossoms and the two hummingbirds that were dive-bombing each other over territorial rights to the sugar water in their feeder. He sat the picture on the seat beside him, leaned back and closed his eyes.

I let you down, Helene. I let you down in so many ways. I didn't fight hard enough to stay out of prison. I was consumed with grief and naive enough that I believed innocent until proven guilty was more than an empty premise.

I wasn't here for the boys. Dakota's stubborn, like I am. I don't know if he'll ever come home and give me a chance to prove I'm not the monster he's convinced I am.

"I thought I might find you out here."

He jumped at the voice, then turned to the glass door he'd left open behind him. "Ruthanne, have you ever heard of ringing the doorbell?"

"I rang it. You didn't answer. But your truck was parked in front so I figured you might be out here."

She joined him in the garden, her high heels clacking against the rough stone walkway. Her straight black skirt was a snug fit on her shapely body and the emerald green of her blouse set off her fiery eyes. She was damned attractive for a woman her age. Too bad she was so annoying.

She took the garden chair and crossed her legs so that the skirt rode up to indecent levels. "You know it's time you stop just sitting around grieving for a woman who's been dead for nineteen years."

"I don't just sit around. I work a ranch."

"You should get out more. The Stevensons are having a cocktail fundraiser next weekend for their son-in-law who's running for agriculture commissioner. You should go."

"I wasn't invited."

"You could go as my guest."

"I'm busy."

"Doing what?"

"I don't know yet."

"You are one hardheaded man, Troy Ledger. Anyway, I didn't just stop by to point out your faults. I came to ask if you'd read the Austin paper this morning."

"No, should I have?"

"There was a brief mention of Dakota in one of the columns in the spotlight section."

He set up straighter, his interest piqued. "What did it say about him?"

"Apparently there's a bull-riding event in San Antonio this week and many of the country's top bull riders are participating. Dakota was one of the ones they named."

In San Antonio and Dakota hadn't even bothered to call, much less come for a visit. Troy tried to hide the hurt from Ruthanne. "What did they say about him?"

"That he was the world champion two years ago."

"I already knew that. My grandson Joey and I caught him on cable TV a few months ago. We've managed to see him several times since."

"He was injured last night. The paper said he was thrown and the bull kicked him in the chest."

Troy got a sick feeling in the pit of his stomach. "Did they say how serious the injuries were?"

"Only that they were bad enough to send him to the emergency room. At the time the article was written, they weren't sure if he'd be able to participate tonight. I thought you'd want to call and check on him if you hadn't already heard from him."

"I hadn't heard." Troy hated to admit that he didn't even know how to get in touch with his youngest son.

Maybe Wyatt could track him down. Or it could be that Dylan or Sean had Dakota's phone number.

Troy wondered what Dakota would say if he just showed up at his hotel room.

"I have the newspaper in the car if you want it," Ruthanne said.

"I'd appreciate that."

"There's also an interesting article on my ex."

"Dare I ask what our illustrious senator is up to now?"

"Another senator filed for divorce and claimed irreconcilable differences. He says his wife is having an affair with Riley."

"Another juicy scandal to entertain those inside the beltway."

"Riley was always good at providing that. Neither he nor your friend Able Drake ever knew when to keep their pants zipped."

"You can't compare Able to Riley."

"Of course I can. You never could see what was going on right under your eyes, but I wasn't that blind."

"What's that supposed to mean?"

"You figure it out." She stepped closer, reached over and let a painted fingernail trail his jawbone. "Let me know what you discover about Dakota. And in the meantime, if you find yourself in need of feminine company, you know where to find me."

"I'll keep that in mind."

He walked to the car with Ruthanne to get the newspaper. If Dakota was seriously hurt, Troy would find a way to see him. Whether Dakota liked the fact or not, he was Troy's son.

"THAT WAS A complete waste of time," Viviana said as they left the police station. "At least it was for me. Hopefully the convenience-shop owner had better luck."

"It's too bad they haven't found your car. It could have usable fingerprints."

"I'm just glad I didn't get in that car with the thug."

Dakota opened the passenger door of his truck and waited while she climbed in. "I'm famished," he said. "How about a late lunch?"

"I'm not sure I can eat. My stomach has been tied in knots ever since I saw that gun last night. I'll sit with you while you eat."

But first she wanted to call and check on Briana. Not that her daughter wasn't perfectly safe and in good hands with Claire.

Viviana's cell phone rang before she got the chance to make the call. This time she checked the caller ID, but to no avail. It said *Unavailable*. "Hopefully, it's news that they've found my car." She flipped it open.

"Hello."

"Is this Dr. Mancini?" The caller was female and her voice was low and shaky.

"Yes, but I'm not on duty. If you're having an emergency, you should call 911."

"It's not an emergency, at least not that kind of emergency. But I need to talk to you. It's important."

"Who is this?"

"Shelby Lucas. You don't know me, but you were my brother's physician last night."

"You're Kevin Lucas's sister?"

"Yes, ma'am."

That explained his last muddled murmurings. He was trying to give her a message for his sister. "I'm sorry I was unable to do more for him, but there was no way to save him."

"I know. That's what the police detective said."

"If you need any information from Kevin's medical file with the E.R., you'll need to check with hospital records."

"Thanks, but I really need to talk to you in person. Can we meet somewhere?"

"I'm not at the hospital today and there's really nothing I can say except that the bullets entered the skull and did extensive damage to the brain tissue."

"I didn't call about Kevin."

"Then I don't understand."

"I called about Hank Bateman." Her voice dropped so low that Viviana couldn't be sure she'd heard her right.

"Did you say Hank Bateman?"

"Yes."

Viviana felt Dakota's gaze boring into her as he turned into the parking lot of a chain steakhouse.

"How do you know Hank?"

"I'll explain, just not over the phone. I can call you back. I have to go now."

"Wait. We're stopping for lunch. You can meet us at the restaurant."

"I need to talk in private."

"That's not possible, but anything you have to say you can say in front of my friend. He knows about the trial and my dealings with Bateman. You can trust him as much as you trust me."

"Which restaurant?" Shelby's voice had dropped to a whisper, as if she were afraid someone would overhear her conversation.

Viviana gave her the name and the address and described the sapphire-blue blouse and the white capris she was wearing.

She heard a man's booming voice and then a click as Shelby broke the connection. She had a growing suspicion that Shelby Lucas would not keep their rendezvous.

She went back and saved the number Shelby had called from. Any information about Hank Bateman might come in handy before the trial was over.

It was midafternoon and the restaurant was quiet. Viviana tried to remember what Dakota liked to eat, but she wasn't sure they'd had a real meal the entire six days they were together. She'd been too infatuated to think of food and her stomach, like the rest of her, had swirled in a constant state of fluttering excitement.

It had been February and a cold front had moved in. They'd stayed inside and nibbled on cheese and crackers for energy. Once after making love, they'd cooked pancakes as the sun was coming up. Dakota had spilled flour down his bare chest and it had stuck like snowflakes on his dark hairs.

She had a sudden craving for pancakes now. Fortunately, they weren't on the luncheon menu. Instead she ordered a grilled chicken salad. Dakota ordered a porterhouse steak with a baked potato.

She'd barely nibbled at her meal and Dakota was half-through with his when a reed-thin young woman with punky red highlights in her black hair entered the restaurant. She wore oversize sunglasses, tight denim shorts and a white cotton shirt that was so big it fell off her narrow shoulders. Her belly had a swell to it that indicated she was a few months pregnant.

"Ten to one that's your girl Shelby," Dakota said.

"I'm inclined to agree with you. She doesn't look

like your typical steakhouse clientele, especially for this neighborhood."

Viviana stood and waved so that Shelby would see them tucked away in a back booth. Shelby put her head down, crossed the room and stopped near Viviana. A tissue clutched in her hand was twisted into shreds.

"You must be Shelby," Viviana said.

"Yes. And you're Dr. Mancini. I recognize you from a picture that Hank has." Shelby's voice was as shaky and unsure as she seemed.

"Hank carries my picture around?"

"Not exactly, but he has it at the house."

Not comforting. "I would think he had better things to do with his time."

"He just doesn't want to go back to jail."

He should have thought of that before he started shaking Leslie Compton, Viviana thought. She kept that to herself. No use upsetting Shelby any more than she already was, especially before she heard what the woman had come to say.

Viviana kept her tone congenial. "Did you have trouble finding the restaurant?"

"No. I knew where it was. I used to date one of the cooks. That was a few years back."

"Dr. Mancini told me about your brother," Dakota said, breaking into the conversation. "I'm sorry for your loss. This must be a very difficult time for you."

"It's hard. Kevin had problems, with drugs, you know. He liked to get high. But he never hurt anyone. He didn't deserve to get shot."

"Do you have any idea why someone shot him?" Dakota asked.

Shelby finally looked up to face Dakota. "Are you a cop or a lawyer or something?"

"Nope. I'm just a cowboy."

"You ask questions like a cop. Anyway, I didn't come here to talk about Kevin."

"So tell me about Hank Bateman," Viviana said. "How do you know him?"

"I'm his woman."

Obviously post Karen Compton. "How long have the two of you been together?"

"Ever since Karen dumped him. I stood by him."

"Hasn't he been in jail most of that time?"

"Yeah, but we still talked. His friends looked out for me while he was locked up."

"Looked out for" most likely meant supplied her with drugs. Now she was emaciated, unsteady and fearful… and probably barely out of her teens.

"What is it that you feel I should know about Hank?"

"He didn't kill that baby. He wasn't even home that night."

"He brought her to the hospital," Viviana reminded her.

"I know, but that was because he came back and found her like that."

Shelby was either extremely naive or lying. Or else Hank Bateman had brainwashed her.

"That's between Hank and the police, Shelby. All I can testify is the condition of Leslie Compton when she was admitted to the E.R."

The waitress stopped by to see if Shelby was joining them for lunch.

"Nothing for me," Shelby said.

"Are you sure?" Dakota asked. "You might feel better if you eat. My treat."

"No. I couldn't keep anything down, what with Kevin getting killed. A diet cola would be good, though."

The waitress nodded and left a napkin for Shelby.

Shelby smoothed the cotton square with her fingertips, rubbing so hard the pressure against the plastic counter made a squeaking noise. "Don't testify against Hank, Dr. Mancini. Please, just tell the attorney you changed you mind."

"Did Hank ask you to talk to me?"

"No, and he wouldn't like it if he knew I was here. Please don't tell him."

"Did you ask Karen Compton not to testify? Is that why she left town?"

"No. I thought…" She shook her head, her eyes downcast. "I didn't know she'd left town. I haven't seen her in months."

"But you know her."

"We were friends once. She doesn't have anything to do with me since Hank took me for his girlfriend."

"Maybe she just doesn't want to be around Hank since he killed her baby," Viviana said. "Maybe you should think about finding someone else to be with, too. What if he took a notion to shake your baby to death?"

Shelby started to shake. "He wouldn't hurt his own kid. He's not like that. Please, just tell the attorney you changed your mind and they'd probably just call off the trial."

"I can't do that, Shelby. I have to testify and I have to tell the truth about what I know. I won't be cajoled or frightened out of it. I have to do what's right."

"If something happens… Well, just remember that I

begged you not to. I have to go now, but don't tell anyone I talked to you, especially not Detective Cortez."

"I take it you've met the detective."

"Yes, he came by this morning to tell me about Kevin getting killed. He even tried to blame that on Hank, but I know Hank didn't do it."

"What makes you so sure?"

"Hank was with me last night."

"What time did you talk to Detective Cortez?"

"Early this morning, around eight."

That was before the detective had turned up at Viviana's house, yet Cortez had indicated he had no idea what Kevin Lucas was referring to when he mumbled *Shell*.

Detective Cortez was the one person she'd trusted to level with her. Now she had to wonder if she could even rely on him.

"Did the detective say who he thought killed your brother?"

"No, but I think he's the one who came to tell me about his death because he's talked to me before about Hank."

The waitress returned with the drink, but Shelby ignored it in her hurry to leave.

"She's a wreck," Dakota said as he watched Shelby bump into and almost knock over a chair on her way out.

"She's scared, but I don't know if she's afraid for me or for Hank."

"I think she's afraid for you," Dakota said.

"How can you tell?"

"Just a hunch. Have you thought about backing out?"

"And let Hank Bateman get away with murdering that helpless infant? I couldn't live with myself if I did that."

"I understand, but if Bateman is behind everything that happened last night, he's a dangerous lunatic. Which means you're stuck with me for eight more days, so we might as well work at being friends again."

"We were never friends, Dakota. We were madly infatuated lovers from practically the moment we met."

"We could always give that a try."

"You can barely move."

"Then we can at least be civil to each other, which means no more locking yourself away upstairs as if being near me is going to contaminate you. We're parents. We should at least be able to talk."

"Deal," she agreed.

And for eight days she'd go through the torment of being near Dakota without touching him. Hearing him in the shower without joining him. Sleeping in the same house without crawling into his arms.

Eight days of agony in order to keep Briana safe while not falling helplessly in love with the wrong man all over again.

The trial could not come too soon.

THE SUN WAS low in the sky by the time they'd picked up Briana from Claire's, stopped at the market for a few groceries and driven back to Viviana's town house. Dakota hadn't complained but Viviana could tell he was still in significant pain. He was constantly rubbing his right shoulder and she'd seen him wince over nothing more that hitting a rough spot in the road. Worse, he cringed at times just trying to take a deep breath.

"I have some pain meds," she said as he pulled into her driveway. "You need to take two tablets and go to bed."

"Does that mean I'm no longer relegated to the couch?"

"I'll have to change the sheets but then you can have Claire's room."

"Is that your best offer?"

"Dakota, don't—"

"I know. I know," Dakota interrupted. "I was just trying to inject a little levity into what has been a harrowing day for both of us. You need to relax a little, too. If I say I'll protect you, I will."

He killed the engine and climbed out of the truck.

He'd made a valid point. Why couldn't she just relax and accept his protection? She was the one who'd ended their relationship and he'd merely stayed away as she'd asked. She was the one who hadn't found a way to get word to him that he was a father.

But she couldn't relax around him, would never be able to joke about his coming to her bed. The memories of their time together were too potent. The attraction between them was still far too dynamic.

She got out of the truck, opened the back door and began to unbuckle Briana from her car seat.

"Let me help you with her," he said.

"I don't think you should be lifting yet."

"Briana doesn't weigh much more than those ice packs you keep pushing on me."

"You'd be surprised. But if you insist on trying, I'll get the groceries."

"I'd forgotten about those."

"I can handle them. I'm used to it. Just don't try to pick up Briana with your right arm."

"You got it, Doc."

Viviana snagged the bag of groceries, then waited

while Dakota removed Briana from her car seat. The darling kicked a few times in protest. Then she dropped her head to his shoulder, as if it were the most natural thing in the world for this cowboy with a smile that matched her own to be carrying her into the house.

Briana would easily learn to love Dakota, but could he love her back? Would she be able to count on him or would he provide only broken promises and rejection? Would she grow up believing there was something wrong with her that kept him from loving her?

Viviana pulled her new set of door keys from her handbag and hurried to unlock the door. She noticed the doll almost at once, at the edge of the walkway next to a pot of blooming mandevilla. It wasn't Briana's and it hadn't been there when they'd left.

Apprehension made her palms clammy as she stooped to pick up the plastic-and-fabric doll. It wasn't until she'd lifted it that she realized that the back of the doll's head had been crushed. Fake blood dripped down the collar of the doll's delicate sky-blue dress.

This was pathetically sick. She started to slam it back to the walk. That's when she spotted the square of paper tucked inside the doll's cotton panties.

Carefully maneuvering the groceries to free her fingers, she retrieved the note and began to read. The words blurred. Her hands began to shake. And then she felt the earth moving beneath her feet and the walkway rushing toward her face.

CHAPTER NINE

THE DIAPER BAG hadn't been zipped all the way, and when Dakota grabbed the strap to sling it over his free shoulder, two bottles fell and bumped along the driveway before rolling beneath the car. Briana started to wave her hands in the air and do her best to squirm from his hold.

"You think that's funny, do you? I guess you want to crawl under the truck and get them?"

"Duuuuu."

"Chanting won't help, sweetheart. I'm on to you, little Miss Viviana, Jr."

She pushed a thumb into his cheek and smiled. His breath caught and all of a sudden the significance of the moment hit him. He was holding his daughter for the very first time. Not as a newborn, the way most fathers did it, but as a seven-month-old with an attitude and a personality.

She was a real person. She'd have needs. She'd have expectations. Could he be the kind of father she deserved?

You're your father's kid, Dakota. Unless you continuously fight it, the evil will take control of you one day, just like it did him.

He cringed as his uncle's condemning voice echoed in his head.

There was a splat and the sound of breaking glass. Dakota spun around. Viviana was lying on the walkway, her leg twisted beneath her. The bottle of blackberry jam was shattered in jagged shards next to her. Two oranges rolled toward him.

The sights registered as he raced toward Viviana. He knelt down beside her, dropping the diaper bag to the grass and bracing Viviana against him as best he could with Briana's short arms wrapped around his neck.

"Viviana. What happened? Talk to me."

She blinked rapidly and her eyes fluttered open. "Dakota."

"I'm right here. Did you trip? Are you hurt?"

A tinge of color returned to her pasty face. "No, but I've had all I can take of Hank Bateman." She held up the broken doll as if it were evidence to justify her statement.

"Did you trip over the doll?" He hadn't a clue what that had to do with Hank.

"Read the note." Viviana's voice was shaky. She pushed a small square of paper into Dakota's hand.

Briana began to cry and reach for her mother.

"I'll take her," Viviana said.

"Okay, but don't try to stand with her. And watch for the broken glass." Dakota handed Briana over and read the scribbled words.

Testify and your daughter's head will match the doll's.

Viviana was right. This time Hank Bateman had gone too far.

"Briana's down for the night. At least I hope she is. Can we talk?"

"Sure." As long as it wasn't about the relationship

they no longer had. Dakota looked up from the beer he'd been drinking as Viviana entered the kitchen.

They were practically the first words Viviana had spoken since Dirty Harry had left. He'd come over to examine the doll and had taken it and the note with him. Since then, Viviana had been upstairs with Briana, not to avoid him this time, but just to regroup.

That left him alone to stew about what he could do to stop Hank Bateman, short of cracking the back of *his* skull. That possibility was steadily gaining favor.

"How about a beer?" he offered. "Or maybe something stronger?"

"A beer would be good." Viviana slid into a kitchen chair.

He took a beer from the refrigerator and set it in front of her before getting another for himself.

"I've made a decision."

Viviana's somber tone made him edgy. He remained standing. "Let's hear it."

"I'm leaving town."

He hadn't expected that. "What about your job?"

"I have vacation time banked, and I've been granted approval to take it starting as soon as my break is over. Even if I didn't have the time coming, it wouldn't matter. Briana is my life. I have to protect her at any cost."

"Have you given any thought to where you want to go?"

"I have." Viviana took a sip of the beer. "My dad has a sister who lives in a small Texas town not too far from here but off the beaten path."

"Are the two of you close?"

"Closer than I am to anyone else in my family. She pretty much held me together when my mother died. She even took care of the funeral details and paid for everything. She said I'd need the little money Mother had left after her illness for med school."

"I can see why you'd think of her at a time like this."

"Mother didn't stay in touch with any of Dad's family after the divorce. Apparently, neither did Dad. Aunt Abby hasn't heard from him in years. She thinks he may have moved to Mexico."

"Does that mean you never hear from him, either?"

"That's exactly what I mean. I used to receive a Christmas card once a year. Now I don't even get that."

There were obviously enough dysfunctional families to go around.

"Does she know why you're coming?"

"I told her everything. I thought that was only fair. She offered to drive down and pick me up, but I told her you'd drive me. Not that you have to. My insurance will cover a rental car."

"I thought we'd agreed that I could protect you here."

"That was before the doll. I'm not making light of your offer, Dakota. This just seems the better solution to the problem for both of us."

"You might have given me a vote."

"That would have only complicated matters. Aunt Abby has a small house, but she said she'll make room for me and Briana. She even has a neighbor whose kid just outgrew his baby bed. She's going to borrow it for Briana to use."

So that was the plan. Ditch him and turn to the aunt. His blood began to boil. Viviana's life might be hers to do with as she pleased, but Briana was his daughter. He had a say in keeping her safe.

"If dear Aunt Abby only has one extra bed, you better hope it's big enough for two."

She looked at him as if he were speaking Greek. "That's just the point, Dakota. If I'm with Aunt Abby, you won't feel compelled to stick around to protect us."

"I never said I was compelled. I just made that choice. And your aunt may be as good and as trustworthy as gold, but she's no match for Hank Bateman."

"She won't have to be. Hank will never look for me there. No one in San Antonio even knows I have an aunt. Besides, you said the first time we were together that you lost your edge if you stayed away from bull riding for any extended period of time."

"We're only talking about a week. Once the trial is over, either Hank goes free or he's locked up for years. Either way, the need to keep you from testifying becomes a moot point."

"If you really want to go with us, I suppose that can be arranged."

"Is there another man in your life? Is that why you're so hell-bent on ditching me?"

"No. I told you there's been no one since you. When would I have had time for a man even if I'd wanted one?"

He picked up his beer. "Then what's the name of this safe little town where the three of us will crowd in on poor Aunt Abby?"

"Mustang Run."

Dakota choked on his beer. Viviana jumped up, grabbed a couple of napkins off the counter and handed one to Dakota. While he dabbed the sputtered liquid from his chin and the front of his shirt, she wiped off the counter.

"Are you okay?" she asked.

"Not with this plan. You can just forget about Mustang Run. We are not going there."

"Why? What do you have against Mustang Run? Aunt Abby says it's a charming town. And the sheriff is one of her best friends. She said he'll be there in a matter of minutes if I need him for anything at all."

"If you want to disappear, you need a big city. We can drive to Dallas or fly to Chicago or even New York. I'll take care of expenses. It will be like a vacation."

And if he decided to return to the bull-riding circuit or if he got tired of being the protective father he claimed he didn't know how to be, she and Briana would be stranded in a strange town where they knew no one. Besides, he hadn't objected to a small town until she'd mentioned Mustang Run by name.

"Give me one good reason why I shouldn't go to Mustang Run," she demanded.

He exhaled slowly. "Troy Ledger."

"What does that mean?"

"You asked for one good reason. I just gave it to you. It's Troy Ledger."

"Who—or what—is Troy Ledger?"

"My infamous father. You must be the only person in Texas who hasn't heard of him."

Viviana was certain Dakota had never mentioned any of his family. Another of the problems with jumping headlong into a week of devouring each other. Between the chocolate and whipped cream and myriad other sexual experiences so hot and exciting they had blown her mind, she and Dakota had passed right over all the normal relationship preliminaries.

"What's Troy Ledger's claim to infamy?"

"He was sentenced to life in prison."

"On what charges?"

"Murdering my mother."

It took a few seconds for the shock to settle. "I had no idea. I'm so sorry."

"Don't be. It was a long time ago."

Yet he was clearly still traumatized by it. "Do you want to talk about it?"

"Not much point."

"Have you seen or been in contact with your father since he went to prison?"

"No. The last time I saw him was at his conviction. I'd just turned seven at the time. Before that, I hadn't spoken to him since the day my mother was killed. I haven't until this day, and I'm perfectly happy keeping it that way. I'm not looking for pity. I'm also not looking to reconnect with Troy Ledger."

"Isn't he still in prison?"

"He was released a year ago on a technicality. He returned to the ranch in Mustang Run and is now living in the house where my mother was shot and killed."

"Maybe you should go back to Mustang Run, Dakota. It might give you some closure."

"I'm not looking for closure, and I don't need you to serve as my shrink."

"Do you have other family in Mustang Run?"

"I do now. My brother Dylan and his wife live on Willow Creek Ranch with my father, though they have their own house. My brother Tyler is in the army and stationed in Afghanistan, but his new bride, Julie, is living on the ranch in a starter house Troy, Dylan and Sean built for her and Tyler."

"Who's Sean?"

"Another brother. He's a horse whisperer. He married Dad's prison psychiatrist and they bought a horse farm in Bandera."

"How many brothers do you have?"

"Four. Wyatt's a homicide detective in Atlanta. He and I are the only two siblings who haven't jumped on the big happy family bandwagon."

She wondered if Wyatt was as bitter as Dakota…and why the others weren't. "Aunt Abby probably knows your father and your brothers. She owns a diner in town, so she knows almost everybody for miles around."

"I'm sure she knows them. Dylan's married to the sheriff's daughter. I'm going with you when you leave here, Viviana. So pick any town other than Mustang Run."

"I can't, Dakota. It's all arranged. I'll feel safe there and I'm close enough to come back to San Antonio if the prosecutor needs me for any reason. And if the hospital falls into a serious bind due to some kind of catastrophe or natural disaster, I could leave Briana with Abby and return to work, even sleep at the hospital if I think it's necessary."

Those were all valid reasons, but just as importantly, she was getting an uncanny premonition that they were meant to go to Mustang Run. "If three of your brothers have reconnected with Troy Ledger, then it can't kill you to at least make a visit home, Dakota."

"I have no home."

He turned his back on her and walked away. For the first time, she'd glimpsed a part of Dakota that lived beneath his almost impenetrable shell. He was more vulnerable than he wanted anyone to know.

It changed things between them, connected them in ways the initial spontaneous and fevered attraction hadn't. They could never go to back to the purely physical relationship, to desire so primal it defied reason.

That didn't mean they couldn't move on to something even better.

But she definitely wasn't counting on that.

DAKOTA STRETCHED OUT on the bed that unofficially belonged to the nanny. It was far more accommodating of his size than the sofa had been, but there was still no way to get comfortable.

He was used to aches and pains. It went with the bull-riding territory. Some days it was worse than others. Today it was a killer. Thank God he'd been wearing the protective vest.

Truth was, though, that it wasn't the soreness that had him tense and edgy. It was everything coming down on him at once. Running into Viviana and finding her in danger. Learning he was a father. Actually holding a beautiful baby born of his own seed.

His seed. The Ledger legacy.

You're cursed, Dakota Ledger. You got a killer's bl running through your veins.

His uncle's words echoed through his mind as they had so many times before. At six, they'd terrified him. That was before he'd learned what real terror was.

His cell phone vibrated, making a clacking sound against the wooden nightstand. He grabbed the phone quickly before the noise woke Briana.

"Yo."

"Dakota, hi, it's Dylan."

Dread swelled inside him. Surely Dylan hadn't already heard he'd be in Mustang Run tomorrow. "What's up?"

"We heard you got thrown hard last night and ended up in the hospital."

"Bad news travels fast."

"It did this time. You were mentioned in the morning newspaper."

"Must be a slow news day for the sportswriters."

"How bad were you hurt?"

"I've got a few bruised ribs and a sprained right shoulder. Nothing that won't heal itself in a few days."

"Good. Dad saw it and he got worried."

Sure he did. "You can tell him I'm fine. I'll take a few days to heal and then I'll be back on the bulls."

"Since you are so close and not competing for a few days, why not spend that time here at the ranch? I'd love for you to see what we've done with the spread. And we have two new colts that were foaled last month."

"I'd love to see you and the horses, and meet your wife, but I need to stick close this week in case I need some physical therapy."

"Is this about therapy or about Dad?"

No use to deny the truth. "You know how I feel about him."

"Bitterness is a heavy load to tote through life, Dakota."

"Don't get preachy on me."

"Okay, but I think you're making a mistake in not giving Dad a chance."

"It won't be my first one."

"So how about I drive over to San Antonio and meet you for lunch? We're brothers. We should be able to talk."

"Maybe next time. I've got business that needs taking care of."

"If you change your mind, I'd love to see you. We all would."

"If I change my mind, I'll call."

And look out for the ice storm if he did, 'cause hell would surely be freezing over.

DAKOTA HAD PULLED his truck into the garage when he started loading it for the trip to Mustang Run. On the outside chance someone was watching the house, there was no point in announcing they were leaving town.

He'd packed his one bag into the truck first, glad he'd made use of Viviana's washer and dryer last night to launder his lucky red shirt and the rest of his dirty clothes.

Next he lifted the cooler with Briana's bottles into the backseat of the truck and then slung two huge suitcases into the truck bed.

"I told you to let me put that luggage in the car," Viviana protested as she rolled out yet another bag.

"I used the good shoulder."

"Well, get out of the way, because I intend to put this one in the truck myself."

"Are you planning on changing clothes every five minutes?"

"No, but sometimes Briana does. Plus I have to take her bottles and food and diapers and toys and—"

"Bricks," Dakota added. "I'm sure that brown carry-on is full of bricks."

"Books from my TBR pile. I haven't finished a book since Briana was born. A week in exile should give me a chance to do that. And my weights are in there. I have to stay in shape and there's no time for the gym with Briana around."

Gym or not, whatever Viviana was doing worked. She'd added a few pounds since he'd seen her last, but they looked good on her. He was pretty sure her breasts were a little bigger, too. He'd know if…

The image of her naked slipped into his mind. He shook his head to clear it. Start thinking like that and he'd get so worked up it would make driving all but impossible.

"I need to make one last trip through the house to make sure everything is turned off and all the doors and windows are locked," Viviana said. "Then I'll get Briana from her playpen and we'll be ready to roll. Except that I need to fold the playpen and put it in the truck. Oh, no. I almost forgot her jump chair. That's a lifesaver when she gets too fussy for words."

"Keep going and I'll have to rent a moving van."

Viviana leaned against the truck. "Are you sure you want to do this?" she asked. "There's still time for you to back out."

"I don't relish spending any time in Mustang Run. But I'm not backing out. I'll see this through until the trial is over."

"I just don't want you to think that…" She hesitated.

"To think that this means I can jump your bones."

"I wasn't going to put it that way."

"I believe in telling it straight. I'm not looking for a roll in the hay as thanks, Viviana. When and if we ever make love again, it will be because we both want it. We've had delirious perfection. Duty sex won't cut it."

"You do believe in telling it straight."

Ten minutes later, they were buckled in and backing out of the driveway. A car pulled up behind them, blocking them in.

"The return of Dirty Harry," Dakota said. "Did you tell him you were leaving town?"

"No, but I guess I will now. I'd planned to give him a call later."

"Since he doesn't know you're leaving, I guess he's not just dropping by to say adios."

Dakota and Viviana both got out of the truck while Detective Cortez lumbered toward them.

The detective glared at Dakota. "I see you're still here."

Dakota decided against the first smart-ass reply that popped into his mind and settled on something slightly less obnoxious. "Do you have a problem with that?"

"Not as long as I don't have to do business with you."

"Did you find my car?" Viviana asked.

"Yep, we did. That's the good news. Now for the bad."

CHAPTER TEN

"YOUR CAR IS TOTALED," Cortez said. "An off-duty police officer spotted a flume of black smoke off a dirt road near his fishing camp about ten miles west of the city. At first he thought it was just someone burning trash. He checked it out and found the car completely gutted by flames."

"How can you be sure it's mine?"

"The VIN number was still decipherable."

Tears burned at the back of her eyes. This was totally mad. And for what? "I loved that car. I looked for weeks to find just the right color and model. I hadn't even made a payment yet. It was the first non-junky car I'd ever owned in my life."

"I guess that rules out any chance of the vehicle providing fingerprints," Dakota said.

The detective nodded.

Briana began to fuss in her car seat. She'd start to scream any minute if they didn't get moving. Viviana felt that same urge.

"Why steal my car only to set it on fire? If Hank Bateman is responsible for this, his actions are having just the opposite effect of what he intends. This makes me more determined than ever to see him in prison. It's where that lunatic belongs."

"There's no proof he's behind it. He definitely didn't set the car on fire himself."

"How can you be so sure?" Dakota asked.

"We have a tail on him. Your car was set on fire sometime during the night and Hank hasn't left his house since yesterday afternoon."

"What time yesterday?"

"Somewhere around 3:00 p.m."

That left Hank plenty of time to drop off the doll and the note before his movements were being monitored.

Harry Cortez stretched his arms out in front of him, then relaxed them and popped his large, knotty knuckles. "There's more."

"Oh, joy." The wisecrack fell flat. Frustration was making her ill.

"The charred remains of a body were found in the front seat."

Viviana closed her eyes and tried to obliterate the sickening image that filled her head. Being an emergency medicine specialist, she'd seen her share of victims of gruesome accidents. That didn't make the image of a fatally burned body any easier to swallow.

Dakota wrapped a steadying arm around her waist. "Has the victim been identified?"

"Not yet. It may take several days. The M.E. will likely need a dental record match."

"Male or female?" Dakota asked.

"Male. The M.E. could tell that much."

"Not likely that the thief set the car on fire and then got back in it," Dakota said.

"Not likely," the detective admitted. "We'll know more when we get the autopsy."

"This makes absolutely no sense," Viviana said. "I

go months without threats of any kind, then all of a sudden, horrors are pounding me like ice in a hailstorm."

"We'll get to the bottom of it," Cortez said. "In the meantime, I'm requesting an officer be assigned to protect you. It's either that or have you checked into a safe house. That can be pretty complicated when it involves a baby as young as yours. It can be done, though. In fact, the chief may order it."

"She has a bodyguard," Dakota said before she had a chance to answer.

"You? A rodeo jockey?"

"That's right."

"Face it, Ledger. Viviana needs a professional in charge of her protection."

"I appreciate the offer of protection," Viviana said, "but right now, I'll stick with Dakota."

The detective's expression said it all. He thought she was making a big mistake. If she was, Briana's safety would also be at risk.

But so far Dakota had a winning record. He'd saved her life two out of two times. If she'd gotten into the car with that gunman, her body might have been the one found burned to a crisp. If Dakota hadn't chased off the man at her window, he'd have gotten inside her house where she, Briana and Claire would have been at his mercy.

"Call me if you change your mind," Cortez said. He turned to walk away.

She started to shake. Dakota pulled her into his arms and held her close until the shudders ripping through her settled into a numbing stillness.

Crazy, but in spite of all the times she'd thrilled at

Dakota's touch, she'd never realized how safe it felt just to have his arms around her.

DAKOTA PARKED IN the center of the old downtown section of Mustang Run at ten minutes after one in the afternoon. From the looks of things, they'd time traveled back to the early days of the preceding century. Only instead of honky-tonks and livery stables, the one-story buildings housed small boutiques, antique shops, an ice-cream emporium, a tempting bakery and, of course, Abby's Diner.

"Just in time for lunch," Viviana said.

Dakota turned the key and killed the engine. "The sign says home cooking and fresh-baked pies. I can go for both of those." He might as well try to keep a positive spin on the whole Mustang Run adventure until it turned sour on him.

Viviana had Briana out of her seat by the time he rounded the back of the truck. "Smelly time," she said. "Can you grab the diaper bag for me? There should be a changing station in the ladies' restroom."

He retrieved it, flicked the lock button on his key and followed them inside. It didn't look like the kind of town where you needed to lock doors, but he was taking no chances.

The odors, boisterous voices and clattering of dishes attacked as the bell over the door announced their entrance. Dakota glanced at the crowded counter, where an eclectic mixture of businessmen in suits and ranchers in jeans were immersed in their meals. Several were digging into mouthwatering piles of meringue.

"If the food tastes as good as it smells and looks, I'm

destined to gain a few pounds around Aunt Abby," Dakota said.

"The smell I'm getting is not that appetizing," Viviana said. "But I am hungry and thirsty. Why don't you snare that empty booth near the window? If the waitress stops by, order me a diet cola while I change Briana."

"You got it. When do we meet the illustrious Aunt Abby?"

"She's probably in the kitchen. I'll check when I get back."

Dakota claimed the booth and then turned his concentration to the food being served by hustling waitresses. A plate of chicken and dumplings with sides of greens and fried okra looked tempting. So did a tray carrying a plate that spilled over with a huge chicken-fried steak topped by a mountain of cream gravy, all cozied up next to a mound of sliced beefsteak tomatoes.

He scanned the men at the counter with a more discerning eye. No one looked even vaguely familiar, not that he'd expect them to. Nor would he look familiar to them. He'd changed a lot since age six. If he kept a very low profile, maybe he'd actually make it through the week without his family knowing he was around.

A whiff of fried catfish had him practically drooling. His gaze followed the waitress carrying the tray of golden brown filets and crispy French fries.

She stopped at his booth. "I'll be right with you. Today's specials are listed on the board over the counter, but I'll bring menus."

Dakota scrutinized the rest of the customers. The waitress served the catfish to a man reading the newspaper in a booth across from the door to the restroom.

The man looked up as she set the plate in front of

him. He ignored her. Instead his penetrating gaze fixed on Dakota.

Dakota's mouth went dry. A roar filled his head, as deafening as the tornado he'd lived through when he was ten. He watched, muscles clenched, as Troy Ledger stood and started walking toward him.

There was no doubt it was him. Dylan had sent a picture of the three forgiving brothers and Troy via cell phone. Even if he hadn't seen the picture, Dakota would have recognized Troy. The Ledger features that were so prominent in him were also undeniable in Dakota and his brothers.

Dakota slid from the booth as Troy extended a hand.

"You were the last person I expected to run into in Abby's," Troy said.

The same was true for Dakota. Otherwise, he wouldn't be here.

"For a few seconds there, I was afraid to believe my eyes," Troy continued. His voice was husky with emotion.

Dakota swallowed hard. He so did not need this. "It's a spur-of-the-moment trip," he offered.

"That works. I'm just glad you changed your mind about driving over for a visit."

"Actually, I'm not really here to visit."

His father looked hurt, or maybe just confused.

"I'm in Mustang Run to take care of some business," Dakota said.

"What kind of business?"

"Personal."

"I see. Does that mean you weren't going to call and tell your brothers or me that you were in town?"

"I wasn't sure I'd have time for visiting." That wasn't a total lie, but it felt like one.

Troy worried an old scar that dominated the right side of his face. "Then I guess I'm lucky I ran into you here."

Great reunion they were having so far. Dakota had no idea what Troy expected of him. Whatever it was, he couldn't deliver. His right shoulder began to throb. He massaged the painful area.

"Looks like you're having trouble with that arm. The newspaper said you got roughed up pretty bad a couple of nights ago," Troy said.

"Reporters tend to exaggerate."

Thankfully, a waitress approached. She didn't have menus, but she did have a gleam in her eye. She flashed a smile that lit up her plump face as she caught hold of Troy's arm.

"Glory be and bringing in the sheaves. Tell me my eyes are not lying, Troy Ledger. This has got to be Dakota." She wiped her hands on the front of a bleached white apron.

Before Dakota could react, the matronly woman pulled him into a hug. Then she backed away and looked him over as if he were a breed bull she was thinking of buying.

"I swear you look just like your dad did at your age."

"You say that about all my sons," Troy said.

"Well, they do. I'm Abby," she said. "I know you don't remember me, Dakota, but I sure remember you. You hit me with a spitball one day in church, you little stinker. But you sure grew up nice. That you did. A darn good bull rider, too, I hear. Helene would be proud as punch of all her boys."

"Aunt Abby."

"Ba ba ga ma."

Viviana and Briana pushed into the awkward circle. It was too late to run. The party Dakota had hoped to avoid was now in full swing.

TROY STRUGGLED TO get a handle on his emotions. Dakota was actually here, standing less than a foot from him. Not the mischievous little kid who'd made them laugh with his nonstop antics. Not the boy who could make Helene cry with a bouquet of weeds picked from the yard and a sticky hug around the neck.

He was a man now. There was so much Troy needed to say to him, but it would be a waste of time. Dakota wore his resentment on his sleeve, more obvious than a tattoo, more cutting than a Bowie knife.

And Abby was going on and on, gushing over some cute, jabbering kid and preventing any chance Troy had for a conversation with the son he hadn't seen in eighteen years.

"Have you met Dakota?"

Troy studied the woman who'd asked the question. She looked like a model for one of those slick women's fashion magazines. Flawless olive complexion. Dark, curly hair that tumbled around her slender shoulders. Long, dark lashes that outlined the most expressive eyes he'd seen in many a moon.

"I've known Dakota Ledger since he was born," Abby said. "I grew up with his mother, grade school right through high school. I've been knowing Troy since he came into town and swept Helene right off her feet. 'Course they both dropped out of my life for many a year."

"So you're Troy Ledger," the young woman said. She

eyed him warily. He was used to that from strangers. It went with the murder conviction.

"I'm Troy Ledger."

"I'm Viviana Mancini. I'm very glad to meet you." Her circumspection transformed into a smile.

Abby coochie-cooed the baby and then looked back to its stunning mother. "How do you know Dakota?"

"He's the friend I told you I was bringing with me."

"Well if this old world isn't shrinking to the size of a dried-up walnut. I never dreamed Dakota Ledger was the friend you were talking about."

Troy looked at Viviana's ring finger. It was bare, which didn't necessarily mean anything these days. He hoped that Dakota's business wasn't rendezvousing in Mustang Run with a married woman who had a young kid.

"I need to finish up a couple of things in the kitchen while you kids get something to eat. Then I'll run you over to my place so you can get settled in," Abby said. She reached over and rustled the baby's thick, dark curls. "And you, Miss Briana Mancini, can have a nice long nap so you can be wide-awake to play with your great-aunt Abby when I get home tonight."

Viviana looked Troy square in the eye. "Actually, it's Briana Marie Ledger."

Shock left Troy speechless. He looked to Dakota, but his son was staring at Viviana as if she'd just committed treason. He glanced at the dark-haired baby. There were resemblances.

"Are you saying that Briana is my grandchild?"

The couple in front of them turned to stare. That was the least of Troy's concerns.

Dakota straightened and finally met Troy's gaze. "Yes, Briana's my daughter."

"Don't that beat all?" Abby said. "My grandniece is a Ledger." She punched Troy in the arm. "We're practically kin."

"It looks that way." Troy got a funny feeling in his chest. He stared at the baby. Amazed. And suddenly enchanted.

"If you're here with Dakota, then why in the world do you want to be cooped up in my little house?" Abby asked. "Not that I'm not glad to have you but Troy's got a big, rambling house out there on Willow Creek Ranch. And you'd have at least three tough cowboys to protect you and Briana from that baby killer back in San Antonio."

Troy's ire fired like an explosion. "What's this about a baby killer?"

Now everyone in the restaurant was starting to stare.

"I think we'd best finish this conversation in the kitchen," Abby said.

"Anyone who tries to hurt my granddaughter better have his will made out."

VIVIANA KNEW SHE hadn't played fair. She might feel a lot guiltier about that had it not been for the body that had burned along with her car. Hank Bateman might not have lit the fire himself, but he was behind it. It was the kind of act she'd expect from a man sick enough to kill a helpless infant.

Dakota was strong, tough and willing to protect her and Briana, but he was only one man. She liked the odds a whole lot better with four Ledgers to fight off the bad guys.

If there was more to her reasoning, she wasn't admitting it yet. But she had liked Troy from almost the minute she'd met him. So had Briana, and babies were seldom fooled. Dakota might not need a father, but Briana could use a doting grandfather and she'd never get that from Viviana's dad.

"Do we have much farther to go?" she asked.

"About five miles." Dakota kept both hands on the steering wheel and didn't glance her way.

"Are you going to pout and not speak to me the whole time we're on the ranch?"

"Don't tell me you're going to start worrying about my feelings now."

"Staying at the ranch makes sense and you know it, Dakota. We'll each have our own bedroom, even Briana. We'll be on an isolated ranch with no one around to see and identify us in case Hank Bateman or one of his henchmen happens to come snooping around."

"And I'll get to roam the house where my mother was murdered. We'll just have a jolly old time."

Viviana had been so focused on doing what was best for Briana, she hadn't even considered that. Guilt set in, causing her to rethink her impulsive decision. "I'm sorry, Dakota. If you don't want to stay at the ranch, turn around and we'll go back to Abby's. That was our original agreement. I had no right to change it against your will."

He nudged his Stetson back an inch or two. "No. You were right. The ranch makes more sense and I was probably going to have to face my dad one day just to get my brothers off my back. It may as well be now."

"You might consider giving him a chance. Innocent

men have been convicted before. Your father could be telling the truth."

"He's definitely convinced Dylan, Tyler and Sean that he is."

"And they know him a lot better than you do," she reminded him.

"Okay, I concede that he might be innocent. Are you happy now?"

"If you think he might be innocent, then I don't see why you're so dead set against at least trying to reconnect with him."

"He doesn't need me. And I don't need him. That's just how it is."

"But not how it has to be."

Dakota turned into a dirt drive and stopped at a metal gate. The sign hanging above it read Welcome to Willow Creek Ranch. A large black crow set atop the sign. It cawed loudly, almost as if it were warning her to stay out.

A shiver crept up Viviana's spine. What if she'd been wrong in insisting they come here? Evil had visited this ranch the day Helene Ledger had been brutally murdered. What if it came again?

She was being foolishly superstitious now. Evil didn't hang around like a ghost waiting until the perfect victim came its way.

Hank Bateman was the only evil she had to worry about, and it was extremely unlikely he'd show up here. If he did, the Ledgers could handle him. Actually, Dakota probably could singlehandedly take care of a rat like Hank.

But why take that chance? Why risk Dakota's life

when all the backup he needed was waiting right here on the ranch he refused to call home?

"THIS IS THE guest room," Troy said. "Helene planned this wing of the house. The master bedroom is right on the other side of that courtyard garden. That was Helene's favorite spot. Dakota used to take his dump truck out there and move dirt around. Told us he was fertilizing."

The house held few memories for Dakota. Either he'd been too young when his mother had died or else he'd blocked them from his consciousness. He stepped back into the hallway.

Viviana seemed fascinated by the house's history. He doubted either of them would miss him.

He wandered back down the hallway and paused at a closed door. Impulsively, he opened it and stepped into the room. Finally the familiarity spurred a few haunting memories. This had been his room. The twin bed next to the window had been his bed. He'd kept all his treasures in the bottom drawer of that old pine dresser. He'd even put a little grass snake in there once.

He ran his finger along the back edge of the dresser until he felt a small niche. He'd carved it there with Wyatt's scout knife.

Wyatt had found him with the knife and told him he'd be in big trouble if his mother found out he was playing with knives and cutting up furniture. Wyatt had never told on him.

Odd that he remembered something as mundane as that when he couldn't remember anything about his mother's murder. He didn't really remember her, but he knew what she looked like.

His grandmother had made sure of that. She'd given

him a scrapbook of pictures of him with his mother so that he'd never forget her. He'd slept with that scrapbook under his pillow for years.

There was something else behind the old chest. He could feel it with his fingertips but couldn't tell what it was. Pain seared through his chest as he scooted the heavy wood furniture away from the wall. Oddly, the pain was a relief. It brought his focus back to the present.

The object was nothing but a book. He stooped and picked it up. *Mike Mulligan and His Steam Shovel*. Just a kid's book, but as fast as quicksilver a memory leaped from the crevices where it had been in hiding.

His mother had read that book to him over and over. She'd try to talk him into something else, but he'd always wanted Mike. He couldn't have been more than three years old then.

A mother who read to you. Brothers who played with you and helped keep you out of trouble. A ranch to explore. Horses to ride. A father to teach you guy things.

That was the life he would have had if his mother had lived. Dakota's chest tightened and hot flashes of pain slashed at the muscles around his rib cage. The tension was adding strain to the injured areas. Riding bulls would be easier than facing this.

He stuck his hat back on his head, walked to the kitchen and out the back door. He needed fresh air and space to breathe.

TROY TIGHTENED THE last bolt. "All done. The crib is ready for Briana. It's a good thing Abby found one because there's none in my attic. We got rid of it after Dakota outgrew it. He was the caboose."

"Dakota has issues with you," Viviana said, for some

reason thinking she should explain his walking out without saying a word to either of them.

"He has reason to," Troy said. "I'd probably feel the same if I was in his place. Don't apologize for him. He'll come around if and when he's ready."

"Okay." Viviana shook out the nice clean crib sheet and fit it on the mattress. "This bed is in great shape."

"Louella had five grandchildren. She probably bought it new when the first one came along."

"I'm glad she's not using it now."

"I could use a cup of coffee," Troy said. "How about you? I could make some fresh."

"I'm not much of a coffee drinker after that first cup in the morning, but I'd love a diet soda if you have one."

"So happens I do. Sean's wife, Eve, is a soda drinker."

"Let me check on Briana and I'll meet you in the kitchen," Viviana said.

As Troy gathered up his tools, Viviana walked back to the cozy bedroom with the garden view. Briana was fast asleep in her playpen. Maybe she knew she was safe on her grandfather's hill country ranch. Viviana was even beginning to relax herself.

Her soda was open and waiting, accompanied by a glass of ice. She drank too many sodas, a habit picked up while she'd been cramming her way through med school. She'd actually been making progress toward cutting back when the Hank Bateman nightmare had started.

Troy poured himself a cup of stale coffee and joined her at the kitchen table. Apparently he'd decided not to bother with making a fresh pot. The conversation they'd started in the bedroom was still bothering her.

"Stop me if you think I'm interfering where I'm not

welcome, but I don't think Dakota's issues with you are all about his mother's murder."

"That's good because I didn't kill Helene. I'm innocent on that count."

His tone disturbed her. "Are you guilty of something else?"

"I'm guilty of blind complacency."

"I'm not following you."

"I didn't fight hard enough to prove my innocence. I'm not sure I cared what became of me at the time. I loved Helene so much that when I lost her, I wanted to die. My boys should have been reason enough to fight for my freedom, but I simply couldn't face life without her."

"So you just let them convict you without mounting a defense?"

"I'm not sure I could have turned the tide of suspicion, but, yes, basically, I didn't fight for my freedom. I was so depressed I didn't even cooperate with my attorney. I just clammed up or else I would have gone berserk that no one was finding her killer."

"Dakota said he never heard from you when he was growing up."

"Once the depression and grief became tolerable, I tried to get in touch with the boys. Helene's parents filed a lawsuit claiming they were terrified of me and that contact with me was too upsetting. To tell the truth, I figured the boys were better off with me out of their lives. I was in prison for life. I had nothing to offer. The best thing I could do for them was let them have a normal life."

Briana was only seven months old, but Viviana couldn't imagine going through life and never knowing if she was healthy or sick or if her heart was bursting with happiness or breaking into tiny pieces.

"I can't undo what's done," Troy said. "Dakota is a grown man. He'll make up his own mind about whether or not he wants me in his life, just as my other sons have done. I have no choice but to accept that."

Troy sipped the stale coffee. "So let's talk about something we might be able to do something about. Tell me about this trouble you're having."

She explained as succinctly as she could, filling him in on the gory details.

"Hank Bateman." Troy chewed on the edge of his bottom lip as if deep in thought. "For some reason that name sounds familiar."

"Maybe you've met him. Do you travel to San Antonio often?"

"I haven't been there since my release from… Prison. That's why the name sounds familiar."

"Was Hank in prison with you?"

"Not that I recall, but there was a George Bateman. Big guy. Mean as a snake. Got in a fight once and killed a guy with his bare hands. He said it was self-defense. Nobody who saw it was brave enough to say he was lying."

"Intimidating witnesses. That sounds like Hank, but you said your prison mate was named George."

Troy nodded. "But he talked about a brother and I'm almost sure his name was Hank. I know George was from San Antonio."

"Is George still in prison?"

"No, he was granted parole a good two years before I was released. I can check, see what I can find out about him. I don't see offhand how knowing about George could help you, but more information never hurts."

Viviana looked up at the sound of footsteps at the

back door. Dakota stepped inside, took off his hat and tossed it onto a chair. "Am I interrupting anything?"

"No," Troy said. "We were just talking."

"Troy put the crib together," Viviana said.

"Thanks. I was coming in to do that now."

"It was no trouble," Troy said. "Fact is, it was kind of fun. It's the first time we've had a baby around the house since you were born."

"Briana's only here for a week," Dakota quickly reminded him.

"This time," Viviana corrected. "But she'll come back to visit her grandfather." She knew Dakota's feelings toward Troy, but she thought he was being grossly unfair to the man. Based on first impressions, she liked Troy a lot.

"When do I get to meet the rest of the family?" she asked.

"Tomorrow evening," Troy said. "Family dinner right here. Eve says Joey is so excited about meeting his bull-riding Uncle Dakota that she'll be surprised if he sleeps tonight."

"Joey I haven't heard about," Viviana said.

"That's Sean's stepson. He's seven and a bundle of energy. He'll bring Sparky with him, too. He takes that golden retriever everywhere he goes except church and school."

"I can't wait to meet him."

"There's coffee in the pot and soft drinks and beer in the fridge," Troy offered his son.

"Thanks." Dakota got a beer from the refrigerator but didn't join them at the table. Instead he went back and stood near the back door, staring out at the summer landscape as if he were planning another escape.

"Did you go to Dylan's while you were out?" Viviana asked him.

"No, I just took a short walk to get a breath of fresh air."

Viviana finished her drink as the tension built in the kitchen. Perhaps the men needed time alone. "I should unpack before Briana wakes up. Thanks for the cola, Troy."

"You help yourself to another soda or anything else around here you want. Think of this as home while you're here."

"I appreciate that."

There was dead silence between the two men as Viviana walked away. But at least they were in the same room. That was progress.

She started to unpack, but mean-as-a-snake George Bateman stayed on her mind. If Hank wasn't doing his own dirty work, then maybe his brother George was doing it for him.

She took her cell phone from her purse to call Dirty Harry. He'd know if Hank had a brother who'd been in prison. The display informed her she had received three new messages since she'd arrived at the ranch a few hours earlier.

She called her voice mail, punched in the code and listened to the first message. It was from the detective.

"Hank's still being tailed. He's mostly hanging out with his girlfriend. There's been no sign of trouble and no attempt to flee the area. The cops are monitoring your place. All clear there."

Dirty Harry might not be the neatest of souls, but he appeared to have everything under control. After a year of bureaucracy and postponement, this trial might actually get under way one week from today.

The second message was from Betsy, a nurse in the E.R. She wanted to know why Viviana had taken her vacation on such short notice. Was Viviana all right? Was Briana?

Viviana would text her back later that she was fine. She wouldn't mention she was with the "gorgeous" cowboy Betsy had tended to at the hospital.

The third message was from the prosecuting attorney. Nick Jefferson had bad news.

The nightmare had gone prime time.

CHAPTER ELEVEN

DAKOTA TOOK THE cell phone Viviana handed him with shaking hands.

"It's from the prosecuting attorney," she said, "so I'm sure the facts are correct."

The message began to play.

"This is Nick Jefferson. I wanted you to hear this from me before you hear it on the news, Viviana. Harry Cortez was shot a few minutes ago as he was leaving a crime scene. He's in surgery now, but his condition is listed as critical.

"Nothing indicates the shooting was related to the Compton case, but on the off chance that it was, I'm going to request short-term witness protection for you and Briana until after the trial. Call me back as soon as you get this message."

Viviana dropped to the edge of the bed. "I can't believe it. Why would someone try to kill Detective Cortez? I can't even see how that would help Hank's position."

"Cortez puts killers behind bars. That had to make him a few enemies along the way."

"I don't know which hospital he's in, but I can make a few calls and find out. Physicians have privileges when it comes to obtaining patient information."

"You need to call the attorney back, as well," Dakota said. "Does he know that you're in Mustang Run?"

"No, and frankly I'm surprised by his sudden concern about my safety. He never even calls me about the trial. I usually talk to his assistant."

"He wants that case to go to trial next week and he plans to make sure his number-one witness is there."

"No one wants that case to go to trial more than I do. Who knew just putting a guilty man behind bars could be this difficult?"

Troy would tell her it was easier to frame an innocent man. But Dakota understood Viviana's frustration and fear. He was feeling the heat of battle himself right now. He had to ask the question, though he dreaded her answer.

"Do you want to accept the attorney's offer of protection, Viviana?"

She looked up and met his gaze. "Do you want to get rid of me?"

"No. I want you and Briana right here with me. I can even tolerate staying at the ranch if it means keeping you both safer."

"Then why ask?"

Because his reasons for wanting her here weren't all noble. "I just want you to feel safe."

Viviana stood and fit herself against him, wrapping her hands around his waist. "I've never felt more safe in my life."

He held her close, feeling her heart beat against his chest, drinking in the flowery fragrance of her hair, remembering the taste of her lips on his.

He hated to let her go.

Briana had other ideas. Her high-pitched wails echoed down the long hallway.

Viviana slipped from his arms. "Nap time has officially ended."

She rushed off, leaving him to swallow the desire that was swelling inside him and go to work on discovering who shot Dirty Harry. He figured he'd start by harassing the SAPD and by alerting his brothers that the heat had been turned up a notch.

THREE OF THE five Ledger brothers and their father were present and accounted for in the newly constructed ranch headquarters by eight o'clock Saturday morning.

Headquarters consisted of two rooms, built as an extension off the back of Dylan's house. One was a small office with the usual business equipment and a functional desk.

The second room was a spacious area with a rectangular metal table and an assortment of mismatched chairs that looked as if they had come from a used furniture store. Books on cattle selection, maintaining cattle health, growing your herd and countless other ranching topics half filled a large wooden bookshelf.

A huge interactive map of the ranch covered most of one wall. Dylan had explained its significance while they were waiting for Sean to arrive. The map divided the ranch into sections, each one labeled as *E, W, N* or *S* followed by a number. Flagged pins denoted which pastures held what percentage of the cattle at any given time.

The Willow Creek Ranch was a much more impressive operation than Dakota had anticipated. Under other circumstances, Dakota would have enjoyed hearing more about it. Today, though, his entire focus was on making sure that neither Hank Bateman nor any of his hit men set foot on the ranch.

If Hank was behind the attack on Harry Cortez, then his desperation level had just spilled over the top. Obviously he was willing to go to any length to stay out of prison.

As soon as the brotherly arm punches, back-whacking and hand-shaking were done, the men settled in chairs around the table and got down to the business at hand.

"I have bits and pieces of the situation," Sean said, "but I'd like to hear the full story."

Dakota recapped, leaving out nothing except the fact that being with Viviana and not really being with her was driving him crazy.

Sean scribbled a few notes on a pad he'd pulled from his shirt pocket. "So you just found out a few days ago that you're a father?"

"Yeah. Sounds strange, I know, but Viviana and I had decided to end the relationship. She was doing her residency. I was on the road all the time."

"Dakota's personal life isn't up for debate," Troy said. "If Viviana and Briana were virtual strangers when they showed up on this ranch, we'd still feel duty bound to protect them."

"Point made," Sean said. "So where are Viviana and Briana now?"

"They're in the house visiting with Collette," Dakota replied, realizing he was grateful for the distraction that Dylan's wife provided Viviana.

"And you're sure she wants to turn down the offer of temporary protection from the authorities?" Dylan asked.

"She says she'd rather stay here on the ranch."

"Can't say I blame her." Dylan nodded and leaned back in his chair. "I took the liberty of talking to Collette's father last night. Glenn's been the sheriff in this county for decades. He says he can guarantee that if the government offered witness protection, they're convinced that Viviana and Briana are in imminent danger."

Dakota was well aware of Glenn McGuire's longevity and reputation. He'd been sheriff when Dakota's mother was murdered. In fact, he'd arrested Troy. If it bothered Troy to have Glenn McGuire brought into this, he didn't show it.

"What was McGuire's take on the situation?" Sean asked.

"He thinks we should hire Daniel Riker to set up a protection plan on the ranch with the primary emphasis being on watching the house where Viviana is staying."

"What kind of qualifications does Riker have?" Troy asked.

"He retired last year, but he was in special operations with the Dallas Police Department for the last ten years of his career. He was on the SWAT team in Garland before that. He's won countless titles in sharpshooting competitions with other law enforcement personnel."

"What about Trent Fontaine?" Sean asked.

Neither name registered with Dakota. "What's Trent's claim to fame?"

Troy rubbed the scar that trailed from his right cheek to his breastbone. "He's the retired Texas Ranger who's been helping me look for your mother's killer. I gave him a call last night, as well."

"He's a good man, too," Dylan said. "Did he have any suggestions?"

"He said pity the man who went up against the Ledgers."

"Damn straight," Dylan said. "Was that all Fontaine had to say?"

"He said watch each other's backs, expect the worst of anyone we don't know who tries to set foot on the ranch and if we had any questions, we could call him anytime."

"Was Trent interested in working protection at Willow Creek?" Sean asked.

"He's currently under contract to a private group along the border, trying to keep the illegal drug traffickers from killing the ranchers and their families and taking control of their land."

"That rules him out," Sean said.

"I'm willing to consider having a professional coordinate the protection efforts," Dakota said. "But when push comes to shove, I have the final say on everything."

"That goes without saying," Troy said. "Viviana's the mother of your child."

"We're pushing around ideas," Dylan said, "but it's your call, Dakota. We can chase this horse in circles for another couple of hours or you can just tell us how you want us to help. We're behind you all the way."

"I appreciate that," Dakota said. "But I'd like to hear your opinions on hiring Riker or going it alone." He meant it and those were words he'd never expected to come out of his mouth.

He was a loner. He made friends, but he kept them at a distance, never sharing too much of himself, never wanting to know much about them. Never fully trusting anyone.

He'd come close with Viviana. That had cost him his heart and his chance to make the world finals last year.

But it had given him a daughter.

"My vote is that we keep this in the family and we take care of things ourselves," Dylan said. "If we need law enforcement to come and make an arrest, we go to the sheriff."

Dakota turned to Sean. "What about you?"

A hairy, black spider made the fatal mistake of crawling too close to Sean. He lifted his foot and squashed it beneath the heel of his boot.

"That's my decision." He lifted his foot and kicked the dead spider across the floor. "If that baby-murdering bully shows up here, we'll squash him the way I did that spider. I relish the chance. And I won't need an outsider to tell me how to do it."

They all looked to Troy, even Dakota. He didn't need his father, but Troy had spent years in prison. He had far more experience with the depraved factions of the human race than the rest of them put together.

"I'm with you, but never underestimate a desperate enemy. Most men will go to any lengths to avoid a life in prison, especially if they know the hell it really is."

Yet from what Dakota had heard from his uncle, Troy hadn't fought at all.

But then his uncle had a way of seeing whatever he chose in any situation.

"I'm with you," Dakota said, "except that I'd like to hire some off-duty cops to work under my command and keep a close watch on the house or any other place on the ranch where Viviana might choose to go. I'll want that 24/7. I'll pay all the expenses."

Sean nodded in agreement. "I can arrange for off-duty cops out of Austin if you want. I trained a couple of problem horses for their chief of police."

"Then I'll leave that up to you," Dakota said. "I'd like them on the job no later than tomorrow morning."

"I'll let you know if I run into any problems."

Within an hour the rules of operation had been established. Julie was to stay at Sean and Eve's for a few days. Collette was to have either Dylan or a couple of their most dependable wranglers with her at all times. Dakota wouldn't leave Viviana or Briana alone unless he'd notified Troy so that he could be available for any emergency.

That left Troy and Dylan free to run the ranch for most of the day, though they both wanted to be alerted by cell phone if any problems developed.

Dakota's brothers had come through for him. So had Troy. And yet Dakota still felt as if they were miles apart. The intervening years had taken too much of a toll on his ability to think of himself as part of a family. Closing the gap would be next to impossible.

"I'M GONNA BE a bull rider when I grow up, too, Uncle Dakota."

"It's not all fun. Those bulls can sure kick hard." Dakota looked down at the cute little towheaded nephew who'd been following him around ever since he arrived, staring up at him as if he were a superhero in jeans. This time he'd followed Dakota out the back door to take out the trash.

"I'm already practicing for the rodeo, but all Daddy will let me do so far is barrel riding for little kids."

"That's a good start. There's lots of coordination involved in getting that horse to do exactly what you want him to do. Plus, you learn to react to the animal's movements and mood."

"My daddy knows all about horses. He's a whisperer."

"I know. Now that takes real skill."

"He says the horses talk to him. They just don't use words. He says they talk to everybody, but some people just don't listen."

Sean joined them on the back porch. "Speaking of horses, why don't we take a walk to the horse barn and you can show Uncle Dakota the two young colts that were born last month."

"The walk would do me good," Dakota said. He'd been cooped up in the house all afternoon and his injuries were tightening up on him. "Give me a minute to see if Viviana needs help with Briana."

He found Viviana in the dining room, spreading a large plaid tablecloth over a massive oak table. His daughter was nowhere in sight. "Where's Briana?"

"Meeting all her new aunts and being spoiled rotten. Collette has her at the moment. They're in the garden cutting a bouquet of fresh blossoms for the table."

An uneasy feeling ripped through him. "A grandfather. Aunts. Cousin Joey. You're rushing into this family concept awfully fast."

She smoothed the cloth. "You're Briana's father. This is your family. It's a package deal. Besides, I was an only child. I love the warmth and openness of family, especially this one."

"Don't get too comfortable with this."

"Don't worry. I have no expectations of home and hearth with you. The bulls would wreck the floors."

Now he'd irritated her. "Sean wants me to walk down to the horse barn with him."

"Great idea." She dismissed him with a toss of her head.

He rejoined Sean on the back porch and they started

down the well-worn path to the horse barn. Dakota had no memories of the old one, but Dylan had mentioned that they'd doubled the size of it since he'd married Collette. She loved raising and training the animals and she'd learned a lot about both from Sean.

Joey ran ahead of them with his dog, Sparky, at his heels.

"Your stepson seems crazy about you," Dakota said. "He told me what a great whisperer you are."

"I can't seem to get away from the term *whisperer,* though I've tried. It makes me sound like I put some kind of magic spell on the animals. Believe me, I deal in common sense, not mumbo jumbo."

"Stick with *whisperer,*" Dakota teased. "It has a much better ring to it than common-senser."

"Good thinking. And even whispering is not quite as high on the hero list as bull riding."

"Less risk to the family jewels, though."

"There is that. Though I've had a wild stallion or two try to make a steer of me."

Dakota smiled. "You don't want that to happen, not with a woman like Eve to go home to every night."

"She is remarkable," Sean agreed. "I had no intention of ever saying 'I do.' And then I met Eve and suddenly that was all she wrote. I bit the dust with little more than a whimper."

"It sounds like you're a lucky man."

"Very lucky, which is not to say that Eve and I agree on everything. Not to change the subject, but what's the latest on Detective Cortez?"

"Viviana checked a couple of hours ago and his nurse reported that he's in and out of consciousness but still critical. It will be touch-and-go for the next twelve hours."

"Any word on who shot him?"

"Nothing official, and, apparently, he's too out of it to even remember getting shot. A detective named Gordon Miles is handling that investigation and also replacing Cortez in investigating the recent threat and attacks against Viviana."

"But the case is still on the trial docket?"

Dakota nodded. "Jury selection starts on Friday."

Joey reached the horse barn and disappeared inside. Loud neighing and some snorts welcomed his arrival.

"Joey loves horses, and he's a natural in the saddle," Sean said.

"I get that part of the family picture," Dakota said. "It's the way you all rally around Troy I find hard to buy. Even if he didn't kill Mother, he didn't give a damn what happened to us and you know it."

The anger erupted before Dakota could stop it, but he wasn't really sorry he'd said how he felt.

"He tried to get in touch with us. Our grandparents got a court order to stop him. They even went so far as to falsify a letter from Wyatt telling him that none of us wanted to hear from him."

"All I know is that I was six years old and nobody cared what happened to me."

"How can you say that? You were the only one of us who got to go home with Grandma."

"Who immediately went into a deep depression."

"We only heard she was sick at the time. But then you got to go and live in Montana with Uncle Larry."

"Yeah, good old Uncle Larry." Sarcasm cut through his voice.

"Guess that didn't go so well, either, huh?"

"Hardly."

"No one knew that," Sean said.

"No one bothered to find out."

"I'm sorry."

"Not your fault. Just don't expect me to suddenly start thinking of Troy as this great father figure of the Ledger clan."

"No one's selling that story, Dakota. Dad's not a saint. He's just a man. But he loved Mom. And he's doing what he can now. I guess that's good enough for me."

"I may have missed the forgiveness gene."

"Give yourself time. Viviana and fatherhood may change your way of thinking about a lot of things."

"You do know that Viviana and I aren't really together."

"Aren't you? She trusts you enough that she's here with you instead of in a safe house. You're here protecting her and Briana instead of chasing another world championship buckle."

"That's all temporary."

"All I'm saying is, don't go yanking the saddle off the bucking horse before you've done all you can to ride."

"Advice from a whisperer?"

"Common sense from a brother."

Joey stuck his head out from the barn. "Are you guys coming?"

"Yep. I was just telling your uncle what a great little horseman you are." Sean threw his arm around Dakota's shoulder and lowered his voice. "Don't be so hard on Troy or yourself. You're a Ledger. You'll do what's right for Viviana and Briana."

To Dakota's way of thinking, being a Ledger had never been a plus. He had little faith in that changing anytime soon, if ever.

VIVIANA JOINED EVE and Julie on the wide front porch. "Briana is already sleeping soundly. I think all the activity wore her out."

"She's so adorable," Julie said. "I can't wait for Tyler to return from Afghanistan so that we can start a family."

Viviana settled on the top step next to Julie. "When will he be discharged?"

"He has nine more months of active service, but he may return to the States before that. That's the day I'll truly start celebrating."

And between now and then Julie must be living in fear that Tyler might be killed or maimed while fighting for his country, Viviana thought. She had to wake to that possibility every day and go to bed with that apprehension hanging over her every night. Yet, her blue eyes danced with excitement when she talked about him.

Collette pushed through the front door carrying a tray. "Dessert," she announced. "Cookies, compliments of Eve. The citrus slush is my concoction. All healthy and cooling."

Eve's brows arched. "Is the evening too hot for your usual coffee?"

"I'm trying to cut down on my caffeine, but there's coffee brewing in the kitchen if you'd rather have it."

"No, I'm fine with half-frozen lemonade," Eve assured her. She stood and helped pass out the drinks and the cookies before she and Collette both settled onto the porch swing.

Viviana was amazed by the way the three sisters-in-law got along, especially when they were all so different in looks and personalities.

Dylan's wife Collette was friendly, yet cautious. She seemed to fit into ranch life as if it were a second skin, especially when she talked of the horses. Yet she looked like a confident model tonight with her thick red curls tumbling over her beautiful bare shoulders and the white sundress dancing about her knees.

Eve was quieter, soft-spoken, insightful. At least that was Viviana's first impression of her. Her brown hair was cut into a sensible bob that fell to her chin. She clearly adored Sean and had a warm and loving relationship with Joey.

Julie was a vivacious blonde. Full of energy. Quick to laugh. Madly in love with her soldier husband.

"Isn't it great when the men offer to do cleanup?" Collette commented. "It gives us a chance to gossip."

"Speaking of which, what happened with Troy's housekeeper?" Eve asked. "All I heard was how wonderfully she was working out and the next thing I hear she's quit."

"It's the haunted-house rumor," Julie said. "Some woman in town told her how she'd seen a woman in white standing in the window one night and it scared the wits out of her."

"That story's been circulating ever since Helene's murder," Eve said. "You'd think it would die down now that people are living in the house again."

Fortunately, Viviana did not believe in ghosts.

Julie wrapped her hands around her legs and leaned against the post at the top of the steps. "On the more notorious gossip front, Troy's former neighbor, Senator Foley, made the news again."

"Not another conquest?"

"Yes, and as usual, the love interest is married and half his age."

"Have any of you ever met the senator?" Eve asked.

"I've met him several times," Collette said. "I've been one of his constituents for years."

"What's he like?"

"He's charismatic, but not particularly handsome."

"I think his ex-wife is after Troy," Eve said.

"I agree," Julie said. "You should see the blouse she wore over here last week. It left little to the imagination. But I'm not sure I blame her. She is very attractive, and Troy would be a great catch if it weren't for the fact that he's obsessed with finding Helene's killer."

"For some reason, Sean doesn't like Ruthanne Foley," Eve said. "He never says why, but I can tell he doesn't like it when Troy mentions that she's stopped by."

"Enough about Ruthanne Foley," Julie said. "Viviana is going to think we're a bunch of catty snobs."

"No way," she assured them.

Actually she knew that they were intentionally trying to keep her mind off her own situation and she appreciated their efforts. It didn't work, of course. How could it, when even now Dakota and his brothers were likely talking about Hank Bateman and speculating as to what heinous act he'd resort to next?

The women jumped from one topic to another over the next half hour, starting with Eve's volunteer work with an agency dedicated to finding adoptive parents for handicapped youngsters and finally getting to Collette's announcement that she and Dylan were planning to start a new wing on their house.

"You just added an office wing for ranch headquarters," Eve noted. "Aren't you tired of all that construction?"

"No. I like the idea of more room."

"For the two of you?"

"We won't always be just two."

Julie jumped up from the step and walked over to stand next to the swing. "You're pregnant, aren't you?"

Collette rubbed her hand over her belly. "Do I look pregnant?"

"Yes. You're glowing," Julie said. "Besides a new wing, a sudden need to cut down on caffeine. You may as well wear a sign."

Collette flashed a conspiratorial smile. "Okay, since you dragged it out of me. I'm pregnant."

Julie squealed as she tugged Collette from the swing and into a bear hug. "I'm so happy for you."

"Does Dylan know?" Eve asked as she threw her arms around Collette.

"He does. He's deliriously excited. We were going to tell all of you this weekend at dinner, but then he thought we should wait until the threat of danger to Viviana and Briana is past. But I couldn't hold it in another second."

"I've disrupted all your lives," Viviana said, walking over to join them. "I guess I was selfish in not thinking—"

"Nonsense." Collette pulled her into a hug and interrupted her apology. "We all came into the Ledger family the same way. I'm beginning to think that the only way you can win a Ledger's heart is by needing his protection."

"It's that cowboy-code thing," Julie said. "They're all a bunch of heroes just waiting to be needed before their passion can be unleashed."

That hadn't been the case with Dakota. With him, the passion had been explosive from day one. Then came fatherhood. And then danger. Love and commitment showed no sign of emerging.

"Dakota is definitely protective," she said and left it at that.

The chatter and easy camaraderie continued until Sean joined them and said it was time to go. Julie left with them. She was spending a few days with Eve and Sean at their horse farm in Bandera.

"You're very quiet," Collette said to Viviana once the others had left. "Is there anything you'd like to talk about?"

"No, I'm just tired. The last few days have been trying and exhausting."

"I'm sure. We didn't get to you with that talk of the house being haunted, did we?"

"No. I don't believe in ghosts or spirits."

"Even if you did, there's nothing to fear. Helene's spirit might be intrusive and a bit creepy at times, but it's not dangerous."

The comment surprised Viviana. Collette seemed so levelheaded. "Are you telling me that you believe Helene's ghost still haunts this house?"

"No. Pay no attention to me. It's just that sometimes I have a very active imagination."

Viviana had enough real trouble in her life without looking for spirits or letting her imagination run wild. She said good-night and went inside. Dylan, Troy and Dakota were still talking in the kitchen, but she didn't disturb them to say good-night. For once her thoughts weren't all centered on the upcoming trial and Hank Bateman.

It was Helene Ledger's murder that stalked her mind as she walked down the long, dimly lit hallway to the guestroom, the room directly across from the master suite that Helene had shared with Troy Ledger so many years ago.

VIVIANA WAS TUBING down the Guadalupe River, the swiftly flowing water carrying her faster and faster, rushing past people on the banks frantically waving and yelling for her to get out of the river.

The water that had been warm at first grew colder and colder until the chill seeped into her bones....

Viviana jerked awake and reached for the quilt she'd kicked to the foot of the bed. Only remnants of the nightmare remained but a cold draft swept across her shivering body. Even if a door was open, it couldn't be this cold unless someone had turned the air conditioner on full blast.

She should check on Briana. But when she tried to push to a sitting position, it was as if her shoulders were pinned to the bed.

And then a voice, low and broken, echoed about the dark room.

"I had a baby once, too."

CHAPTER TWELVE

WHITE RIBBONS FLASHED across the room like lightning.

Viviana's heart pounded in her chest so loudly that it echoed about the room.

"You should be very afraid."

"Who are you?" Viviana asked.

"A mother. Babies need their mother."

"Is that you, Helene?"

The ribbons flashed again and then coalesced into a woman's shape that hovered over Viviana's head.

"No one took care of my baby. No one protected him."

"Your baby is Dakota. He's a man, Helene. He's here. He's come home."

"No." The figure disintegrated. When it did the ribbons turned red and cracked like whips above the bed. "Dakota is lost. Find him, Viviana. Find him and bring him home."

"He is home, Helene. He's in the same room where he used to sleep."

"No. He's lost in Montana. Wounded. Afraid. You and Briana must save him."

"Briana's just a baby, Helene. Dakota is strong and protective. He's saving us."

"Hold on tight to Dakota. If you let go of him, he will be lost forever."

The words made no sense. And the room grew colder,

still. Viviana could feel bands of ice forming around her heart. "Did Troy kill you, Helene? Is that why you can't let go?"

Balls of fire darted across the room, dispelling the chill.

"Did Troy shoot you, Helene? Tell me and I can make him pay."

"Love doesn't kill. But it can destroy. Don't destroy my son."

A searing heat shot through Viviana as if one of the balls of fire had cut right through her flesh. The ribbons cracked one last time and then they were gone.

Only the heat remained. For a second, Viviana thought the whole house must surely be on fire. She jumped from the bed. The second her feet touched the floor, the heat dissipated. The temperature cooled to normal in a heartbeat. Viviana's heart found a steady rhythm.

A nightmare. That's all it had been. It had seemed incredibly real, but it was just a stupid nightmare induced by the evening's talk of ghosts, spirits and haunted happenings.

Viviana's cotton nightshirt was damp and sticking to her like syrup. She yanked it open and let it drop to the floor while she reached for the robe she'd left hanging on one of the posts of the antique bed.

Once it was cinched, she stooped to pick up the nightshirt so that she could toss it out of the way. A wide strand of white ribbon clung to the collar.

A shudder ripped through Viviana.

Hold on tight to Dakota. If you let go of him, he will be lost forever.

Only how could Viviana hold on to him if he didn't want to be held?

She tiptoed from the room and stepped across the hall to check on Briana. Her heart jumped to her throat when she saw the shadowy figure standing by the bed.

"I thought I heard Briana cry out, but she's fast asleep."

Dakota. Only Dakota. She took a deep breath and let the air fill her lungs before slowly exhaling.

"I didn't hear her," Viviana said. "I just woke and came to check on her."

"Does she always sleep with her little rump stuck up like that?" Dakota asked.

"Usually."

They stood silently, side by side, staring at the child that seemed to hold them together at the same time she pushed them apart.

"Did you hate me when you found out you were pregnant?" Dakota whispered.

"I've never hated you, Dakota."

"You chose not to have me in your life."

"I didn't want to love you when you were never going to be mine."

"I was yours."

"For a week. But you'd made it clear from the first day we met that you were addicted to bull riding and to…"

"Never sleeping too many nights in the same place," he whispered, finishing the statement for her. "That was the code I've lived by since I ran away from home at sixteen."

He reached into the crib and let his fingers entwine with the soft locks of Briana's dark, curly hair. "You were right to send me away. I have nothing to offer. I wouldn't be good for you or Briana."

Hold on tight to Dakota. If you let go of him, he will be lost forever.

"I think you have a lot more to offer than you realize. We could start over, Dakota, this time as friends and see where it goes from there."

"I'm not sure I could stop at just being friends." He bent closer to her, so close she felt his breath on her skin, so close she could almost taste his lips.

Her knees grew weak. Any claim to control vanished, and she closed her eyes in anticipation.

The kiss never came.

When she opened her eyes, Dakota was staring at the display on his cell phone.

"Good that I had it on vibrate," he whispered. "I'm sorry, but I have to take this call."

"Go right ahead."

She followed him into the hallway and watched as he retreated to his room. She wondered if there had really been a call or if he'd just needed an escape.

Not that it mattered, she told herself.

There had been no ghostly vision and Dakota wasn't lost. He was exactly what he wanted to be. Sexy as hell. Brave enough to take on anything…except commitment.

BRIANA MADE UP for going to sleep early by waking at six. Viviana dragged herself from bed, pulled on her robe and went to get Briana before she woke Troy and Dakota. Troy needed his rest and Viviana had no interest in talking to Dakota after the way he'd wormed his way out of the kiss.

"Good morning, sweet angel. You slept well last

night. I think ranch living agrees with you. Or do you just like having Momma here instead of Claire when you wake up?"

Briana kicked her feet and legs, then rolled over and got up on her hands and knees as if trying to help Viviana get her out of bed.

"First we'd best get rid of that wet diaper. Then we'll go find breakfast."

Briana cooed and uttered a string of baby gibberish, bouquets of sounds that Viviana always hoped would come out as *Momma*. It hadn't happened yet, but Viviana knew it would come any day now.

The neckline of Briana's pajamas was wet, as well. Cutting teeth were accompanied by excessive drooling. Viviana slipped a cute polka-dot knit top over Briana's dry diaper.

"Now you're ready to enchant the world."

Troy was sitting at the kitchen table sipping coffee and poring over the morning paper when she and Briana entered. "You're up early," he said.

"I could say the same for you."

"Rancher's hours."

"It's Sunday."

"The cows don't know that. But actually Dakota got me up even earlier than usual this morning."

"Don't tell me he's ranching?"

"No. He left for San Antonio about thirty minutes ago. Didn't he tell you?"

"No." Apprehension settled in the pit of her stomach. Briana began to squirm and she switched her to the other hip. "Why is he going to San Antonio?"

"He said he had a call from one of his bull-rider friends and he needed to go and help him with a problem."

Maybe that had been a legitimate call he'd gotten in Briana's room last night. But what could a bull-riding friend want that was so important that Dakota had to drive to San Antonio at daybreak?

Surely Dakota hadn't just decided to dump her and Briana on his family while he reentered the competition.

"Da pa ba a da."

Viviana frowned. *You better not even think of muttering "Dada" before you say "Mama." I'll sell you to the highest bidder.* She took Briana's plastic cereal bowl and coated baby spoon from the bottom shelf of the cabinet.

Troy stood, walked to the counter and held out his hands to Briana. "Why don't you come to Grandpa while your mother gets your breakfast ready?"

To Viviana's surprise, Briana went right to him.

She poured the cereal into the bowl and then took a jar of pureed applesauce from the refrigerator. "Did Dakota happen to mention which friend he was going to see?"

"No, he just wanted to make sure I would be here to keep a close watch on you and Briana."

Troy stayed to visit while she fed Briana.

"I don't know if this is the best time to go into this, but I had a call from my son Wyatt last night after both you and Dakota had gone to bed. He was able to find out quite a bit about the George Bateman who was in prison with me."

"Like what?"

"For starters, he is the brother of the Hank Bateman accused of killing Leslie Compton."

"So we know criminal behavior runs in the family. What else did Wyatt discover about the Batemans?"

"George was in prison with me. He'd been convicted of armed robbery of a small mom-and-pop grocery store.

But robbery wasn't enough for George. He tied up the couple who owned the place, tormented and tortured them for hours and finally shot both of them in the stomach. Then he set fire to the building and left them alive to burn to death."

"How sick and depraved. Two murders should have earned him at least life in prison. How is it that he's already a free man?"

"The couple escaped and survived so he was tried on a lesser charge than murder one. He was sentenced to twenty years and served ten. It's how the system works."

"If fire is George's weapon of choice, then it's not surprising that Hank would have my car set on fire. He's learned from the best of the worst. He might have even had George do that bit of depravity for him." She shook her head, as if to erase the image.

"Does Dakota know any of this?"

"He knows all of it. I relayed it to him just as he was leaving for San Antonio. Now tell me more about the death of that infant," Troy said.

"Hank Bateman brought the child into the E.R. about one in the morning."

"Where was the mother?"

"Working. She was a prostitute. Hank didn't tell us that, but Cortez discovered her profession in his investigation. She'd been arrested several times."

"Was the baby still alive when Hank showed up at the emergency room?"

"Alive, but unconscious. Hank claimed she'd rolled onto the floor from a bed where she'd been sleeping. I knew from the excessive retinal hemorrhaging and the pattern of bruising that he was lying. I notified the police department and they assigned Harry Cortez to the case. The autopsy findings bore out my claims of non-accidental trauma to the brain."

"How did Hank react that night?"

"He was nervous. He even seemed a little panicked—more for himself than the child."

"But it was his kid?"

"Yes. DNA testing has proved that Leslie Compton was his biological child, but he and the mother were not married."

"Are they still together?"

"No."

"Will the mother testify against him?"

"That was the original plan, but now Karen Compton's disappeared. The prosecutor believes she's off on a drug binge."

"I'd say it's more likely Hank got to her."

"You think he abducted her?"

"It's possible. That might have been what the gunman in the E.R. parking lot had planned for you."

"He would have likely been successful if Dakota hadn't shown up when he did."

"Dakota's a good man, Viviana. I know things aren't right between the two of you, but he'll be a good father to Briana. He just needs time to adjust to the idea of fatherhood."

"I'm sorry now that I didn't find a way to contact him when Briana was born."

"We all have regrets, Viviana. Don't waste time worrying about what might have been or what could have been. Take the advice of a man who lost almost two decades of his life. Time is much too precious to waste."

Was that what she was doing? Losing the present? Destroying the future?

Hold on tight to Dakota.

Had that been her own good sense speaking, trying to break through to her consciousness any way it could?

DAKOTA STOOD AT the door to Jim Angle's hotel room, his temper exploding as he plunged into a state of absolute fury. "Why didn't you tell me they'd beat the hell out of you when you called last night?"

"Because all they'd done then was make a phone call and demand I tell them where you and Viviana had gone." Jim dabbed at the blood spilling from the space where a front tooth used to be. "They made personal contact this morning to finish making their point."

"When were they here?"

"You missed them by about ten minutes. If you'd driven a little faster we could have made it a real party."

"I don't suppose you caught their names?"

"Nope, but one of them has a killer right punch."

"What did they look like?"

"Two thugs in ski masks."

"Any identifying marks? Tattoos? Scars? Blemishes?"

"One of them has a black eye. I got in one good left hook before I went down. But the guy who did the punching was the same one who made all the threats on the phone last night. I recognized his voice. The bastard who did the holding didn't say much."

"Exactly what was their message?"

"The same as I told you last night. If I liked waking up mornings I'd best tell them where you and Viviana had gone."

"Did you tell them?"

"Do I look like a damned traitor?"

"You look like you just got run over by a cement truck."

"Either that or by Devil's Deed on steroids. You look like you're recovering, though."

"I'm well enough to take care of the men who did this to you."

"That's not your job."

"Says who?"

Dakota pulled out his cell phone and made a call to Detective Gordon Miles. He got nothing from him except the assurance that Hank Bateman was not at his brother's apartment. If he was, they would have found and arrested him by now. It had been the first place they'd looked for Hank when he'd slipped his tail.

Dakota's next call was to his brother Wyatt.

"It's Sunday. I'm off duty. Take two aspirin and call me in the morning."

"Sorry, bro. I've got an emergency."

"Dakota. It's you. What's up?"

"I need an address for George Bateman. Can you get that for me?"

"I gave it to Dad a few minutes ago. You two should try conversing."

"I'm not at the ranch, but he did give me the rest of the scoop on George Bateman before I left."

"Okay. Hold on a minute."

Dakota held for two.

"Sorry," Wyatt said when he got back to the phone. "The street number was buried in one of the files. But I found it."

Dakota scribbled George Bateman's address on the hotel notepad when Wyatt repeated it.

"Tell me you're not going to do anything stupid like go visit George Bateman without backup."

"I'd never tell you that."

"Putting our lives on the line is why we cops make the big bucks. Call them."

"I tried that. They're uncooperative."

"Then take friends or family."

"I'm taking two friends. Smith and Wesson. And I'm just going to have a little chat."

"Stay alive, Dakota. It's the best way to make the criminals really mad. Plus dead heroes never get the woman."

"I'll make a note of that."

Jim had pulled off his bloody shirt while Dakota was talking to Wyatt and was trying to shrug his arms into a clean one. "If you're going to see George Bateman, I'm going with you."

"As the poster child for the importance of avoiding bullies?"

"As your backup."

"Fine. Let's go. My truck is waiting."

GEORGE BATEMAN STOOD at the front window, watching as Dakota Ledger climbed from his fancy new pickup truck. The dope was really making this convenient.

George pulled his gun and aimed it at Dakota's head. He could put the bullet right between the cowboy's eyes. Seeing him dead would be a kick but getting rid of the body would be the really fun part.

He'd deliver it to Dr. Mancini and leave it in her bed. What a homecoming present that would be. And next time somebody told the bitch to mind her own business, she might pay attention.

One step inside the door and then George would have to shoot the trespasser. In fear for his life. Even if he got caught, no judge could argue with that.

He didn't plan to get caught. He was much too smart to let that happen again. Murder and payback had become a cottage industry for him.

CHAPTER THIRTEEN

DAKOTA HAD MADE three stops on the way to the home of George Bateman. The first was to the E.R., where he had forcefully dragged Jim out of the truck and left him yelling curses a few feet from the front entrance.

The second stop was to a Walmart, where he'd purchased a lightweight windbreaker. The third had been to pawn shop that was open on Sundays, where he picked up a shoulder holster that fit over his lucky red shirt and beneath the light windbreaker that was already causing him to sweat profusely.

George's apartment was on the first floor, right side, of a fourplex. The windows of the left side had been boarded over and the building looked as if it had recently been gutted by fire. He wondered if the tenants had gotten on George's bad side.

It was twenty minutes before ten and the streets were deserted except for two kids who looked to be about ten years old. They were riding their bikes down the middle of the street and popping wheelies. Dakota would have to make sure the boys weren't hit by stray bullets if his chat with George turned into all-out war.

Hank might not be around, but someone was home at the Bateman residence. Dakota had seen the blinds shift slightly in the front window when he'd driven up.

He rang the bell and waited. Shelby Lucas came to the

door. He hadn't been expecting her. Her face was swollen, her right eye circled in purplish bruises.

She looked to her left as if waiting for a signal. "Come in," she mumbled and stepped aside.

Dakota smelled the trap as surely as if it had been set with Roquefort cheese. He pulled his gun. George's was already pointed at his head. Neither backed off.

George smirked. "Had I known there was going to be a duel, I would have dressed for the occasion."

"Had Jim Angle known he was going to be jumped by a couple of worthless thugs, he'd have given you a better fight."

"Sorry, Dakota Ledger, but I don't know a Jim Angle."

"I don't suppose you know Dr. Viviana Mancini, either."

"I've heard of her. She's the bitch who's trying to frame my brother for murder when none was committed."

"A jury will decide that. Five days from now, George. There *will* be a trial. Dr. Mancini *will* testify."

"*Dr. Mancini*. That's rather formal for a woman you're sleeping with. You bull riders amaze me. You reek of bull dung while putting on airs."

"And we have extremely itchy fingers when they're resting on triggers."

"Just say what you have to say, Ledger. You're starting to bore me."

"Hank needs to turn himself in so that this trial can take place as scheduled."

"You're talking to the wrong person, Dakota. I'm not my brother's keeper."

"Then let me put it another way. If that trial doesn't start as scheduled, I'm going to hold you personally responsible. And if Hank or anyone else harms Dr. Mancini or her daughter, they *won't* live to regret it."

"Is that it, Ledger?"

"For now." Dakota started to back from the room when he saw the clench of George's jaw and the flick of his wrist. Dakota fired first, shooting the pistol from George's hand.

Shelby screamed.

George let out a stream of curses and grabbed his bleeding hand. "Get out of my house, you son of a murdering wife killer."

Dakota kicked George's gun beneath the couch. "Leave my dad out of this."

"Why should I, you pious fool? Troy bragged to everyone in prison that he'd killed your mother. She was a no-good tramp who was about to leave him for another man. He wasn't about to let her get away with that."

Rage consumed Dakota. He ached to pull the trigger again. He wanted so badly to kill George Bateman that his finger shook on the trigger.

One pull and he could blow the bastard into tiny pieces. He took a deep breath, then forced himself to switch the pistol to his right hand. He punched George as hard as he could. His fist connected with Bateman's jaw with enough force to knock him against the wall.

George staggered for a second and then came back swinging. He caught Dakota in his bruised chest with a left jab. The pain was so intense Dakota couldn't breathe for long suffocating seconds.

George took advantage of the moment and wrestled the gun from Dakota's hand. It went off in the process and the bullet ricocheted about the room.

The next bullet hit the wall just past George's head, but that bullet had not come from Dakota's gun.

They both turned and stared at Shelby. She was standing just out of George's reach, his own gun aimed at his right temple. Somehow she'd retrieved it without either of them noticing.

"Drop the gun, George," Shelby said. "There's too much killing. Too much."

"Stay out of this, Shelby."

"No. Drop the gun before I count to five or I swear I'll kill you."

"You don't have the guts."

"One. Two."

Dakota looked Shelby square in the eye and the cold, hard glaze convinced him that the timid and fearful woman had finally been pushed over the edge.

"Three."

"Put the gun down, Shelby," George ordered. "You'll never shoot me and you know it."

"Four."

George lunged at Shelby and she pulled the trigger. The bullet missed his chest by inches, digging into the muscle of his forearm. It was far from a fatal injury but it was enough that he dropped the gun and bolted for the door.

Shelby collapsed into a ball, crying as she rubbed her stomach.

Dakota started after George, but changed his mind. He'd said what he'd come to say. If he went after Bateman now and killed him, it would be cold-blooded murder.

With full malice intent. The same way Troy had killed Dakota's mother.

Dakota would never leave that legacy to Briana.

He holstered his gun and then knelt beside Shelby. She was still rubbing her stomach and crying.

"It's okay, Shelby. You shot George to keep him from killing me and maybe even you. You can't go to prison for that. Even Hank will understand."

"Hank killed Leslie Compton." Her voice was shaky and hoarse. "I lied before when I said he didn't. I was trying to save him. Now he won't have anything to do with me. That's the thanks I get."

"Were you there when Hank killed the baby?" Dakota asked. "Can you testify as an eyewitness?"

"I wasn't there, but Hank told me he did it. The baby wouldn't stop crying so he started to shake her. And then something just came over him and he shook her until she went limp."

Dakota put an arm around her shaking shoulder. "You can't keep protecting him, Shelby."

"I know."

"You have to tell the police what Hank told you about killing Leslie Compton."

"The police won't believe anything I have to say."

"A jury might."

Dakota put in another call to Detective Gordon Miles. "I think you may want to meet me at George Bateman's apartment. I may have another witness for you in the Leslie Compton case."

WHEN DAKOTA HADN'T returned by noon, Viviana was seriously apprehensive. He'd been at her side almost constantly since coming to her rescue in the parking lot. So what had happened to cause him to leave for hours without telling her where he was going and why?

She stretched out next to Briana's quilt, but even Briana's antics and babbling couldn't take her mind off Dakota.

Her pulse quickened when she heard a vehicle pull up and stop in the driveway. She picked up Briana and raced to the door. It was only Collette and Dylan with their hands full of covered bowls and pans with their handles cradled in hot pads.

"We brought lunch," Collette said.

"Enough for a week," Troy said, walking up behind Viviana.

"Or for three hungry men," Collette corrected.

"Right now there are only two hungry males," Troy said.

"Where's Dakota?" Collette asked after she said hello to Viviana and gave Briana a kiss.

"He went into San Antonio on business," Troy said.

Dylan's eyes reflected the concern that Viviana was feeling. "What kind of business?"

"He didn't say, but I got the idea it was urgent."

"Then he should have said where he was going and had one of us go with him. Either we're in this together or we're not. How long has he been gone?"

"Going on six hours now."

They started back to the kitchen with the food. "Dakota's not used to family," Troy said. "Cut him some slack. It takes a while to learn to trust. You remember how things were between you and me when I was first released from prison."

"This is different. Dakota should have called."

"He hasn't had to check in with me since he was six," Troy said. "I reckon he doesn't figure he has to start now."

Viviana placed Briana in her jump chair so that she could help serve the home-cooked meal of baked macaroni and cheese, salad and fried chicken. She was just about to sit down to her plate of food when the front door creaked open.

She stepped to the kitchen doorway in time to see Dakota turn the corner to the back of the house without even a glance toward the kitchen.

"It's Dakota," she announced to the others. "Collette, would you mind watching Briana for a few minutes?"

"Of course, I'll watch her. But don't be gone too long. The macaroni will get cold."

"No, I'll just be a minute or two."

Dakota tossed a pistol to the bed just as Viviana stepped into the room. Her apprehension became tangible. "Where have you been?"

"Taking care of business."

"With a gun?"

"As a matter of fact, that's exactly how I took care of it. But strike that panicked expression from your face. I haven't killed anyone. Yet."

She dropped to the side of the bed. "If this has anything to do with me or the trial, I have a right to know."

"You have a right to know a lot of things. And it's time that they were said."

VIVIANA SAT DUMBSTRUCK as she listened to Dakota's account of his morning's adventure. He'd taken on a hardened criminal all by himself, stood there with a gun pointed at him by a man who'd have had no qualms about killing him. Yet Dakota hadn't backed down.

He was fearless. Brave and courageous. A protector

who didn't just wait for trouble to appear but went after it at its source.

She started to shake. "You could have been killed."

"I could have sat back and done nothing while the Brothers Gruesome beat up my friends and planned a way to keep you from testifying in court. I may not have accomplished much, but at least I let them know that I don't plan to roll over and play dead while they run over you."

"You did a lot, Dakota. You stood up for your friend. You stood up for me and you gave Shelby Lucas the courage to stand up for herself against the father of her unborn child."

"I think Hank did that when he proved to her what a perverted jerk he really was."

"But she might never have had the courage to act if you hadn't shot the gun from George's hand first. You let her know that neither he nor Hank were invincible."

"There you go making me into a hero when I'm just doing what needed to be done."

She fought tears and a surge of passion that triggered a myriad of mixed emotions. She stood and pressed her body against his, wrapping her arms around his neck. "You are a hero, Dakota."

She touched her lips to his and this time he didn't worm his way out of the kiss.

He took her mouth hungrily and she exploded with a need that rocked clear through to her soul. The kiss intensified and she reveled in every sensation it created. Her breath mingling with his. His tongue pushing its way into her mouth. The salty sweet taste of his lips. The hard, wanton heat of his need for her swelling between them.

His fingers tangled in her hair and then slid down her spine, pressing and kneading until they slipped inside the waistband of her white shorts and worked their way inside her panties.

He pressed her against his erection. Her heart beat so fast and so strong it felt as if it might burst from her body.

It was the middle of the day in his father's house, but Viviana could no more hold back the driving need inside her than she could stop time or reverse the spin of the earth. She yanked her shirt over her head and wiggled out of her bra so that her breasts were free.

Dakota cupped her breasts with his hands and gingerly sucked and nibbled the right nipple until it was rock hard and perfectly erect.

She felt the hot rush building inside her core.

"Take me, Dakota. All of me. I've waited for this for so long. Waited even when I told myself I didn't need you to make me complete."

Dakota pulled away as if her words had been thorns… or a trap.

"I can't do this, Viviana. Oh, God, I want you so badly, but I can't do this to you."

His rejection ripped at her heart like a jagged knife. "You can put your life on the line for me, but you can't make love with me. Are you that afraid you might actually find out that you need me?"

He shook his head and raked his fingers through his hair. "It's not that. It's nothing like that."

"Then what is it, Dakota? Talk straight like you claim you always do because I can't begin to figure out what you want from me. I thought it was sex without strings. But then I throw that at you and you turn it down."

"I'm Troy Ledger's son, Viviana."

"If that's your excuse, I'm not buying. Dylan and Tyler and Sean are Troy's sons and they lead perfectly normal lives. They may face a few negative comments from time to time, but they're man enough to take it. I'm sure you are, too."

"They're not Troy's sons the way I am. I wanted to kill George Bateman today. Not in self-defense. In rage. When he called my mother a tramp and said Troy bragged all over prison about how he'd murdered her, it was all I could do not to pull that trigger."

"But you didn't pull it, Dakota. You drew from something deep inside you and punched him instead."

"But one day I might not. I might give in to the rage just as Troy did. He must have tried to stop himself, yet when he flew into the rage, he pulled the trigger three times and left my mother lying in a pool of blood."

"You don't know that. Just because a lying, scumbag brute said it, that doesn't make it true."

"Why else would Troy have turned his back on us unless he knew he'd killed our mother, unless he knew that he had no more to offer us than I have to offer Briana?"

"So that will be your justification for turning your back on Briana? Some crazy notion that you have murderous tendencies in your DNA?"

She pulled on her clothes, hating that she'd bared her body and soul to him. "I thought you were brave, Dakota. I thought facing a killer for us demonstrated your courage. But that was the easy way out for you. It's like riding bulls. You relish the risks, as long as you don't ever have to put your emotions on the line."

"My emotions are on the line. They have been since the day I met you."

"Then be a real man, Dakota. Talk to you father one-on-one and then put the past behind you. Do it for you. Do it for Briana. Do it for us."

Hold on tight to Dakota. If you let go of him, he will be lost forever.

She was trying, but Dakota was slipping from her grip.

CHAPTER FOURTEEN

HANK BATEMAN WAS sick of covering for his brother. George always had to be the tough guy. He started trouble everywhere he went.

But it was never knowing when to keep his mouth shut that was bringing them both down. Hank had a couple of small details to take care of and then he was cutting out and leaving George behind.

There were still a couple of kinks to work out but nothing he couldn't handle. He already had a map with the back roads to Willow Creek Ranch.

He knew he'd find Dr. Mancini there, thanks to the notes he'd lifted from Detective Cortez's notebook. The other reason was far more pressing. They were closing in on him and George. Time was running out.

A few more days and his new life would start. Him and Karen, finally together. She needed him the way no other woman ever had. The authorities would search for them in Mexico, but they would never find them.

His flights to Switzerland were already bought and paid for. The fake IDs were almost ready.

The only task left was to kill the good doctor. Slow and painful. The kind of murder he'd always liked best.

CHAPTER FIFTEEN

DAKOTA SPENT THE next hour sitting in the shade of a tree, whittling a broken limb with his pocketknife. He used to whittle a lot back in Montana.

There was never a pattern to his cuts. There was no skill involved. It was just watching the knife slit into the wood and seeing the chunks fall to the ground that tended to clear his mind when his thoughts became so muddled he couldn't think straight.

It might have all begun with Wyatt's knife and the niche Dakota had carved into the old dresser. He wondered how much of what he'd learned in those early years on the ranch were part of the man he was now even though he didn't remember most of that time.

The chunks were flying fast and furious today, but the muddle refused to clear. Maybe Viviana was right. He needed to level with his father.

There were things that needed to be said. Hurtful things. Painful truths. Difficult questions that had tormented Dakota since he was six years old.

He found Troy in the workshop, making what looked to be a rocking horse from knotty pine.

Dakota leaned against the carpenter's bench. "Have you got a minute?"

"I've got all the time you need."

Troy laid down the plane he'd been using to smooth

the horse's wooden mane. "I guess this talk has been a long time in coming."

Dakota brushed some sawdust from the edge of the table. "About nineteen years."

"Ask whatever you want."

"Tell me how you met Mother?"

"That's an easy one. I was working as a wrangler at the Black Spur Ranch to earn money for my rodeo fees. I was a bull rider, same as you, only not nearly as good.

"I wasn't from Mustang Run but I'd become good friends with Sheriff McGuire, though Glenn wasn't a sheriff back then. He was a student at UT. He kept telling me about this wonderful girl he was dating. Finally he brought her home for me and his parents to meet."

"And that was Mother?"

Troy smiled and nodded. "One look at her and I knew she was the woman I wanted to spend the rest of my life with. Her parents were against the marriage from the beginning. They were from Boston and hated that their beautiful Helene was going to settle for a poor cowboy."

"How did you get the money to purchase Willow Creek Ranch?"

"Your mother worked until Wyatt was born. We scrimped and saved part of the down payment. A good friend of mine named Able Drake backed me for the rest of it."

"Were you happy before the trouble started?"

"What trouble?"

"Whatever trouble drove you and Mother apart."

"Nothing drove us apart. Our love was as strong the day she was killed as it had ever been. The night before, we'd danced to music on the radio until past midnight. I can still remember how she'd fit in my arms."

Troy turned away, but not before Dakota glimpsed the moisture in his eyes. If he was faking the way he'd felt about Helene, he was doing a bang-up job of it.

"I loved your mother with all my heart. I can't control what you believe, Dakota. But I won't apologize for sins you think I may have committed. Not here in this house where we made love and gave life to you boys. I won't have her memory tainted by misconceptions and lies."

His dad had a point, but the resentment that had festered inside Dakota for so many years wouldn't be abated by mere words. He knew that. Still, the questions persisted.

"I was six years old. Just a kid. Did you ever once think that it was your duty to make certain I was safe?"

"What are you saying, Dakota? Were you abused by your uncle?"

"It's a little late in the game to worry about that now. I just wondered if it ever crossed your mind that I was still your son and not a fruitcake that you could just pack off and mail to a distant family member who no one else in the family even talked to."

"Were you abused?" Troy persisted.

"Let it go, Dad. I'm a man now and Uncle Larry is dead. I no longer need a champion. I'd just like to hear your side of this."

Troy worried the scar on his face, tracing the jagged outline all the way to his breastbone. "Not a day went by that I didn't think about you, Dakota. I wasn't as close to any of you guys as your mother was. I admit that. I worked the ranch most days from sunup to sundown, trying to keep our heads above water. She spent a lot more time with you."

"So when Mother died, you just turned us over to her

parents. Didn't you have a say in what happened to us? Couldn't you have made them keep us brothers together so that we could watch each other's backs?"

"I had no say. Your grandparents were granted custody by court order. I assumed at first they'd take all of you to live with them."

"Why would you assume that?"

"They were constantly begging Helene to leave me and take you boys to Boston so that they could give you the material things I couldn't. But then when your mother died, apparently your grandmother let the grief kill her."

"Was Mother leaving you?"

"To go back to Boston? No. Hell, no. Helene had gone to school at UT to escape her mother's dreams for her. Helene was beautiful. Your grandmother expected her to marry well and move up the societal ladder in the way she hadn't been able to do herself.

"Helene wanted no part of Boston. She loved the ranch. She loved me. Most of all, she loved you boys. You were the center of her life, especially you, Dakota. You were her baby." Troy smiled. "I took you with me whenever I could just to keep her from spoiling you even more than she already had."

That pretty much summed it up. His mother would have kept him safe, but his mother was dead. No matter how Troy dressed it up, the truth was more likely that nobody but Uncle Larry would take the spoiled brat of the family. Dakota had been thrown to the wolves.

"I know I let you down, Dakota. If I could go back and change things, I would. But the past is the past. The only thing I know to do to help make things right is to find your mother's killer. I swear I'll never give up until I do."

"I guess that about covers it," Dakota said. It didn't change the past or the present. In fact it gave him surprisingly little satisfaction. Laying the blame at Troy's feet wasn't the end-all solution Dakota had always imagined it would be.

Troy picked up the plane and went back to the task Dakota had interrupted. "I'm making this horse for Briana. I know she's not old enough for it yet, but when she is, she'll have it. I can't get a do-over with my sons but I plan to be the best grandfather I can be. I want to enjoy every minute of it."

"I'm sure Briana will like the horse," Troy said. "Viviana will be thrilled with it. She's already claimed all of you as family."

"You have a precious daughter," Troy said. "You'll make some mistakes, but this is your chance to be the parent you wish I'd been. Go for it. And if you mess up with Viviana, then I have to say you're a damn fool."

And that might be the most significant piece of wisdom Dakota had ever gleaned from his father.

"You don't know how much I hate making this call, Dr. Mancini, but we can't have a trial without a suspect. Hank Bateman can't be found, therefore the case against him has been removed from the court's docket indefinitely."

As soon as Viviana ended the conversation with Melody Hollister, she turned off her phone and tossed it onto the bed. She didn't need to hear anything else.

The threats. The gunman. The attempted break-in.

The doll with the crushed head. Everything she'd endured was for nothing.

Tears of frustration filled her eyes. She had to get out of this house.

She should never have come here, never told Dakota that he had a daughter. He was too screwed up by his past to ever love her or Briana.

She wasn't doing that much better with her own stinking past. And now a fine pair she and Dakota had turned out to be. So hot for each other they sizzled and not enough sense to turn the heat into something sane and lasting.

She lifted Briana from her crib and went to look for Dakota. It was time for her and her daughter to go home. Alone. And Dakota could take his lack of closure and killer reputation to the bulls. She and Briana didn't need an emotional attachment with him.

PANIC WAS STARTING to buck inside Dakota by the time he finally found Viviana. She was sitting on a bale of hay just outside the horse barn, rocking back and forth and cradling Briana in her arms.

Briana was sucking her thumb and waving her plastic keys, seemingly oblivious to the tears that were rolling down Viviana's cheeks. He knew he'd upset her earlier, but he hadn't expected this.

He went and sat down by Viviana, half expecting her to slam him off her bale and knowing he deserved it. "Is this a private crying jag or can anyone join?"

"Don't lecture me."

"I wouldn't dare."

"Then you can stay."

He eased an arm around her shoulders.

"I always thought he hated me," Viviana said, "but you know what? He didn't. Hate would have required caring and he barely knew I existed."

Dakota was thoroughly confused. "Are we talking about anyone I know?"

"I'm talking about my miserable excuse for a father. My mother worked at least two jobs all her life just to make ends meet. He never worked one for more than a few weeks at a time. There was never even money for rent. That's why we had to move so often. Do you know how embarrassing it is to be evicted and have your friends see your clothes piled out on the street?"

"Can't say that I do." And even if he did, he wasn't getting into a childhood-horror contest with her. He could win that hands down.

"We never knew if he was coming home or not and then one day he didn't. Not just any day, mind you." The tears fell harder. "It was the day Mom was diagnosed with cancer."

Maybe he wouldn't win hands down.

Briana began to squirm. He took off his shirt and spread it over a grassy spot next to Viviana's hay bale. He took Briana from her and set her on the soft denim shirt.

Briana rolled onto her stomach and pushed up into a crouching position. "Ba ba ba ga."

"You're welcome." Dakota resettled next to Viviana. "What brought this on? Did you hear from your father?"

Viviana buried her head in her hands. He hugged her close while she sobbed. Finally, she sniffed a few times and wiped her eyes with the heels of her hands. "I don't know how my father got into this, except that I keep comparing him to your family."

Falling apart over nothing didn't sound like Viviana. "Is that the only thing that prompted the tears?"

"No. It's just the first time I've cried since right after my mother died, so I guess I just pulled out all the stops."

"What's really wrong, Viviana?"

She took a deep breath and exhaled as if she were blowing rings of smoke. "The trial has been postponed indefinitely. No suspect, no trial. Hank Bateman just walks free to kill again and then harass and intimidate witnesses so that no one will dare testify against him."

Dakota's muscles bunched into tight knots. He'd been mad when he'd wanted to kill George Bateman this morning. Now he was really pissed off.

Viviana had been through hell because she'd been determined to do the right thing. Dirty Harry had been shot. Kevin Lucas had been murdered. Some guy had been set on fire in Viviana's new car.

All likely connected to Hank Bateman. And those were just the crimes they knew about. Now the cops had let Hank Bateman slip through their hands. The trial for a killer had been postponed the way you might call a baseball game because of rain.

"Not this time." The words came out like curses.

"There's nothing we can do about it," Viviana said.

"Don't be so sure. I'm willing to bet George knows where Hank is. And I know where George lives."

"You're not confronting George again. It's too risky. That's police work."

"Then maybe I'll just have to give the cops a nudge."

Ideas filtered through his mind in rapid succession as they walked back to the ranch house. Only this time, he wouldn't go it alone. The first thing he'd do was call Wyatt.

All his brothers were strong, capable and eager to help. Wyatt was the only one who had the determination of a Ledger plus the experience of a big-city homicide detective.

And Dakota had the determination of a jackass. If the two of them worked together, how could they fail?

IT WAS EIGHT O'CLOCK before Wyatt returned Dakota's phone call. Dakota was on the porch having an after-dinner bourbon while the electric ceiling fan whirred monotonously above him.

"Sorry to be so late getting back to you, but I was at a grizzly crime scene when you called and just now got my messages. The criminals in this state are getting more brazen and just plain crazier every day."

"And getting away with murder," Dakota said.

"Not if we cops can help it. What's the latest with Viviana's situation?"

"Hank Bateman's given the cops the slip. As a result the trial has been postponed indefinitely."

"I was afraid of that when the judge let him out on that penny-ante bail. That made no sense. Unless…"

"Unless what?" Dakota questioned.

"Probably nothing. I tend to jump to the realm of bizarre possibilities. I guess Viviana and her daughter will be returning to San Antonio?"

"Do you think the danger's past?"

"It should be, but you can't be sure. Hank may figure he has a score to settle with Viviana. George may be looking to settle one with you. You know the routine."

"Actually, I don't. The villains in my life are mostly bulls."

"Best to keep it that way. Let the cops handle the Batemans."

"I like the odds better if at least one of the Batemans is in jail. I'm thinking of going after Hank myself."

"That's a very dangerous idea."

"Would you do it, if Viviana were your daughter's mother?"

"That's an unfair question. I'm a cop."

"Would you?"

"The truth?"

"Yeah."

"In a heartbeat."

"That's what I thought. I'm open to advice on how to apprehend Hank. I figure you know as much about that as anyone in this part of Texas."

"Let me think on it tonight. I'll call you first thing in the morning."

"I guess I can wait that long."

"In the meantime, don't let down your guard at the ranch. By now the Batemans may have figured out that's where you are."

"I wish Hank would show up here," Dakota said. "It would save me the trouble of tracking him down."

"Sleep with your gun loaded, one eye open and never underestimate the enemy. That's the first lesson in Survival 101."

"What's lesson two?"

"Sleep with your gun loaded, one eye open and never underestimate the enemy."

"Got it."

Dakota finished his bourbon and stared into the darkness. The night was eerily quiet and an oppressive layer of clouds had blacked out the illumination of the moon and stars.

An owl hooted from a branch of a nearby mesquite tree. Something rustled the grass beneath the thick thorny bushes near the driveway. A coyote howled in the distance.

Nothing unusual or alarming, but Dakota had an uneasy feeling as he went inside and locked the front door behind him. He'd definitely sleep with one eye open tonight…if he slept at all.

THE WIND PICKED UP, blowing dust into vicious whirlwinds that clogged Viviana's lungs and burned her eyes. She tried to run for the house but the dust was so thick she couldn't see to get her bearings.

She fell and her knee slammed against something with a sharp edge. Blood spurted in her face and sprayed the top of the casket. A tiny casket. A baby's casket.

She lifted the lid. Leslie Compton stared back at her accusingly.

The wind died and the sand fell to the earth like blood.

The air grew instantly frigid….

Viviana opened her eyes. There was neither sand nor a casket, but shadowy veils floated about the room. The faint odor of summer flowers wafted on the icy breeze.

The ghost had returned, but this time Viviana wasn't afraid.

"I know you're worried about Dakota, Helene. I'm worried about him, too. I love him just as you do, but I can't reach him."

The veils began to crackle. The figure of a woman materialized in the fog.

"Time is running out. Danger is near."

"Danger to whom? Dakota? Briana? Me? You have to tell me, Helene. You have to help me save us all."

The figure floated toward the glass doors that opened to the garden. The veils followed.

"Follow your heart, my dear. Follow your heart."

Blistering heat suffused the room. Viviana kicked off the sheet and jumped from the bed. This time she didn't bother with the robe.

Her bare feet were all but soundless on the polished hardwood floors. She paused at Dakota's door for only an instant before she opened it and stepped inside.

"Viviana." Dakota jerked to a sitting position. "Is something wrong?"

"Yes. But it's time to make it right." She unbuttoned her freshly laundered nightshirt and let the soft pink cotton pool at her feet. She stood in front of him naked, exposed in every way.

Then she slid beneath the sheet and into Dakota's waiting arms.

QUESTIONS AND DOUBTS exploded in his brain. Viviana silenced them with the touch of her lips to his.

Desire coursed through him so instantly and completely that he forgot everything except the thrill of Viviana. He kissed her, ravaging her lips while the excitement she incited reached every part of his body.

She reacted with the same delirious passion and brazen inhibition that she had before. Her hands tangled in his hair as she slid her tongue between his lips. They kissed until his lungs burned for air.

He wanted her all the way and all at once, but he forced himself to slow down. He kissed her mouth, her eyelids, her nose, then laid her on her back so that he could taste and explore every inch of her beautiful body.

Kicking out of his boxers, he trailed kisses down the smooth column of her neck to her perfect breasts. Her hand slid between their bodies, touching her most private parts and then massaging her slick moisture onto his throbbing erection.

"You make it difficult to go slow," he whispered.

"Then don't. Take me the way you did before, as if you'd never get enough of me."

"I never did. And I haven't wanted anyone since."

"Nor have I, so we can forget protection."

"What about getting pregnant?"

"I'm on the pill. I held on to the dream that you'd come back one day and want the same things I did. That all you'd need was me and Briana."

He pulled away. "I can't give you…"

She kissed the protests from his lips. "I'm not looking for forever tonight. I just need this moment and you."

"And I need you, more than you'll ever know."

Passion took over, whipping Dakota into a frenzy of desire so intense he couldn't hold back. He lifted himself over Viviana. She cradled his throbbing erection and guided it into her before wrapping her arms and legs around him.

Blood rushed to his head as he thrust deeper and deeper inside her. His heart pounded, his body exploded and Viviana rode with him straight over the top.

He held her close as the afterglow settled over them. He'd thought she'd fallen asleep until she began to stir again. She kissed his stomach and twirled a finger inside his navel.

"Do you remember the night we got whipped cream and chocolate syrup all over my sheets?"

"And in my ear," Dakota said.

"And in my hair. All of my hair," Viviana teased. "It took three showers and half a bottle of shampoo to get it out."

"I remember," Dakota said. "I helped. Those were the top three showers of my life."

His body began to come alive again, probably a new record for recovery time.

Any thought of danger had moved to the back of his mind.

The sound of gunfire brought it crashing down on him again.

CHAPTER SIXTEEN

DAKOTA LEAPED FROM the bed and pulled on his jeans. "Lock yourself in Briana's room," Dakota ordered as he grabbed his gun.

There was more gunfire and the sound of breaking glass at the back of the house. Dakota raced down the hallway.

By the time he reached the kitchen, a man was lying facedown in a pool of blood. Troy was leaning over him, checking for a pulse. A rifle was propped against the chair next to him.

"Two of them were breaking into the house," Troy said. "The other son of a bitch got away." Blood wet Troy's left sleeve and trickled across his hand.

"You got hit."

"Friggin' flesh wound. That's all."

"Call an ambulance."

"Too late," Troy said. "This dude is dead."

"Call it for you. In the meantime, Viviana's a doctor. Just protect her and Briana while she tends to that arm."

"Take the deer rifle," Troy said. "It's loaded and more accurate at a distance."

Dakota exchanged weapons and left through the back door at a dead run. He spotted a pickup truck near the horse barn, picking up speed as it bounced and rocked along the rocky surface toward the ranch road.

He fired once and hit nothing.

Dylan's pickup roared toward him from the west and skidded to a stop next to him. "Get in."

"How the hell did you get here so fast?"

"I thought I heard something go past on the road near the house. Never saw lights. Called the guard. No answer. Decided to check it out myself. Heard gunfire and saw you."

He fired the explanation at the same speed he was driving—as fast as he could go. He quickly narrowed the distance between him and the escaping pickup truck.

Dakota lowered the window and pushed the gun outside. He'd never shot from a speeding vehicle before, but he took aim as best he could. There was a loud clunking sound as the first bullet ricocheted off the back fender of the truck they were chasing. The truck left the road, taking down a fence as it cut across the rolling pasture.

"Go for the tires," Dylan shouted.

"I was."

Dakota fired in rapid succession. One of the bullets finally took out a rear tire.

With one tire flat, the truck began to skid but didn't stop. Dakota reloaded and shot another round into the back of the truck, taking out the other tire.

The driver brought the truck to a jerky stop.

"Save your bullets," Dylan said. "We've got him now."

"And we need him alive," Dakota said. "The other one's dead."

"There's another one?"

"The one who shot Troy, but don't panic. Troy's injury is only a flesh wound. He's there with Viviana and Briana."

The man jumped from his truck and took off running toward a cluster of cedar trees. Dakota took off after him. The chest injury fired up again, and he felt as if he were breathing flames. He ran all the harder. He was not letting the guy get away.

He dived for the man football-style and managed to tackle him to the ground just before he reached tree cover. The man went for his gun.

Dylan arrived just in time to stamp the man's gun hand into the rocky earth. The pistol fell from his smashed fingers and Dylan kicked the weapon into the trees.

There was just enough light that Dakota could tell this was not Hank Bateman. He toed the man's arm. "Start talking."

"Keep your foot off me. I've got rights."

"Yeah. Try this *right* on for size." He propped the barrel of his rifle against the man's chest. "You have the right to start talking or I'll see if I can put a bullet right through the center of your heart."

"There wasn't supposed to be any trouble."

"What was there supposed to be?"

"I was told everyone would be asleep and we would just break in and abduct the doctor and her kid."

"Told by whom?"

"I said all I'm saying. I'm not naming names. I'm not that stupid."

Dakota poked his chest with the barrel of the rifle. "Who sent you?"

The guy shook his head. Dylan aimed his rifle at the man's head. "Let me have this one."

"Go ahead. He's no good to me. Take him out." Dakota turned as if he were ready to walk away and leave the guy with Dylan.

"Okay, okay," the man sputtered. "It was Hank Bateman who gave the orders."

"Are you a friend of Hank's?"

"Hank doesn't have friends."

"So what's your connection?"

"I owe him."

"For drugs?"

"Ask Hank."

"I'd love to. Where do I find him?"

"You could have found him right here on Willow Creek Ranch if you hadn't come after me. I'm sure he's finished taking care of his business and is long gone by now."

Damn. Hank had been on the spread and Dakota had missed his chance. Instead of guarding the place himself, he'd been in bed with Viviana.

Never underestimate your enemy.

He'd failed Survival 101.

So had his guards. They hadn't answered Dylan's call. They hadn't shown up at the first sound of gunfire.

Unless the guards had been Hank's business.

Dylan pulled out his cell phone and started punching in numbers.

"Who are you calling?" Dakota asked.

"My father-in-law. This is his turf and I think we need some local law enforcement on the scene."

"Agreed."

The call took less than a minute from beginning to end.

"McGuire and three deputies are driving onto the ranch right now," Dylan said.

"Where was he, sitting outside the gate waiting on you to call?"

"Collette called him the second I left the house. He was riding rounds with a new deputy tonight and they were in the area. He called in two more who were working a car break-in on Hutchens Road."

The gang was all here...after the fact.

Except that his hired guards were still unaccounted for. And Hank Bateman could be anywhere, regrouping for his next attack.

But why go to these extremes to silence a witness in a trial that wasn't going to be held?

Whatever the reason, Hank Bateman had to be stopped.

He was the bull that Dakota had to ride to the ground. The cost of failure could be Viviana's life.

THE COFFEE WAS still brewing and the first rays of morning sun were painting golden squares on the kitchen table when Dakota's cell phone announced an incoming call from Wyatt.

"I just had a call from Dylan. He says Dad got shot last night during a rip-roaring, old-time western gun battle."

"Sadly, with a body count of two. Things have deteriorated fast since we spoke last night."

"Two? I thought I counted three when Dylan was giving the wrap-up."

"Our guard who took the knife to the gut is in the hospital but holding his own. The guard whose throat was sliced died on the scene. And the guy Dad shot through the window died from a piece of jagged glass that sliced through his windpipe."

"Tough way to go."

"So is having your throat slashed."

"How's Dad?"

"He had to have a few dozen stitches in his arm, and he'll have another scar to add to his collection, but he's fine. Already hollering to come home."

"Can't blame him. He's got a doctor staying in his house."

"A very upset doctor. Viviana thinks the deaths are her fault. She's lamenting that she came to the ranch."

"If she hadn't come there, she'd probably be dead."

"I know. I get sick just thinking about what Hank Bateman would have done to her and Briana if his henchmen had abducted them."

"Luckily Dad was awake and in the kitchen when they attempted the break-in, at least that's the way I heard it."

"That's the way Dad told it," Dakota said. "He said he woke from a sound sleep. He thought one of us had come to his room, but when he turned on the light to look, there was no one there. He went to the kitchen for a glass of water and saw the shadow of a guy as he skulked from that storage building out back toward the house."

"I heard Dad shot him with a rifle."

"He did. When he saw the shadow, he took the rifle from the locked case and waited until the guy was at the window. He didn't see the second guy until he took off running."

"And that was the guy you and Dylan chased down?"

"Right, the one who admitted Hank is behind all of this. So have you come up with ideas for locating Hank?"

"About that… I did some checking. You really don't want to get involved with him or his brother, Dakota."

"I don't have a choice."

"You do. Just give it some time and I think it will take care of itself."

"Why would you think that?"

"I shouldn't be telling you this so keep it under your hat. Both brothers are being investigated by the Feds. Arrests may be in the foreseeable future."

"Which also means arrests may not be made in the foreseeable future."

"True. I'm giving you the best scenario."

"Help me here," Dakota said. "How did killing Leslie Compton became a federal case?"

"It didn't. The Feds are investigating them for something else altogether. The Batemans will get taken off the streets eventually and in the meantime, you don't want to become a statistic."

"I don't want Viviana or Briana becoming statistics, either."

"Then persuade Viviana to stay at the ranch awhile longer."

"Why are the Feds after them?"

"I can't talk about the case against them. I've already said more than I should have. They're in big trouble. Viviana is just fun and games for them and there won't be any more fun and games once they're arrested. So just give this some time."

"I appreciate the advice."

"I hope that means you're going to follow it."

"I'll give it some thought."

"Don't make me have to come down there."

"Why not? Then we'd have the whole gang down here."

"The sons of Troy Ledger ride again."

"Sounds like a movie title."

"Let's make it one with a happy ending, Dakota."

"Wouldn't have it any other way."

VIVIANA PLACED THE stack of neatly folded panties in the suitcase. Briana reached over and pulled them out.

"I know you don't want to leave the ranch, sweetheart, but we have to. Mama is trouble, trouble, trouble."

"Ma-ma. Ma-ma."

"You said it! You said 'Mama.' On the day I needed good news the most." Viviana picked up Briana and hugged her tight.

Dakota stopped in the doorway. "Did I hear shouting in here?"

"Briana just said 'Mama.' Say it again, sweetie. Mama. Mama."

"Ab a ca oo."

"Well, she said it twice, so that means it wasn't just an accident," Viviana said.

"I'm not doubting you." Dakota stepped into the room. "Why are you packing? Are we going somewhere?"

"I'm going away for a while."

"Going where?"

"To California."

"That's not just another state. It's another world from Texas."

"I appreciate everything you've done, Dakota, but I can't keep living in this constant state of flux and I certainly can't expect it of your family."

"Coming here was your idea."

"Yes, and it seemed to make sense when we were talking about a week at the most, but this is a nightmare with no termination date."

"When did you plan to tell me this?"

"When I finished packing. I have a car coming to pick me up at eleven and I have a flight from Austin to Los Angeles at two-thirty this afternoon."

"Do you have a place to stay in L.A.?"

"One of my friends from med school is there. She says the hospitals out there need emergency medicine specialists and that I'll have no trouble getting a job. Briana and I can stay with her until I find a place of my own."

"I don't blame you for giving up on me as a protector. I've failed you miserably, but don't you think quitting your job is going a bit too far?"

"You didn't fail me or Briana. We're both safe. It's just that keeping us safe has become too costly and dangerous for everyone around me."

"No one wants you to leave the ranch."

"They should be demanding it. Two men are dead. Another may not make it. Your father is in the hospital. And what if Hank had stopped at Dylan's and sliced his and Collette's throats? Do you think I could ever live with myself after that?"

He walked over and took her free hand. "Look, Viviana, I admit that this isn't working, but we'll come up with another plan."

"You have bulls to ride."

"Three more days. Give me three more days to come up with a plan. If I don't have one by then, L.A. will still be there." He leaned over and kissed her.

Briana grabbed his nose, making the kiss more of a challenge than an act of passion. Still, it took her breath away.

Her cell phone rang. She checked the caller ID. "It's Shelby Lucas."

"I'll take Briana while you talk, but put the phone on speaker so I can hear what she has to say."

Briana put her short, chubby arms around Viviana's neck as she tried to pass her to Dakota. Somehow he managed to charm her into letting go.

Viviana dropped to the side of the bed and switched the phone to speaker. "Hello."

"Hi. This is Shelby. We talked at the restaurant."

"Yes, I remember you well. You're Hank Bateman's girlfriend."

"I *was* his girlfriend."

"Did you break up with him since we talked?"

"He dumped me for that slut Karen Compton."

"Leslie's mother?"

"Right. I found out he's been seeing her ever since he got out of jail."

Surely Karen hadn't gone back to Hank after he'd killed her baby, but then Viviana shouldn't be that shocked at anything that happened in Hank's world.

"Why are you calling, Shelby?"

"I overheard Hank talking to George. He's planning to kill you and your baby. There's been too much killing. That's why I wanted to warn you."

"Why would he kill me?"

"To make you pay for calling the police on him and saying he killed Karen's baby."

"I only reported the cause of death. The police connected Hank to the death on their own."

"Whatever. I thought with him wanting to kill you and all, you might want to know where Hank is hiding."

Dakota motioned to Viviana and whispered instructions.

"Yes. I'd love to know where Hank is."

"It's an abandoned house in a wooded area near the river. I can't tell you where it is, but I can show you. You might want to take that cowboy with you. He's not afraid of anything, not even George. He's a good shot, too."

"Why didn't you go to the cops with this information?"

"I don't deal with cops. If I show you and that cowboy where Hank is, you have to promise no cops."

"What do you have against cops?"

"It's what they have against me."

"Warrants for your arrest?"

"Yeah. For writing bad checks, shoplifting. Stuff like that. Nothing big. I'm calling 'cause I want to help you, Dr. Mancini. But it's also because I need money real bad."

"So you expect me to pay you for showing me this house in the woods?"

"One thousand dollars in twenties. That's enough for me to get back to Mississippi. I've got family there. But you have to show up with the cowboy even if you don't go after Hank with us. I have to know you're in on this. I trust you not to tell the cops."

Dakota nodded his approval but this sounded like a trap to Viviana.

"I can meet you at that same restaurant where we met before," Shelby said. "Can you make it by three o'clock this afternoon?"

"I haven't agreed to anything yet."

"Okay, but if you want to get Hank before he kills you, bring the money to the restaurant at three. I'll be parked near the front entrance so you won't even have to go inside. If you're not there, that's okay, too. I'm leaving town with or without the money. I'm tired of getting pushed around by the Batemans."

Shelby broke the connection before Viviana could give her an answer.

"I'll be there," Dakota said, as if Shelby could hear him.

"I don't trust her," Viviana said. "This is either a trap or just a ploy to get cash."

"Maybe it's not a trap. Hell hath no fury like a woman scorned, you know."

"A woman whose fury can be lessened with a thousand dollars."

"I'll make sure that I'm ready for any trick she might try. I just have a few details to work out. I'll have the sheriff and his deputies come out and stay with you and Briana. He's offered to help in anyway he can."

"Not so fast," Viviana said. "If you're determined to meet with Shelby, I'm going with you. Collette, Dylan and her sheriff father can take care of Briana."

"No. You said yourself that this could be a trap."

"I'm the one Shelby trusts, Dakota. I'll see if Collette will watch Briana while we're away."

"You're not going, Viviana. Final answer."

"It's either the flight to Los Angeles or the steak restaurant. You decide."

"Did anyone ever tell you you're a hardheaded woman?"

"All the time, and thank you."

He kissed her again, slower, sweeter, wetter than before. Briana bit him on the nose.

"Be ready at one," he said and then turned and walked away.

WHEN THEY WERE within fifteen minutes of arriving at the restaurant, Dakota made one last call to Detective

Gordon Miles to make certain that the details of the plan were in place.

"Everything's a go," the detective assured him. "I'm parked across the street in an unmarked car. You won't see me en route, but I'll stay just close enough that I don't lose you."

"What about the guard for Viviana?"

"Sergeant Blake will keep her in his sights. He'll pull in front of the restaurant exactly five minutes after we pull out, also in an unmarked car and wearing street clothes."

"How will Viviana recognize him?"

"He'll be driving a dark blue Ford Taurus and wearing jeans and a blue polo shirt. He'll stop near the front door of the restaurant, get out and put a black laptop bag in the backseat of the car. That will be her signal that it's safe to get in the car. Then they'll go to her town house and wait for you to come back for her."

"At that point, you should have Hank Bateman in custody," Dakota said.

"If all goes as planned."

Dakota pulled to a stop at a red light. The restaurant was just ahead. "Have you heard anything new on Harry Cortez's condition?"

"Yes, good news. He not only started talking today but he's also finally making sense."

"Did he ID his shooter?"

"Yep. Guess who?"

"Hank Bateman."

"You got it. I hope to go by the hospital tonight and tell him Bateman is locked up and that we threw away the key. Even better news would be that we had to shoot the bastard in self-defense."

The light turned green. Dakota pulled across the intersection. "Any luck yet with identifying the man who was burned in Viviana's car?"

"Also just in. His name is Ronnie Pellor. He was a stoolie for one of our narcotics agents, same as Kevin Lucas was. I'm sure one of the traffickers put out a hit on them."

Dakota hadn't heard that about Kevin Lucas but it would explain why Detective Cortez didn't admit knowing who Kevin was referring to when he'd muttered "Shell." The cops protected pigeons.

"I'm pulling into the restaurant parking lot now," Dakota said.

"I've got you spotted."

"Shelby's parked near the front entrance just as she said she'd be," Dakota said.

"In the red Jeep?"

"Yep.

"I figured that was her."

"Looks like she may be sporting some new bruises," Dakota said, "though it's hard to tell from here."

"She pulled a gun on George Bateman the other day," Miles said. "I'm sure that didn't earn her flowers. Now, remember, make sure the backseat and the trunk are empty before you get in or hand over any money. And keep your pistol ready, just in case Shelby's packing and lying."

"Got it," Dakota said. "See you in the little house in the big woods."

"And here's hoping we also see Hank."

SHELBY DROVE AT least ten miles over the speed limit, recklessly switching lanes and barely avoiding a collision with a semi. She surfed the radio channels every time a song finished until she finally settled on a heavy rock station that played nothing Dakota would consider music.

"You seem nervous," Dakota noted, baiting as much as questioning. His suspicions of this being a trap were growing stronger with each mile they traveled.

"Wouldn't you be nervous if you were ratting out Hank Bateman?"

"Probably. Is he the one who did that to your face?"

"Do you recognize his artistic touches?"

"Just a lucky guess." He looked out the window, then back to Shelby.

"How did you learn Hank's location?"

"I've got my ways of finding out things," Shelby said.

Yep. He was being driven into a trap, but this time he and Detective Miles would be ready for whatever surprises Hank threw their way. At least he hoped they would.

Thirty minutes after they'd left the restaurant, Shelby stopped the car at the end of a deserted road. Beyond them was a thick wooded area. There was no sign of the detective.

Dakota was starting to get a tad nervous.

"I don't see a house," he said.

"We took the back roads. You can't see it from here but it's about a ten-minute walk through the woods. Just stay east of the tree line. You can't miss it."

"I thought you were here to show me the way."

"I'll stay here with the car. When I see you coming, I'll start the engine for a fast getaway."

He waited. There should be some sign of the detective by now.

"Are you going to get out or not?" Shelby asked, clearly impatient.

"I'm thinking about it." He lowered the window. The air was hot and humid. A murder of loud crows darted in and out of the branches of a scrawny oak tree. A lone butterfly fluttered among the honeybees sipping nectar from the honeysuckle vines that climbed a nearby fence.

There was a whir in the distance, growing louder as it came closer. Maybe a motorbike. Dakota opened the car door and stepped out, his hand resting on the butt of his gun.

He was usually comfortable trusting his instincts, but they seemed off-kilter today.

He caught sight of movement in the trees. Could be a deer but Dakota figured it was Hank.

"Afternoon, Ledger." George Bateman stepped into the clearing, his pistol pointed at Dakota. "You just can't stay away from me, can you?"

The sound of gunfire blasted through the still air. Crows scattered in every direction. The gun George had been holding fell from his hands and at least ten men in SWAT suits surrounded him.

Detective Miles drove up and stepped out of his car. "Good work, Dakota."

"Thanks. Now would someone mind telling me what the devil's going on?"

Shelby gunned her engine and threw the car into Reverse.

"Let her go," Miles called loudly enough for everyone to hear. "She's small potatoes. We can pick her up anytime."

Miles walked over to where Dakota stood as two helicopters landed a few feet from the tree line.

"This is a federal operation that's been in the works for months," Miles explained, yelling over the helicopters' roar. "They finally got the evidence they needed to tie George and Hank to several dozen cartel-related murders over the past two years. That's why the judge agreed to set bail for Hank so close to the trial. They needed a few more pieces of evidence that Hank conveniently led them to."

"I still don't get it."

"It's kind of a trade-off. They arrest Hank and hope for him to provide info to catch one of the big guys who's ordering hits on police officers all along the border."

"And George?"

"He's a worker bee. He does as he's told, but he's not connected the way Hank is. Up until he was arrested for Leslie Compton's murder, Hank was moving into the upper echelon of one of the biggest cartels."

"And he blew all that by killing his girlfriend's baby. He doesn't sound that smart to me."

"I'm sure he never thought he'd go to jail."

"Because he and George would intimidate the witnesses. I'm still not sure why you included me in any of this."

"The Feds have been searching for Hank for two days. Every time they think they have him cornered, he fools them. You called and offered to deliver. The Feds decided to take you up on it."

"The house is empty," someone yelled. "There's no sign of Hank."

Gordon Miles muttered a string of curses a mile long. "He's slipped through our fingers again." The detective went toward his men.

Dakota leaned against Miles's unmarked car. All this

and no Hank Bateman. So where was he? Apprehension settled like lead in Dakota's gut. He took out his phone and called Viviana.

No answer.

He tried the number again, letting it ring until it switched to her voice mail.

This wasn't like her, not when she believed that Dakota might be walking into a trap.

He scanned the area, searching for the detective. Miles was nowhere in sight and there was no time to waste looking for him.

Dakota opened the door to the detective's car. The keys were in the ignition. That was all the invitation he needed.

VIVIANA SERVED A cup of the fresh-brewed coffee to Sergeant Blake. "Feel free to turn on the television over the counter," she said, "or you can watch the one in the living room."

"No, I'm good. I like to keep my mind on the job."

"Do I have to sit with you or is it okay if I go upstairs?"

"You have full run of the house. I've already checked inside every closet, under every bed and even looked inside those two big chests you have at the end of the hall."

"In that case I think I'll go upstairs and lie down until Dakota gets back. I got very little sleep last night."

"Do whatever you want. If you need me, I'll be right here."

"Help yourself to more coffee whenever you want it."

"Yes, ma'am."

She did try resting, but she was so nervous she couldn't even close her eyes. Dakota and the detective had both assured her that nothing could go wrong this afternoon, but she couldn't get last night out of her mind.

In a matter of minutes two men had been killed and Troy had been wounded.

She needed this to be over. They all did. She couldn't think beyond that.

She went to the bathroom and washed her face. When she turned off the water, she heard a noise as if the detective had dropped something. She went to the head of the stairs and looked down.

"Are you all right?"

The house was deathly quiet.

"Sergeant Blake?"

The lack of a response and the quiet set her nerves on edge. She had to settle down. The officer was likely in the bathroom or checking something in the garage.

She took the stairs slowly, stopping on the landing to call again.

"Sergeant Blake? Are you in the kitchen?"

This time she heard whispered voices.

The television. He must have changed his mind about it and turned it low so as not to disturb her. She hurried into the kitchen. The sergeant was in the same chair as she'd left him.

Only now his hands were duct taped behind his back and his eyes were rolled back in his head as if he were drugged…or dead. A bloody knife lay next to him and there was a jagged cut down one arm. The blood had soaked into his uniform.

CHAPTER SEVENTEEN

VIVIANA'S HEART POUNDED fiercely against the wall of her chest, the fear so strong her feet refused to move. Hank Bateman was somewhere inside the house. And not alone. She'd heard voices. Male and female. And he must have heard her calling.

He'd stayed out of sight, intentionally playing a vicious game of cat and mouse, no doubt delighting in her horror at the sight of the sergeant in her kitchen.

She checked Sergeant Blake's pulse. It was weak but not in the danger zone. She tiptoed past him and pulled a clean, bloodless chef's knife from the block on the counter.

"I know you're here, Hank. I know you see me."

There was still no response.

Holding the knife in her hand, she began to tiptoe toward the back door. If she could just get outside, she could run and scream for help.

Her left hand was on the doorknob, the right still clutching the knife when she felt the sharp point of a blade prick the skin at the base of her skull.

"It's too early to leave, Dr. Mancini. The party is just beginning."

He'd sneaked up behind her, which meant he'd been hiding in the laundry room. But for how long? She was sure the sergeant had checked that room when they'd come in.

He wrapped his right hand around hers. "I'll take that knife before you hurt yourself and rob me of the pleasure."

She tried to swing her arm backward and hit him with the sharp blade. If she could just buy time the way she had with the key in the E.R. parking lot, she'd have at least a chance of escape.

He was too strong for her. He crushed her hand in his until she screamed from the pain and the knife clattered to the floor.

"How did you get in?" she asked.

He slid the point of the knife up and down her neck, drawing beads of blood that slid down her flesh.

"It's quite easy to pick a lock when you know how, but this time I climbed in through the kitchen window."

"I don't believe you. Sergeant Blake would have heard you before you could get inside."

"That's why I came early. I knew I'd have plenty of time since Shelby wasn't meeting you until three."

He'd put Shelby up to this, which meant Dakota had surely walked into a trap. Her stomach began to roll.

"You made Shelby do this, didn't you?"

"Yes, the scared, fearful little dimwit is disgustingly easy to manipulate."

"She's in love with you."

"She's pregnant with my brother's child. They deserve each other. Karen, come in here. The doctor needs someone to help her undress before we practice our surgery."

"If you hurt me, Dakota Ledger and his brothers will hunt you down and cut out your heart."

"They may hunt, but they won't find me." Hank led

her toward the table as Karen Compton joined them in the kitchen.

"Start with the blouse. I'll watch and decide where we should cut first."

Hank took a step away from her, removing the knife from her flesh for the first time since he'd come into the kitchen. But he was close enough that she'd never be able to get away before he caught her. She had to think, had to find a way to escape.

Karen's hands shook as she slipped the first pearl button of Viviana's blouse through the hole. Hank had claimed Shelby was easily manipulated. Perhaps Karen was, too.

Viviana put her mouth close to Karen's ear. "How can you stay with a man who killed your baby girl?"

Karen moved on to the next button, but now her hands were shaking so badly, she was having difficulty maneuvering the button through the hole.

"Your baby girl is dead," Viviana whispered. "She is gone from you forever. Hank did that to you."

Karen stepped away from Viviana. "Stop. Make her stop, Hank."

"No more talk of babies, Doc, or I'll skip right over the fun part."

"Baby killer," Viviana whispered.

Karen shoved Viviana into the table. "Hank didn't kill my baby. He didn't, so stop saying that. I killed her. Me. Her mother. She wouldn't stop crying. All day, all night, she just wouldn't stop. And then finally she did."

Karen fell to the floor sobbing.

Hank kicked Karen in the stomach. "I should have let you go to jail for killing that kid and then I wouldn't have to listen to your constant wailing about it."

He took the knife and sliced Viviana's blouse down

the front so that it gaped open. Then he fit the blade inside her bra and sliced through it.

"Does that make you feel like a man?"

"I am a man. And you can shut up, too."

"Why should I do what you say when you're going to kill me no matter what I do? You're a monster, Hank, a certifiable beast. How does anyone ever get to be as heartless and evil as you are?"

He rolled the point of the knife across her nipples. "I'll tell you how, sweetheart. You have a dad who gets drunk two or three times a week and comes home and beats the living crap out of you. And if you whimper, he hits you that much harder. If you cry, he pokes you with his lit cigarette until you pass out from the pain."

Viviana backed up slowly as he talked, finally getting close enough to reach the bloody knife Hank had used on the cop. She picked it up and threw it at Hank, blade first. It impaled his chest and he stumbled backward. She dashed past him and ran for the door.

Hank grabbed her from behind, the knife still in his chest.

"Don't kill her," Karen begged. "She just wanted to help our baby."

"If you say one more word, I'll kill you, too."

He knocked Viviana to the floor then straddled her, holding her down with his knees while he yanked the knife from his bloodied chest and then held it to her throat.

One swipe across her jugular and she'd bleed to death.

She didn't want to die. She wanted to raise Briana. She wanted to hold tight to Dakota and love him.

She closed her eyes and thought of her cowboy and her baby while she waited for the sharp, quick slice of death.

CHAPTER EIGHTEEN

"Answer the phone, Viviana. Please answer the phone and tell me I'm going crazy for nothing. Tell me you are sitting there drinking a diet soda while you entertain the cop with stories of life in the real E.R."

The phone switched to her voice-mail message once again. He didn't bother to leave one this time.

Dakota had made a grave error in judgment. He'd thought he had everything under control, but once again he'd underestimated the enemy.

He parked a few doors down from Viviana's town house. He'd circle the house first and try to assess what was going on inside. Play it smart and not just burst in and get shot before he could save Viviana.

He cut through the neighbor's yard and slipped through the hedges to the bay window in front of the house. The living room was empty. Creeping as stealthily as he could, he skirted the side of the house and moved to the back. He stayed low as he neared the kitchen window.

Finally, he straightened and looked inside. The first thing he saw was the cop, his head rolled back, blood rolling off his chin and down his neck like a gaudy ruby necklace.

His heart plunged when he spotted Viviana. She was on the floor, her eyes closed, with Hank Bateman pressing a bloody kitchen knife to her throat.

Hank looked up, saw Dakota watching and threw back his head and laughed. Fury exploded like a bomb inside Dakota, and adrenaline coursed through his veins in angry waves. But this time he couldn't just act on impulse. This time it was Viviana's life on the line.

"So glad you made it in time to watch her die, Dakota. But if you make one move toward us, I'll have to kill her so fast it won't be fun for either of us."

A woman who seemed to materialize from thin air walked over to Hank. She was holding a knife to her own throat.

"I'll die with you, Viviana. I killed my baby. I don't deserve to live."

Hank reached up to grab the knife from her hand. When he did, Viviana rolled from beneath him.

Dakota flew into action. He ripped off the screen with one quick jerk and smashed the butt of his pistol through the glass.

His gaze met Hank's for one split second before Dakota pulled the trigger and fired.

Hank fell back, dead before he hit the ground, thanks to a bullet between the eyes.

Heart pounding, Dakota climbed through the window, crossed the room and dropped to the floor beside Viviana. He took her into his arms and pulled her to him.

"I should never have left you," he said, "should never have trusted anyone to watch over you but me."

"You're here now, Dakota. You're here now and you have never looked or felt so good."

"AND THEN WHAT HAPPENED?" Collette asked.

Viviana sipped her ice-cold diet soda. "Detective Miles showed up. He'd come to the same realization that Dakota had about the time he looked up and saw Dakota speeding away in his unmarked vehicle."

"When he couldn't reach Blake, he called me," Dakota said. "He called for backup but by the time they arrived at Viviana's the ambulance had already picked up Blake and Hank Bateman. There was nothing for them to do but arrest Karen for assisting Hank in today's assault."

"And for the death of her daughter nearly a year ago," Viviana added, "though I don't think there's any punishment they can give her that is worse than the one she's given herself."

"How did you find out she was the one who killed the baby and not Hank?" Troy asked.

"She admitted it to me before Hank kicked her and long before my hero here showed up on the scene."

"It doesn't quite add up," Troy said. "Hank was a ruthless, heartless killer yet he took the blame for the baby's murder when it was Karen who killed her."

"Maybe he really loved her in his own way," Collette said.

"If that's love," Dylan said, "I hope to never have any part of it."

"I feel the same," Viviana said. "Now if you'll all excuse me, I need to check on Briana and then go to bed. I'm cratering fast."

Viviana got ready for bed first and then spent long minutes staring at Briana, grateful that she'd stayed alive to come home to her tonight. Helene Ledger had once faced a killer in this very house, but she hadn't tucked her kids in bed that night or ever again.

No wonder her spirit lingered and still worried for her boys.

When Viviana returned to the guest room, Dakota

was standing at the glass door staring out at the court-yard garden his mother had loved so much.

"I'm glad it's finally over," he said. "I never want to be as afraid again as I was when I saw that knife at your throat."

"I was afraid, too. I wasn't ready to die. Now I'm more than ready to live my life to the fullest. But I can't help but feel just a little sad for Hank Bateman when I think of the way he grew up. Can you imagine being beaten almost daily by the one who should be keeping you safe?"

"I don't have to imagine it. I lived it."

Viviana's insides quaked at the sadness in Dakota's voice. She walked over and put her arms around his waist and rested her face against his back. "Do you want to talk about it?"

"I thought I wanted to. I thought I wanted to throw my past in the face of everyone in my family and punish them for letting me suffer at Uncle Larry's hands. It turns out I don't."

"What changed your mind?"

"Finding you again. Becoming a father. Meeting my family. All of the above in differing measures. When my mother died, life changed for all of us. None of us will ever get back what we lost. For me it was growing up without ever feeling safe."

"That must have made for a frightening childhood."

"It did. The only thing I loved growing up was the rodeo. That was my escape. It was pain with a purpose."

"Now I understand why you love it so much."

"I'm not sure about that but it may have kept me from turning out like Hank Bateman."

"Or it might have been the six years of your mother's love that saved you."

Dakota put an arm around her shoulder. "I've been thinking a lot these past few days and I've made a couple of major decisions, Viviana."

"It may have been the stress," Viviana suggested cautiously. "Perhaps you should wait to tell me until you're sure the changes are what you really want."

"I'm sure now. I want us to be a real family. You, me and Briana. I want wedding bells, cake and a gold band. I'm ready to go whole hog. That is if you'll have me."

"What about bull riding?"

"If that's what it takes to be a family, I'll give that up, too."

"No. I've changed my mind about a few things, too. You can keep your bull riding. All it takes for us to be a family is love. But I would like that wedding you mentioned."

"Any kind of wedding you want—as long we have whipped cream and chocolate for the honeymoon."

Viviana melted into Dakota's arms and into his kiss, sure she'd never been this happy in her life.

She lingered at the door to the garden after Dakota released her.

Hold on tight to Dakota. If you let go of him, he will be lost forever.

"I have him, Helene," she whispered. "You can let go now and rest in peace. But I didn't save Dakota. Love saved us both."

"Did you say something?"

"I said let's go to bed. I can't wait to sleep in your arms tonight and forever." Her forever had just turned to pure gold.

* * * * *

Two-time RITA® Award-nominated and award-winning author **Linda Warren** loves her job, writing happily-ever-after books for Harlequin. Drawing upon her years of growing up on a farm/ranch in Texas, she writes about sexy heroes, feisty heroines and broken families with an emotional punch, all set against the backdrop of Texas. Her favorite pastime is sitting on her patio with her husband watching the wildlife, especially the injured ones that are coming in pairs these days: two Canada geese with broken wings, two does with broken legs and a bobcat ready to pounce on anything tasty. Learn more about Linda and her books at her website, lindawarren.net, or on Facebook, LindaWarrenAuthor, or follow @Texauthor on Twitter.

Books by Linda Warren

Harlequin American Romance

The Christmas Cradle

The Cowboy's Return

Once a Cowboy

Texas Heir

The Sheriff of Horseshoe, Texas

Her Christmas Hero

Tomas: Cowboy Homecoming

One Night in Texas

A Texas Holiday Miracle

Texas Rebels: Egan

Visit the Author Profile page at Harlequin.com for more titles.

TOMAS: COWBOY HOMECOMING

Linda Warren

To my wonderful editor, Kathleen Scheibling, for creating the Harts of the Rodeo and giving us such interesting characters to develop. And a temperamental black stallion to tame.

To Johanna Raisanen for editing the books to make them the best they could be.

To the men and women in our military. Thank you.

Acknowledgments

Thanks to all the people who answered my many questions about rodeo, especially Catherine Laycraft from the Calgary Stampede. And a special thanks to Rogenna for sharing her knowledge of the military.

And for all the info available on the internet about rodeo and PTSD.

All errors are strictly mine.

CHAPTER ONE

HOME TO THUNDER RANCH.

In a coffin.

The only way Marine Staff Sergeant Tomas "Tuf" Hart ever saw himself returning to the place of his birth from the battlefields of Afghanistan was in a pine box.

Draped with an American flag.

Every time his unit engaged the enemy, bullets whizzed past him as mortar fire exploded in his ears. Two of his buddies died not twelve feet from him, but he'd been spared. Unscathed. Except for the invisible wounds on his soul that would be with him a lifetime. He'd seen too many innocent women and children killed for them not to.

But that was behind him and he was ready to see his family again. Though he'd been out of the Marine Corps two years, he hadn't been home. Explaining that wasn't going to be easy, but talking about the war was something he didn't do, and he hoped his family respected that.

The sleepy town of Roundup, Montana, nestled in the pine-clad valley of the Bull Mountains. The town got its name because the valley near the Musselshell River was a natural place for ranchers to round up their cattle.

It was three days after Christmas and the town was quiet as he drove down a snow-covered Main Street,

tire-track trails visible in the slush. Red-and-green dec-
orations still fluttered from every building. Familiar
storefronts. He noticed a redbrick building with black
trim—Number 1 Diner. That was new, but otherwise
the place was the same—his hometown.

He left town and turned south, taking the county road
leading to the ranch. A light snow began to fall and he
flipped on the windshield wipers. As he rounded a corner, he saw a little girl about four or five walking on the
side of the road. She wore a heavy purple coat with a fur-
lined hood, but the hood wasn't over her head. Flakes
of snow clung to her red hair, gathered into a ponytail,
as she purposefully marched forward in snow boots.

A flashback hit him. He hadn't had one in months.
He could see the little girl in Afghanistan, hear the rapid
spatter of gunfire, the shouts, the screams and then an
unholy silence. Stopping the truck in the middle of the
road, he gripped the steering wheel with clammy hands.
He took a quick breath and closed his eyes, forcing happier memories into his mind as his counselor had taught
him.

He was fishing on Thunder Creek with his dad.
"Come on, boy. The big ones bite early. Throw your
line next to that old stump." Tuf would grin and throw
the line where his father had showed him.

"That's my boy."

He opened his eyes as the flashback ebbed away. The
little girl trekked forward in the snow, a good distance
from him now. He eased the truck closer and got out.

What was she doing out here all alone? Buddy
Wright's was the closest place, and he didn't have any
young kids Tuf knew about.

"Hey," he called, but the girl ignored him. She did

move farther into the ditch, though. His boots slipped and slid on the snow-slick blacktop, but he made it to her without falling on his ass. "Hey, what are you doing out here?"

The little girl frowned up at him, her green eyes narrowed. "I'm not 'posed to talk to strangers."

"Listen…"

"Sadie! Sadie!" a frantic voice called, and Tuf turned his head to see a woman running toward them. She was dressed in a denim skirt, brown boots, a suede vest and a white blouse. No coat. And the temperature was below freezing. Her deep red hair, the color of cinnamon, glistened with snow.

Cheyenne Wright.

He'd know her anywhere.

Even though she was a year younger, he'd had a huge crush on her in high school. Since he was a bareback rider and she was a barrel racer, he saw her often at rodeos. He had asked her out twice and she'd said no both times. Figuring third time's a charm, he'd asked again and got the same answer. Puzzled and frustrated he'd asked why. Her response was "I don't like you, Tuf Hart."

That had dented his puffed-up seventeen-year-old ego. He didn't get it. He was reasonably good-looking, well liked by everyone in school and he had his own pickup. Back then that was a sure thing to get a date. Not with Cheyenne. But he didn't think it to death because he was aware the Hart and Wright families didn't get along. Buddy was an alcoholic and had served time in prison for stealing cattle. John Hart hadn't wanted the man on his property.

So Tuf, as teenage boys are known to do, moved on. He never forgot the shy, untouchable Cheyenne, though.

Since he was twenty-eight, she had to be about twenty-seven now, and she still looked the same with dark red hair and green eyes. And a slim curved body he'd spent many nights dreaming about.

She squatted and pulled the child into her arms. At that point, Tuf noticed an identical little girl running to catch up to Cheyenne. *Twins.* This one had the hood over her head and was bundled up tight in a pink winter coat.

"Mommy," the second twin cried.

"It's all right, Sammie," Cheyenne said in a soothing, soft voice. "I found Sadie." Cheyenne brushed the snow from Sadie's hair and covered it with the hood, securing it with the drawstring. Her fingers shook from the cold as she touched Sadie's red cheeks. "I've been looking all over for you. What are you doing out here?"

"I'd like to know that, too."

Cheyenne stood, holding on to the girls' hands. Her eyes narrowed much as her daughter's had. The sparkling green eyes of the cool, aloof Cheyenne from high school were gone. Now he saw only disillusionment in their depths. A look he knew well. He saw it every morning when he looked in the mirror. What had happened to her life?

"I'll take care of my daughter," she replied, as cool as the snowflakes falling on her hair.

"I hope you do. I could have hit her. Anyone driving on this road could have, and then two lives would have been changed forever."

"I'm sorry if she disturbed...your drive."

He heard the derision in her voice and he relented a little. "It's dangerous out here."

"I'm aware of that." She looked down at her daughters and ignored him, much as she had in high school. "Let's go home where it's warm." They walked away, Cheyenne holding the girls' hands.

"I didn't talk to him, Mommy, 'cause he's a stranger," Sadie said.

"Good, baby."

Cheyenne started to run and the girls followed suit. Sadie glanced back at him as they disappeared into the Wrights' driveway.

Tuf pulled his sheep-lined jacket tighter around him to block the chill of a Montana December.

Welcome home, Tuf.

Some things just never changed. Cheyenne still didn't like him.

CHEYENNE USHERED THE girls into the living room and sat them down by the fire. For a moment she let her chilled body soak up the warmth. When she stopped trembling, she hurried to the bathroom for a towel. Rushing back, she removed the girls' new Christmas coats and dried Sadie's hair and face, as well as her own. Her clothes were damp and she needed to change, but she had to talk to Sadie first.

She sat between them. "Sadie, baby, why do you keep running away?"

Sadie shrugged.

Cheyenne brushed back one of Sadie's flyaway curls. "Mommy is worried. Please stop this."

Sammie crawled into her lap. "I won't run away, Mommy."

She kissed Sammie's warm cheek. Their father's death had affected the girls so differently. Sammie clung to her while Sadie was defiant and seemed determined to get away from her. Cheyenne was at her wit's end trying to get Sadie to talk about what was bothering her.

Gathering the girls close, she whispered, "I love you guys."

"I love you, too, Mommy." Sammie was quick to say the words.

Fat tears rolled from Sadie's eyes. "I…I…" she blubbered.

Cheyenne held her tighter, feeling hopeless. Why couldn't she help her child? She smoothed Sadie's hair and kissed her forehead. "You love Mommy?"

Sadie nodded and Cheyenne held her daughters, wondering how she was ever going to reach Sadie. The fire crackled with renewed warmth, and she leaned against her dad's recliner holding the two most important people in the world to her. They snuggled against her.

Cheyenne's body was so cold she didn't think she'd ever get warm again. The fear in her slowly subsided. They'd been in town and on the way home when Sammie suddenly had to go to the bathroom. Running into the house, she'd turned on the TV for Sadie and helped Sammie out of her coat. When they'd come out of the bathroom, Sadie was gone. Cheyenne was frantic, calling and calling for Sadie.

It wasn't the first time Sadie had disappeared, and Cheyenne had tried to breathe past the fear. But Sadie wasn't in the yard or at the barn. Sammie trailed behind her crying. Cheyenne made her go back into the house for her coat. It was cold. The only place left was the road, and it had started to snow again.

When she saw a truck stopped and a man talking to

her child, real terror had leaped into her throat. She had to do better than this.

And the man had turned out to be Tuf Hart, the last person she'd thought she would ever see again. She was too worried about Sadie to give him much thought. He'd changed, but she still knew who he was. He was the only man who ever made her nervous and excited at the same time. One thing was clear, though: the skinny, affable boy from school had returned a man, with broad shoulders and a muscled body that was toned from rigorous training. She knew that from her marine husband, Ryan. He'd hated the training, but Tuf seemed to have flourished in it.

Tuf is home.

His family would be so relieved. He'd called his mom two years ago to let her know he was out of the marines and okay. After that, there'd been no word until his cousin Beau had seen him at a rodeo in November. Tuf still didn't come home, though. The family was worried. Understandably so. Beau had assured the family that Tuf looked fine. Cheyenne could attest to that. Tuf Hart looked very fine. Yet different somehow. Being a marine changed men. It had changed Ryan and not for the better. Mentally it had destroyed him. And their marriage.

The front door opened and her dad came in after wiping his boots on the mat. He removed his hat and coat, hooking them on the wrought-iron coatrack. Tall and lean with a thatch of gray hair, Buddy Wright's rugged, lined face showed a life of too much alcohol and too many days on the wrong side of the law.

Cheyenne thought she'd never return to Roundup. As a young girl, her dream was to leave and get far away from her alcoholic father. He'd caused her and her brother, Austin, so much heartache. Yet when she was at her lowest, she'd come home to the only parent she had.

He'd finally stopped drinking and gotten his life together. It couldn't have happened at a better time for both his children. Austin had married Dinah Hart, and the Wrights were now included in the Hart family circle. It was a what's-wrong-with-this-picture type thing. When John Hart was alive, he made it clear Buddy was not welcome at Thunder Ranch. That was the main reason she would never go out with Tuf. The Harts were a prominent family and the Wrights were from the wrong side of the tracks. She would not expose her wounded pride to the Harts, especially Tuf.

"I thought you were coming to the celebration," her dad said.

"I was, but—" She got to her feet and flipped on the TV. The girls scurried to sit in front of it. "Sadie ran away again."

"Again?" Her father followed her into the kitchen and watched as she made coffee. "I wondered what had happened. Leah was asking about you, and Jill wanted to know when the twins were coming, so I thought I'd better come check."

"Tuf Hart found her walking in the ditch by the road."

"Tuf?" One of her father's shaggy gray eyebrows rose as she placed a cup of hot coffee in front of him. "Are you sure?"

"Yes, Dad. I know Tuf Hart." She stirred milk and sugar into her coffee and sat at the table with him. "He's changed, though. He's not that laughing, fun-loving kid anymore. He seems so serious now."

"War does that to a man." Her father took a sip of his hot coffee, making that face he always made when he took the first taste. That oh-I-needed-this look. He sat the mug down. "The family must not know he's coming or Sarah would have been so excited. He must be planning a surprise visit."

She toyed with her cup. "I thought of calling Dinah, but if Tuf wants to surprise them, that's his business. I'm not getting involved."

"Wise decision." Her dad frowned. "Wonder where he's been for two years."

"Dinah thinks he was wounded and in a navy hospital somewhere recovering and didn't want the family to worry."

"Did he look like he'd been wounded?"

"He seemed okay."

"He'll have some questions to answer, but like you said, it's none of our business."

"No."

Her father eyed her. "So you're not going to the party?"

"I'm not rewarding Sadie with fun time. I have to start disciplining her." And that would just about kill Cheyenne. "I'm going to fix them something to eat and put Sammie to bed. Then Sadie and I are going to have a talk. She'll shrug and start crying like always. Honestly, Dad, I don't know what to do anymore."

He patted her hand on the table. "Just love her."

She nodded and got to her feet. "I imagine there's a lot of celebrating going on at Thunder Ranch right about now. I hope for Tuf's sake everyone is glad to see him."

"Sarah will be happy to see her youngest child."

"But what about the rest of the family? The ones who have been struggling to save John Hart's legacy?"

Cheyenne took their cups to the sink. "I'm glad we're not there. This is family time."

"You bet. I'm going to check on the horses." He ambled back into the living room to get his hat and coat.

Tuf Hart was home and that didn't mean a thing to her. She planned to stay away from him, just as she had as a teenager.

TUF TURNED ONTO Thunder Road that led to the ranch. He stopped the truck once again and stared. The big two-story house he'd grown up in was lit up like a Christmas tree, and the driveway was full of parked trucks and cars. What was going on? His mom always had Christmas on Christmas day, so they couldn't be celebrating the holiday. Not wanting to deal with a crowd, he drove to the barns, parked and got out.

He breathed in the heady scent of the ponderosa pines and saw the snow-covered Bull Mountains in the distance. He was home. No more war. No more killing. No more dying.

It had stopped snowing and the air was fresh and invigorating. Glancing toward the house, he decided to wait a while before making his appearance. An agitated neighing caught his attention and he walked toward the corral attached to the barn. A beautiful black stallion circled the pen. At the sight of Tuf, the horse reared his head and pawed the ground with one hoof.

Tuf leaned on the fence and watched the black horse with the flowing mane. He was magnificent and Tuf wondered what he was doing on Thunder Ranch. The more he watched, the more agitated the horse became, snorting, his nostrils flaring as he pawed the ground. Finally the horse trotted over to a dun mare drinking from a water trough. The mare's rounded belly indicated she was pregnant. The two neighed back and forth and the black horse seemed to calm down.

"Tuf?"

He looked over his shoulder to see Royce, one of the ranch hands, staring at him. "Hey, Royce."

"Man, it is you." Royce vigorously shook his hand. "Your mom's gonna be beside herself. I'll give her a call." Royce reached for his cell.

"No." Tuf stopped him. "I'll surprise her in a minute." He glanced toward the house. "What's going on?"

The other man frowned. "You don't know?"

"What?"

"Beau got married today and your mom threw him and Sierra a big reception."

"What?" He'd seen Beau at a rodeo in November, and he hadn't said anything about getting married, but then, Tuf hadn't given him time to talk. Beau had been full of questions and Tuf couldn't answer them. He wanted to go home but couldn't, and Beau wouldn't understand that. Making a quick exit was all he could do.

"Go on up to the house and join the celebration," Royce urged.

Feeling chilled, Tuf pulled the collar up on his coat, his eyes centering on the black horse, who was watching him as Tuf had watched the horse earlier. "What's the story on the horse?"

Royce leaned on the fence. "That's Midnight. Ain't he a beauty? Your mom and Ace bought him at an auction when his owner died. The foreman mistreated him so he's a little gun-shy, if you know what I mean. His lineage goes back to the great bucking horse Five Minutes to Midnight and they paid a pretty penny for him."

"Yeah. He's prime horseflesh."

"Ace outbid ol' Earl McKinley, and Earl wasn't too happy." Royce shook his head. "Midnight has caused a whole passel of problems. Went missing for a while and upset the whole family. Turned out thieves who were stealing tack left the gate open and Midnight sprinted for freedom. The horse turned up at Buddy Wright's place. That gave everyone pause, but Buddy just patched up the horse's wounds and kept him safe. Ol' Buddy has changed a lot."

Tuf digested that for a minute. It would be nice if the Hart and Wright families could exist in peace. Life was too short for petty grievances.

Royce watched the horse. "Very temperamental and hard to handle, but Ace and Colt are working wonders with him."

"Is he for breeding or bucking?"

"Depends on who you ask. Ace wants to keep breeding him, but Colt's entered him in a few rodeos. Midnight twisted his left knee in November, and the family is at odds on what to do with him now. Ace doesn't want to risk getting him injured again. The family has a lot riding on that black horse." Royce peered at him. "You do know the Harts are in the rodeo contracting business?"

"Mom mentioned that."

"Things have changed since you've been gone."

"Mmm." He'd spent six years fighting in a war-torn country, sometimes sleeping on the ground and living off military-issue food not fit for a dog, but it kept him alive. It was always a celebration to get back to base for real food. He'd almost forgotten what it was like to live in the real world and to enjoy the freedom he'd been fighting for. His adjustment was yet to come.

Midnight reared up on his hind legs, pawing at the air, clearly upset at the stranger eyeing him.

"Calm down," Royce said to the horse, and Midnight trotted back to the dun mare.

"Do you leave him out here all night?"

Royce slapped him on the back. "Man, you have been gone a long time if you've forgotten what Ace is like." Royce pointed to the right of the barn. "See that opening? It goes into Midnight's personal oversize stall. Once the mare goes inside, he'll follow. She has a calming effect on him."

"I noticed."

"Midnight hates being penned up. He likes open spaces. When he injured his knee, we closed the doors and Midnight went crazy. Ace had to sedate him to keep him calm so he wouldn't injure the leg further. That horse is either gonna make or break Thunder Ranch." He held out his hand to Tuf. "Glad to have you home. Go join the celebration and make your mama happy. I'm feeding the pregnant mares, but I'll be up for some grub as soon as I finish."

Tuf nodded and breathed in the crisp air off Bull Mountains. Time to face the family, but he couldn't take his eyes off Midnight, who continued to circle the pen.

"I've dreamed of riding a horse like you all my life," he muttered under his breath.

Midnight flung his head and stomped his hoof again in protest as if he understood every word.

"Tomas. Tomas. Tomas!"

Only one person called him that. His mother. Damn! Royce had called. He turned around as his mother flew across the yard in a dress and heels. At the sight of her silver hair and smiling face, his heart thumped against his ribs. Oh, how he'd missed his mom.

How did he explain the past two years?

CHAPTER TWO

"TOMAS!" HIS MOM grabbed him in a bear hug. He held on with arms that felt weak, but he was buffeted by a strength he couldn't describe. Being over six feet, he leaned down so she could kiss his cheek. He'd started doing that when he was about fourteen.

Sarah stroked his face and then ran her hands over his shoulders, arms and chest, much like when he was younger and a horse would buck him into the dirt. "Are you hurt? Are you okay?"

"I'm fine, Mom." The family stood behind her all dressed in their Sunday best. Some of the faces he didn't recognize. The guys were in pressed jeans, pristine Western white shirts with bolo ties. The women were in dresses or suits. Before he could see anything else, his brothers, Aidan and Colton, nicknamed Ace and Colt, barreled into him with fierce hugs, and then twin cousins Beau and Duke and Uncle Josh. He'd missed this connection to family.

Someone grabbed his arm and jerked him around. His sister Dinah's fiery hazel eyes flashed up at him. "Where have you been? You've had us all worried sick."

"Hey, sis." He reached for her and lifted her off her feet into a tight embrace.

"Be careful. She's pregnant," Sarah warned.

"Oh." Tuf eased her to the ground.

Dinah laughed. "Get that look off your face. I'm respectably married." She pulled a guy forward. "This is my husband, Austin. You remember him?"

Austin Wright. His sister had married Austin Wright, Cheyenne's brother. How did that happen?

Before he could find an answer, his mother linked her arm through his. "Let's go to the house. It's cold out here. We have a lot to celebrate. My baby is home."

Baby. Usually when she called him that, it would cause sparks of resentment to flash inside him. Thank God he had finally outgrown that reaction.

Dinah also linked her arm through his, and they made their way into the house through the spacious, homey kitchen to the great room. He barely had time to remove his hat. People milled around him. To the right was a long buffet table laden with prime rib and all the fixings. In a corner stood a ten-foot spruce fully decorated. The piney scent mixed with vanilla and cinnamon filled the room with a relaxing feeling of warmth enhanced by the fire in the river-rock fireplace. A large maple mantel showcased rodeo trophies from every member of the Hart family.

He was home.

But he felt as if he'd been dropped into enemy territory and he was waiting for the first round of fire. This time, he knew, he would be hit. There was no way of escaping the inevitable.

Ace approached him, carrying a baby in a pink blanket. "I want you to meet Emma, the first Hart grandchild."

"You have a daughter?"

"Yep. Isn't she beautiful?"

Tuf looked at the perfect baby face with swirls of blond hair. "Yes, she is. Does she have a mother?"

Ace frowned at him in that familiar way Tuf remembered well, especially when Tuf had done something to displease him, like wearing Ace's best boots to a rodeo. "Of course—Flynn."

"McKinley?"

Ace's frown deepened to a point of aggravation until Flynn walked up. "Don't look so surprised, Tuf," the beautiful blonde said.

"How did you manage to lasso him?"

She leaned over and whispered, "It wasn't easy, but I finally found the magic rope." She winked and gently took her daughter from Ace. "She's only three weeks old and all this celebrating is too much for her. I'll put her in the bassinet in Sarah's room."

"Congratulations," Tuf said to his brother.

"Thanks. Glad you're home," Ace replied, but Tuf felt he wanted to say a whole lot more. They both knew this wasn't the time. Ace was the oldest, the responsible one and the head of the family, next to their mom. And Ace would hold Tuf accountable for two years of silence, two years of ignoring the family and two years of shirking his responsibility to said family. Accountability was coming but it would not be tonight.

His other brother, Colt, edged his way toward them. "Now, Ace kind of fibbed about the firstborn Hart grandchild." Colt pulled a boy of about eleven or twelve toward him. "This is Evan, my son."

Tuf stared at the boy and then back to his sandy-haired, handsome brother. Love-'em-and-leave-'em Colt—that's how he was known around the rodeo circuit. Romancing the ladies came easily to him, while

Tuf found it almost painful sometimes. Maybe because his brothers cast long shadows and it was hard to walk in their wake. Seemed as if all his life he'd been trying to prove he was tough enough to match his older brothers and cousins.

"Nice to meet you," the boy said and held out his hand.

Tuf took it. "Nice to meet you, too, Evan." The last time Tuf was home, there had been no mention of Evan, and now wasn't the time to point that out.

Reaching behind him, Colt pulled a brown-haired woman forward. *Leah Stockton.* "You know Leah. We're married and these are her kids, five-year-old Jill and three-year-old Davey."

Tuf touched his forehead. "Am I in another time zone or something? Colt is married with a ready-made family?"

Colt punched Tuf's shoulder. "You bet."

Leah hugged him. "Welcome home, Tuf."

After that he was lost in a sea of unfamiliar faces. His cousin Duke strolled over with his new wife, Angie, and her eight-year-old son, Luke. He also met the new bride, Sierra, and his uncle Josh's wife, Jordan, who walked with a white cane and had a yellow Lab Seeing Eye dog named Molly. He didn't get the whole story, but he could see Uncle Josh was very much in love.

Seemed Sierra owned the Number 1 Diner in town and Jordan was her aunt. He was beginning to think there was something in the water. In the past year, his whole family had gotten married.

His mom shoved a plate of food into his hands. "Eat. We'll talk later."

He picked at the food, his eyes going to Dinah and

Austin. That marriage still puzzled him. Buddy Wright was an alcoholic. Austin had said many times he would never be like his father, but Tuf had seen him at rodeos where he could barely stand. Tuf liked Austin, even though he had a problem holding his liquor. He didn't understand how he and Dinah had gotten together.

Finding a vacant chair, he sat down and continued to nibble at his food. Dinah slipped into the chair beside him.

"You know, you have a lot of explaining to do."

"Yeah." He speared a piece of prime rib. No one had enough guts to bring up the past two years tonight but his sister. She always danced to the sound of an offbeat drummer.

"But I'll give you time to settle in before I grill you."

"I'd appreciate that."

"You do know I'm the sheriff now, right?"

He glanced at her. "Mom mentioned it. If I see you in town with a gun on your hip, you'll have to forgive me if I laugh."

She frowned. "You better not."

"So you and Austin, huh?"

"Yeah. I love him and he's changed. He really has."

He stirred the meat into mashed potatoes. "A lot of that going around." Home was different now and he wondered how he'd fit in. They'd all moved on without him. He felt a little lonely in a room full of loving family.

"Mmm." Dinah kissed his cheek. "Welcome home, lil' brother."

Soon after, he said his good-nights and made his way to the stairs. His mom followed.

"Your room is ready. I washed the sheets every week just in case you'd come home."

Guilt the size of a boulder landed on his chest and he took a deep breath. The worry he must have caused her was too painful to think about.

His room was the same as he'd left it. Horseshoe patterns decorated the curtains and comforter. Horseshoes were branded into the headboard and the dresser—something he'd done when he was about twelve, much to his parents' disapproval. He had a thing about horses. All the Hart kids did, but he was the only one who'd branded his furniture.

Chaps lay across a chair and he picked them up. "I don't think these will fit anymore."

"No, you've filled out."

On a bulletin board attached to the wall were newspaper clippings of some of his rodeo adventures in bareback riding. Belt buckles lay in a tray. His youth was in this room. He turned to see his mom staring at him.

"Go back to the party, Mom. I'm tired from the long drive and I'm just going to bed."

She lifted an eyebrow. "I would ask a long drive from where, but I know you'll tell me when you're ready."

"Mom…" That boulder got heavier on his chest.

She wrapped her arms around him and hugged. "I'm so happy you're home, my son."

He swallowed. "I'm home to stay."

"Good." She touched his face. "I'll see you in the morning."

As the door closed, he laid the chaps on the bed and walked over to the window. His room faced Thunder Road. Pushing the curtains aside, he glanced toward Buddy Wright's place and thought of Cheyenne. What was she doing back in Roundup? Was it for a visit? Or was she here to stay? He couldn't seem to get her out of his head, especially that tortured look in her eyes.

Almost ten years and he was right back where he'd started—dreaming of Cheyenne.

IN THE DAYS that followed, everyone gave him his space, even Dinah, and he was grateful for that. He was used to getting up early and was usually out of the house by 5:00 a.m. Since it was still dark, he'd jog around the barns and inspect all the new additions. An updated mare motel had been built to house pregnant mares. Webcams monitored the activity of the mares. Ace had his vet practice set up in another barn with private stalls for his four-legged patients. The office for the ranch was next to that.

Cattle carriers, trailers and trucks were parked to the right of the barn. They sported a new logo: Hart Rodeo Contractors arched across the top, the lettering green. In the center was the Bull Mountains shadowed by a blue cloud with a bucking horse and bull in front. Below was etched Roundup, Montana. Very impressive. The family had invested heavily in the contracting business.

As soon as the sun peeked over the Bull Mountains, he saddled up Sundance, his brown quarter horse with a white blaze on his face, and galloped off into miles of Thunder Ranch. Snow blanketed the ground, but in places winter grass poked through. He stopped and sucked in the fresh, cold air. There was no scent anywhere like winter in Montana.

He kneed Sundance and rode along Thunder Creek. The snow-banked water was frozen in places. Sundance picked his way through the snow and Engelmann spruce, and they came across a herd of cattle huddled together near a windmill. At the sight of horse and rider, the cows bellowed. Tuf dismounted and saw the water trough had frozen over. Picking up a pipe left there for such purposes, he broke the ice. Cows milled around for a drink.

He swung into the saddle and was surprised not to see more cattle. The herd must have been downsized—more changes. He rode back to the house in time for breakfast.

When Tuf was in Afghanistan, he often dreamed of his mom's warm yellow kitchen with the pine plank floors, the natural butcher-block counters and cherry-stained cabinets. It relaxed him and he'd wondered if he'd ever sit at the family table again.

He ran his hand across the butcher-block table and felt the warmth of being home.

His mom watched him while he ate. She did that a lot, and he felt guilt press on his chest again.

Picking up his mug of coffee, he asked, "What happened to all the cattle?"

She shrugged. "The economy tanked and cattle prices dropped and I made the decision to downsize. The contracting business is time-consuming, and we need every available hand to make it a success."

He pushed back his plate. "Then I'll take care of the cattle. That should help."

"Yes, but I'd rather you enjoy life for a while. There's no rush for you to do anything."

That puzzled him. Growing up it was always important that everyone pulled their weight. "Come on, Mom. I need to stay busy. What is everyone else doing?"

"Ace handles the breeding program while Colt's in charge of Midnight and handles the rodeo bookings and transporting bucking horses. Beau and Josh take care of the bulls, though Josh is cutting back to spend more time with Jordan."

"Is anyone rodeoing?"

"You bet. There's a lot of rodeo talent in the Hart and Adams families. All the boys are riding to earn extra money for the ranch, except Duke. He's given up bull riding for Angie, but he's still helping to transport stock to rodeos."

He got up and poured another cup of coffee. "I never thought Duke would give up bull riding for love."

His mother carried dishes to the sink. "His heart was never in it like Beau's." She shot him a glance as she rinsed dishes to go in the dishwasher. "Like you."

"Yeah." He leaned against the counter. "I loved bareback riding."

"Your father said you're the best he'd ever seen."

He thought for a minute. "If everyone's rodeoing to make money, I can, too."

His mother had a way of not frowning, but she made up for that with a disapproving look.

"What?"

"For eight years I've gone to bed every night wondering if I'd ever see my youngest again."

"Mom…" His heart twisted.

"I just want you safe."

He smiled at her worried face. "We're the Harts. Rodeo is in our blood."

"Mmm. I guess it's safer than what you were doing."

"I want to help out." He tried to ease the tension.

"As long as I know someone's not pointing a gun at you, I…" She reached for a dish towel, wiped her hands and then dabbed at her eyes.

His heart twisted so tight he could barely breathe.

Ask me questions. Ask me. Let me get it off my chest.
But she didn't.

As she loaded the dishwasher, he had second thoughts. She was all alone in a five-bedroom house and that bothered him. His mom was used to having family around her. Ace had lived in the house with a separate entrance until his marriage. Now he lived at the McKinley place with his new family. Colt and Uncle Josh had houses nearby, but it wasn't the same thing.

There was a housekeeper, Lisa Marie, but she was only there a few hours a day to help his mother. He found that odd since his mom had always refused help. What had happened to change her mind?

She straightened and hugged him. A whiff of gardenia reached him. It was a scented lotion she'd used ever since he could remember.

"Take all the time you need. When you're ready, you'll know. Now I have to get dressed and go to work. Lisa Marie will be here soon and Leah's probably already in the office."

"Leah takes care of the books now?"

"Yes, and she's been a blessing. All this new technology goes over my head sometimes. You'll have to check out the updated office. With the rodeo contracting business we have to keep up-to-date records and know exactly where and when our animals go to rodeos. It takes all of us to accomplish that."

"Mmm. When are Uncle Josh and Beau coming back?" Seemed his uncle had gotten married a few weeks ago and they had gone on a honeymoon, too.

"Any day." His mom moved toward her bedroom.

"Mom, I need some new clothes. Is there anyplace in Roundup I can buy them?"

She glanced over her shoulder. "Austin carries nice things at his Western Wear and Tack Shop. It's not a law but a rule that you support family."

He grinned. "Yes, ma'am." He reached for his hat, slipped into his jacket and headed for the door. As he walked to his truck, he saw Midnight in a pen, and Gracie, one of the ranch hands, watching him. He strolled over to take a look. Gracie was somewhere in her forties and she knew her way around horses and cows. Bundled up in a heavy winter coat, she had a wool scarf looped over her felt hat and tied beneath her chin to cover her ears.

"Mornin', Tuf," she called and opened a large gate to a big corral. Midnight trotted through and galloped around kicking up his hooves in the nippy morning air.

"Mornin'." He leaned on the fence and watched. The stallion circled the corral, his muscles rippling with restless energy.

"He's easy to exercise," Gracie said, "as long as I don't try to box him in. Though he loads pretty nicely into a trailer for Colt. You just have to know what to do and what not to do. The horse is temperamental, to say the least."

"But a gold mine if he performs as planned."

"You got it."

Midnight threw up his head, steam coming from his flared nostrils, but it was clear the horse reveled in the cold.

"He was born to buck," Tuf murmured.

"The family still hasn't decided yet." Gracie shoved her gloved hands into her jacket pockets. "It's cold. I hope Buddy gets here soon so I can go to the mare barn where it's warmer."

Tuf frowned. "Buddy Wright?"

"Yeah. When Midnight went missing, he showed up at Buddy's place with a few cuts. Buddy doctored his wounds and took care of him. He was afraid to tell anyone where the horse was because he feared everyone would think he'd stolen the Harts' prized stallion."

Tuf remembered Royce saying something about that.

"But Dinah got to the bottom of everything, and your mom was very grateful to Buddy. She encouraged him to visit Midnight at Thunder Ranch whenever he wanted. And he does about two or three times a week. It helps me out a lot."

Before Tuf could sort through this new information, Ace drove up to his clinic area and Colt pulled in behind him. They waved and went inside. They were giving him his space, and he should be happy about that, but in truth, he didn't understand it. If one of them or Beau or Duke had disappeared for two years without a word, he'd be mad as hell. But he was the one who'd left Thunder Ranch and his family. They had gotten used to life without him. Deep in his heart, though, he knew this standoff wasn't going to last. Soon someone would pop the cork of their bottled-up emotions and Tuf would be held accountable for his decisions.

ON HIS WAY into town, he passed the Wright property. All was quiet, not a soul in sight. It was nice to know the Harts and Wrights were getting along so well. Very nice. He wondered if Cheyenne's husband was with her. Or if she had a husband. From the look in her eyes, he knew something bad had happened in her life. What?

He was thinking too much about her and turned his attention to the view. It hadn't snowed in days, but it still lingered across the landscape and nestled in the ponderosa pines. The chilly blue sky went on forever, and he was sure it reached into eternity with its wondrous breadth and depth. There weren't skies like that in Afghanistan.

As he turned onto Main Street, he looked for a parking spot near Austin's store. He swerved into a space and removed his keys. He'd purchased the silver Ford Lariat pickup in Maryland because he needed a way to get around. First new truck he'd ever owned, but he figured he'd earned it, since his pay had been piling up in his checking account. But he should have thought that over a little more. His mom said things were tight and the ranch could have used the money. Readjusting to the real world was a hell of a blow.

Getting out, he locked the doors, pocketed the keys and walked into Wright's Western Wear and Tack. A bell jangled over the door and the scent of leather reached him. He came to a complete stop.

Cheyenne was behind a counter, arranging colorful jewelry in a glass case. She looked up, her green eyes startled. Her red hair was clipped behind her head and strands dangled around her pretty face. A flashback hit him that had nothing to do with Afghanistan. He was seventeen years old and sitting in the school auditorium right behind Cheyenne Wright, staring at the back of her hair pinned up much like it was today. Several loose strands curled against the curve of her neck, and he'd wondered if he reached out with one finger and gently tugged her hair toward his lips if it would taste like cinnamon. Which was odd, because Cheyenne never gave him any indication she wanted him to taste any part of her.

Strange how that memory lingered in his mind.

"Can I help you?" she asked in the coolest voice he'd ever heard.

CHAPTER THREE

CHEYENNE'S HEART POUNDED in her chest at an alarming rate—too alarming to suit her. What was Tuf doing here? And why was he still standing at the door?

Closing the glass case with a snap, she asked again, "Can I help you with something?"

He removed his hat like a true gentleman and stepped closer to her. Well over six feet with wide shoulders, he was a little intimidating, which she was made very aware of by the flutter in her stomach. His dark brown hair was cut short and neat, and the lines of his face were all sharp bones and angles. A tiny scar over his left cheek added to his manly image.

The scar wasn't something new. He'd had it in school. Rumor was he'd fallen off a horse when he was about three and hit a water trough.

"Is Austin here?"

She cleared her throat. "No...no, he's over at the diner having coffee with Dinah. He should be back shortly."

"Oh." He looked around. "I need some clothes. Do you mind if I look around?"

"Um...no." Was she supposed to help him? Why couldn't he wait until Austin returned?

He settled his hat onto his head and glanced at the items on racks and shelves. Without taking time to look at anything, he grabbed T-shirts, socks, long johns and Jockey shorts.

He wears briefs.

Cheyenne took a deep breath. She really didn't need to know that.

After laying his load on the counter, he walked to a round rack of Western shirts. He found his size and reached for a handful. Good heavens, he didn't even look at the style or the color. Unable to stand it, she made her way to his side and tried not to frown.

"Don't you want to look at the shirts?"

"No. Why?"

She suppressed a groan. "They're different. Some are solids, prints, plaids and checks."

"Doesn't matter. It's a shirt."

She gritted her teeth. "Some have snaps. Some have buttons."

"Doesn't matter. I can handle both."

"This is ridiculous. No one buys clothes without looking at them."

He shrugged. "I've been buying my clothes since I was about sixteen and that's my method."

That would account for that god-awful shirt he wore in school.

He pointed to her face. "You're frowning. What's wrong with the way I buy clothes?"

Now she'd stepped in it. Why was she even talking to him? She should have stayed at the counter. She bit her lip and stepped in a little deeper. "I was remembering that bright pumpkin-orange shirt with purple piping you wore in school. Evidently you had on sunglasses when you bought it."

He gave a cocky grin. "Ah, the orange shirt. My

friends and I were in Billings getting rodeo supplies and they had that shirt in the window. I said someone would have to pay me to wear something so gaudy. Well, that's what my friends did. They bought it and paid me twenty bucks to wear it to school. It got a lot of attention and laughs. I'm sure I still have it. My mom never throws anything away. It's too small for me now, but you can have it if you like." He lifted a daring eyebrow.

"No, thanks." She took the shirts out of his hands and held one up. "This is a solid baby-blue Western with pearl snaps. It comes in white, yellow and pink. You might prefer the yellow."

His grin widened and she felt a kick to her lower abdomen. "No. I prefer the blue."

"See. That's shopping. Making a decision." She held up another. "This is a light blue check. We have it in dark blue, too."

"I'll take the dark blue."

"And this—" she pulled a shirt off the rack "—is red, white and blue. It was made popular by Garth Brooks. Since you're a former marine, you might like it."

"I do." He glanced at the shirt and then at her. "But don't you think it's a little loud?"

It was, but she wasn't going to admit that after the orange-shirt comment. "It's fine."

"Good. I'll take three."

She had a feeling he didn't really care. To him it was just a shirt, like he'd said. She found that so strange. Her husband, Ryan, had been a picky dresser. Sometimes she took shirts back three or four times before she could find one he liked. And they had to be starched and ironed before he'd wear them. If they weren't... Her hand instinctively went to her cheek.

"Do you have any chambray shirts and jeans?" He glanced at the shirts hung against a wall.

"Yes." She waved her hand. "And Austin has a lot more on this round rack. What color?"

"Light blue."

"Not red?"

"No. That's Colt's trademark. Too flashy."

"Yeah, right." She reached for two. "Jeans are here." She pointed to her left. "The size is beneath each stack. Do you know your size?"

He stared directly at her with steamy dark eyes. "Doesn't every man?"

She felt dizzy, but she just shrugged. "You'd be surprised. A lot of women buy their husband's clothes."

"I don't have a wife, and like I told you, I buy my own clothes." He studied the sizes and fit and pulled out five pairs.

"Mommy, Sadie's coloring on my page."

"Excuse me." She took the shirts and jeans from him, and as hard as she tried not to touch him, his hand brushed against hers in a fleeting reminder of the difference in the texture of male skin. She drew in a breath, laid the merchandise on the counter and went to her daughters, who sat at a small table in a corner.

"Sadie, color in your own book." She homeschooled the girls, and while she worked in the store, they did their lessons. Today they were coloring a picture according to the colors Cheyenne had marked on the page.

"Sammie doesn't know how to color. I'm just showing…" Sadie's green eyes widened and her mouth fell open. Cheyenne knew why. Tuf was standing behind her. She could feel his warm vibes.

She stepped aside. "I don't believe you've formally

met my daughters. Girls, this is Tuf Hart, Aunt Dinah's brother. And this is Cassandra and Samantha. Otherwise known as Sadie and Sammie."

"Why not call her Sandy or Cassie?"

Cheyenne tensed. "It's a name her father gave her."

Tuf nodded and looked at the girls. "Nice to meet you."

Sadie scrunched up her face. "I don't like you."

"That seems to be a unanimous opinion in the Wright family."

Cheyenne forced herself not to smile. "Sadie, that's not nice. Apologize."

Her spirited daughter hung her head.

"Sadie."

Sadie mumbled something, and Cheyenne went to the checkout counter with Tuf. "My name is Sundell now," she said and was unsure of the reason why she needed to mention that.

"So you and your husband moved back to Roundup?"

Cheyenne kept scanning the items into the cash register, trying not to react. Trying to be cool. "No. Just the girls and me."

There was a pregnant pause filled with all kinds of questions. But again, she didn't react. "Will there be anything else?"

"I need PRCA regulated rowels and spurs."

"Austin orders those."

"I figured." He reached for his wallet in his back pocket and pulled out a credit card.

She totaled his purchases, swiped his card and ripped off a receipt for him to sign. She watched as his strong hand slashed out *Tomas Hart*. No one around here called him that. Even in school he was always known as Tuf, the youngest Hart.

As he slipped the card back into his wallet, he said, "I was out of line the other day. Your child is your business and I shouldn't have said a word."

She was taken aback by the apology, but all of Sarah Hart's children had good manners. "No, you shouldn't have, but I appreciate your concern. Sadie always tests my patience."

He nodded and picked up the big bag from the counter as if it weighed no more than his wallet. "Thanks for the help."

Even though she told herself not to, she watched through the display window as he took long strides back to his silver truck.

"Mommy, who's that man?"

Cheyenne looked down to see Sadie staring up at her with big green eyes.

Someone I knew a long time ago. Someone I wished I'd had the courage to date.

"He's Aunt Dinah's brother."

Sadie bobbed her head. "Aunt Dinah gots lots of brothers."

Sammie leaned into her, wrapping herself as close as she could to Cheyenne, needing attention, love and reassurance that their world was still okay. Sometimes she didn't know if she had that much strength because she struggled every day to make sense of a life blown apart. But for her daughters she would do everything possible to hide her fears.

Her eyes strayed to the window. If only she could go back in time…

TUF GLANCED ACROSS the street at the redbrick building that used to be the home of the old newspaper but was now the Number 1 Diner. Sierra, Beau's wife, owned it, and Tuf's mother raved about the home cooking. He swung the bag of clothes into the backseat of his truck and walked over.

Inside, the diner was decorated in a mining theme, and he remembered his mom saying it had been named in honor of Sierra's grandfather, who'd died in a mine. On the walls were mining photos and a long shelf held mining artifacts. The tables were red and the chairs had black leather seats. The place had a rustic, homey appeal, and the scent coming from the kitchen made him hungry.

He spotted Dinah and Austin sitting close together in a booth. Not wanting to interrupt, he started for the counter to order coffee, but Austin eased out of the booth, so Tuf strolled over to join them.

"Hey, Tuf." Austin shook his hand.

"I was just over at your shop to order some rowels, spurs and chaps."

Austin's eyebrows rose. "Getting back into rodeoing?"

"Yeah."

"Come back and I'll get you set up."

"Okay. I'll visit with my sister first."

"Good deal." Austin leaned down to kiss Dinah and then made his way toward the door. Dinah's eyes followed him and she had a dreamy look on her face.

Tuf slid into the booth. "You've got it bad, Sheriff."

Her gaze swung to him. "Yes, I do."

Tuf removed his hat and placed it beside him. Before he could say anything, a young girl in jeans with a red apron trimmed in black appeared to take his order.

"Just coffee, please."

When the girl left, Dinah asked, "So you're getting back into rodeoing?"

"Mom and I talked about it. She'd rather I take it easy for a while, but I need to be busy."

"Maybe you've been taking it easy for two years. Who knows?"

This was the Dinah he knew, the one who came straight to the point, spoke her mind and didn't pussy-foot around.

"But I'm not going to grill you because I know you've been through a great deal."

Damn. She was folding like a greenhorn in Vegas. He didn't expect that. He should just tell her where he'd been, and he didn't understand what was holding him back.

The waitress placed a cup of hot coffee in front of him, and his hand gripped the warmth of the cup. But words lodged in his throat.

"Are you okay?" Dinah asked in a concerned voice. "That's all I want to know."

"I'm fine." He took a sip of coffee and thought it best to change the subject. "I saw Cheyenne over at the store."

"She helps out when Austin needs her. Aren't her little girls adorable?" Dinah looked down and rubbed the swell of her stomach. "I hope our little one is as cute."

"How could it not? His or her mother is a natural beauty."

"Stop it." Dinah wrinkled her nose. "You're my brother. You have to say that."

He grinned. "Not really. That's Austin's job. Me, I can poke fun all I want. It comes by right of birth." He pointed to her chest. "Love the way that badge sparkles on your khaki shirt there." He leaned over to see her waist. "Damn. No gun."

"Will you stop?" Her voice was stern, but her eyes sparkled.

He took a sip of coffee, remembering all the times he'd teased her as a kid. It was part of his job as little brother. Her teen years were a nightmare. John Hart kept a tight rein on his only daughter, and Dinah rebelled over and over. Tuf often wondered if Dinah would make it through those turbulent times. He would tease her just to see her smile.

Dinah scooted to the end of the booth. "I have to get back to work."

"What's Cheyenne's situation?" he asked before he could stop himself.

She sighed. "Please tell me you've gotten over that teenage crush."

"I have." He twisted his cup. "I'm just curious. She's different."

"She's going through a rough time."

"She said her husband wasn't with her in Roundup."

"No." Dinah dug in her purse and laid some bills on the table.

"Are they divorced?"

She frowned at him. "No. He died."

"Oh." He wasn't expecting that. "Cancer, heart…"

"Tuf." His sister actually glared at him. "Cheyenne's emotions are very fragile right now and…"

"What happened to her husband?"

Her glare was now burning holes through him. "You can't let this go, can you?"

"Like I told you, I'm curious. There's a certain sadness about her, and I know something traumatic has happened in her life."

Dinah zipped her purse. "Okay. But what I tell you, you keep to yourself. Very few people in Roundup know this, and I don't want people gossiping behind her back."

"Have you ever known me to gossip?"

"No, and that's why I'm telling you." She drew a deep breath. "Her husband was a marine."

"He died in combat?"

"No. He was out for six months and had severe PTSD. Austin said he had terrible nightmares and was sometimes violent."

A knot formed in his stomach and bile rose in his throat. He fought the terrible memories every day, and he vowed they would not bring him down. He'd stand strong. He was a marine. But there were days…

"What happened?"

"He left a note for Cheyenne saying he was leaving and not to try and find him. He added they were better off without him. Two days later he was found in a motel. He'd shot himself."

"Oh, God." Now he knew what the look in Cheyenne's eyes was about. The life she'd planned was not the life she was living. She'd learned that there was hatred and evil in the world and it had spread to the most innocent victims like herself and her daughters. Her belief in life had been shattered, and she was struggling to make sense of it all—like he was.

"I'm sorry she had to go through that," he murmured.

"We all are." Dinah reached across the table and rubbed his forearm. "Are you sure you're okay?"

"Yep." He reached for his hat. "I'll walk you to your office."

Dinah got to her feet. "Oh, please. I'm the sheriff, remember?"

Tuf stood with a smile. But he still had an ache inside for all the soldiers who had come home and were still fighting that terrible war in their minds.

"Look," Dinah said, and he followed her gaze to the kitchen area. Beau stood there. He kissed Sierra and headed for the front door.

"Hey, Beau," Tuf called.

Beau swung around and walked toward them with a grin on his face.

"You're home," Tuf said.

"We got back late last night. I spoke with Dad, and he and Jordan just drove in, too. I'm picking up Duke at the sheriff's office, and we're going out to welcome them home."

"Sounds like a plan." Dinah stepped toward the door. "I'll go with you to the office to make sure we don't have anything pressing. See you at the ranch." She waved to Tuf.

Tuf made his way across the street to his truck. As he was about to get in, he noticed Sadie and Sammie looking through the glass door of the shop. He raised a hand in greeting. Surprisingly, they both lifted a hand, but they didn't smile. He knew without a doubt they were affected by their father's death. Cheyenne shooed them back to their seats, and their eyes locked for a moment. So much sadness clouded her beautiful face. He got in his truck and drove away, telling himself it was none of his business.

And he was real good at lying to himself.

WHEN HE REACHED the ranch, he saw Ace's and Colt's trucks parked near Ace's vet office. He drove there, too.

As he got out, he heard loud voices coming from the barn attached to the office.

"It's time, Ace," Colt was saying. "Midnight has healed and we need to get him on the rodeo circuit as soon as February."

"No way. I'm not risking him getting hurt again. Breeding season is about to start and he'll be busy."

"Damn it. Can't you see how restless he is? He needs the excitement of the rodeo."

"I agree," Tuf said before he thought it through.

His brothers swung around to stare at him. It wasn't a good stare. His settling-in period was over.

Ace's eyes narrowed on him. "You haven't shown any interest in this ranch for eight years and now you think you have a say?"

"Yeah, Tuf," Colt added. "We understand about the first six years. You were fighting a war, but where in the hell have you been for the last two?"

Ace had a lot more to say. "Do you even realize how bad it's been around here? We had to lease a lot of our land and take out a mortgage with my vet business on the line to survive. Everyone pulled their weight to make sure Thunder Ranch didn't go under."

"I didn't know."

"No, because you never called home to find out." Cool, collected Ace had reached a breaking point, and Tuf knew he had every right to be upset. "You never even called home to check on Mom. That I can't forgive. Do you know she had a spell with her heart and was hospitalized for a few days? We had no way to get in touch with you."

He felt as if he'd been kicked in the gut by the wildest bronc in Montana. He swallowed. "Mom had my cell number. I gave it to her when I called that one time."

"No." Ace shook his head. "Mom would have told me."

"I had it," their mom said from the doorway. Uncle Josh, Beau, Duke and Dinah stood behind her.

"What?" The color drained from Ace's face. "But you asked me to call his friends to see if Tuf had contacted them."

The group walked farther into the barn until they stood in a circle. Horses neighed, and Royce and Gracie came in through a side door. But everyone was staring at his mom.

"Yes, I did," Sarah admitted. "I was worried and wanted to know if Tomas had reached out to some of his old buddies. They would talk to you quicker than an overprotective mother. I'm sorry, Ace. I know I lean on you too much."

"It's okay, Mom," Ace assured her. "It's not your fault. It's Tuf's."

Tuf took the blow to his heart like a marine, like a cowboy, without flinching. It was his fault, and it was time to open that wound and let it bleed until he couldn't feel the pain anymore.

Uncle Josh patted his shoulder, and Tuf hadn't even realized he'd moved toward him. "We don't mean to pressure you, Tuf, but you're a part of this family and we've all been worried. It's not like you to shut the family out. If you found someone and wanted to spend some time with her, we'd all understand. We just need to know why you've ignored us for two years."

"There isn't anyone," he murmured under his breath.

"Were you injured and in a hospital?" Dinah asked.

"No. It wasn't that."

He looked at their expectant faces and knew he had to tell them. They deserved the truth. But once he did, they would look at him differently.

And he didn't know if he was ready to handle different.

CHAPTER FOUR

TUF COULDN'T PUT it off any longer.

Accountability had arrived.

He held up his hands and took two steps backward. "Okay. Just listen. Don't say anything until I'm through."

Everyone nodded, except his mom.

"This is ridiculous," she said. "You don't have to tell us a thing if you don't want to."

Ace flung a hand toward Tuf. "Stop protecting him. You always do that. Tuf's old enough and strong enough to take responsibility for his own actions."

"Why did you start this?" his mom demanded of Ace. "I told you to leave it alone."

Ace sighed and turned away.

His mother instinctively knew he'd been through something horrific, and she was doing everything she could to protect him. Shielding her kids from pain had been her life's work, but Tuf couldn't take the easy way out. Not this time.

"Ace is right," he told his mother. "I have to take responsibility for the last two years, so please just listen." He stared down at the dirt floor. "I was all set to come home. My commander said the paperwork was in order. One more mission and I was going to be flown to Germany for evaluation and then to a base in the U.S. and finally home. I couldn't wait to get back to Thunder Ranch and family."

He took a deep breath and stared at the corner post of a horse stall. "The insurgents had attacked a small village that they suspected of giving aid to U.S. Marines. Most of them were able to get out but two families were trapped. Our orders were to go in a back way in the dead of night and rescue the Afghans. An Afghan soldier guided us through rocky terrain to the village. Getting in undetected was no problem. We found four adults and three kids in a mud-walled hut. Dawn was about to break and we had to get them out quickly. Then we were informed by the Afghan soldier that there was an elderly woman trapped in another hut. We found her and brought her to the others.

"When we were finally ready to leave, daylight broke. For some reason a little girl about three darted for the doorway. PFC Michael Dobbins was closest to her and he jumped to grab her. But it was too late. The insurgents knew we were there. They fired at Michael and he went down and fell on the girl. We immediately returned fire, but Michael was taking the brunt of the hits. His body jerked every time a bullet struck him. I told the corporal to call the commander and let him know what was happening and to call for mortar fire. We needed help."

His lungs expanded and his hands curled into fists as red flashes of gunfire blurred his eyes. "Then I charged out that door, firing blindly, and covered Michael's bloody body."

"No," Sarah cried, and Josh put his arm around her.

Tuf didn't pause or look at his mother. He couldn't. He had to keep talking.

"The rest of my unit joined me, and we made a wall in

front of Michael to keep more bullets from hitting him. We just kept returning fire, and we all knew we were in the open and could very well die there. Then the order came, charge up that hill and take out the insurgents, so we hauled ass. A marine was hit and then the Afghan soldier went down. We found shelter behind some rocks and then we waited, hoping and praying that the attack chopper would come in soon with mortar fire."

He paused. "As soon as the blasts started, we continued our surge to the top. When we got there, six heavily armed insurgents came out of a cave. They fired on us, but we had the upper hand. It was over in seconds. We ran down that hill, picked up our two wounded men and headed for the rescue chopper. Everyone was shouting, 'Run, run, run,' but I kept thinking about Michael back at that hut. I couldn't leave him in that hellhole."

He unclenched his numb hands. "I ran in the other direction, and I could hear my men shouting for me to come back. We didn't know if more insurgents were in the area, and we were ordered to get out fast. But I still kept running toward that hut. I fell down by Michael. The mother and father of the little girl were there desperately trying to lift Michael's body off their child. He was a big man and deadweight. I helped them and the girl was still alive. On the ground was some sort of Muslim toy. The girl must have dropped it when they'd rushed into the hut to escape the insurgents. I handed it to her and realized the toy was the reason she'd run for the door. I pointed in the direction where the chopper was landing and told them to go. Then I hoisted Michael's blood-soaked body over my shoulder and followed.

"Everyone had already boarded, but the chopper waited for me. Two marines helped to carry Michael inside. I watched as a medic covered Michael's body with a blanket. He was dead. He was finally going home, too."

"Oh, no," his mother cried.

Tuf kept talking because he knew if he stopped he wouldn't be able to start again. "I leaned my head against the chopper wall, closed my eyes and imagined I was back at Thunder Ranch in Mom's kitchen eating peanut butter from a jar with my finger. I could see that look on Mom's face when I did things like that and I relaxed, wishing and praying I was away from that awful war. Away from the killing.

"I don't remember much about the next few days, but I was flown to Germany for evaluation and then to the San Diego base. I was going home and putting it behind me was all I could think about, but first I planned to go to the commander's office and ask for Michael's parents' address. I wanted to go see them and tell them what a hero their son was in saving the little girl's life. Before I could do that, I got a message my presence was requested in the commander's office. I thought he wanted to wish me well or something. I was unprepared for what he really wanted. He said to call my folks and let them know I wasn't coming home just yet. A plane was waiting to take me to the naval hospital in Bethesda, Maryland. Michael Dobbins was asking to see me."

A collective "oh" echoed around the dusty barn, and Tuf noticed Royce and Grace had taken seats on bales of alfalfa, listening intently.

"I was stunned but glad he was alive. I figured he wanted to thank me for carrying him out of there. I was mistaken. The doctor advised me to be prepared for the worst. But nothing could have prepared me for the sight of Michael. He was bandaged from head to toe. Tubes seemed to be attached to every part of his body. The gunfire had blown off the left side of his face. They'd amputated his left leg and he was in danger of losing his left arm. But Michael was refusing any more surgeries. He wanted to die."

He gulped a breath. "I stood there staring at his one good eye. The right side of his face and mouth were the only parts of him that weren't bandaged. A suffocating feeling came over me, and I didn't know what to say or what to do. Michael had plenty to say, though. 'Why couldn't you have left me there? Why did you have to play the hero and come back for me?' His strained voice demanded an answer. Again, I didn't know what to say. 'I hate you,' he screamed at me. 'I'd rather be dead. I have no life like this. Why did you have to save me?'

"I couldn't answer so I walked out. The doctor informed me that Michael was refusing to see his parents, his wife and their three-month-old son. I was the only one he'd asked to see. The doctor added that I was Michael's only hope. I was overwhelmed by the responsibility, and I wanted to leave that hospital and never look back. But I found I couldn't. All the years of Mom and Dad preaching morals, values and honor must have reached me. I went back into that room prepared for battle.

"As soon as I entered, Michael screamed, 'Get out.' I told him no. He'd asked for me and I wasn't leaving. He looked at the ceiling and refused to speak. I searched my brain for something to say, something to get his attention. I just started talking off the top of my head, telling him the cowboys around the rodeo circuit have a saying—when things get rough, 'cowboy up.' I reminded him it was time to 'marine up,' to fight for the most precious thing he had—his life. He kept staring at the ceiling, and I kept talking, saying stuff like cowboys and marines don't give up and if he did, he wasn't the man I thought he was."

Tuf felt as though he was back in that hospital room. He could smell the antiseptic, hear the beep of the heart monitor. He swallowed hard.

"Out of the blue Michael asked if cowboys died with their boots on. 'Hell, yes,' I said, 'and it's even better to die in the arms of a beautiful woman.' He seemed to relax and I could swear he was smiling. I felt I was getting through to him so I kept pressuring him, telling him how much he needed the surgeries. Finally, I asked in a loud voice, 'Marine, what's your answer?'

"He didn't say anything for a long time and then he asked if I would stay with him. That threw me. I reminded him that his wife and parents were waiting. He said he didn't want them to see him like he was. I heard the pain in his voice and I found myself agreeing to stay. I told the doctor the surgeries were a go and then I called Mom to tell her I couldn't come home, but I would as soon as I could. I gave her my cell number in case she needed to get in touch with me."

Nobody said a word and Tuf forced himself to finish the story. "After the first surgery, I figured I'd leave, but it took six surgeries to repair his arm. Janet, Michael's wife, haunted the lobby, but Michael refused to see her. I felt sorry for her and I didn't know how to get through to Michael. I slept on a bed in his room, and every night I pushed him about seeing his wife. He finally admitted his fears about his face. A part of his jaw and cheekbone were missing as was his eye. He was going to look different and he wasn't sure his wife could take that. In a way I understood his fears, and I stayed as the doctors started reconstructive surgery to his face. Days turned into weeks, weeks into months. Thanksgiving and Christmas came, and I sat through every painstaking surgery praying and hoping that Michael was going to find the strength to live again."

He drew in deeply. "After calling Mom, I'm sorry I never called home again. I felt guilty and conflicted about Michael. I kept wondering if I'd done him any favors by saving his life. I kept thinking it was my fault he was going through so much pain. If I hadn't played the hero, like he'd said, he wouldn't be suffering, but I could never make myself believe that. All I knew was I had to stay there to help him heal. I had to really save him this time. If I had spoken to anyone here and heard of Mom's health scare or the ranch's financial situation, I wouldn't have been able to do that because I wanted to come home so badly."

"Oh, my poor sweet son." His mother rushed to him and wrapped her arms around him. He clung to her because his legs felt weak. "Don't you apologize for a thing."

"Did Michael recover?" Ace asked in a low voice.

"Yes. It was difficult, but the reconstructive surgeries to his face were amazing. They rebuilt his cheekbone and jawbone, and he received a new artificial hand-painted eye. It looked real. There were scars, but they were hardly noticeable. This was when I told Michael it was time to see his wife. He didn't know it, but I'd been sending her pictures of Michael from my phone when he wasn't looking. She needed to see that he was alive and healing. I told him if he didn't see her, I was leaving. He sat in a chair stone-faced and I headed for the door."

His mom patted his chest. "He saw her?"

"Not until I forced him," he replied. "Before I could reach the door, he reminded me I'd told him that cowboys live by a code of honor and they always keep their word. He added I wasn't a true cowboy if I left. He had me and it made me mad. I pulled out my phone and informed him that this is how a cowboy would handle the situation. I sent a text to Janet to come to the room. Now Michael was angry, but I told him not to worry. I had his back.

"It was a Saturday, and Michael's parents had brought his son to visit Janet. When she entered the room, she held the boy by the hand. He was over a year old now and walking. He tottered over to Michael, who was sitting in a chair, and said 'Da-da.' A tear slipped from Michael's right eye and I quietly left the room. The counselor wanted to see me so I went to his office. He said it was time to wean Michael away from me. I was all for that. I never slept in Michael's room again. Janet finally moved in and I slept down the hall.

"The counselor advised me to do something I enjoyed away from the hospital. For me that's rodeoing, but I didn't have a way to get around so I bought a truck, got my rodeo card and signed up to ride. When Michael's parents came to see him, I thought I'd go home for a visit. I got as far as Wyoming, and I saw Beau at a rodeo and knew once I reached Thunder Ranch, I'd never be able to leave. I'd given Michael my word, so I headed back to Maryland. I'm sorry, Beau. I couldn't talk about it at the time."

"Don't worry," Beau said. "I was just concerned. You weren't yourself."

"He's home now." His mom patted his chest again. "That's what matters."

"As soon as Michael walked out of that hospital on his prosthetic leg with his wife and parents by his side, I headed for Montana." He reached into his pocket. "My unit was awarded the Bronze Star for bravery in protecting Michael. And Michael received the Silver Star for bravery in saving the little girl." He opened his hand to reveal a Silver Star encased in a clear plastic sheath. "I was awarded the Silver Star as well for covering Michael's body and for carrying him out of there." He held it out to his mother. "I want you to have it."

"No, no." She shook her head. "You keep it. You earned it, my son. You're the hero."

Suddenly, there was that silence he dreaded. He glanced at their familiar faces and saw the look he dreaded, too—hero worship. He shoved the medal into his pocket and took a step backward. "I'm not a hero. Michael is. I did what I was trained to do. Anyone here would have done the same thing. Any marine in my unit would have done the same thing."

Uncle Josh put his arm around Tuf's shoulders. "But no one in your unit covered Michael's body. No one in your unit ran back for him. They were running for the chopper and safety. You did that. Why is *hero* so hard for you to accept?"

"Because you're looking at me different. I'm not different. I'm still the annoying younger brother."

Ace approached him on the left side. "Yep, you're still that annoying kid who had the nerve to wear my best boots to a rodeo, like I wouldn't see the mud and the scuffs. But you'll forgive me if I see a man where a boy used to stand."

"Yeah." Colt moved closer.

Dinah, Beau and Duke echoed the sentiment.

Some of the tension left him. "I know none of you understood my reasons for joining the marines, but when Dad died, I lost my love of rodeo. It wasn't the same without him there. I was always in the shadows of my brothers and cousins. I had to get away to find my own niche in life. I just never planned on being away so long." He sucked air into his starved lungs. He never talked this much. Ever. "I'm home now and I'm ready to start rodeoing again to help out." He looked at Ace. "Just how bad are the finances?"

After a round of hugs and shaking hands, he, Ace and their mom walked to the office. For the next two hours, they went over the books with Leah. They'd leased three thousand acres to a man from Texas who was always late with the lease money. That put a strain on making the payment on a three-hundred-thousand-dollar note at the bank. Seemed the economy, a flood and bad decisions made by their father had left the ranch deep in debt.

Tuf rose from his chair. "I'll go to the house and get my checkbook. I have some money in my account, and I'll sign it over to the ranch."

"Absolutely not," his mom said.

"Sorry, Mom, it's my money and I can do what I want with it and I can sell my truck."

"Slow down," Ace advised. "You're going to need a dependable truck if you start rodeoing."

"Yeah. I hadn't thought of that."

Ace patted his back. "I'm sorry I was short with you earlier."

"Come on, Ace, don't do that. Don't treat me with kid gloves. You've never done that before."

Ace nodded. "Okay, then get your ass to rodeoing and see how much money you can win."

"That I can do."

"But I want you to know I'm proud of what you did for Michael. Dad would be, too."

"Thank you." Emotions clogged his throat for a second, and he wondered why it had been so hard to open up and share his experience with his family. In the end it had been cathartic.

His family might look at him differently, but he knew they would never treat him differently.

That he could handle.

CHAPTER FIVE

MOST OF JANUARY Tuf busied himself learning the rodeo contracting business. Leah had a huge whiteboard in the office listing rodeos and horses and bulls to be delivered to said rodeos. He didn't see Midnight's name on the board. His mom hadn't made her decision yet.

"Tuf Hart, get away from my board," Leah said, walking into the office.

"Yes, ma'am." He grinned. If anyone got too close to that board, Leah was on the alert. She didn't want anyone messing with it. She was organized and thorough.

Since Uncle Josh wanted to spend more time with his wife, Tuf took over a lot of his chores, like taking care of the cows, but Ace planned to hire another hand when Tuf hit the rodeo circuit. Colt and Beau came in, and the three of them sat at the computer picking rodeos they were going to participate in and coordinating many events with the delivery of Hart animals to the rodeo.

"I'll participate some," Colt said, "but I got a kid and two stepkids, not to mention a wife I'm not getting far from."

"Thank you, honey," Leah said from her desk, not even raising her head.

Beau leaned back in his chair. "Sierra and I talked, and I'm going to give it my all this one last year."

Tuf knew Beau was worried about not being home

for Sierra. She had a genetic eye disorder and would eventually go blind, but she was very independent and intended to stay that way.

"You and me, huh?" Tuf asked.

Beau thought for a moment. "Sierra's my top priority, but I'll stick with you as long as I can."

"What's your goal, Tuf?" Colt asked.

The answer was easy. "To make as much money as I can."

"How about the nationals in Vegas?" Colt pressed.

Tuf shrugged. "I'm a little rusty. We'll see how the year goes." Tuf leaned forward. "Can we use your Airstream trailer if we need it?"

"Sure."

"We're set, then." He slapped Beau on the back. "I run at five in the morning. Want to join me?"

Beau frowned. "Are you crazy? At five in the morning, I'll be wrapped around my wife."

"Wimp." Tuf laughed as he left the office.

AT FIVE THE next morning, he got up and did his squats and stretches and then dressed in heavy sweats, sneakers, gloves and a wool cap. The temperature was in the thirties, but it wasn't snowing. To combat the darkness, he had reflectors on his jacket and sneakers. He planned to stay physically fit to compete. The cool morning air burned his lungs. Yet there was something uplifting about running when the world was asleep. An occasional truck sound and a coyote yapping accompanied him.

When he reached Roundup, the sun burst through the clouds, bathing the town in a misty yellow glow. He stopped at the sheriff's office to take a breather and had a cup of coffee with Duke, who had night duty.

"I—I don't know what to say to you," Duke mumbled, sitting at his desk. "I'm blown away by what you did in the Marine Corps."

"Seems like it happened to another person." It was always easy to talk to his quiet cousin. "I'm glad to put it behind me."

"Do you think about it much?"

"I try not to." He took a swig of the bitter coffee. He thought about it all the time, but no one needed to know that. And his greatest fear was sleep. That's when the nightmares came.

"If you need to talk, I work a lot of nights."

"How does Angie feel about that?"

"She's the best."

"Mmm." Tuf took another swig and got to his feet. "Thanks." He raised a hand in farewell. "See you later."

He ran toward Thunder Road and thought how nice it was that Duke had found the perfect partner, his soul mate. Ace, Colt, Beau and Dinah had also found their other half. He wasn't sure that was ever going to happen for him. It would have to be someone special—someone who was willing to share his nightmares.

The wind picked up, but he pressed on, monitoring his breathing, reserving his strength, something he'd learned in the marines. Suddenly he came to a complete stop. Up ahead, Sadie, wrapped up in her purple coat, was walking on the side of the road, head down, and trudging straight for him. Cheyenne was nowhere in sight.

About four feet from him, Sadie jumped back as she realized someone was standing in front of her.

He squatted. "Hey, munchkin, where you going?"

She shrugged.

"Where's your mother?"

She shrugged again.

"Let's go find her." He stood.

Sadie looked up at him. "Are you a stranger?"

"No. I've known your mother since we were kids."

"Oh."

He reached for her hand and she didn't object. Slowly they made their way to the Wright entrance and driveway. Cheyenne ran to meet them, Sammie trailing behind her.

"Sadie, where have you been?" she asked.

Sadie shrugged.

"I'm getting really upset by this behavior, Sadie. I…"

"I gotta pee, Mommy." Sammie clutched her crotch. "I gotta pee."

"Run to the house," Cheyenne told her.

"No. I'm scared." Sammie started to cry.

Turmoil etched Cheyenne's face as she struggled with her emotions, her attention split between her daughters.

"I'll watch Sadie," he offered.

"Thanks. We'll only be a minute." She grabbed Sammie's hand and they ran for the house.

Tuf still held Sadie's hand, and he led her to the steps on the front porch. He sat on the top one and she perched beside him. It was evident that something was bothering Sadie. He didn't have to be a psychologist to know that. Going on a hunch, he tried to draw her out.

"When I was six, I ran away from home."

"You did?" Today Sadie had the hood over her head and the white fur lining circled her face. She looked like an angel.

"Yep."

"Why?"

"Well, I have two older brothers, an older sister and

two older cousins. I was the youngest and I wasn't allowed to do what they did. I was too small. I wanted to be big and tough like them. When my dad wouldn't let me round up cows with them, I decided to leave and find a family without older, bigger kids."

The little girl watched him intently. "Where did you go?"

"I didn't get too far. My dad drove up and asked if I needed a lift into town. I got in the truck and he drove to Roundup. He asked if I wanted an ice cream at McDonald's. I said yes, and after that he said he was going to the feed store and I went along. A man with a horse in a trailer drove in behind us."

"Was it a pretty horse?"

"Oh, yes. A chestnut mare and she had a white star on her face. The man said his son went off to college and the horse was for sale. I told my dad we needed to buy it. He said he'd buy the horse if I'd take care of her. I agreed and named her Star. On the way home, Dad told me I wasn't always going to be little. Someday I'd be as big and tough as my brothers and cousins. I just had to be patient."

"Did you get big enough?"

"You bet." He looked into her bright eyes. "When someone runs away from home, they're usually running from something or to something." He paused. "What are you running to, Sadie?"

She shrugged.

"No." He shook his head. "Don't do that. Tell me. It's just you and me."

She scooted closer and whispered, "I have to find my daddy so he can come home and tell my mom he's sorry for hitting her."

Cheyenne gasped behind them. She sat by Sadie and gathered her into her arms. "Baby, I told you Daddy died. He's not coming back."

"But…but…you only said that 'cause he was mean to you," Sadie blubbered.

"No, baby, Daddy died."

Sammie whimpered behind her, and Cheyenne enfolded both girls as close to her as she could get them. Again, turmoil was etched across her beautiful face. He felt his heart contract. So much pain and they were still suffering. He should get up and walk away. This was none of his business, but something held him there.

He cleared his throat. "Where is your husband buried?"

"Uh…" Her watery green eyes stared at him. "In Billings. The aunt who raised him lives there and it was her wish."

"Have the girls been to his grave?" He didn't know why he was persisting. He should be halfway home by now.

"No," she replied, her frosty voice signaling for him to butt out.

He ignored the warning. "It might help."

She glared at him.

Sadie raised her head. "Does Daddy have a grave like Grandma?"

"Baby…"

"Is his name on it like Grandma's?"

Cheyenne swallowed, clearly torn by the questions.

"It might help," he repeated.

"Mr. Hart, don't you have to leave?"

"No, Mommy. He has to go with us to Daddy's grave."

That threw him, but he knew one thing: Sadie was

searching for answers, and she'd somehow connected getting those answers to him. It was about time to start his day and he should be at the ranch. Yet, he stayed.

"Sadie, calm down and we'll talk about this."

But Sadie wouldn't be deterred. "Where's Daddy's grave, Mommy?"

Cheyenne sighed, giving in to the inevitable. "I'll get my jacket."

Sadie and Sammie huddled together, their arms locked around each other. They looked so sad and once again his heart contracted. He got to his feet, not sure whether to go or to stay.

Cheyenne came out the door shrugging into a brown wool jacket, a purse in her hand. "Let's go."

Sadie jumped to her feet and took his hand.

Cheyenne frowned. "Mr. Hart has work to do."

"He has to go," Sadie insisted.

He reached for his cell in his jacket pocket. "I'll let Ace know I'll be late."

Cheyenne didn't say anything. She walked to a dark blue Jeep Durango parked in the driveway and opened a back door. He noticed two car seats. The girls hurried and climbed into their seats. Cheyenne buckled Sammie in, and he went around to the passenger side and did the same for Sadie. Crawling into the front passenger seat, he realized he had a problem. The SUV was small, and he had to adjust the seat as far back as it would go to fit his long frame inside.

The interior was small, too. Only the console was between them. He could have actually reached out and touched the angry lines of Cheyenne's face. She was upset with him. That was obvious.

He removed his wool cap and gloves and stuffed them

into his pocket. He felt out of place in sweats. A hat and boots would do a lot for his confidence. As she drove out of the driveway, he noticed her white-knuckling the steering wheel. She was nervous and afraid. He was sure she had her reasons for not taking the girls to their father's funeral. He should have respected that and kept his mouth shut. But he would see this through to the end, hoping she wouldn't hate him forever.

CHEYENNE DROVE STEADILY toward Billings, trying to ignore the man sitting next to her. The SUV was small, though she never realized how small until Tuf's six-foot-plus frame was within touching distance. His outdoorsy, masculine scent was appealing, but she wasn't in a mood to be tempted.

She was in a mood to smack him.

How did this happen? One minute she was frantically searching for Sadie and the next she was taking her girls to see their father's grave. When Ryan had committed suicide, she'd been devastated. After the horror and the grief, her only thought was to protect her girls.

Sadie and Sammie chatted to each other like they always did, and she tried to relax.

Tuf leaned over and whispered, "It will be okay."

She glanced at him briefly. "You don't know that."

"Evidently they didn't attend their father's funeral."

"No. They were three years old and I thought it was best. I didn't want them to have those kinds of memories of Ryan."

"Kids are very resilient."

"How many kids do you have?" she asked, not bothering to hide her annoyance at his interference.

"None. But it doesn't take someone with kids to see something is bothering Sadie."

She clenched her hands on the steering wheel and forced herself to relax, which was almost impossible. Why couldn't Tuf stay out of her life? "I've done everything to protect them," she found herself saying and didn't understand why she was explaining anything to him. "But it hasn't helped. Sadie keeps running away, and Sammie is clingy and cries all the time. I had no idea Sadie was trying to find her father."

"That's why seeing his grave will help."

"You don't know that. It could make it worse, and if it does, I'm going to blame you."

"I have broad shoulders."

"I've noticed." The words slipped out before she could stop them.

His brown eyes caught hers, and her heart raced as traitorous feminine emotions blindsided her. Damn!

"Mommy," Sadie called. "Can we get flowers like we get for Grandma's grave?"

"Sure, baby."

She negotiated traffic and pulled into a grocery store she knew carried flowers. Her hand shook as she reached for her purse. Damn him!

Tuf stretched his legs while they went inside. The girls argued over the flowers. Sadie wanted red tulips and Sammie wanted yellow. She bought both colors to save time. They ran outside to show Tuf their treasures. He seemed genuinely interested as he helped to buckle them into their seats.

Nothing was said as she drove to the cemetery, and she liked it that way. She drove through the double arcs and parked to the side as she neared the grave. Her stomach formed into a knot like it always did when she came here, reminding her of the hopes and the dreams that had died with Ryan.

Tuf stood by the car as they made their way to the site. Sadie and Sammie clutched their flowers. The dry winter lawn was neatly kept, some lingering snow nestled against the bottom of the headstone, and the flowers Cheyenne had put there at Christmas looked faded. She didn't visit the grave much because the girls, mostly Sammie, became upset if Cheyenne was out of their sight. But they'd fallen asleep while Christmas shopping in Billings, and Cheyenne had hurriedly bought and put the flowers on the grave. She felt she needed to at the holidays.

She squatted and had to swallow before she could speak. "This is where your daddy is buried. See—" she pointed to the headstone "—there's his name."

Both girls leaned in close to her, not saying anything, and she feared this was a bad idea. She had to swallow again. "Go ahead, put your flowers by the red ones."

To Cheyenne's surprise, Sammie was the first to act as she gently laid her yellow tulips by the poinsettias. Sadie was always the leader, but today she held back. Cheyenne waited, not wanting to push her. Slowly Sadie moved forward and placed her flowers by Sammie's.

"Do you have any questions?" she asked once Sadie was back in her arms.

Sadie twisted her hands. "Daddy's dead?"

Cheyenne tightened her arm around her. "Yes, baby."

"Did he love us?"

"Oh, yes. You were the light in his eyes."

"Did he love you, Mommy?"

Her throat went dry and words were now an effort.

For her girls, though, she had to answer. "Yes, but Daddy was sick, and he said and did things he didn't mean."

"He's not sick no more?"

"No, baby, Daddy is at peace."

Tears rolled from Sadie's eyes and she started to cry. Sammie joined in and Cheyenne held them close. "It's okay. It's okay," she cooed.

Suddenly Sadie tore away from her and ran to Tuf, who was leaning against the car with his sneakers crossed at the ankles, observing the whole scene. Sadie took his hand and led him to the grave.

Looking up at Tuf, Sadie asked, "What's your name?"

"Tuf," he replied.

Sadie pointed to the headstone. "My daddy is dead."

Tuf squatted beside Sadie. "I know. Now you don't have to search for him anymore. You know where he is."

"Right there." Sadie pointed again.

"Yep. Do you want to say something to him?"

Sadie twisted her hands again. "L-like what?"

"I love Daddy," Sammie said.

"I love Daddy, too," Sadie added.

Tuf stood. "Tell him goodbye and we'll go get ice cream."

"Goodbye, Daddy," they chorused, and ran to the car.

Cheyenne got to her feet and Tuf reached out to help her. She didn't pull away or act insulted. "Thank you," she said. "I just never realized they needed to see their father's grave. I thought I made the right decision at the time but…"

"Don't try to second-guess yourself. Let's just hope Sadie doesn't run away anymore. Now, let's get ice cream."

"Do you know what time it is?"

"When you do something out of the ordinary, ice cream makes it that much more fun."

"Really?"

"Yes."

As they walked to the car, Cheyenne knew that Tuf Hart was a very nice man. She'd probably known that from the first day she'd met him—back in school many years ago.

But he was a man who took control—like he had today, not giving her much choice in the situation. That brought back painful memories of Ryan. He had controlled every facet of their lives, even choosing the color scheme and the furniture for their home. Her opinions didn't count.

If she'd learned anything from her disastrous marriage, it was that she'd never let another man control her.

And that included Tuf Hart.

CHAPTER SIX

IT WAS AFTER ten when Tuf hurried through the back door. He heard a vacuum cleaner in another part of the house and darted up the stairs for a shower and a change of clothes. As the warm water ran over his body, his thoughts turned to Cheyenne and the hell she was going through and the hell she'd lived through.

PTSD was common among the soldiers returning from Iraq and Afghanistan. Killing and watching people being killed was a nightmare in itself. His counselor had encouraged him to talk about the nightmares, his feelings, and to get them out into the open. Keeping the horrific details of battle bottled up inside was a recipe for disaster. Soon they would bubble to the surface and destroy and disable a man more than the war. That's the reason Tuf had opened up to his family. He had to get all the pain and anguish out of his system, as his counselor had advised.

But it would never truly be out of his system. It was there lurking beneath his thoughts of family and home, making an appearance like a coward in the dead of night when his defenses were down. Then moments of horror would vividly flash before his eyes, and he'd bolt awake screaming, fighting for a way to survive.

He picked up his Silver Star from the dresser and tucked it into his jeans. He never understood his need to keep the medal close. The counselor had said there was nothing wrong with that as long as he talked about it. He wished his mother had taken it, then he wouldn't cling to it like a baby to a pacifier. Or some such crap.

With a sigh, he jerked on his boots and wondered about Ryan. Was he one of the marines who couldn't share or talk about his experiences and in the end they had destroyed him? He'd taken his frustration out on Cheyenne. How often did he hit her? A shudder ran through Tuf as he slipped into a clean shirt. He prayed he never slid that far into the nightmare. Cheyenne and the girls deserved better. They deserved happiness.

And, once again, he was getting in too deep. Concerned. Caring. Worried. When he himself was loaded down like a U-Haul truck with life's problems.

In the hospital in Maryland, the counselor kept throwing the same question at him. "Your family is waiting in Montana, yet you're here helping a fellow marine. How does that make you feel?"

"Like hell," he'd muttered.

Honor and loyalty had kept him there. Didn't mean he didn't want to leave. He'd made it to the front door several times. He'd always turned back. Those two years had taken a toll on his emotions, but in other ways it had helped. He'd been forced to see a counselor, forced to talk, forced to open up. If he hadn't, he probably would have turned out like Ryan, keeping all the garbage inside.

But he could never see himself taking his life. He'd never do that to his mother or his family. Life to him was living, and he planned to do that the best he could manage. And if he could see Cheyenne occasionally, well, life would be like winning a gold buckle every day.

He dreamed big.

Tuf STROLLED TO the office. Hearing voices, he made his way to a corral on the other side of the main barn. Colt, Beau and Royce leaned on the pipe fence, watching Ace with a brown-and-white paint. Ace was well-known for his horse-whispering skills.

He had a bridle on the young gelding and was speaking softly to him. Every now and then the horse would rear his head, resisting.

Tuf leaned on the fence next to Colt.

"You keeping banking hours these days?" Colt asked.

"Yeah," Beau added, "I've already fed the bulls and the cows."

"Sorry, I got hung up." Tuf was glad his family wasn't treating him differently. That day in the barn when he'd spilled his guts was probably on their minds, but they never let it show.

"How do you get hung up on a run?" Colt asked.

"Someone needed help."

Beau looked at him. "Was that someone a woman?"

"Yep."

Colt slapped him on the back. "Every single woman within a hundred-mile radius is going to be after you."

"I can handle that." He grinned. But there was only one woman he wanted. Yet Cheyenne seemed a little distant on the return to Roundup. The girls chatted incessantly, and he wasn't sure if Cheyenne was still upset with him or not. Seeing Cheyenne might not be as easy as he'd like.

He turned his attention to his older brother. "Ace trying to break the horse?"

"Yeah, but the horse is nervous and temperamental. Ace is working his magic."

Just then the horse flung his head and jerked away

from Ace, trotting to a corner of the corral. Ace walked over to them.

"I left this one too long. I should have been working with him months ago, but I had too much to do."

"No worry, big brother," Tuf said. "I'll break him the old-fashioned way."

"You need to save that vim and vigor for the rodeo," Ace told him.

"What better way than to start now?"

Ace narrowed his eyes. "You serious?"

"Yep."

Ace looked from the horse to Tuf. "Well, I need to be in my office, so go right ahead."

"Hot damn. It's rodeo time." Colt sailed over the fence and Beau followed. They managed to herd the horse into a chute, but the horse was frightened, nervous, jumping, throwing up his head, desperately trying to get out.

Tuf climbed the chute. "Easy, boy, easy."

Royce reached for the reins that were hanging to the ground. "Okay, Tuf. When you're ready."

Tuf eased over the railing and slid onto the horse's back. Powerful muscles rippled beneath him. He anchored his hat and reached for the reins. "Okay," he shouted. "Open the chute."

Colt and Beau swung it wide, and the horse leaped out and bucked with a force Tuf had forgotten. He found himself on the ground, staring up at a blue, blue sky.

"Damn, Tuf." He heard Colt's amused voice. "If you can't do any better than that, you're not going to make a dime."

Tuf staggered to his feet and picked up his hat lying in the dirt. He dusted it off and slapped it onto his head. "Get him back in the chute. This isn't over."

"You're a glutton for punishment," Ace said from the sidelines.

Colt and Beau hurried the horse into the chute before he could break free. Tuf crawled onto the fence and eased onto the horse's back again. Royce handed him the reins.

"Open the chute."

The gate banged against the chute and the horse burst out like a rocket from a launchpad. Tuf held on for about two seconds before he found himself in the dirt again.

Laughter echoed on the sidelines. Leah, Flynn and his mother had joined the group.

"Tomas Hart, what are you doing?"

For the first time in his life, he ignored his mother. Well, maybe not the first. There were a couple of other times he pretended not to hear. He signaled to Colt and Beau to put the horse back in the chute. They shook their heads but did as he requested.

His body felt tight and achy, but he climbed onto that horse one more time. He was ready for the surge of power and stayed on as the horse bucked, twisted and did everything he could to get Tuf off his back. Finally, the horse galloped around the pen.

"Open the paddock gate," he yelled.

Colt ran and swung it wide. The horse bolted through with Tuf on his back. Sensing freedom, the paint's hooves slammed against the dirt and charged full speed ahead. Wet and sweaty, the horse's flowing mane slung droplets against Tuf's face. Just as Tuf decided to pull the reins, the horse stopped along Thunder Creek, breathing deeply.

Tuf stroked the wet neck. "Easy, boy, easy. We can either be friends or enemies. I prefer friends." The paint snorted and trotted to the creek to suck in water.

Tuf gave him time, talking soothingly to him, some-thing he'd learned from Ace. After a few minutes, the horse raised his head and Tuf turned him from the creek. "Let's go home, boy."

Slowly the paint picked his way through the winter grasses and spruces. Tuf liked the horse. He had speed like Tuf had never seen. Maybe he came from racing stock. Since Sundance was getting older, he'd talk to Ace about making the horse his own.

Tuf guided the paint into the corral without incident. The guys must have been watching for him because they came out. Beau closed the gate and Tuf slid to the ground. The horse didn't move.

Colt climbed onto the fence. "I thought he'd come back alone and we'd have to go looking for you."

"I was worried about that, too," Tuf replied. "That's why I didn't get off of him in the pasture." He stroked the paint's face. "What are your plans for him, Ace?"

"He came with a group of mares Mom and I bought. I just wanted to get him broke before too much more time passed."

"I'd like him."

"Sure. He doesn't come from bucking stock, so we don't plan to use him for rodeos."

"He's fast and I like that. I'm calling him Ready to Run. I'll rub him down and feed him. Later this after-noon I'll try to put a saddle on him."

Tuf worked with the horse the rest of the day, and by the end of the week, he had Ready trained to a saddle. The more he worked with the animal, the more he felt Ready came from quarter-horse stock. He instinctively re-sponded around cattle and he wasn't frightened of a rope.

After Ready was fully broken, Tuf turned his attention to the rodeo. They were headed to Bozeman, Montana, in a week with a load of stock for a rodeo. Tuf, Colt and Beau were scheduled to ride. They'd be away overnight, so they were taking Colt's Airstream trailer.

Tuf continued to run every morning, but he hadn't seen Cheyenne or the girls. The place was always dark when he passed by. This morning there was a light on, and since he had more nerve than common sense, he jogged down the driveway, up the steps and knocked on the door.

CHEYENNE WAS BUSY gluing stones onto a cuff bracelet. She could get a lot done before the girls woke up. Designing and making cowgirl jewelry was her livelihood now. She had her own website and advertised at rodeos and craft stores. Clunky bling was in, and she had several orders to fill before the twins demanded her attention.

She jumped at the knock at the door. Who could that be? It wasn't even six yet. Her dad had gone out to check on a mare that was about to foal. The knock came again. She got to her feet and tightened the belt of her green chenille robe. She hadn't combed her hair, so she tucked it behind her ears and trudged to the door in the bright psychedelic-green fuzzy slippers the girls had gotten her for Christmas. They actually glowed in the dark.

"Who is it?" she asked.

"Tuf."

Tuf? What was he doing here? She was a mess, with no makeup and her ever-present nemesis, the dreaded freckles, skimming across her nose and cheeks. She couldn't see him like this.

"It's Tuf," he called as if she hadn't heard him.

She sighed, knowing she had no choice. She smoothed her flyaway curls. He might as well see the real Cheyenne: the anxious, stressed mother of two active, fatherless little girls. Most days she didn't have time to put on lipstick, so what did she care if Tuf saw her looking less than her best? Oh, yeah, that might get her a time-out in her daughters' tell-no-lies world.

"Cheyenne."

Leaning her head against the door, she counted to ten. Maybe he'd go away. Austin had told her about Tuf's bravery in Afghanistan and it hadn't surprised her. She already knew he was that kind of man. She hoped he was seeing someone to talk about his experiences. PTSD would destroy him otherwise.

"Cheyenne."

Good grief! The man was tenacious. She opened the door, trying to hide behind it as much as she could.

His eyes slid over her disheveled appearance. "Sorry. Did I wake you?"

"No, I was working. Is there a reason you stopped by?"

"I wanted to check on Sadie."

"She's fine, and she hasn't run away again."

The cold air wafted through the door, and he looked beyond her to the fire in the living area. "May I come in?"

No. No. No! But she realized that reaction was a little insane. She stepped aside. "Would you like some coffee?" She marched into the kitchen, uncaring of what she looked like. Almost.

"Love the slippers," he said, following her.

She poured him a mug. "They were a gift from the girls. Let's just say they like bright."

As she turned around, she saw he was staring at her jewelry-making supplies on the table. "I make cowgirl jewelry," she explained.

"Oh." He took a seat and removed his cap and gloves.

Suddenly the kitchen was too small, too hot and way too intimate. Strong male vibes seemed to close in on her, reminding her that she was young and not immune to the male species. And Tuf Hart was all male.

She placed the mug in front of him with a shaky hand and slid into her chair. Picking up the leather cuff, she continued to glue the flat rhinestones around the edges.

"What is that?" he asked.

"It's a cuff made out of leather, conchas and rhinestones. I also make a light metal cuff and add whatever a woman wants."

"And women wear this?"

"Yes."

He fingered a reddish necklace lying on the table. It had five rows of red coral teardrop beads interwoven with silver spacers and pink feathers. A rhinestone boot decorated with the teardrop beads hung from it. "And this?"

"Yes."

"It looks big."

"Women like big and bold." She turned the laptop on the table so he could see her website. "The bigger pieces are my most popular items."

"Cheyenne Designs. Nice. Do you sell mostly online?"

"At Austin's store, a couple more stores in Billings and at rodeos."

He picked up a pair of round-nose pliers. "What do you do with these?"

"I use them to bend jewelry wire, make eye loops, P loops, wrapped loops and all sorts of things." She pointed to other tools on the table. "That's a cup bur for rounding the end of cut wire, and that's a flush cutter for cutting wire and—"

"Okay. I get it." He wrapped his hand around the mug, and she marveled how the mug seemed to disappear in his strong grasp. "Did you do this when Ryan was alive?"

His question startled her and she paused, laying the cuff carefully on the table. That was really none of his business, but she supposed he was only curious and didn't mean anything by it. And she could be a little touchy about the subject. She was willing to admit that.

She folded her hands in her lap. "Not at first. Both of us were eager to start a family, and Ryan wanted me to be a stay-at-home mom. I couldn't get pregnant, and Ryan…"

"Blamed you."

She caught his brown gaze, and a shiver ran through her. Was he psychic? "Yes. But we both saw a doctor and were told we were fine and we had to be patient. It wasn't long after that I became pregnant but I…I miscarried at three months."

"And Ryan blamed you for that, too?"

She balled her hands into fists and wanted to reach across the table and smack him with one. "I'm not discussing my marriage."

He quirked an eyebrow. "They say talking is good. I've had every snippet of my life pulled out of me by a compassionate psychologist with the insights of Dr. Phil and the patience of Mother Teresa."

"I'm glad you got help. Ryan resisted every step of the way."

"It's not easy opening up and revealing painful things."

She reached for a loose rhinestone on the table. Something in the way he said that made her curious. "You know what happened to Ryan?"

"Yes."

She didn't look at him. She kept playing with the shiny stone.

"And you know what happened to me?" he asked so low she almost didn't catch the words.

"Yes. It's hard to keep secrets when our families are now so closely entwined."

His eyes caught hers and she couldn't look away. "I'm sorry for what you had to go through."

"And I'm sorry you had to witness so much carnage." She glimpsed a shadow of pain, which was quickly replaced by a teasing glimmer.

"So why don't you take pity on this cowboy/marine and go out with him sometime?"

She melted into his warm gaze for a second but was quickly slammed against the hard facts of reality. Ryan's suicide had crippled her emotionally. At times she felt dead all the way to her soul, and she fought that feeling for her girls. For them she went through the motions of everyday life. For them she smiled and pretended she was happy because they needed to see that. For them she would do anything to ensure their happiness.

How did she explain that to Tuf? And why did she feel she had to explain it?

"Don't say you don't like me. We both know you'd be lying."

She shrugged. "That was just a way to protect my pride," she admitted. "Our families didn't get along, and our dating would have only caused more problems."

"Problem solved. Our families have united in a way no one would have ever expected."

"It's not that simple."

"Why isn't it?"

"Because everything I do is for my girls. They're my focus, my life. I don't have time or energy for anything else."

"I understand that, but I've learned one thing from counseling—you can't keep all those emotions inside. You have to share, open up and live life. Otherwise you live in a vacuum, and that's not good for you or the girls." He blew out a breath. "And that's the longest speech you'll ever get from me."

"Tuf…"

He held up a hand. "Okay. Can we be friends? Can I stop by here every now and then and have a cup of coffee? No strings. No attachment. No making out. Just friendship."

She stared into his stubborn brown eyes. "You're very persistent."

He grinned and her heart hammered wildly. Oh, he was good.

"My dad used to say I was like an old hound dog with a juicy bone. I could never let go of anything."

"I hope I'm not a juicy bone." She tried very hard not to smile, but she felt the corners of her mouth twitch.

"The very best."

As tempting as he was, she had to say no. Even though it had been more than ten years, their situation hadn't changed much. They still weren't right for each other. They had too much baggage and heartache to deal with. They had to conquer their demons alone.

Then he did something unexpected. He reached across the table and ran one long finger across her freckles. His touch was light and gentle. He'd never touched her before, and a sea of emotions swamped her, emotions she'd just sworn she didn't have. Why was she suddenly hot all over and had the urge to giggle?

"In grade school, I thought your freckles were cute. I actually tried to count them one time when we sat across from each other in the cafeteria. You frowned at me, so I had to stop counting. In high school you covered them with makeup, but I like the freckles."

Was he for real? Ryan never cared for her freckles. He preferred her in makeup.

"I'd like it if we could be friends. Do you think that's possible?"

No. No. No!

But the word that slipped from her dry mouth was "Yes."

CHAPTER SEVEN

TUF WATCHED THE startled expression on her pretty face and wondered if she was confused by her decision to see him or guilty she'd agreed to see someone other than her deceased husband. Before she could change her mind, he said, "I've got to run. Busy day at the ra…" His words trailed away as he heard childish chatter.

"The girls are awake," Cheyenne murmured.

Two whirlwinds blew into the kitchen and abruptly stopped when they saw him. They stopped so fast Sammie ran into Sadie. They both wore one-piece pajamas. Green frogs danced on Sadie's purple ones and Sammie's were pink Barbie all the way.

Sadie's eyes opened wide. "You came to see me?"

"Sure did, munchkin. How you doing?"

"Good. Sammie's good, too."

Their red hair was everywhere, and Sammie kept brushing hers out of her eyes. Sammie whispered something in Sadie's ear.

"Sammie wants to know why you call me munchkin."

"Because you're cute and small."

Sammie whispered in Sadie's ear again.

"Sammie wants to know what you call her."

He studied Sammie's face, the same as Sadie's. "Well, I think I have two munchkins here. You're identical."

They giggled and Tuf felt like laughing, too. They were so darn cute.

Sammie whispered to Sadie again.

"Stop it, Sammie," Cheyenne said. "You can talk. Sadie doesn't need to speak for you. Now, what do you want for breakfast?"

The whispering started again as the two debated this in their own twinlike language. Finally, Sadie said, "We want pancakes."

"Go wash your hands and comb your hair," Cheyenne instructed.

They darted off, but Sadie turned back. "Bye, Tuf." Their heads were together again and they could hear Sadie. "You better say it."

"Bye, Tuf," Sammie said.

"Bye," he called and then looked at Cheyenne. "Are they always like that?"

"Yes, and it gets annoying. Sadie's the dominant one and Sammie relies on her for everything."

Tuf drained his mug. "Are they in school?"

"They should be in pre-K, but after Ryan's death they were very clingy and cried all day in class so I took them out and I'm homeschooling them. When they start kindergarten, I want to separate them, but I don't know if they're ready. Sammie has to find her own identity, though."

"Since Sadie has accepted her father's death, maybe they'll both grow stronger in the months ahead."

"That's my hope."

He stood and pulled his hat and gloves out of his jacket pocket. Slipping his cap over his head, he said, "I'll see you later."

"Tuf…"

He could hear the hesitation, the fear in her voice, and he wasn't letting her go back on her word. He leaned over and whispered in her ear, "Later." A flowery, feminine scent weakened his knees and he had trouble moving away. "Tell that to the other Cheyenne who is scared to death of life." He walked toward the door, shoving his hands into his gloves.

"I'm not scared." Her words followed him.

"Good."

"Tuf Hart…"

He closed the door and smiled as he went down the steps and all the way to Thunder Ranch. He didn't know what he expected from their friendship. All he knew was that he liked Cheyenne. He always had and he wanted to get to know her better.

She was right about one thing: they both had a lot of emotional baggage. Maybe they could work on lightening the load together or whatever. So far things were going good and he wanted to keep it that way. Friendship was a good start, but he knew and she knew that he wanted a lot more.

As Tuf hurried through the back door, he met his mom in her customary jeans and flannel shirt.

"Tomas." She glanced at her watch. "You're running late. We have a business meeting in ten minutes."

"I was talking to Cheyenne and…"

"Cheyenne." A sharp note ran through her otherwise calm voice. "She wouldn't go out with you in high school. The nerve! Who wouldn't want to go out with my handsome son?"

He tried not to smile at her offended expression. "Well, Mom, your handsome son's father was John Hart, and Dad didn't like Buddy's thieving ways. Do you see the conflict?"

"Yes." She shook her head. "Things sure have changed. Not sure how your father would take that, but I like Austin and I've always liked Buddy."

His mom liked everybody. That's why he was startled by her reaction to Cheyenne's name.

She looked up at him, her eyes worried. "Are you and Cheyenne friends now?"

"Yeah, we're friends."

Suddenly, she wrapped her arms around him and hugged. "I don't want anyone to hurt you ever again."

"Mom, you can't always protect me. I'm old enough to handle anything life throws at me."

She pulled back and brushed away a tear. Sharp, needlelike pains shot through his stomach.

"We can talk about Afghanistan if you want to." Since that day in the barn, she hadn't mentioned it, and she seemed to purposefully avoid the subject.

"Why would I bring up that subject? I do not want you to relive any of it."

But I do. In the darkest of night.

"I'm fine, Mom." He felt he needed to reassure her. "I've checked in with the VA in Billings, and I can see a counselor anytime I feel the walls closing in."

"You can talk to me, too."

"I know, Mom."

She patted his chest. "You're home now and safe. That's what matters." She reached for her Carhartt jacket on the wooden coatrack. "Do you ever hear from Michael Dobbins?"

He fished his phone out of his pocket. "I got a text from him yesterday. See." He punched a couple of buttons and showed her the message: Farmer again. Never felt so good. "Here's a picture." He brought up a photo of Michael on a tractor. "His family are farmers in Kansas."

"He looks quite normal."

"He is, except for the artificial leg and eye and numerous other scars, but he's living life again."

"All because of you."

Tuf swallowed, not really wanting to talk about that heartbreaking time or take credit for it, but he'd encouraged her to talk. Luckily, her cell buzzed.

She grabbed it off the counter. "Yes, Aidan, we'll be right there." Clicking off, she said, "Get dressed. I'll stall."

He ran upstairs, and in ten minutes he walked into the office, which was filled with family, even Dinah and Duke.

"Still keeping those banker hours," Colt commented.

"Shut up." Tuf grinned.

His mom started the meeting. "I won't keep everyone waiting. Josh and I have talked, and I've made a decision about Midnight. That horse has caused us so many problems that at times I wanted to strangle the poor thing. But we have a lot invested in him, and I intend to see that horse doing wonders for Thunder Ranch and Hart Rodeo Contracting Company. That's been my goal from the start."

She took a moment. "I know all of you have different opinions about Midnight's role in the rodeo. Mine has changed several times. Midnight getting injured could thwart all our plans. That's been a big factor, but Aidan has been able to collect semen from Midnight. At first, he was unable to do this because the animal was too unpredictable, and we didn't want Aidan or a handler getting hurt." She looked around the room. "So I've decided to enter Midnight in rodeos to see if he can live up to his reputation as an exceptional bareback bronc."

"Hot damn." Colt raised a fist in the air. "Time to rodeo."

"Colton." His mother's stern voice brought Colt down to earth quickly. "It will be your job to keep Midnight as calm as possible and living up to his potential."

"Yes, ma'am."

Everyone got up from their seats, preparing to leave.

"Wait a minute," Dinah called. "I have news."

Now everyone stared at her, and she rose to her feet, her hand on her stomach. "Austin and I found out that we're having a…girl. We're so excited."

Everyone jockeyed for a position to hug her.

"Another granddaughter," Sarah cried, squeezing the daylights out of her daughter. "How wonderful. They'll grow up as best friends."

Tuf was the last to hug her. "How are you going to handle your sheriffing duties while—" he glanced at her rounded stomach "—you're pregnant?"

"I got the okay to hire another full-time deputy, and I'm on office duty for now."

"What a relief." Sarah sighed.

The family dispersed to start their day. Tuf helped Beau feed the rodeo bulls. He brushed hay from his clothes and watched the bulls tearing into the alfalfa.

"That brown-and-red one looks mean."

Beau leaned on the fence beside him. "That's Bushwhacker and he is mean. His main goal is to gore you as soon as he can. I drew him once. Didn't make the ride, and I got the hell out of his way as fast as I could."

"That's what I like about horses. Once the ride is

over, they're searching for the open gate to get out of the arena. They're not looking to maim you for life."

"I just like riding bulls."

"Well, coz, let's see how we do in the next few months, and hopefully we make it home in one piece."

Later that afternoon, Tuf worked with Ready. The horse rode as smooth as Mrs. Worley's Cadillac. Brad, her son, had been in his class, and Mrs. Worley always drove them to school outings in her big smooth-as-a-glider Cadillac. Yep, Ready was a Cadillac horse.

The cows needed hay, so he cranked up the tractor and carried a round bale of hay to them. As he worked, he thought of Cheyenne. Hell, there wasn't a minute of the day that he hadn't thought of her. Was he still infatuated with her? Or was it something more? He wasn't sure, but he was willing to find out.

THE NEXT MORNING Cheyenne was up early, brushed her hair and clipped it back. All the while she resisted the urge to put on a touch of makeup. Tuf liked her freckles. She stopped. What was she doing? She couldn't keep saying no and feeling excited at the same time. Picking up her box of supplies, she headed for the kitchen in her first-thing-in-the-morning look.

Her dad had made a fire in the fireplace and she could smell coffee. He was an early riser, but this morning he'd gone to Thunder Ranch to check on Midnight. It was one of his favorite things.

Cheyenne fixed her coffee and laid out her supplies. She had ten sparkly stretchy bracelets in different colors to make, and she could whip them out in no time. As she worked, she kept glancing at the clock. Six-fifteen—no

Tuf. Six-thirty—no knock on the door. By seven, she
knew he wasn't stopping to visit.

Finishing the bracelets, she placed them in a small
box and stored them inside her big box, trying to figure
out why she felt hurt. She liked Tuf, even his weird shopping habits. She liked his compassion for her girls, his
selfless bravery and his inherent strength. But after what
she'd been through with Ryan, she wasn't ready for any
kind of intimate relationship, even if Tuf was charming,
caring and unbelievably heart-stoppingly good-looking.

"Oh, oh," she groaned. She needed something stronger than coffee to deal with her unsettling thoughts.
Getting up, she stood on tiptoes to reach the top cabinet
door. She pulled out a bowl of candy—the girls' stash
that she gave them when they were good.

Tootsie Rolls, M&M'S, bubble gum, Dots, gummy
bears, Twix and Milky Ways. She grabbed a Milky Way,
tore off the wrapper and took a bite. Oh, yeah, just what
she needed. Almost.

After her sugar high, she put Tuf out of her mind.
They'd agreed to be friends, and anything else was out
of the question. That was her bottom line and she was
sticking to it.

The next morning she heard his knock and calmly
walked to the door and opened it, uncaring of her gaudy
robe and slippers.

Tuf brought the cool outdoors in with him. He removed his gloves and held his hands to the fire.

"I need new gloves. I think I've worn these out. Feel."
He cupped her face with his hands and she lost all train
of thought. The roughened male skin against her soft
face shot her adrenaline through the roof. She knew he
intended to show her how cold his hands were, but all

she felt was warmth all the way to her toes. His dark eyes stared into hers, and the world stopped turning for a brief moment as she realized just how much she liked Tuf Hart. *Friends.* She kept trying to remind herself. Friends wasn't even on her radar. Friends with benefits wasn't even an option. How did she get from *no* to the delicious thoughts in her head?

She hated that he could make her so wishy-washy when she intended to be firm in her decision.

"W-would you like a cup of coffee?"

"As long as it's hot."

He followed her into the kitchen and sank into a chair. "Making jewelry, huh?"

"Yes."

He stared at her. "You seem tense."

"I want to make it clear that we're just friends."

"Okay." His gaze grew intense. "Something else is bothering you."

"Yes, it's about the cemetery the other day. I should have mentioned it sooner, but you put me in a difficult position. I make all decisions concerning my girls, and I do not appreciate you taking control."

His eyes narrowed. "Did something happen?"

"No, except they want to go to the grave site every day. I told them it was too far and we'd go once a month. We circled a date on the calendar. They haven't mentioned it since."

"So?"

She could see the confusion on his handsome face. She placed a cup of coffee in front of him and slid into a chair feeling foolish. Ridiculously foolish. Before she knew what she was doing, she started telling him about her marriage and Ryan. She didn't sugarcoat anything.

"Ryan was a control freak in every way and it only grew worse."

"Did you ever think of leaving him?"

"He was in so much pain I couldn't bring myself to do that until…until one day he became enraged that I hadn't taken his clothes to the cleaners. Sammie had the flu and I wasn't taking her out. He hit me so hard I fell in the kitchen and hit my head on the table. Blood ran into my eyes, and I knew one of us had to leave or he was going to kill me. I told him to get out and not to return until he got some help. I thought he was going to hit me again, but he walked out. That was the last I saw him." She gripped her hands until her knuckles were white. "It breaks my heart that Sadie saw that."

"She just wanted her daddy to say he was sorry so he could come home."

"I know but…"

"Sadie will be fine." Then he told her the story about the little girl in Afghanistan. "The girl went through a horrific event, but the moment she saw her toy, the horror was forgotten."

"That's why you were so stern that day you saw Sadie walking on the road?"

"Yeah."

She stared into his brown eyes and saw a vortex of dark emotions that still lingered from the war. But he wasn't trying to hide them like Ryan had.

Suddenly the darkness faded. "I'm not trying to control you, Cheyenne. I'm really not that type. I was just trying to help Sadie."

Seeing the turmoil on his face, she knew she had to be honest. "I'm a mess. My emotions are helter-skelter, and I do my best to get through each day for my girls.

But—" she shifted uneasily "—earlier when you cupped my face, I felt warm and feminine again."

"Is there something wrong with that?"

"Yes. I'm an emotional wreck, and I'm finding every excuse I can to stay away from you."

"Well, then, stop nailing up excuses like barbed wire to keep me away. Let's just take this one day at a time. What do you say?"

She licked her dry lips. "Tuf...why would you want to do that? I can't see any kind of future for us. We both have too much baggage."

He twisted his cup. "But there's an attraction between us. It's been there since we were teenagers." He looked directly at her, and his dark eyes were as inviting as the chocolate on a Milky Way bar. "Can you deny that?"

"No, but I'm scared." Oh, God! Had she said that out loud?

"I know. I am, too."

His honesty startled her, and she just stared at him, all her defenses down. But she didn't feel weak or vulnerable. She was uplifted knowing she wasn't alone in her fears.

"Is it okay if I continue to stop by?"

"Yes," she replied, and meant it.

"Tuf," Sadie screeched from the doorway and jumped onto Tuf's lap. "You came to see me again?"

"Yep. How you doing?" He cradled her close as if he'd been doing it all his life.

"Good." Sadie bobbed her head.

Cheyenne wondered where Sammie was. The girls were inseparable. She stood to go check when a loud scream was followed by wails. "Mommy! Mommy!"

She sprinted to their room and found Sammie standing in the middle of Sadie's bed crying her little heart out.

"Baby, it's okay. Mommy's here." She gathered her child into her arms.

"Sadie left me." Sammie hiccuped. "I'm scared."

"Mommy's here. There's nothing to be afraid of." She reached for tissues on the nightstand between the beds and wiped Sammie's wet face. The girls had twin beds, but Sammie always crawled into Sadie's during the night. At times like this, Cheyenne became so angry at Ryan for doing this to his kids.

She carried Sammie to the kitchen, and Sammie was on full attack as they often were when the girls were mad at each other. "You left me, Sadie."

"I had to say hi to Tuf."

"I want to say hi to Tuf," Sammie mumbled.

Cheyenne stood her on her feet, and she climbed onto Tuf's other leg, but her attention was on her sister. "You left me."

"You're a big baby," Sadie spat.

"Am not." Sammie slapped her sister's chest.

Sadie hit her back. "Am, too."

"No hitting," Cheyenne said. "Now make up."

"She's a big baby," Sadie insisted, resisting, as always.

"You're mean!" Sammie cried.

"Girls, did you not hear what I said? Make up and be nice."

They glared at her and then at each other. Slowly their foreheads met and they started to whisper. Tuf rolled his eyes over their heads, and Cheyenne smiled, feeling lighthearted and silly. She hadn't felt that way in a long time.

"I've got to go to work, girls," Tuf announced, and they scrambled from his lap, staring up at him.

"When you coming back?" Sadie asked.

The back door opened, and Cheyenne's dad stomped in, wiping snow from his boots. He stopped short in the doorway. "Tuf." A startled expression flashed across his face.

Tuf walked over and the two men shook hands. "Mornin', Buddy."

"Mornin'. I was just at Thunder Ranch exercising Midnight."

"Gracie said you took care of him when he went missing."

"Yeah. Grew kind of fond of the horse."

"You're welcome anytime. Now I've got to run," Tuf said and looked at her. "See you later."

She nodded and wondered if she was just weak or if she was glimpsing a light through the darkness that surrounded her heart.

The girls ran behind him to the door. "Bye, Tuf," they called and then ran to the bathroom to get ready for breakfast.

"Tuf Hart?" Her dad lifted a shaggy eyebrow when the door closed.

"Take that pained look off your face. We're just friends."

He poured a cup of coffee. "Mmm. I'm glad he helped with Sadie. We didn't know what else to do."

"I'm grateful for that, too." Her conflicting thoughts she kept to herself.

He sipped his coffee. "Just take it slow. Tuf's been through a war, and you've been battered and bruised."

Her dad rarely offered parental advice. He figured

he'd lost that right many years ago, so for him to speak up she knew he was worried.

She kissed his cheek. "Dad…"

"I just don't want to ever see you like you were when you came home over a year ago—totally defeated and withdrawn."

She didn't, either. She wouldn't survive another debilitating heartache like that. "I'm taking baby steps," she told him. "I better check on the girls."

As she walked toward the bathroom, she felt Tuf's hands cupping her face. Why was that feeling so strong?

CHAPTER EIGHT

TUF AND BEAU checked Tuf's rigging for bareback riding. They sat at Beau's workstation in the barn next to the old foreman's house. Beau had converted the small barn into a saddlery. A gorgeous saddle Beau had just finished sat on a large sawhorse. The scent of leather filled the room and cuttings lay on the floor.

They examined the Barstow rigging that Austin had ordered for Tuf. The leather strap placed around the horse's withers had a luggagelike handle made out of rawhide. The underside was sheepskin to protect the knuckles. Slipping his gloved hand into the handle, Tuf gripped it tight.

"Just right," he said. "I have a good grip, and I can get my hand in and out without a problem."

Beau nodded. "That's why it's the best."

"I'll put it in my truck with the rest of my gear."

"Wait. I have something else for you."

Tuf walked back in, and Beau grabbed a package wrapped in brown paper. "I made this for you."

Tuf glanced at the package and then at Beau. "Now, that's too little for a saddle."

"I made you a saddle years ago."

"And I still use it." He stared at the package, wondering what was inside. For some reason he was hesitant to take it. He was sure it was something special, and guys didn't do special. They laughed, joked and horsed around. Special meant his heart was about to take a hit. That's why guys like him avoided it.

"Open it." Beau shoved it at him.

Slowly, he laid the rigging on the table and took the package. Ripping off the paper, he could only stare. He held up the item and felt his heart take a nosedive, just as he'd foreseen. Red chaps with white fringe and blue stars ran down each side—red, white and blue for an American marine.

"I don't know what to say" was all he could manage.

"If you don't like them, you don't have to wear them. I thought they would give you a brand—cowboy marine."

"They're nice, really nice. I appreciate it and I'll definitely wear them. Thanks, coz." Tuf held out his hand.

They shook hands and then did a brief hug and laughed.

"We're hopeless," Tuf said.

"Now, if you were Sierra, I'd hug you like crazy."

"Let's remember I'm not when we're sleeping in that small Airstream trailer."

"Let's go see what time Ace wants us to leave for Bozeman on Friday morning."

"Do you want to guess?" Tuf asked.

"Early."

"Yep." They walked out of the barn toward the office.

Ace wanted them on the road at six. He was staying behind to keep an eye on a mare that was showing signs of distress with her pregnancy. Since it was one of Midnight's offspring, Ace wasn't taking any chances.

Tuf had a lot to do before they left. His last rodeo had been in November, so he was a little rusty but felt his technique would come back. He intended not to think

too much about it. He didn't want to leave without seeing Cheyenne and the girls.

He hated she was in so much turmoil, and he didn't
want to push or control her. Her husband had really done
a number on her. Tuf just wanted to help her. As Ace
and Beau talked, he tried to figure out why that was so
important.

IN THE LATE AFTERNOON, Tuf drove to the Wright place.
Cheyenne, the girls and Buddy were at the corrals. He
parked by the old tin-rusted barn and walked over.

"Tuf!" The girls squealed and ran to him.

"What's going on?"

"Grandpa bought us horses," Sadie informed him.

He took their hands and walked closer. Cheyenne
smiled at him, and his heart kicked against his ribs like
a bronc about to be broken. Damn, she was beautiful
with the sun glistening off her hair. Today none of her
angst showed on her face.

"Hi," she said in that soft voice that made his insides
feel like jelly.

Before he could say anything, Buddy led the horses
over. One was white with black flecks and the other a
muted gold with a white blaze face.

"Hey, Tuf," Buddy said.

He nodded. "Where did you get the horses?"

"Over at Angie's animal rescue. They've got some
age on 'em and are gentle. I thought they'd be perfect
for the girls."

"I don't want to ride," Sammie said, clinging to Cheyenne's leg.

"It's okay, baby. You don't have to," Cheyenne told her.

Sadie climbed onto the fence. "I'm gonna ride."

"Since Sammie's not, you get to choose," Buddy said to Sadie. "Which horse do you want?"

Sadie shrugged.

"Come on, munchkin," Tuf urged. "Which one do you like?"

"That one." She pointed to the gold one.

Buddy tied the white horse to the fence and led the gold horse closer. A child's saddle was on both horses. "You ready?"

Sadie looked at her mother, then at Tuf and back at the horse. Her eyes flickered with uncertainty. "Come with me, Tuf."

Tuf was startled. He thought Sadie would want her mother to ride with her because Cheyenne was an expert horsewoman. But with Sammie attached to her leg, she could barely move.

He looked at Cheyenne for approval. He wasn't doing anything without her okay. That lesson he'd already learned.

"Baby, are you sure?" she asked Sadie.

"Yep." Sadie bobbed her head. "If Tuf helps me."

"Okay," Cheyenne said.

He leaped over the fence and then plucked Sadie off her perch. "Let's get acquainted with… What are you going to name her?"

Sadie shook her head.

Tuf stroked the horse's face and Sadie tentatively stuck out her hand. "Don't be afraid," he said. "I'm here."

She touched the face and then started petting in earnest. "See, she likes me."

"Yes, she does," he agreed and wondered how old the animal was. She seemed almost sedated, which worked well for a scared little girl.

"Now I'm going to put you in the saddle, and I'll swing up behind you. Okay?"

"'Kay."

"But first we have to give her a name."

Sadie looked at Cheyenne and then at Buddy. "Grandpa, what's her name?"

"She's just an old horse without a name. You have to give her one."

"'Kay." She touched the horse's face. "I wanna call her Tuf."

"Sadie, baby, you have to give her another name. That's Tuf's name."

He glanced at Cheyenne and saw she was smiling. He was smiling, too. He'd never been around kids that much and found he liked it, especially Cheyenne's girls.

"I wanna call her Tuf," she insisted with a stubborn lift of her chin.

"How about if we call her Toughie?" he suggested.

"'Kay. I'm gonna ride Toughie."

"Here we go." Tuf lifted her into the saddle and held on in case Sadie started screaming. She gripped the saddle horn with both hands but didn't make a sound. He adjusted the stirrup to her leg length and slipped her purple boot in. He didn't have to look to know that Sammie's cowgirl boots were pink.

Buddy adjusted the other side and Tuf swung up behind Sadie. Buddy handed him the reins.

"How do we start her, Tuf?" she asked.

He suppressed a laugh. "Like this." He kneed the horse and was surprised when the horse actually moved. He could have sworn he heard a snore. They trotted around the corral and Sadie finally let go of the saddle horn. He showed her how to use the reins and she caught on quickly.

"Look, Mommy, I'm riding."

Sammie had finally let go of Cheyenne's leg, and they had climbed the fence to watch. "I see, baby."

Sadie pulled up the horse and turned to look at him. "I can drive by myself now."

"No," Cheyenne was quick to say.

"I can do it by myself," Sadie shouted.

"The horse barely moves, girl. She'll be fine," Buddy said to his daughter.

Indecision filtered across Cheyenne's pretty face so Tuf made it easy for her. He slid to the ground. "Go slow," he instructed in a stern voice. Around and around the corral Sadie guided the horse, even being bold enough to stand in the stirrups. He followed her on one side, and Buddy was on the other just in case she took a tumble. When it was clear Sadie had it mastered, he strolled over to Cheyenne.

"I can't believe she learned so quickly."

Tuf pushed back his hat. "Look who her mother is."

She smiled, and he couldn't look away from the light in her green eyes. "That was a long time ago."

He pointed to the barrels outside the fence. "They're getting rusty. You might spray paint them and see what Sadie can do."

"I don't think she's ready for that."

"Sammie," Sadie called. "Ride with me. It's fun."

Sammie's eyes were glued on her twin. Tuf saw the fear in her eyes and knew that was the worst feeling in the world. He'd felt it many times. Mostly when high-powered bullets were whizzing past his helmet or when he had to tell a wounded buddy that everything was going to be okay when in truth he was scared out of his mind. There was only one way to conquer fear—to not let it have control. Sammie was only four, but the fear was just as real.

He walked to the white horse and led her over. "This is your horse. Do you want to pet her?"

Sammie's eyes opened wide and Tuf glanced at Cheyenne. She nodded.

"Does she bite?" Sammie asked, shocking both adults.

"Um…no," he said with certainty. He wasn't sure the horse was even breathing much less have enough energy to injure someone.

"Her name is Princess," Sammie announced, shocking them again.

Tuf lifted the girl off the fence and felt her tremble. "You don't have to ride if you don't want to."

"I know," she replied and reached out a hand to touch the horse, and then she stroked her. "She's pretty."

"Yes, she is." He gently placed her in the saddle and waited for the crying. None came. He adjusted the stirrup and slid her pink boot in. Buddy hurried to adjust the other side.

"That's my girl," Buddy encouraged her.

Tuf swung up behind her and kneed the horse. The horse trotted off and Sammie's trembling grew severe and he held her tight. He didn't stop the horse or take her off because he knew it was important to her to do what her twin was doing. Tuf knew that feeling, too.

After about the third trip around the corral with Sadie constantly passing them, the trembling stopped. He showed her how to use the reins and she grew confident. When she looked back at him, he knew it was time to get off, which he did, but he followed along the side.

Once Sammie had it mastered and Buddy was watching both of them, Tuf walked over to Cheyenne. "You can breathe now."

"I can't believe she did that. Since Ryan…she's been so clingy and needy, but look at her." He followed her gaze to see Sammie following Sadie around the corral. "She's having fun." Her eyes caught his, and he got lost in her rapturous expression. "All because of you. Neither one of them would have gotten on a horse for Dad or me. We tend to pamper them, but they wanted to impress you."

"So they like me?"

"Yes."

He leaned on the fence about six inches from her and stared into her gorgeous eyes. "How about their mother?"

"She does, too," she whispered.

Her pink, full and inviting lips were inches away. He pressed closer, needing to breathe the same air.

"Cheyenne," Buddy called, and a curse word slid down Tuf's throat. "It's getting late. We're taking the horses in to rub them down, and Angie sent some horse cookies the girls can feed them."

"Okay, Dad."

Tuf raised a hand. "Bye, girls." He hadn't paid any attention to the time, but the sun was about to slam-dunk another day.

The girls clamored to get off and Buddy helped. In a split second they charged toward Tuf. He squatted and held out his arms to catch them. "Thank you, Tuf," they chorused.

"I'm proud of you. You both did really good."

Sadie kissed his right cheek and Sammie kissed the

left. Then they ran after Buddy. Tuf swung over the fence and landed by Cheyenne.

"I'm fixing to start rodeoing so I'll be gone quite a bit. Do you mind if I call to see how the girls are doing?"

"No. They would love that." She gave him her cell number and he entered it into his phone. "My cell is at the house, but when you call I'll have your number."

He slipped his phone back into the case on his leather belt, and his eyes caught hers. The light he saw there gave him the courage to say, "When a cowboy rides away, he usually gets a kiss from a pretty cowgirl."

She lifted an eyebrow. "Are you riding away?"

"Temporarily."

'Well, then." She stood on tiptoes and gently touched his lips. He cupped her face, needing her touch, her caress a little longer. His lips took hers with the same gentleness but he was unable to disguise the fire leaping within him. He pulled away like someone who had just been given CPR. He had what he needed for now—to survive. He strolled toward his truck.

"Bye, Tuf," she called in a wistful voice.

He didn't turn back. The best was yet to come.

CHAPTER NINE

CHEYENNE CLOSED *SLEEPING BEAUTY,* kissed her daughters and tucked them in for the night. Out of all the new books they had, the girls preferred her to read the classic fairy tales at night. They were from the Little Golden Books collection Cheyenne had as a child. Just like her daughters, she'd dreamed of a prince, too. That was in books, though. In the real world, a prince was very rare. Or realistic.

Flipping off the light, she watched to make sure the night-light was on, and then she went to the kitchen to prepare the girls' lesson plan for tomorrow. Her dad was asleep in his chair.

In the utility room, she pulled a box of school supplies out of a cabinet. In the morning they'd work on motor skills, and in the afternoon they'd color and read. Marbles in a jar, nuts and bolts so they could pick up and screw on, and then pipe filters and beads to make a bracelet. They'd read *The Very Hungry Caterpillar* and *If You Give a Mouse a Cookie.* That settled in her mind, she went to her bedroom to finish several jewelry orders.

But her thoughts kept straying to Tuf and the kiss. She didn't think twice about kissing him. It felt natural and right. And damn good. She'd been resisting an obvious attraction since she'd met Tuf. Placing her pliers on the table, she decided to stop resisting, to stop comparing Tuf to Ryan and to stop looking for fault where there was none. And to stop being afraid of a simple thing like falling in love. Again.

Six months ago she would have said that it wasn't even a possibility.

But now...she was starting to believe.

THE NEXT MORNING everyone was up early getting ready for the trip to Bozeman. Tuf swallowed one last sip of coffee.

"Mom, you sure you're going to be okay?"

She turned from putting dishes in the dishwasher, giving him one of those looks. "Tomas Hart, I'm fine. I have my nitroglycerin pills in my pocket, in my bedroom and in the office. I wish you kids would stop worrying."

He placed his cup in the sink. "Did you ever stop worrying about me?"

"I'm your mother, and mothers never stop worrying."

He kissed her cheek. "I want you around for a long, long time."

"I don't plan on going anywhere."

"Good." He reached for his hat. "I just hate you being alone in this big house."

"If it will make you feel better, Leah and the kids are spending the night."

"Yep. That makes me happy."

She pushed him toward the door. "Now make your mama happy and focus on the rodeo."

"Yes, ma'am."

For the next hour, Ace and Colt shouted orders like drill sergeants, but everyone did his or her job without complaining. Colt backed the cattle carrier up to a chute attached to a corral. Tuf rode Ready and herded the saddle broncs into the corral and into the chute. They loaded easily, and Royce closed the first compartment gate. He did the same with the bareback horses. Beau and Gracie followed with the bulls, and they charged into the carrier without a problem.

That left Midnight to occupy the last compartment alone. Colt ushered him into the corral and managed to get him in the chute, but that's where Midnight balked. He stopped short, refusing to budge.

Colt climbed onto the pipe railing. "C'mon, boy." He rubbed Midnight's back and the horse reared his head. "C'mon, boy. You've done this before. It's rodeo time. Don't make me look like an ass."

"You don't need any help from Midnight," Ace remarked.

Colt shot him a killer glance. "C'mon, boy," he said again and slapped Midnight on the rump. The horse darted into the compartment, and Royce slammed the door closed before Midnight could change his mind.

"Let's go," Colt shouted, swinging over the fence.

Tuf hooked up to the Airstream trailer. The truck bed was loaded with hay and feed and covered with a tarp in case of rain or snow.

"Let's go," Colt shouted again.

The cattle carrier pulled away from the corral and Tuf followed. They settled in for the long ride. Country music blared on the radio. Tuf sipped his coffee and stayed as close to the cattle carrier as he could.

But his thoughts were on Cheyenne. He could see her at the kitchen table making jewelry in her green robe and bright slippers. They were friends, and slowly that friendship was developing into something more. He felt it yesterday when she'd kissed him, and he really hoped he wasn't misreading the signals. The memory of her kiss had to last for a while. That was the easy part. All he had to do was close his eyes and she was there in his arms, touching her sweet lips to his.

Beau took the wheel of Tuf's truck for the last leg of the trip. Tuf catnapped. He wasn't sure how much time had passed when Beau said, "Hey, we're heading into Bozeman."

The sign for Bozeman appeared ahead, and the right blinkers on the carrier came on.

Tuf sat up. "Everything okay?"

"Yep, except Midnight keeps staring at me."

Ever since they'd left Roundup, the horse had been watching the truck. "He's a little restless on the road."

"On the road? He's restless all the time," Beau told him.

"Yeah, Ace said they knew that when they purchased him, but they've worked wonders since then. If he doesn't perform well, though, it will be a big loss for Thunder Ranch."

"A lot rides on that horse."

"You bet."

They pulled into the fairgrounds. Colt jumped out of the carrier and walked over. He took a moment to make sure Midnight was okay.

When Colt reached Tuf, he thumbed over his shoulder. "You do realize you'll probably have to ride him one of these days."

"Yep." Tuf shoved his hat back on his head. "I'm hoping it's not this rodeo."

Colt laughed. "I'll check with the coordinator and see where we need to unload."

Tuf stretched his legs, as did Beau, who was on his cell with Sierra.

Colt came back with instructions. They unloaded Midnight in a separate pen because he was a stud and there were too many mares around. Once in the pen, he charged around the perimeter looking for a way out. When he found none, he settled down and drank from a water trough. The rest of the unloading went smoothly.

They found a spot to park and hook up the Airstream trailer. After that, they fed the animals. His mom had stocked the trailer with food, so they went back to eat and rest before the rodeo.

Bareback riding was first, and Tuf took his rodeo gear to the cowboy-ready area. Colt and Beau handled the stock.

Tuf took a moment to look out at the stands, full of eager rodeo followers. Sponsors' signs were plastered around the arena. Vendors sold hotdogs, sandwiches, cotton candy, pretzels and more. The scent of popcorn mixed with the foul odor of manure and rawhide wafted on the air.

Yep, it was a rodeo.

The press box was above the chutes, and a Garth Brooks tune played on the loudspeakers. The announcer came on and introduced the cowgirls, who were dressed in white. Circling the arena on horseback, they carried both the Montana state and U.S. flags. They formed a line in the center of the arena and stopped.

"Ladies and gentlemen—" the announcer's voice came on "—please stand for the national anthem. Our own Marsha Gates will sing it."

Tuf stopped adjusting his chaps and stood with his hand over his heart as the words to "The Star-Spangled

Banner" rang out. Someone called his name but he didn't move nor did he plan to. In his mind's eye he could see Corporal Charles Hoffman lying with a hole in his chest, blood gushing out.

"Tuf Hart!"

Tuf pulled the marine's body behind a rock to safety. "Everything will be okay," he promised. But it wasn't. Charles closed his eyes and died in Tuf's arms. Nothing would ever be okay again.

The song ended and Tuf turned to the man calling him.

"Hey, didn't you hear me?" a man with a clipboard asked.

Tuf poked a finger hard into the man's chest. "Didn't you hear the national anthem being sung?"

"Huh?"

"The national anthem. Don't you have enough respect to stop for a moment to honor the men and women who died for your freedom?"

The man drew back with a scowl. "You talk as if you were in the service."

"I was. Marines. Staff Sergeant Tomas Hart."

The man's ruddy complexion turned a funny shade of white. "Look, man, I'm just trying to find Tuf Hart."

"That's me."

"Oh. I…I just wanted to tell you you'll be the fifth rider and the horse you drew is Teddy Bear."

"I already know that."

"Just making sure so everything will run smoothly. Bareback riding should start in about five minutes." The man walked away.

Colt strolled over. "Lighten up. You scared him to death."

"I wanted to drive my fist through his face."

Colt shook his head.

"I'm sorry. I lost it for a moment." He bent to finish strapping on his chaps, trying to blend reality with the horror of war.

"Tuf…"

"Don't worry," he told his brother. "I'm not a violent person. The man's disrespect just got to me."

"If you want to talk, I'm here."

"I know, and thanks, but I'm fine." He exhaled a harsh breath and tried to push the incident out of his mind. "Let's rodeo."

Jesse Hobbs was up first on Powder Puff. He made the ride and scored a 79. Trey Watson was next with a 79.5 ride. Bossy Lady charged into the chute, and Colt climbed the steel rail to help Cory Kinney prepare to ride. The horse bucked wild, but Cory managed to stay on and scored an 80.

Beau took over the job of helping the cowboys. The next rider bit the dust, too, on a horse named Dixie Chick. Then it was Tuf's turn. Teddy Bear was in the chute. Tuf donned his protective vest and climbed the steel rail. At the top, he blocked the crowd, the sounds and the scents from his mind. The horse fidgeted, not liking the chute.

"Stay focused," Beau advised.

Tuf slid onto the horse and checked his rigging. It was cinched tight around the horse's withers. Tuf slipped his gloved hand into the handle and gripped with all his strength. He got his legs into position, leaned slightly back and raised his left hand. Ready, he nodded and the gate flew open. When the horse's front hooves hit the ground, Tuf marked the horse at the shoulders with his spurs. Before he could get a rhythm marking, the horse gave a wild buck, and he found himself lying flat on his face in the dirt.

"Damn!" He got to his feet, dusted off his new chaps and picked up his hat.

The rest of the rodeo he helped with the Hart stock, getting them in chutes and out. Colt made his ride, as did Beau. They'd probably place in the money if they made their ride tomorrow night.

They were dog-tired by the time they made it to the trailer for the night.

"Who gets the bed?" Beau asked, removing his dirty shirt.

"Since it's my trailer, I get half the bed." Colt made his opinion known.

"That's cool," Beau said. "I'll sleep on the kitchen-table converter bed. I'll be talking to Sierra before I go to sleep and that way I won't disturb anyone."

A knock sounded at the door. Tuf looked at Colt and Beau. "Expecting anyone?" They shook their heads. Tuf turned the latch to find two girls standing there, one blonde and the other brunette, in tight jeans and even tighter blouses. They wore cuffs like he'd seen Cheyenne make on their wrists.

"Is Colt Hart here?" the blonde asked.

"Uh…" He glanced over his shoulder to see Colt waving his arms above his head and mouthing *no*. "Uh… he's unavailable."

"That's a pity. We're going to a party and Colt loves parties."

"He's married now."

The girl cocked an eyebrow. "Married? When did that happen?"

Tuf didn't know the exact date, and before he could reply, Colt walked up. "Hi, Cindy, Mallory."

"Colt," the girls screeched in unison.

Colt shoved his hands into his jeans. "Sorry, I'm a family man now. Got kids and everything."

"Oh, we hadn't heard." The blonde made a face. "Such a shame. We could have had a great time."

"Hope you enjoy the rodeo." Colt backed into the trailer like an inchworm.

Cindy batted her eyes and looked Tuf up and down. "How about you, cowboy? Would you like to go to a killer party?"

"Uh…no, but thanks."

"Why doesn't anyone want to have fun anymore?" Cindy mumbled.

"Uh…night." Tuf closed the door and looked at his brother. "I'm proud of you."

Colt shrugged. "Figured it was time to stop hiding and be an adult."

"You know, Colt," Beau said from his perch at the kitchen table, "you should have some flyers printed up announcing your marriage so all the girls on the rodeo circuit will know, because clearly some haven't heard the news."

Colt raised his hand but restrained himself from shooting Beau the finger. Instead he headed for the bedroom. "Think I'll call my wife and tell her what a catch she's landed."

Tuf sank into the booth at the table. "Yeah, that's going to go over big." Colt laughed as he closed the small door. Tuf glanced at Beau. "Want to flip a coin to see who gets the shower first?"

"Nah. You go first. I'm waiting for a call from Sierra."

After his shower, Tuf pulled on jeans, a T-shirt and a jacket. Colt and Beau were each on the phone with their wives. He slipped out the door and sat on the trailer step. The night was chilly but not uncomfortable. He wrinkled his nose. Since the stock pens were a short distance away, the scent of alfalfa and manure wafted on the breeze.

Sticking his hand into the pocket of his jacket, he found his cell and clicked Cheyenne in his address book. She answered immediately.

"Hi, Tuf. How did you do?"

He grimaced. "I got bucked off."

"You'll do better. I know you will."

Her warm voice was soothing. "I hope it's not too late to call."

"No. The girls are out for the night and I'm making jewelry."

He settled against the trailer door. "Did they ride today?"

She laughed softly and it eased every ache in him. "I could hardly keep them focused on their lessons today. They wanted to ride instead. Guess why it was so important?"

"Why?"

"So they can show Tuf how good they can ride all by themselves."

Tuf grinned up at the twinkling stars.

"I made a short video with my cell. I'll send it to you."

"Okay." He clicked off and waited for the beep. Then he opened the video. Astride the horses, dressed in matching pink and purple outfits, including hats and boots, Sadie and Sammie waved excitedly at him. He could hear their voices.

"Hi, Tuf," Sadie said. "We can ride real good."

"I was 'posed to say that," Sammie complained.

"No, I was," Sadie corrected her.

"I was," Sammie insisted.

"Girls." Cheyenne's voice rang out. "Do you have anything to say to Tuf? Sammie first."

"She's a big baby," Sadie grumbled.

"Am not."

"Sammie, say something quick." Mother director was on the job.

"I love you, Tuf."

"I love you, too, Tuf." Sadie wasn't going to be outdone.

"I love you, too," he murmured as the screen went black. Holding the phone in his hand, he wondered how that could have happened so quickly. They'd stolen his heart, much as their mother had years ago. His cell buzzed and he clicked on.

"I forgot to tell you they weren't on their best behavior."

"I thought they were cute."

"You would."

There was a long pause, and he could feel her doubts seeping through.

"Tuf...we agreed to be friends, but things are changing too fast. My girls are becoming attached to you and..."

"What?"

"I don't want them to get hurt."

His hand gripped the phone. "You think I'd hurt them?"

"Not intentionally, but you're a former marine and

you've been through a great deal. I couldn't help Ryan and…"

"Cheyenne…" The only thing he could do was be honest. "Yes, I came back scarred, but I had a counselor at the hospital in Maryland and I see one in Billings. I've done everything I can to heal."

"Oh, Tuf."

He held the phone a little closer to his ear. "If I thought for one minute I could harm you or the girls, I'd walk away now."

"I…I don't want you to walk away."

"Good." He relaxed. "Then let's go on a date, the four of us."

She laughed, a tingly sound that seemed to light up the night.

"And don't you dare say no."

"Yes, Tuf Hart, I will go out with you."

He never realized until that moment that he'd been waiting ten years for her to say that.

CHAPTER TEN

THE DARKNESS OF the trailer threw him as he slipped back in. A tiny light burned in the kitchen area. Beau slept on the makeshift table bed and Colt was out in the bedroom. Had he and Cheyenne been talking that long? Yanking off his jacket and jeans, he crawled over Colt and snuggled under the blanket. Colt didn't even stir. He always slept like a log.

As sleep claimed him, he heard her words, *"Yes, Tuf Hart, I will go out with you."* That would sustain him for a while.

Sometime toward dawn when his defenses were down and he was weak, bad memories snuck through like thieves stealing his well-earned peace of mind. He was back on that hill in Afghanistan where Michael had been shot, bullets blasting all around him. Frank Bigby screamed and went down. Tuf and another marine dragged Frank behind a rock, out of the line of fire.

"I'm hit, Tomas. It hurts."

"I know. Take a deep breath. Stay here. We'll pick you up on the way down."

"Tomas…"

"You're fine. It's just a shoulder wound."

Mortar fire exploded above them. "Stay down. Stay down!" he shouted to his men. When there was a lull, he jumped to his feet. "Let's go. Let's go!" They charged forward, avoided enemy fire when they could. The Afghan soldier went down.

He had to stay focused. He'd check him once the battle was over. They were almost at the top. A few more feet and they could take out the enemy. "No, no, no!" He had to look. "No!"

"Tuf! Tuf! Tuf!"

Someone held him down. Had the enemy captured him? He had to fight. He had to get away.

"Tuf, damn it! Wake up!"

He opened his eyes and saw Colt sitting on top of him. Beau held his arms. "Oh, no!" They released him and he sat on the side of the bed, his head in his hands. Colt and Beau sat beside him.

"Do you want to talk?" Colt asked.

"No."

"You were screaming and thrashing about. I think you were back in Afghanistan."

Tuf jumped to his feet and grabbed his clothes. "I have to get out of here."

"Tuf."

Within a minute he was dressed and hit the door.

"Tuf!"

He ran until his lungs could no longer hold air and then he sank to the cold ground. The stock pens were in front of him. Midnight stared at him and suddenly the nightmare eased. He was home, away from the horror.

Brushing the nightmare from his mind, he got to his feet and walked over to Midnight. "Good morning, boy."

The horse pawed the ground and Tuf relaxed, but he still didn't understand why he was having the debilitating dream again. He hadn't had one in months. Something must have triggered it. A gush of air left his throat in realization—the man who wouldn't pause for the national anthem. That had to be it.

Slowly, he made his way back to the trailer, feeling trapped in a war he couldn't escape. Last night he'd been so happy, but now he couldn't see any kind of relationship with Cheyenne. She'd had one marine who'd suffered from PTSD. He couldn't do that to her again.

When he entered the trailer, Colt and Beau were at the table eating breakfast tacos and drinking coffee. No one said anything and he sat down next to Beau. Colt slid a taco and a cup of coffee toward him. He wrapped his hands around the warm cup and took a swallow. Then he undid the tin foil around the egg-and-sausage taco and ate it. Still no one spoke.

Tuf set his cup on the table. "Somebody say something. Please."

Colt shrugged. "We don't know what to say."

"Just don't look at me like that."

"Like what?"

"With pity."

Colt sighed. "Tuf, I can't even imagine what you've been through, but last night Beau and I got an up-close-and-personal view of something horrific. We're not looking at you with pity. We're looking at you in awe."

"Yeah," Beau agreed. "Do you want to talk?"

He shook his head. "I've talked to a counselor about my experiences until I'm blue in the face. I guess some of those memories are always going to be with me." He wadded the tin foil into a ball. "Could we talk about something else now?"

"Sure." Colt settled back. "Last night after I finished talking with Leah, I took a shower and noticed you weren't in the trailer. I looked outside and saw you on the step talking on your cell. Who were you talking to?"

"Cheyenne," he admitted.

"Ah." Colt nodded. "Leah mentioned you came to the rescue of the infamous runaway Sadie."

"Yeah. Cheyenne and I are friends. We're just talking."

Beau punched his shoulder. "Well, that's a lot more than you did in high school."

"You had a big crush on her back then," Colt added.

He frowned. "Did everybody in Roundup know that?"

"Everybody but Cheyenne." Colt pushed away from the table. "We have to get to work. We have a rodeo tonight."

"Let's go," Tuf said and paused briefly as a tiny remnant of the dream lingered. He pushed it away and hoped it was gone for a long, long time.

The rest of the day went smoothly. They had two jobs: getting the animals into the chute to ride and supporting each other and the cowboys. Then they had to make sure the animals made it back to the stock pen without injury. After a ride, an animal was usually hyper, hard to settle down. But there were several handlers to help. They trusted no one with Midnight, though. Ace would be proud of the way Colt took care of the horse that the future of Thunder Ranch rode on.

The spotlights came on and people filed into their seats, chattering. Noise erupted around the arena. "Should've Been a Cowboy" by Toby Keith blared over the speakers. In the cowboy-ready area, it was a whole different scene. The chutes banged while cowboys worked on their gear, psyching themselves up for a good ride. Tuf was no different. As he tightened the straps on his spurs, the announcer asked for everyone to stand for the national anthem. Standing, he once again placed his hand over his heart and remembered his buddies and other soldiers who had died in the line of duty for their country.

When the music ended, he turned to see the man with the clipboard. Tuf nodded and squatted to finish adjusting his spurs.

"Mr. Hart, I…um…"

Tuf rose to his feet and stared at the man, realizing for the first time that he was probably about twenty years old.

"I…I'm sorry about last night. I have a cousin in the navy and I would never disrespect our military. Working the rodeo is a dream job for me. I got so busy with details, I wasn't paying attention. I won't make that mistake again."

"I appreciate that."

The kid glanced at the clipboard. "You're second up tonight on True Grit. You got about five minutes."

"Thank you." Tuf held out his hand and the kid shook it vigorously.

"Thank you, sir," he said and walked off.

Colt hurried over. "Did you get into it again with him?"

"No. He apologized."

"That's good." Colt looked him up and down. "You ready?"

"Yep." They strolled to the chutes and watched as Jesse Hobbs slid onto Naughty Girl. The horse burst from the chute and bucked one way, and Jesse went in the opposite direction, landing on his stomach.

True Grit waited in the next chute. Tuf anchored his

hat and climbed the chute. The horse was restless, moving about. Carefully, he slid on, balancing himself on the cold steel of the chute. True Grit jerked his head, not liking the baggage. Tuf tested his rigging and stuck his right hand into the handle.

"Stay focused," Colt suggested. "This horse is not known for consistency. Be prepared for anything."

"Got it." He placed his legs into position and raised his left arm. When he nodded, the side of the chute opened, and True Grit leaped out and bucked into the arena. Tuf held his feet in position over the break of the horse's shoulders until the horse's front feet hit the ground. He marked the horse, and while maintaining control, he moved his boots in a toes-turned-out, rhythmic motion in tune with the horse's bucking motion.

Three seconds. Four seconds. His muscles stretched, and he felt like his arm was being pulled out of its socket, but he kept marking the horse with his spurs. Eight seconds. The buzzer sounded, and he leaped from the bucking bronc and landed on his feet. Yes! He'd made the ride. Walking toward the chute, he watched for his score on the board. Seventy-eight. Not bad.

He swung over the arena fence and made his way to the cowboy-ready area. Removing his chaps and spurs, he placed them in his bag. Beau would take his rigging off True Grit. He hurried to help Colt, and he wanted to be there when Midnight made his appearance. Cory Kinney had drawn Midnight and he was scheduled to go last.

Tuf remembered Cory. He'd made it to the national finals last year and had placed sixth overall. He was an up-and-coming bareback rider, and Tuf wondered how he'd do on Midnight.

"Great ride," Colt said as Tuf climbed the chute. Trey

Watson was about to ride. "Take over. I have to get Midnight ready."

They watched as Trey scored a seventy-nine, putting him ahead of Tuf. That was okay because Tuf knew he wasn't going to win tonight. His no-ride last night had put him out of the money.

Midnight shot up the alley leading to a chute. Tuf quickly opened the gate and slammed it shut behind the black horse. Colt was already on the chute getting Midnight geared up to ride. Tuf didn't get too close because his presence always seemed to rile the horse, as if he knew they were adversaries and would one day challenge each other.

Once Midnight was reasonably calm, Colt motioned to Cory, who climbed the chute. Colt attached the flank strap lined with fleece, and Midnight jerked his head up. Carefully, Cory climbed on. Midnight's body trembled with restless energy. Several minutes passed as Cory adjusted his rigging. Once he gave the signal, the chute opened, and Midnight reared up on his hind legs and leaped forward, kicking out with his powerful back legs. One strong kick and Cory flipped over backward, landing near the chute. Midnight ran wild in the arena and the crowd roared.

"Damn, what a ride," Colt said.

"I think you mean a no-ride," Tuf corrected him.

"I better get Midnight settled down before it's my time to ride."

Tuf continued to take care of the animals in the chute. Colt had a good saddle-bronc ride and he'd place in the money. When barrel racers came on, Tuf watched for a moment and remembered Cheyenne. He'd been forcing himself not to think of her, but suddenly he could see

her racing into the arena on Jewel and flying around
the barrels in graceful movements. No one rode a horse
like Cheyenne. He took a deep breath and forced those
thoughts away. They would haunt him later, though.

It was almost midnight when they made their way
to the trailer. They were bone-tired, but Colt and Beau
had a spring in their steps because they'd earned some
money for Thunder Ranch. His brother and cousin were
talking to their wives so he took a quick shower and
crawled into bed. He paused for a moment and thought
of calling Cheyenne, but it was late and he wasn't sure
what to say to her now.

Was he always going to be trapped in that war?

TUF LAY STARING into the semidarkness. Colt and Beau
were in the kitchen area, still talking to their wives. The
light from the sink spilled across the bed, but it didn't
bother him. He welcomed it. If he closed his eyes and fell
asleep, he was afraid the nightmare would return. The
only way to ward it off was to stay awake. And that was
crazy. His counselor had said he had something deep-
seated in him that he didn't want to face. He'd gone over
every horrible moment of his stint in the marines, and
he still didn't know what it was.

He flipped onto his side, intending to stay awake as
long as he could. He didn't want to subject Colt and Beau
to a repeat of last night. And he never wanted Cheyenne
to see a glimpse of his hell. What were his options? Not
many. He'd have to stop seeing her. A new kind of pain
twisted his gut. Everything he'd ever wanted was just
out of his reach.

THE NEXT MORNING they were up early to load their stock
and make the long trip home. Tuf's plan of staying awake

hadn't worked. He'd been too tired. The next thing he knew, dawn had arrived, peeping in at a new day. After a quick breakfast, they loaded the stock and prepared to leave Bozeman. They stopped for gas and then rolled onto the U.S. 191 and headed for home.

After almost four hours, they turned the trucks onto Thunder Road. Tuf parked the Airstream in its spot, and Colt backed the cattle carrier to the chute. Once Midnight was unloaded and in his paddock, Colt turned to Tuf.

"Can you handle it? I want to see Leah."

"Go." He waved a hand. "You, too, Beau. I got it."

He didn't have to tell them twice. Colt grabbed the zipped leather bag with the money and paperwork and dashed to the office to leave it in the safe. A few minutes later, Tuf saw him sprinting across the yard to his double-wide. Beau had disappeared faster than he could blink. Evidently, the honeymoon wasn't over.

After unloading, he parked the cattle carrier in its spot. He then fed the animals and made his way to the house. He heard voices in the backyard and went there. His mom sat in a redwood recliner, watching Jill and Davey playing in the yard with a ball.

"Tomas, you're back." His mom smiled.

He kissed her forehead and sat in a chair beside her.

She turned to face him. "I saw Cheyenne and her girls in church this morning."

His stomach tightened.

"When Cheyenne told them I was your mother, well, one of them, I can't tell them apart, was Tuf this and Tuf that. Soon the other twin joined in. They're waiting for you to come home to show you how good they're riding." She lifted an eyebrow. "Shouldn't you be over there?"

Clasping his hands between his knees, he didn't respond.

He could feel his mom's eyes on him. "Tomas, do not disappoint those little girls."

He stood to make a quick getaway.

"Tomas Hart." She stopped him in his tracks. "What's wrong with you?"

He took a deep breath. "I have a lot to sort out. I'll talk to you later."

"Tomas…"

He didn't turn back. He was running—running scared. *Coward* echoed through his mind. He never thought of himself as a coward. Placing his hand over his left jeans pocket, he traced the shape of the Silver Star. He wasn't a coward.

But he sure felt like one.

CHAPTER ELEVEN

CHEYENNE KEPT GLANCING at her watch. Almost five. Why hadn't Tuf called or come by? She'd been waiting since she'd seen the cattle carrier and Airstream trailer go by. And the girls kept asking when Tuf was coming. She'd run out of things to tell them. "He's working and has a lot to do" was beginning to sound flimsy. The girls were sitting on the front porch in their boots, jeans and cowgirl hats. What if Tuf didn't come? What was she going to tell them then?

Feeling anxious, she put down the necklace she was working on. She was making a mess of it. The turquoise stones were expensive and deserved her full attention. She placed them in a tray and stored them in her work-box. She'd finish it later.

Tucking her hair behind her ears, she took a long breath. It hadn't been easy to open her heart again. And to another marine, at that, but she felt a connection to Tuf. It was real, as real as anything she'd ever felt. He was kind, patient, understanding and cared about her girls. That was real, too. Before she'd known it, she was taking steps toward him instead of away like her mind had dictated. She'd been burned badly, so why was she exposing her emotions once again to the fire?

She gathered her jewelry-making supplies and took them to her room. They'd had a wonderful conversation on Friday night so she didn't understand his silence today. Something had to have happened. But what? She was tired of trying to figure it out. She'd take the girls to get ice cream or a hamburger or both to get their minds off Tuf. As she placed her box in an old armoire in her room, she heard the girls screech.

They must have spotted a bug. She ran to the front door, preparing to be the bug slayer, but stopped short in the doorway. Tuf stood there with Sadie in one arm and Sammie in the other. *He's here.* Her heart thumped against her ribs in excitement. She grabbed her jacket, slipped into it and stepped outside.

The girls chattered away. When they saw Cheyenne, they squirmed to be let down. Sadie asked, "Mommy, how long is five minutes?"

She understood the question. How long to tell Tuf to wait before coming to the barn to watch them ride. They wanted to get ready.

"Oh, a long time."

"Good." Sadie looked up at Tuf. "Five minutes and then come watch us."

"You got it, munchkin."

Sadie took Sammie's hand and walked down the steps and headed for the barn. Cheyenne reached for her cell in her pocket and called her dad. "The girls are almost there." She clicked off and stared into Tuf's dark eyes. He looked tired...and sad. Something had happened.

"Could we talk for a minute?" he asked.

"Sure." He sat on the step and she sat beside him, preparing herself for his next words.

He clasped his hands between his knees. "I could have come over earlier but...I think it's best if I don't see you anymore."

Her stomach cramped with an old, familiar pain. Ryan had never given her a chance to help him. He'd always pushed her away.

She faced him and wavered at the pain she saw there. "What happened? Just tell me."

He looked at his clasped hands and he seemed to grip them tighter. "I haven't had a nightmare in six months and I thought I was past that, but while in Bozeman, I had a bad one. Colt said I was screaming and thrashing about. He and Beau were holding me down when I woke up."

Unable to stop herself, she placed her hand on the arm beneath his denim jacket. His muscles were rigid, tight. "I'm sorry."

"I don't want you to see me like that. You went through hell with Ryan."

He was trying to protect her, and for a moment she couldn't speak. Ryan never opened up like this or ever gave her a chance to help him. Tuf was different. She sensed it.

"Did you hit Colt or Beau?"

"What?" He blinked in confusion. "I don't think I did. They didn't say. I just wanted to run until I couldn't feel that pain anymore."

"Ryan was the opposite. He'd become violent, throwing and breaking things. When I would try to calm him, he'd hit me and then leave the house and go to a bar and drink. The next day he'd apologize, but it happened over and over again. I stayed because I knew he couldn't control what was happening to him, but as the girls got older, I knew I'd have to go because he was starting to get angry at them." She took a burning breath. "I don't think you're like that. I've known you all my life and

I've never seen you do a violent thing, except ride buck-ing horses."

"Cheyenne..."

She heard the entreaty in his voice. "What's really bothering you?"

He looked down at her hand still on his sleeve. "I don't want to hurt you in any way. And I'm afraid I will."

"Tuf..."

"You've been through enough."

So have you.

His inner turmoil was a tangible thing. He was trying hard to live again, but the war kept pulling him back. She ached to help him. How? She couldn't help Ryan, so how could she help him? A sense of inadequacy swept over her.

He got to his feet. "I'll take a rain check on our date."

She stood, too, and a chill ran through her. Wrapping her arms around her waist, she said, "Maybe that's best."

Without another word, he swung toward his truck.

"Tuf."

He turned around.

"The girls are waiting for you. Please don't disap-point them."

They made their way to the barn, and the girls happily showed off on their horses. Her dad had spray painted the barrels bright yellow, and they slowly made the fig-ure eight around them. Afterward, Tuf walked away to his truck.

This time, she knew he wouldn't be coming back.

THE NEXT DAY after his run, Tuf quickly showered and changed into jeans and a Western shirt. He hadn't stopped at the Wright house. Not that he didn't want to. It would only hurt her more. Snapping the light blue chambray, he paused. Cheyenne had helped picked out the shirt. Maybe then they'd both known their lives would reconnect. The odds were against them, though. He was a mess. She was a mess. And there didn't seem to be a way around all the baggage they carried. It was best to end it now before their hearts were involved. He wasn't so sure that his wasn't already fully committed.

Strolling across the yard, he noticed Ace's, Colt's, Beau's, Duke's and Uncle Josh's trucks parked at his mom's office. It wasn't even seven yet. Something was up.

As he walked in, Colt said, "Finally, Tuf's here. We can start the meeting?"

His mom sat at her desk with Uncle Josh on her right and Ace on her left. The others were standing around the coffee machine.

Tuf made a face at his brother. "I wouldn't have run if I'd known y'all were going to be here this early."

"Hmm." Duke gave a lopsided grin. "I saw you outside Cheyenne Sundell's driveway."

He hadn't even noticed the headlights. He must have been really distracted. "I just stopped for a second." It was one of those moments he didn't want to admit to. He wanted to see her, but knew it was best if he just kept running.

"You seeing Cheyenne this early in the morning?" Colt asked with a mischievous glint in his eyes.

"Stop teasing your brother," his mother broke in. "He has a lot more muscle now, and I'm too old to be breaking up fights."

"Ah, Mom, we don't fight anymore," Colt told her.

"We just bait each other. Ace is best at it. He uses a verbal cattle prod to keep us in line."

"Someone has to," Ace said out of the corner of his mouth.

"See." Colt pointed a finger at his brother, laughing.

Their mother gave them a look that was as quelling as any words she could have spoken. The room became quiet and they pulled up folding chairs to sit around the desk. Sarah slipped on her reading glasses and shuffled through the papers in front of her.

"I spoke with Dinah and she said whatever we decide is fine with her. She has her hands full with the sheriff's job and her pregnancy." She laid her glasses on top of the papers. "Leah and I have gone over the books, and we're still not making ends meet. The economy is killing us. The price of feed and gas continues to rise. We have a balloon payment coming due on our note June first, and we're ten thousand short even with the money Tomas deposited into the ranch account. That's the bottom line. I really thought we could make a success of the contracting business, but all our problems with Midnight have sorely hurt us."

She leaned back in her chair, and Tuf thought how worried and tired she looked. "I'm not sure what to do now. I've thought about this for days, and the only option I see is to sell the three thousand acres we lease and all our cattle and rodeo stock. We could pay off the note, and everyone could start over with decent nine-to-five jobs. And, Ace, your vet business would be safe and unencumbered by ranch debt."

Stunned silence filled the room. No one knew what to say or do. Sarah Hart wasn't a quitter, but it felt as if she held a grenade in her hand and was about to pull the pin to end all their dreams.

Colt leaped to his feet. "Hell, no. I've worked too hard for too long for it to end like this."

"Aunt Sarah," Beau spoke up, "Tuf and I are set to rodeo, and Colt will be catching every rodeo close to home. If we can't earn ten thousand by June, then we're not fit to be called cowboys."

Duke got to his feet. "Aunt Sarah, I'll continue to help transport stock in my off time and help all I can around here."

"Sarah." Uncle Josh put his arm around his sister. "What's going on with you? I want to spend more time with Jordan, but I don't plan to abandon my duties to Thunder Ranch."

"Yeah, Mom, are you not feeling well?" Ace looked closely at their mother.

"I feel fine." She glanced at family photos hanging on the wall. "I'm just feeling a little melancholy." Her eyes swung to a family picture on her desk. "None of you know what day it is, do you?"

That only confused them further.

"It's John's and my fortieth wedding anniversary. We were so young when we got married and money was tight. Land was cheap back then and we saved to buy our own place. Every extra dollar went to buy more land. We lived in a small trailer and survived on beans and rice. It was a struggle but we did it. Cattle prices were good and we started to make money. When I became pregnant, we decided to build the house we wanted. We brought Aidan home to the new house." She paused for a second. "I can't help thinking that I'm back where I started—struggling. I want better for my kids and nephews, so I decided to give you boys a choice. That's what this is about."

Tuf rose to his feet. "No choice, Mom. We're the Harts and the Adams, and we're not looking for a way out. We're in this for the long haul. I know I didn't do too good in Bozeman, but like Dad used to say, 'You get bucked off, you pick yourself up and do better next time.' That's what I plan to do, so stop worrying. If worse comes to worst, I'll sell my truck. But I don't think I'll have to do that. As you know, Midnight did very well at the rodeo."

"That's a small thing, son. The horse could get hurt, as he has before."

"Have you seen how Colt takes care of that horse? He treats it like one of his kids. And Cory Kinney, an experienced cowboy who made it to nationals last year, couldn't stay on after the first buck. That's going to spread around the circuit, and cowboys are going to want to test their skill on the horse. Midnight will gain attention, and Thunder Ranch will gain more rodeo contracts and breeding fees. It's not the ending, Mom. It's the beginning."

"I agree with Tuf." Ace stood. "I know I was worried about Midnight being injured, but Colt has proven he can control the horse. I don't think there's a need for a vote. You know how we all feel, but you have the right to outvote us. What's it going to be?"

For the first time, a smile spread across his mom's face. "I say I got the answer I really wanted. You boys have turned into fine young men and I'm proud of you." She got to her feet. "Flynn is helping Aidan today and I'm playing Grandma." The worry in her blue eyes vanished.

Uncle Josh followed her to the door. "I'll bring Jordan over. She loves babies."

Ace moved to the computer. "We have to figure out what we have to do to ease Mom's mind."

"Let's check rodeo schedules and see where we can make the most money," Tuf suggested.

For the next thirty minutes, they debated rodeos. "Right now the best money is down south, mainly Texas," Colt said.

Ace pondered this. "Tuf and Beau, you can head south. Colt can rodeo here in Montana, South and North Dakota, and Wyoming. That's closer to home. How does that sound?"

"Like a plan," Colt said, "but my rodeo time is limited because of Midnight. The more we get him out there, the more his reputation is going to grow."

"Yeah, we have to consider that, too." Ace pondered some more. "When Midnight bucks, I want you there."

"I plan to be." Colt nodded.

"Okay. The goal is to make as much money as possible."

"We got it," Tuf said, and he and Beau spent time on the computer planning their schedule.

Later he helped with the broncs and the bulls. Then he checked on the cows. When he returned to the house, his mom was playing with Emma, smiling. She was so different than she was this morning. The worry had been lifted from her shoulders. He would make every rodeo he could to earn money to ease her mind. And to make up for all the years he wasn't here.

BEFORE TUF LEFT to rodeo, he saw a counselor at the Veteran's Administration in Billings. He was never good at opening up about his feelings, but he knew if he wanted to be whole again he had to talk.

Since the counselor had his records from the navy hospital in Maryland, he was already aware of Tuf's story, so he tentatively began to tell the counselor about the recent nightmare, and about Cheyenne and the girls. He came away with mixed feelings. The man agreed with the counselor in Maryland—Tuf had something deep inside him that he didn't want to face. After an hour of sharing brutal war memories, it became clear that whatever was bothering him was buried so deep he might never be able to reveal the pain—even to himself.

But the doctor urged him to remember the good things going on in his life, especially his family and rodeoing. And he encouraged him to continue to talk to Cheyenne, but Tuf didn't know if that was possible. At least not until he got his head straight.

CHAPTER TWELVE

THE NEXT MORNING he and Beau saddled up, so to speak, and headed out to hit the rodeo circuit. Tuf hugged his mom, said goodbye to his brothers and slid into the driver's seat.

As they passed the Wright property, he noticed the kitchen light was on. Cheyenne was making jewelry in her green robe and bright slippers. In his mind's eye, her beautiful features and intense concentration were clear, as were the tiny freckles across her cheekbones and nose.

"Why are you slowing down?" Beau asked.

"What?"

"If you want to stop and see Cheyenne, that's okay."

"No. We're just friends."

"Really?"

"Yep."

"From your expression I'm guessing you wish it was a lot more."

"Right now I'm focusing on rodeoing." It wasn't a lie—just not the exact truth.

"If you say so, coz." Beau pulled his hat over his eyes and went to sleep.

After a hundred miles, they switched drivers. Beau sang with the country tunes blaring from the radio. Tuf closed his eyes and tried to sleep, but he kept seeing Cheyenne's face.

On the way to Jackson, Mississippi, for the Dixie National Rodeo, they stopped for small-town rodeos in Wyoming, Colorado, Kansas and Oklahoma. It wasn't much money, but it helped to hone his skills and also helped to pay for food and motel bills. By the time they reached Jackson, he was ready.

The first night he was the sixth cowboy to ride. As always, Tuf had his equipment checked. The rowels had to be filed down so as not to hurt the horse. The stands were full and eager chatter resonated around the arena. Manure and rawhide were familiar scents. The bang of the chutes. The buzzer. It was rodeo time.

His muscles tensed before a ride. Donning his protective vest, he waited for the signal. Standing in the cowboy-ready area, three cowboys walked up to him. He recognized them: Cory Kinney, Jesse Hobbs and Trey Watson. They were dressed like Tuf, except each had their own signature chaps.

"Hey, didn't you ride in Bozeman?" Jesse asked.

"Yeah."

Jesse made the introductions.

"I'm Tuf Hart from Roundup, Montana." They shook hands.

"Wait a minute." Cory Kinney stepped forward. "Your family owns that black stallion."

"The Midnight Express."

"Cory's still talking about him." Trey laughed.

"That horse is powerful," Cory said. "Do you know where he'll buck next? I'd like another chance at him."

"I'll ask my brother." Tuf knew this would happen. News of Midnight was getting around. That was good for Thunder Ranch.

"This is my cousin Beau Adams," he said.

"Any kin to Duke Adams?" Cory asked.

"My brother," Beau replied.

"What happened to him? I don't see him on the circuit anymore."

"He got married." Beau shifted uneasily. Even though he'd come to grips about Duke's decision, there were times Tuf knew it still bothered him. But because of Beau's own marriage, he understood Duke's motivation a little better.

"Man, he let a woman mess with his head."

Before Beau could reply, Trey asked, "Where y'all headed next?"

"Texas."

"We are, too. Maybe we can buddy up and share expenses and fees."

"Fine by me." Tuf loved that about cowboys. They were always friendly and looking for ways to save money. But he worried about the sleeping arrangements and the nightmares.

"Great." Trey nodded. "I drive a 2003 Dodge and it's always breaking down. Probably because it has two hundred thousand miles on it. You drive anything better?"

"I have a decent truck."

The first rider was climbing the chute and they moved closer to watch. When it was Tuf's turn and he slid onto Black Widow, he heard the announcer. "Now we have a young cowboy from Roundup, Montana. He's a former marine and new to the circuit. Let's give a round of applause for Tuf Hart."

He worked his hand into the handle while Black Widow moved restlessly, eager to buck.

"How do they know that?" Tuf asked Beau, who was helping him with his rigging.

"Word gets around, I guess." Beau leaned away. "This horse bucks wild. Be prepared for anything. Just maintain your rhythm."

It was a grueling week and the competition stiff. He finished third behind Cory and Trey and in the money. He was pleased. But it took a toll on his body as every muscle screamed for relief.

Later, they met the other cowboys and headed for Texas. There was a getting-to-know-each-other period. The cowboys teased Beau because he was a bull rider, and he took it all in good nature.

Every night Tuf worried he'd have the nightmare and scare the cowboys to death. But his luck was holding.

Their next stop was San Angelo, Texas, ten days of nonstop rodeoing. He and Cory were neck and neck through the whole event. Cory edged him out on the last night with an 88 ride. But Tuf still placed in the money, and he was able to send almost all of it home to his mom. He kept just enough for gas, food and lodging, which was much cheaper since his new friends were sharing the cost.

Next rodeo was Fort Mohave, Arizona, then Marshall, Goliad, Nacogdoches and Lubbock, Texas. By now the cowboys had bonded, and once they saw Beau ride, they had a healthy respect for bull riders.

Tuf and Cory were fierce competitors, both determined to win and with a little luck make it to the finals in Vegas. Trey was the ladies' man, and after a lot of rodeos, he didn't make it back to the room until three or four in the morning. Jesse was easygoing and rodeos were fun to him.

But the constant traveling was getting to them. At the end of March, Tuf decided they needed a short break.

Beau was about as Sierra-homesick as he'd ever seen.
They dropped the cowboys in Mississippi, and he and
Beau headed for Montana. And home. The first thing
Tuf thought of was Cheyenne. As hard as he tried not to
think of her, she was always on his mind.

CLASS IN SESSION. That's what the sign said on the closed
kitchen door. After breakfast, Cheyenne let the girls play
for a bit, and then she dressed them and they went to
school, which just happened to be the kitchen. Once class
started, the girls knew they had lessons to do. Sometimes
they got sidetracked and wanted to laugh and play, but
Cheyenne was very strict. She wanted them to be ready
for kindergarten in the fall.

"Write your numbers," she said to Sadie.

"I already know my numbers."

"Write them anyway and then we'll count." Sadie
was very good with numbers and counting while Sammie excelled in reading and the alphabet. Sammie followed instructions easily while Sadie usually balked
until Cheyenne had to make her. They looked alike but
they definitely had different personalities.

Sadie laid down her pencil and crossed her arms
across her tiny chest. "I'm not writing no more numbers."

They had this battle almost every day. Sadie seemed
to have a need to test her, and Cheyenne's patience was
wearing thin. "Go to your room and sit in the time-out
chair. You will not get any gummy bears after lunch or
ride Toughie today. Go." She pointed toward the girls'
room.

Tears rolled from Sadie's eyes and sobs racked her

body. At the sight, Cheyenne's resolve wavered but she remained firm. "Go."

Sadie crawled from her chair, her little body shaking, and then she did a quick turn and threw herself at Cheyenne. Sobbing, she blubbered, "I'm sorry. I'm sorry."

Cheyenne picked her up and held her. "You have to mind Mommy."

"'Kay."

"I finished my number," Sammie said.

"Good, baby, you get an extra gummy bear after lunch."

That immediately grabbed Sadie's attention, and she scurried back to her chair and finished her numbers. Sitting back, Sadie asked, "Mommy, when is Tuf coming to see us?"

She wasn't startled by the question because they asked it every day. "I don't know, baby. He's at a rodeo far from home."

"But why doesn't he come home to see us? He likes us."

That was the hard part. Trying to explain something she didn't understand herself. Tuf didn't want to expose them to his nightmares, and Cheyenne wasn't sure if she could live with another marine with PTSD.

She thought of him constantly, though, and she'd been reading about PTSD on the internet. Tuf needed caring and support and for someone to listen when he wanted to talk. It seemed Tuf had done all the right things, but he was still struggling. She wondered if she'd let go of their relationship too quickly because of her own fears. Could she help him? Did she want to help him?

"I miss Tuf," Sammie muttered.

So do I.

In a short amount of time, she and Tuf had formed a special connection, and she missed him. She missed his early-morning knocks, his cold hands and warm heart.

IN THE AFTERNOON, her dad helped Austin at his store, so Cheyenne had the girls' lesson around the coffee table in the living room. They worked on the alphabet. The workbook had the alphabet listed, but several letters were missing and they had to fill in the blanks. Sammie breezed through hers.

Sadie paused. "Mommy, what comes after *G?*"

"Look at the picture below. It gives you a clue."

"It's a hat."

"Think about it and see if you can get the first letter of *hat.*"

Sammie whispered to her sister.

"Sammie," Cheyenne scolded.

"I got it. *H.*" Sadie beamed a big smile.

Cheyenne scooted to sit between them. She wanted Sadie to finish on her own.

Afterward, she gave them a choice. "What would you like to read today?"

"Brown Bear, Brown Bear," Sadie shouted.

"The Cat in the Hat," Sammie said.

"Go to your room and get the books."

They darted off, and she picked up their workbooks and pencils. After she stored everything away, her dad came in.

"Are you finished?" he asked.

"Yes. We're going to read, but we can do that in their room."

"I just came in for some water." He opened the refrigerator and pulled out bottled water. "Austin and I went over to the diner for a cup of coffee, and Beau called

Sierra. He and Tuf are on their way home for a couple of days. Sierra was all excited."

She tucked a curl behind her ear. "Is there a reason you're telling me this?"

"No." He screwed the top off the bottle and took a swallow. "The girls keep asking about Tuf."

"Dad." She sighed. "Tuf and I agreed not to see each other anymore. He has flashbacks just like Ryan and it's hard for both of us."

"But you want to see him?"

"Dad…"

"I'm going to the barn to feed the horses and then I promised Austin to help unload supplies." He looked at her. "I can see you're unhappy. That's all I'm saying."

As he left, she thought about what he said. She did want to see Tuf—more than she ever thought possible. But there was so much heartache standing between them. Was there a chance for them?

THE LAZY SUN hung low in the west as Tuf drove into Roundup. He dropped Beau at the diner and continued on. The girls played on the porch as he passed the Wright house. He had to force himself not to stop.

When he reached home, he left his laundry in the utility room and walked through the kitchen to the great room. The TV was on, and his mom sat with her feet up watching an old rerun of *Bonanza*.

"Now, that's what I like to see."

"Tuf!" His mom jumped up. "You're back." She hugged him.

"Yeah, for a couple of days. How's everything?"

"You boys are working so hard. I couldn't be prouder. Oh." She reached for her cell on an end table. "I'll call Ace and Colt and…"

He held up his hand. "We can meet in the morning. Don't interrupt their family time."

"Okay. Have you eaten?"

"No, but don't fix anything. I'm not hungry. I'll grab a sandwich later." He trudged upstairs and fell across the bed. His muscles ached and he was tired...and lonely. Empty. Lost, even. There. He'd admitted it. How could he feel that way in a big, loving family? Sometimes he'd felt like that as a kid. Ace and Colt were close in age, and Beau and Duke were inseparable. Dinah had her girlfriends. He was always the odd one out.

Joining the marines hadn't helped that feeling. It had only intensified. Maybe he was one of those people who would always be alone. But...when he was with Cheyenne, those feelings weren't there. He felt alive and full of dreams—for the two of them. And the munchkins. He slowly drifted into sleep

When he awoke, it was dark outside. After a shower, he walked over to the window and stared toward the Wright property. He wanted to talk to her so bad he hurt.

His cell buzzed and he hurriedly picked it up from the dresser. *Cheyenne.* He blinked, not sure he'd read the name right. It was her. He answered.

"Tuf, it's Cheyenne."

"Yes, I know." God, he'd know that voice anywhere. He heard it in his dreams.

"I heard you're back."

"Yeah. We leave again on Friday."

"Could we talk, please?"

"Cheyenne..." As much as he wanted to, he hesitated.

"I'd like to talk. That's all."

"I'll be right over." He couldn't keep resisting. But he wondered what they could talk about that wouldn't hurt both of them.

CHAPTER THIRTEEN

CHEYENNE PUT DOWN her phone and a shiver ran through her. She'd done it. She'd made a choice and followed her heart. Instinctively she knew they had something special, and she was willing to work on their relationship. But was he?

She applied a touch of lipstick and headed for the front porch. The girls were asleep and her dad was helping Austin unload supplies for the store.

In minutes he pulled into her driveway. He slid out of the truck and his long, lean legs strolled toward her. The porch light showed off his handsome face and muscled body. Sexy. Brooding. That worked. A flutter of excitement rippled through her lower abdomen.

Without a word, he sank down by her on the step.

"How are you?" she asked before her nerves got the best of her.

"A little tired," he replied and looked at her.

She melted into his tortured gaze. He was hurting. That was obvious. All her feminine instincts kicked in and she wanted to help him. Before one word could leave her mouth, his eyes dropped to the necklace around her neck.

"That's gorgeous. Did you make it?"

She glanced down at the stainless-steel chain with embedded crystals. "Yes. The cornflower-blue crystals are Yogo sapphires. I made a necklace for a lady using the stone, and I liked it so much I ordered the smallest crystals they had. It was all I could afford. They're mined in Rock Creek, Montana."

"They're almost as beautiful as your eyes."

She lifted an eyebrow. "My eyes are green."

"And brighter than any jewel."

She squinted at him. "You are tired."

"Mmm." He drew up his knees and rested his forearms on them. "What did you want to talk about?"

"Us," she answered without hesitation. "I've been doing a lot of thinking and reading about PTSD on the internet."

He turned his head, his eyes wide, but he didn't speak.

She rushed into speech before her brain could shut her up. "We've both admitted that we're attracted to each other and that we're afraid. I let fear control my reaction that day you said we shouldn't see each other anymore. I never wanted to get involved with another marine, especially one suffering from PTSD. But it's different with you and me. We've known each other all our lives, and I know in here—" she placed her hand over her heart "—that you would never intentionally hurt me. Do you think you can trust me not to fall apart when you have a nightmare? Do you think we can see each other again?"

She waited, her nerves stretched taut.

"The counselor said I have something deep inside me that I don't want to face. I feel it's something bad."

Scooting closer, she placed her hand on his tense arm. "Tuf Hart, I don't believe for one minute that you could do anything bad. No one would go back for that marine like you did. And help the man for two years? No one."

"Mmm."

Going on her own feminine intuition, she wrapped her arms around his waist and laid her head on his shoulder. Suddenly his arms cradled her gently against him. The moon engulfed them, and the stars twinkled with a delight that assured her she'd done the right thing. They needed each other.

She lifted her head and he bent his to steal a kiss. Except he didn't have to steal it. She gave freely, tasting the coolness that quickly turned heated and beyond her control. He kissed just as she knew he would—tenderly with a passion that promised pleasures beyond her wildest dreams.

His lips trailed a path to her forehead, and she sucked in air to cool her heated emotions.

"Are we more than friends now?" he asked.

"Definitely."

She stroked the stubble of his face and he caught her hand. "Are you sure, Cheyenne?"

"Yes. Just don't shut me out." She reached up and gently touched his lips. He drew her closer and they shared a long kiss.

They sat cuddled together. Out of the blue, he started talking about the war. "I wish I could remember what torments me in my sleep."

"Don't worry about it so much."

The big ol' moon stared at them and silently lit a path of dreams for lovers. And it was heavenly. A long time later, Tuf got in his truck and drove away.

She wrapped her arms around her waist, watching his taillights disappear out of the drive. But he would return. Oh, yeah!

THE NEXT MORNING Tuf was up early, as usual. Last night there were no nightmares, just visions of Cheyenne's red hair splayed across his pillow. He was acting crazy and it felt good. For some time it had seemed as if a vise was clamped tight around his heart and he couldn't breathe or react in a normal way. It hurt too much.

He was finally free of the restriction. She didn't mind his nightmares. She had accepted him the way he was. He spent every minute of the day with Cheyenne and the girls. Cheyenne gave the twins a day off from school, and they rode their little hearts out for him, showing off. Sammie was a little daredevil at times. She was finally breaking out of her shell.

They had a late lunch at the diner, and the girls giggled and chatted like four-year-olds. Looking across the booth at Cheyenne, he saw his future. And it was normal and real. Something he'd thought he'd never have, but she was willing to take a chance on him. He was willing to meet her halfway and more.

All too soon it was time to leave. He held her, leaning against his truck. "We need time alone," he whispered against her lips.

"Next time you're home," she promised. "It will be X-rated."

After a long, heated kiss, Tuf drove away with that thought in his mind.

Tuf and Beau had to be in Logandale, Nevada, for the Clark County Fair and Rodeo. From Nevada they headed to Corpus Christi, Texas, and then on to Old Settlers Reunion rodeo in Cheyenne, Oklahoma. The grueling schedule was taking its toll on them. Beau almost got trampled by a bull in Oklahoma and Tuf injured his shoulder, but he and Beau went on to the next rodeo. They ate junk food and sometimes slept in the truck.

They both were feeling the strain of constant rodeoing. And eager to get home.

Dusk crept over the landscape as they rolled into Roundup. Tuf dropped Beau at the diner and sped home. He talked to his mom, showered and changed clothes, and was on his way to Cheyenne's in record time.

His cell buzzed. Cheyenne. He'd talked to her about fifteen minutes ago. He hoped nothing was wrong.

"When are you leaving?" she asked.

"I'm on my way."

"I'll be waiting at the gate."

"Why?"

"If the girls see you, we won't be able to get away."

"Oh. Are they staying with Buddy?"

"Yes. They're gonna watch a movie. I'll explain later. Just hurry."

He zoomed down Thunder Road and his headlights caught her standing at the gate. She was beautiful in jeans, boots and a brown leather jacket. Her red hair was up and she was waving. He felt a kick to his heart. He couldn't believe how much he'd missed her. Before the truck came to a complete stop, he jumped out and wrapped his arms around her, pulling her tight against him. A delicate fragrance reached him and for a moment he just held her.

He ran his hands up her back beneath her jacket. "Oh, God, you feel so good."

She kissed his neck. "You feel pretty good, too."

Slightly turning his head, he caught her lips, and the coolness of the night vanished in the wake of heated emotions. She took his hand. "I have someplace much better in mind."

They crawled into the truck, and he couldn't resist stealing another kiss. "Where to, lady?"

"Billings."

"What?"

"I promised you a night alone, and I've booked a room at a hotel there."

He almost ran into the ditch, but he corrected quickly. "Are you sure?"

She cocked an eyebrow. "I am. How about you?"

"I'll see if I can make this thing fly."

She laughed that laugh that warmed his heart. On the way they talked about their lives. He'd talked to her every day, but it was much different in person. He could look at her, touch her.

"The girls are going to be so excited you're home."

"I can't wait to see them."

"You'll see a big difference. The horses and, of course, you got their minds on something besides their father. They never ask to go to his grave anymore. That worries me a little, but in other ways I feel it's good."

"It is." He reached out to touch her cheek, and she caught his hand and kissed it.

"They spent an afternoon with Dinah and Austin, and Dinah said they didn't ask for me once."

She gave directions, and he pulled into a hotel parking lot and found a spot. Hand in hand they went inside. The hotel was nice with large glass windows in the lobby decorated in a Western theme with Montana wildlife scenes and horse sculptures.

"Are we Mr. and Mrs. Jones?" he whispered in her ear.

She smiled. "Behave." The clerk at the counter gave

her a key and they walked to the elevator. "The guy looked at me funny. I feel wicked."

In the elevator, he took her in his arms and kissed her. "I'm feeling rather wicked myself."

She stared at him with luminous eyes. "Don't tell me you haven't taken a girl to a hotel before."

"No. Well, not lately."

"Then we're leading very boring lives." She took his hand and led him down the red carpeted hall and stopped at their room number. "And that's about to change." She swiped the card across the door handle, and they went inside. The room was large with a king bed, sofa and a huge bath with a Jacuzzi. She glanced at her watch. "Home for the next two hours."

For the first time, he noticed she was nervous. A tiny vein in her neck pulsed wildly. He cupped her face. "You don't have to be nervous with me."

"It's just…"

"What?"

"After Ryan, I thought I would never have these feelings again."

"What feelings?" He found he was holding his breath.

She rested her head on his chest. "Overwhelming feelings. I think about you all the time, and it makes me do crazy things, like book a hotel room. But…but I feel that way because…because I love you. I probably have since high school."

His heart pounded so fast it seemed as if it sailed right through his chest into outer space. He lifted her chin so he could look into her eyes. "I love you, too. There's never been another girl for me."

"Oh, Tuf." She stepped back and let her jacket slide to the floor. Then she pressed herself against him. Every soft curve and angle sent his blood pressure soaring. He gently turned her and fell backward onto the bed. Her laughing green eyes stared down at him.

"Undo my shirt," he said huskily.

"That's easy." With one jerk, the snaps flew open, leaving his chest bare. She paused as she saw his bruised shoulder.

"I landed on it. It's fine."

"Tuf…"

"Shh. Kiss me." Her hands and lips touched his skin, and he groaned, quickly pulling her top over her head.

As their lips met, he thought this had to be the best night of his life.

A BUZZ WOKE CHEYENNE. Her cell alarm. She stirred against Tuf, loving the feel of his naked skin against hers. It was time to go, but it was hard to move with this heavenly lethargic feeling clinging to every muscle in her body.

She'd opened her heart to the most wonderful man, the way she should have ten years ago. She never thought she could love again. So much of her pride had been destroyed in her marriage. With Tuf it was different. She trusted him with her heart and her girls. She wasn't quite sure how that had happened so quickly, but Tuf's compassion for other people pulled her in like a big, hungry fish.

The most important factor was he was willing to talk about his PTSD. He wasn't shutting her out, and he listened to her stories about her defunct marriage without judging her. They'd found a way to connect, and it was oh, so great.

She lovingly stroked his dark hair from his forehead.

He opened one eye. "Did I hear a buzz? Or is that sound stuck in my head from so many rodeos?"

"I set my cell alarm. I want to get home by ten." She kissed his forehead, his nose. "That's Dad's bedtime and he won't go to bed unless I'm there, in case the girls wake up."

He hauled her into his arms and kissed her until she was limp with wanting. "Tuf…"

"I know." His lips trailed to the freckles across her cheekbones. "I couldn't resist."

They helped each other dress, and it was more titillating than it should have been. Finally, they were in the truck and they drove into her dad's driveway at five minutes to ten. The house was in darkness except for a lamp in the living room. Arm in arm they walked to the front door.

"Tonight was better than making an eight-second buzzer," he whispered against her lips.

She giggled. She couldn't help herself. "Tuf Hart."

"What? My whole life is defined by eight seconds."

"I hope it's not when we're making love."

"Oh, hell, no."

They laughed and held on a little while longer. "We have a family meeting in the morning to discuss finances, but I'll be here as soon as I can." He cradled her in his embrace. "Thanks for tonight."

"The start of many," she breathed into his neck.

"I better go, but I don't want to."

"Tomorrow," she said before he kissed her one last time and strolled to his truck.

Slowly, she went inside. Her dad was asleep in his chair, but he awoke the moment she opened the door.

"Have a good time?" He pushed to his feet.

"Wonderful. Are the girls asleep?"

"Like angels." He took a step toward the hallway and stopped. "You couldn't find a better man than Tuf Hart in the whole of Montana, and I'm glad you two are back together but, girl, take it slow. He's wounded on the inside and that takes time to heal. Just be careful."

"I will." She walked to the girls' room, straightened their covers and kissed them good-night, but all the while she was thinking about what her dad had said. Tuf *was* wounded on the inside, and she wasn't naive enough to think that love could heal that deep of a wound. But it could help to ease some of his pain.

As she crawled into bed, a niggling doubt persisted. Could their happiness be destroyed as easily as it had begun?

CHAPTER FOURTEEN

TUF WOKE UP full of energy. He hadn't felt this good in years. After dressing, he took the stairs two at a time. The only thing he wanted to do this morning was see Cheyenne. She fulfilled every one of his fantasies and then some. How was he supposed to think about rodeoing today?

In the kitchen, he poured a cup of coffee. His mother gave him a strange look.

"What?"

"You're in a good mood this morning."

"Why? Because I got a cup of coffee?"

"No. You're whistling."

"Oh." He hadn't even realized he was doing that.

"You must have had a good time last night with Cheyenne."

He straddled a chair. "We did."

"Eat your breakfast. We have to go to the office."

As they walked over, Tuf thought he'd give Ready a workout today. He tried to do that every time he was home, but now he just wanted to see Cheyenne.

Ace and Colt were already there. Beau and Uncle Josh strolled from Uncle Josh's house with a coffee cup in their hands. There was a round of good-mornings and his mom took her seat. After everyone had coffee, Sarah opened her ledger.

She shoved her glasses onto her nose. "Leah has all this on the computer, but I still like it on paper where I can see it. That's the way John and I did it for years, and it's hard to break old habits." She squinted at the open ledger. "You boys have been doing a wonderful job, but we're still short. I have no doubt, though, with the way Tomas and Beau are riding, that we'll make the note payment."

There was a round of high fives.

"But we've incurred more expenses. Josh and I purchased two one-year-old bulls out of the same line as Bushwhacker. They were a good price and I felt we shouldn't pass it up. Improving our stock with fresh blood is important. Also, we had to put new tires on the cattle carrier and gas prices have gone up once again, but I'm still optimistic. And Midnight is doing very well rodoeing thanks to Colt and his management of the horse. We get calls every day from cowboys wanting to know where he'll be bucking. They want a chance at the black stallion. I'm happy to say my instincts and Aidan's are paying off."

"Hot damn, I love good news." Colt grinned.

"But we have to keep doing what we're doing." His mom made that very clear.

"Don't worry, Mom," Ace said. "I think everyone realizes that."

"Yep." Tuf pulled up a chair. "Beau and I are making every PRCA-sanctioned rodeo we can. At the start of Cowboy Christmas in July, we'll make the big-money rodeos that count to build our points. With some luck, we'll make the big show in Vegas. If not, we'll still be earning money."

"Yeah," Beau added, "if I have to stay away from Sierra, I want to make it count for something."

"I appreciate what everyone is doing, but we have a long way to go."

Everyone knew that, and their focus was on one thing—saving Thunder Ranch.

CHEYENNE HAD A PLAN—to spend time alone with Tuf today.

She hurried around her bedroom, which was a chore in itself because it was cluttered. A trail led to the bed and a closet. Jewelry-making supplies occupied every other inch. Beads, stones, wire, spacers and tools littered her worktable pushed against one wall. Precious stones, jewels, supplies and expensive chains filled an armoire on the other wall. Next to it, boxes sat on the floor waiting to be mailed. On the far wall were her desk and computer. A dresser with her clothes was on the other side of the bed. The bed partially blocked a double window. Cramped and small, but it was all she had. What would Tuf think of all the clutter?

For a man who didn't care what color shirt he wore, he probably wouldn't even notice. That's why she loved him. He had a unique way of looking at the world. He didn't sweat the small stuff.

She brushed her hair and let it hang loose around her shoulders. Tossing the thick strands, she picked up a green flower clip she'd made and put it in her hair. Her freckles were naked just the way he liked them. As she applied lipstick, she heard a truck. She hurried to the front door.

Her attention was on Tuf getting out of his vehicle. Heavens, he was handsome and sexy with his long legs and muscled body. His Western shirt stretched across his broad shoulders and the Wrangler jeans were oh, so deliciously tight, fueling her imagination, which didn't need any fuel at all. He moved in a slow, easy stride, like a cowboy. She fanned herself and laughed at the same time. An aspirin might be required. She had it that bad.

Tuf bounded up the steps and gently pushed her inside, closing the door. His kiss was sweet, warm and intoxicating. Her head spun.

Between heated kisses, he asked, "Where's everyone?"

"Dad took the girls to buy more horse cookies from Angie and then they're going to the feed store to buy feed for the horses. After that, they're going for ice cream." She held up two fingers. "We have two hours."

He grinned and threw his hat onto the sofa. "I love a woman with a plan."

Tuf never noticed the clutter. His eyes were on her. Cupping her face, he slowly kissed her until she trembled with weakness. All thought left her. They discarded their clothes quickly and soon they were skin on skin, their hands and lips touching, caressing, stroking. She wasn't even aware of them moving to the bed, but she was very aware of his strong body, hot kisses and warm, erotic emotions shooting through her.

A long time later, they lay entwined and he stared into her eyes. "You're beautiful."

"So are you." She touched his bruised shoulder. "Does it hurt?"

"It's a little sore."

Caressing his shoulder, she suddenly stopped. "Your right arm is swollen a little. I didn't notice that last night."

"Maybe." He shrugged. "It gets some wear and tear trying to hold on to a bucking bronc."

"I'll get some ice. It'll help with the swelling." She slipped into a lightweight robe and hurried to the kitchen for a bowl of ice. In the bathroom she grabbed some towels.

After placing some ice cubes in a hand towel and twisting the ends, she straddled his back and massaged his shoulders with the ice pack until her fingers were numb. She placed the ice in a bowl on the nightstand and continued to massage his back.

"How's the rodeo circuit?" she asked.

"Good. Kinney, Watson and Hobbs are the best bareback riders in the country, and I'm finally getting numbers to match theirs."

"I'm so proud of you." She ran her hands down his back, loving the tautness of his skin, his corded muscles. "Feel better?"

"Mmm. You have angel fingers and they've awakened more urgent needs." He reached around and pulled her down beside him and quickly covered her body with his.

Later, she kissed his sleep-filled eyes. "Sleepy?"

"I sleep very little. That's when I'm weak and the nightmares take over."

"Oh, Tuf." She wrapped her arms around his neck. "You don't have to be afraid with me. I can handle the nightmares. Just don't shut me out."

He stared at her for a moment, his dark eyes guarded, and then he laid his face on her neck. "I love you." Almost instantly, he was asleep.

She stroked his hair, loving him more than she ever thought possible. "I love you, too," she whispered and vowed to help him through his fear. The only thing that frightened her was losing him.

THE NEXT DAY, Tuf took time to go into Billings to see a jeweler for an engagement ring for Cheyenne. He hadn't asked her yet, but they both knew it was only a matter of time. It had to be a Yogo sapphire because she loved them. He picked out a greenish-blue one and had it set in a platinum band. The ring wouldn't be ready for a couple of weeks. That was fine. He had the real thing. He had Cheyenne. Every spare moment he spent with Cheyenne and the girls. Their time alone was his little slice of heaven.

In May, Tuf and Beau were home again for a couple of days during the week. The two days passed quickly, and soon they were packing to leave again. Tuf threw his bag into his truck and noticed Ace's truck at the office. Something was up or Ace wouldn't be here this early. It was barely 5:00 a.m.

A wild neighing echoed through the ponderosa pines. What was wrong with Midnight?

He found his brother watching a computer screen.

"What's up?"

Ace glanced at him. "I'm watching Fancy Gal."

"Have you been here all night?"

"I went home for a couple of hours. Royce was here earlier. Fancy Gal's udder is tight and the foal has dropped. It could be any time or it could be later."

Tuf looked at the screen. They had webcams in the mare motel to monitor pregnant mares. Fancy Gal restlessly moved around. Suddenly she lay down in the hay.

Ace watched closely. When the mare stayed down, he leaped to his feet. "Call Flynn. Tell her to get over here…

fast. And call Colt and get him to calm down that stupid horse and let Mom know what's going on."

Tuf grabbed his phone and called. His mom arrived first in her bathrobe. "What's going on?"

He pointed to the monitor.

"Oh, my."

Colt burst through the door in jeans, T-shirt and house shoes. "What the…" He saw the screen and headed to calm Midnight. "I believe that damn horse is half-human."

Flynn rushed in, her hair everywhere, carrying Emma in a carrier. She handed Tuf the baby, who was sound asleep, and ran to help Ace.

His mom was watching the screen. "Ace will take care of Fancy Gal."

Tuf's cell buzzed and he sat the carrier on the desk. He saw it was Austin. "Hey, Austin."

"Tuf, I've been trying to reach your mom, but she doesn't answer."

"She's right here. What's up?"

"Dinah's in labor and I'm taking her to the clinic. I wanted your mom to know."

"I'll tell her. We'll be there as soon as we can." He clicked off, wondering if there was a full moon or something. "Mom, Dinah's in labor. They're on the way to the clinic."

"What?" She jumped up. "I've got to go. I have to be there for my daughter." She clutched her chest.

Tuf was immediately at her side. "Mom, what's wrong?"

She took a long breath. "I'm just excited. So much is happening at once."

Tuf wasn't so sure. "Where's your pills?"

"I'm fine, son."

Uncle Josh appeared in the doorway. "What's wrong with that damn horse?"

The agitated neighing continued.

"Fancy Gal is giving birth," his mom explained. "And Dinah's in labor, too. I've got to go."

"I'll drive you."

"Make sure she has her pills, Uncle Josh."

"Will do."

Colt charged back in. "I can't do anything with Midnight."

A big, slimy blob slid out of Fancy Gal, and Tuf and Colt moved closer to the screen. Ace and Flynn knelt in the hay doing their jobs, and Tuf and Colt couldn't see much. Ace and Flynn stood to watch the newly born black foal. Long legs twitched and the foal raised its wobbly head. After a moment it staggered to its feet. Fancy Gal rose to her feet and licked her baby.

Suddenly the agitated neighing stopped.

Tuf and Colt looked at each other. "I told you he's part human," Colt joked.

Ace and Flynn came into the office. "Everything went fine," Ace said. "Look at that foal. All black. Not a spot on him. I think Midnight has an heir. Hey, that's not a bad name—Midnight Heir." Ace looked around. "Where's Mom?"

Tuf told him about Dinah.

"You're kidding?"

"No. I'm on my way. Just didn't want to leave Emma."

"We're right behind you," Ace replied. "What a morning."

Tuf talked to Cheyenne on the way, and thirty minutes later the whole family stood outside Dinah's door.

The baby had been born ten minutes ago, and his mom and Buddy were inside getting to see their new grand-daughter. Soon they were all allowed in. Austin cradled the baby in a pink blanket. Beads of perspiration pep-pered his forehead and his hands shook.

"Everyone, I'd like you to meet the new member of the family—Aubrey Wright." He pulled back the blan-ket so they could see the baby. She had swirls of damp dark hair.

"Isn't she beautiful?" Dinah said from the bed. Her hair was wet and she looked pale.

Tuf squeezed Cheyenne's hand and walked over to his sister. "Just like her mother." He kissed her forehead. "Sorry, I've got to go."

"I understand," she said. "I was raised in rodeo time."

At the door, he squatted and hugged Sadie and Sam-mie. In front of everyone, he kissed Cheyenne and walked out. This time, leaving was harder than ever.

MAY PASSED IN a haze of roaring crowds, bucking horses and a damn buzzer that sometimes wrecked his whole day. His favorite part was going home to Cheyenne.

In June his mom made the note payment, and they celebrated with a barbecue in her backyard. The sum-mer day was beautiful with a lot of blue sky. It seemed right and perfect sitting and holding Cheyenne's hand as they watched the girls play with Jill, Davey and Luke. Emma sat in a stroller eating Cheerios.

The girls went home with Jill and Davey to watch a movie. Buddy stayed to talk to his mom, and Tuf and Cheyenne hurried to her house to make up for the days they'd be apart.

Cowboy Christmas, a time during June and July

where a cowboy could make a tremendous amount of money because of all the rodeos taking place, was about to start. Tuf wouldn't be home again until after Cheyenne Frontier Days in late July.

That night they tried to love long enough, strong enough, to make the memories last. But as he and Beau left for Reno, Tuf didn't know if he had enough strength to leave. He managed, though.

IN RENO HE came away with a win, and he broke into the top fifteen cowboys in the country for the first time. Kinney was firmly in the number-one spot.

They crisscrossed the country rodeoing, and they met up with Ace and Colt several times when Harts supplied stock to rodeos. So far Tuf hadn't drawn Midnight and he was beginning to wonder if that was ever going to happen. In late July, they ended up in Cheyenne, Wyoming, for Cheyenne Frontier Days. Midnight was scheduled to buck, and once again Tuf didn't draw the horse on any of his rides. The cowboys that did were eager for the chance.

Beau had broken into the top fifteen bull riders, and they both knew unless something drastic happened they were going to Vegas.

This victory he planned to celebrate with Cheyenne. They drove through the night and they cruised into Roundup in the wee hours of Monday morning. He dropped Beau at the apartment above the diner. Now all Tuf wanted was to hold Cheyenne.

CHEYENNE AWOKE TO the buzz of her cell. She glanced at the clock and picked it up at the same time—5:30 a.m. She had a text. I'm on my way. T

What? Tuf must have just gotten back from his rodeo trip. Jumping out of bed, she heard a light tap at the door. He was here!

Wearing pajama shorts and a tank top, she sprinted to the door and yanked it opened. Warm arms engulfed her and she melted into his embrace. Heated kisses rained on her lips, face and neck.

"I've missed you," he groaned.

"Me, too."

He wore jeans and a T-shirt and he hadn't shaved. She stroked his pronounced stubble. "Why aren't you sleeping?"

"I can't until I get my Chey-fix." His dark eyes were hooded, and she wondered if he was already half-asleep. She took his hand and led him to the sofa. They sank into the soft cushions, and he wrapped his arms around her and promptly fell asleep.

She eased out of his arms and gently put a cushion under his head. Then she lifted his boots to the sofa so he'd be more comfortable. She kissed his forehead and went to make coffee.

Her dad walked in with a frown. "Is that Tuf on our sofa?"

"Yes, crazy man hasn't had any sleep."

"When did he get here?"

"About five minutes ago. He needs some rest so let's be very quiet."

"What about the girls?" He poured a cup of coffee. "Once they see him, it'll be shouts, screams, laughs and giggles."

"I'll have to head them off. They usually wake up about six, so I have time to dress before they make an appearance." She dashed to her bedroom and quickly dressed in denim shorts and a green sleeveless knit top. Hearing little voices, she hurried to the girls' room.

"Mommy said Tuf's coming home tomorrow. Is today tomorrow?" Sammie asked her sister.

"I don't know," Sadie replied. "Let's ask her."

Before they could bolt for freedom, Cheyenne walked in and closed the door. Sammie sat in her bed. She didn't climb into Sadie's in the middle of the night anymore and she wasn't clingy. Sadie didn't run away anymore, either, and had accepted her father's death. All because of Tuf. He had made such a difference in their lives and in Cheyenne's heart. He'd made it easy to love again.

She picked up Sammie and sat on Sadie's bed. "I have a surprise."

"Tuf's here." Sadie made to jump off the bed, but Cheyenne grabbed her.

"I need you to listen. Okay?"

They nodded.

She put a finger to her lips. "We have to be very quiet."

"Why?" Sadie whispered.

"Tuf's asleep on the sofa. He's tired from rodeoing and he needs to rest."

Their mouths formed big O's.

"When will he wake up?" Sadie whispered again.

"I don't know, but we have to be very quiet so he can rest."

They put their heads together and did the whispering thing. "We can do it, Mommy," Sadie said.

Cheyenne had no doubt they could. Tuf was their hero. And hers.

She led them to the kitchen in their short cotton nightgowns. They stared at Tuf with their hands over their mouths just in case any words slipped out.

"Grandpa, Tuf's sleeping," Sadie murmured. "You have to be quiet."

Her father nodded with a smile.

She fixed cereal with a banana and juice. The girls' heads were together, and Cheyenne could hear what they were saying.

"What's Tuf gonna eat?" That was Sammie.

"He's sleeping. He can't eat, doofus."

"I'm not a doofus. You're a doofus."

Cheyenne held her finger to her lips and they started to eat. Her father got to his feet. "I'm going to the barn before I bust out laughing."

After breakfast, she herded them to their room. She dressed them in shorts and halter tops and then brushed their hair into pigtails and tied matching ribbons around them. After finding their flip-flops, she ushered them through the kitchen to the backyard. They'd made it without waking Tuf.

She sat on the porch swing as they played on their swing set. They had a small kiddie pool, which they ignored these days. Sarah's pool was much more inviting, and they often went with Jill, Davey and Luke. They were part of the Hart family, and the girls blossomed in the family environment.

School would start at the end of August. She'd enrolled them for kindergarten. Finally, they were ready to go, and Cheyenne was grateful her babies were now typical little girls. They'd gone to Billings to buy school clothes and supplies. With everything they bought, the girls had asked one question: "Will Tuf like it?" They measured everything by Tuf's opinion.

The girls sat in a swing side by side, talking. Their butts were so small they both fit. She wondered if they would always be this close. Would they always have a special language that only they understood? As they grew, would life change them? She hoped not too much. But somewhere along life's journey, she hoped to get them off pink and purple.

Tuf eased onto the swing beside her. "Hey, gorgeous."

She smiled into his dark, tired eyes. "Hey, you." She brushed the hair from his forehead. "Do you even remember coming here?"

"Some. I was tired, but I wanted to see you, and the next thing I remember is holding and kissing you. It was pretty good, too. I hope it was real."

"It was." Her hand caressed his growing beard. "I like this five-o'clock-shadow look. Sexy."

"Want me to keep it?"

"I just want you."

"Mmm. I hope we have plans for tonight." The wicked glint in his eyes caused her pulse to skitter.

"Dad's taking the girls to see their new cousin, Aubrey. They can't say her name so they call her Bre. Then they're going for supper at the diner." She kissed his cheek. "I'm so proud of you. You're one of the top bareback riders in the country."

"I have the aching muscles to prove it."

"I'll take care of that later." She winked. "Now you need to go home and get more rest so you'll be strong for tonight."

"You're teasing me."

"Yes."

He glanced toward the girls. "How long before you think they'll notice me?"

The girls sat with their legs stuck out and they were staring at the ground. Whatever they were staring at had their full attention.

"Must be a bug," she said. "They're frightened of them. It has to be a large one for them not to notice you."

"Mom…eeeek…Tuf!" Sadie leaped from the swing, quickly followed by Sammie. They jumped on Tuf, burrowing against him. For the next hour, he played with them. He swung them in the swings, played kick ball and rolled on the ground with them until all three were exhausted.

She fixed sandwiches for lunch and then put the girls down for a nap much to their protest. Tuf kissed them goodbye.

Watching him with her daughters, she knew she'd found the perfect man for them. Tuf hadn't said anything about marriage, but it was just a matter of time. Wasn't it? A seed of doubt tortured her. No. She wouldn't listen to it. Nothing could burst her bubble of happiness.

Nothing.

CHAPTER FIFTEEN

TUF HURRIED HOME, showered, shaved and changed clothes. He thought of not shaving, but he didn't want to mar Cheyenne's skin in any way. He should sleep, but he wasn't sleepy. Letting out a long breath, he allowed himself to feel the happiness inside. It was the best feeling in the world. He had it all: the woman of his dreams, two little girls he adored, a loving family and a run for a world title. Afghanistan was finally behind him.

His mom wasn't in the house so he walked to the office. Ace and Colt were there.

Colt grabbed him and shook his hand. "Congratulations, hoss. You're sitting at number six for now. You'll inch higher since you're not through rodeoing. That's pretty damn impressive, and you're going to ride in the rodeo of your life."

Ace echoed the sentiments. "You look a little tired, though."

"I feel great." His cell beeped and he reached for it. He had a text. The ring was finally ready. Tonight he was going to ask Cheyenne to marry him.

"I've got to go." He stopped at the door. "How are the finances…in a nutshell?"

"Good." Ace nodded. "You and Beau have built up a big sum, and come December we might make a large payment or actually be able to pay it off. Depends how well y'all do in Vegas and how much y'all put toward the ranch."

"We're paying it off. That's why Beau and I are riding so hard. And if Midnight wins the PRCA Bareback Bronc of the Year and makes it to the NFR, we can up his breeder fees."

"We're keeping our fingers crossed on that one," Ace said. "We won't know until October, but with his record we're almost certain he'll make the NFR."

"In two years." Colt held up two fingers. "We've put this struggling ranch in the black for the first time in ten years. Hell, we need to celebrate. Get drunk or something."

"Drinking is why this ranch was in a mess," Ace quipped.

Tuf knew that was a reference to their dad, but he couldn't dispute it. It was the truth. Somehow, though, it left an ache in his heart. He'd had a different relationship with their father than Ace and Colt. But above everything, they loved their father. Maybe in a different way, yet the love was still there. And they would be better men because of it.

"I've got to run. A beautiful redhead is waiting for me."

"Then what are you doing standing here?" Colt pushed him out the door.

In less than an hour he was in Billings and had the ring. He watched the blue-green Yogo sapphire sparkle. He hoped she loved it. Slipping it into a tiny velvet pouch the jeweler had given him to protect the ring, he let out a long sigh and placed it in his pocket. If he took the box in, she'd know what it was. He wanted to surprise her. This was it and he was never more ready.

He picked up red roses and a bottle of champagne and was at her house a little before four. The door was open, so he went in and stopped short. It was still daylight, but no lights were on—just candles burning on the coffee table, giving off a vanilla scent. The shades were drawn.

Cheyenne appeared in the doorway in a skimpy black negligee that showed off a lot of breast. Her red hair hung around her shoulders. His muscles tensed at her sheer beauty.

"Hey, cowboy." She walked toward him and he noticed her feet were bare—an odd thing to notice when his pulse was about to burst through his veins.

She stood on tiptoes to kiss him and his blood pressure edged up a few notches. The fragrant scent of the roses and her sexy smile blended into a beautiful picture of the evening ahead.

"If I didn't have my hands full, I'd ravage you right now."

She flipped her hair back and took the roses from him. "I'll put these in water. And thank you."

He followed her into the kitchen and held up the bottle of champagne. "Do you want this now or later?"

Settling the flowers into a vase filled with water, she shot him a teasing glance. "What do you think?"

"There's only one thing I want right now, and it's not liquor. I get high just looking at you in that skimpy thing."

Her eyes sparkled with glee. "You'll have to catch me first." She ran around the table and he followed, finally managing to corral her and swing her into his arms. With laughter and giggles smothered with heated kisses, he made his way to the bedroom and dropped her onto the bed. The laughter died away as he joined her.

The first long, drugging kiss faded into an afternoon of pleasure. Tuf fell asleep in her arms, never wanting this moment to end.

Sometime later, happiness dimmed with the sounds of war. Gunfire blasted all around him. His buddy Frank went down.

"Tomas, I'm hit."

He fired wildly at the insurgents as he dashed toward Frank and examined him. "It's a shoulder wound."

"It hurts."

Another marine dropped down beside them and they pulled Frank behind a boulder. "Stay here. We'll pick you up on the way down."

"Tomas!"

"Stay calm. We're waiting for mortar fire." Just then all hell broke loose as a U.S. attack chopper blasted the insurgents.

"Go. Go. Go!" Tuf shouted as they charged up the hill. They reached the top and faced the enemy. "No. No. No!" There was no other way. He had to save his life and the life of his unit. "No!"

"Tuf! Tuf! Tuf!"

Someone was calling him. A woman's voice. *Cheyenne!*

He forced himself awake and found he was at the foot of the bed, covered in sweat, his muscles tight, his hands balled into fists. Cheyenne cringed against the headboard, fear in her eyes. She held one arm against her as if to protect herself. A red welt marred her upper arm.

"Oh, God. Did...did I hit you?"

She crawled toward him. "You had a nightmare and I tried to calm you."

"Oh, no, I hit you."

"It was an accident. Let me hold you. It will be okay."

"Don't touch me." He jumped from the bed and reached for his jeans. "I'm bad for you. Can't you see that?"

"No. I just see a man who's hurting."

He shoved his arms into his shirt. "I saw the look in your eyes. You were afraid."

"Yes, but only for a moment. It brought back a lot of bad memories, but I know you're not like Ryan. You would never hit me in anger."

He stopped buttoning his shirt and faced her. "There's something bad inside me, Cheyenne. It's so bad I can't even think about it in the light of day. It only comes to me in horrifying dreams. I thought happiness had freed me from them, but it hasn't. The horror is still there torturing me, and until I know what it is, there is no future for us."

"What?"

"You were right. You should have never gotten involved with another marine. I'm sorry."

Her trembling hands tucked her hair behind her ears. "You don't mean that."

"Yes, I do." He shoved his bare feet into his boots. He didn't know where his socks were and he didn't care. He had to go. He had to run.

He looked into her eyes and all he saw was the fear. "I can't risk hurting you. I will not put you through that again."

"You're hurting me now."

"I'm sorry. I'm sorry." He hit the door, running to his truck and leaving everything he'd ever wanted behind.

CHEYENNE SAT PARALYZED, and then the trembling set in. Tears soon followed. They ran down her face and onto her hands. She kept wiping them away, but more followed. It was over. Their relationship was over. Just like that. Without warning.

His tossing and turning had awakened her. Then he started screaming, flailing his arms. She tried to hold him, comfort him, but one flailing arm caught her and knocked her against the headboard. All the times Ryan had hit her and she'd tried to protect herself flooded her and she didn't know what to do. She couldn't help him, just like she couldn't help Ryan. Except Tuf hadn't hit her deliberately. But it didn't make a difference. To Tuf it was the same thing.

Her stomach cramped and she wrapped her arms around herself, feeling a pain like she'd never felt before. She eased onto the tumbled peach comforter and let the tears flow until she had no strength left. This time she knew without a doubt she would not recover. Her heart had burst open with pain, and there was no way to put it back together again.

But for her daughters she would find the strength to go on.

Tuf parked his truck at the house and then ran into miles and miles of Thunder Ranch land. He ran until he had no air left to breathe and then he fell to the grass and stared up at the dark sky. Thoughts and emotions warred for dominance inside him but he forced himself not to think. When he could breathe again, he slowly walked home.

Darkness engulfed him and he welcomed it, but nothing could hide the turmoil eating at him. His mother was in the kitchen and he hoped to get past her. That wasn't possible. He hadn't been able to do it as a boy, and he couldn't do it now.

"Tomas, you're home early." She turned from the sink to look at him. "What's wrong?" Her mother's instinct zeroed in on his face.

"Nothing. I'm fine." He headed for the stairs.

"Tomas…"

Voices floated up from the kitchen. "Buddy, what are you doing here…and with a gun?"

Tuf paused at the top of the stairs.

"Where's Tuf? I'm gonna kill him. He hurt Cheyenne. He hurt her bad."

"What are you talking about?"

Tuf, tired and weary, took a few steps down the stairs to face Buddy. His mom, Ace and Colt stood behind Buddy.

He held his arms wide. "Go ahead, Buddy. Fire away. I deserve it."

Before Buddy could move, his mom jerked the shotgun out of his hand. "Nobody's killing anybody. Now tell me what's going on."

"I hit Cheyenne," Tuf said loud and clear.

His mother paled. Even from where he was standing he could see that. He couldn't stop hurting people.

"What?" Buddy seemed confused. "You hit Cheyenne. She didn't tell me that."

"Yes."

"You sorry…"

"Everybody calm down." Colt stepped forward and looked up at Tuf. "You had another nightmare, didn't you? And you hit her accidently?"

"Nightmare? What are you talking about, Colton?" his mom asked.

Colt sighed. "Tuf has flashback nightmares from the war. He had one when we were on the road. In his mind he's still fighting, trying to save his men. Beau and I could hardly hold him down."

"My son is hurting and no one told me. I do not like this and I will not have my sons keeping things from me."

Ace hugged his mother. "We'll talk about this later."

"You bet we will."

"C'mon, Tuf," Colt urged. "You know it was an accident. Cheyenne knows that, too."

Austin slipped into the room. Cheyenne must have called him.

"This can be worked out," Colt kept on.

"I hit her. Do you understand that? She was scared out of her mind, not knowing if I was going to hit her again. There's nothing acceptable about that to me. She doesn't deserve to live with someone like that, and that's all I'm saying. Now please leave me alone."

"Let's go, Dad." Austin put an arm around Buddy's shoulders, and Sarah handed Austin the gun. "What do you mean bringing a gun over here?"

"It's not loaded. I just wanted to scare him."

"You scared Sarah."

"I'm sorry, Sarah."

"Go home and take care of Cheyenne."

Buddy and Austin turned toward the kitchen. "What are we gonna tell those babies?" Buddy asked. "They worship him."

"Cheyenne will handle it, and she and Tuf will work this out."

Their voices faded as they went out the back door. He stared down at his mother and his brothers and then continued up the stairs. He paused when he was out of sight.

"Tomas, I want to talk to you."

"Mom." Ace's voice sounded stressed. "Tuf's running on empty and we need to give him some space."

"Why? He needs our love and support."

"But not right now. He has to sort this out on his own. We all know he loves Cheyenne, but he has to figure out that's all that matters. He needs time."

"My son needs me."

"Mom…"

"And why wasn't I told about these flashbacks?"

"Let's go to the kitchen and we'll talk about it."

Tuf went into his room and closed the door. He stood there feeling as though he was going to pass out from all the emotions churning in him. He backed against the wall and slid down it like a wet noodle. Drawing his knees up, he rested his forehead on them. Why was he always fighting that war? Why couldn't he wipe it from his mind?

He raised his head and stared straight ahead but saw nothing. His thoughts were inward. For the first time he forced himself to finish the dream. What was so terrifying on the top of that hill? So terrifying that it was lodged in the dark crevices of his mind, forgotten until he closed his eyes in deep sleep. What was it? All he remembered was the blasts of gunfire and then running down the hill to pick up Frank, the Afghan soldier, and check on Michael.

What was it? With the ball of his hands, he rubbed his eyes hard, but there was no answer. He was stuck in this hell that had no end.

The door opened, and Ace and Colt walked in. Colt sank down on one side of him and Ace on the other. They stretched out their legs and didn't say a word. No one spoke. It stayed that way for about fifteen minutes.

Finally, Ace said, "I can't believe Mom hasn't changed this room. It's the same as when you were twelve years old."

"Wonder if my room is the same," Colt mused. "I haven't been up here in ages."

"I'm sure Mom took down the naked women a long time ago," Ace retorted.

"Nah. She found them a week after I put them up and they're history. Your room is probably the same since you lived here until a year ago, but I bet that photo of Flynn is still hidden in your dresser."

"Nope. I took the picture with me when I moved."

The more his brothers talked, the more the pain loosened its grip.

Ace drew up his knees. "I remember how furious Dad was when you branded your furniture."

"Yeah. I was grounded for a month. I couldn't go to rodeos. That was tough."

"Did you buy the curtains and comforter?" Ace asked. "I can't remember."

"Hell, no. Mom and Dinah did that. Horseshoe sheets included."

"You still sleep on horseshoe sheets?" Colt was trying very hard not to laugh.

"Yes. What's wrong with that?"

"Davey has horses on his."

"Shut up." But from somewhere dark and deep within him where all the pain lived, a light found its way out. A light of laughter.

They laughed and it seemed so ironic for this traumatic day.

"You know, life wasn't so bad when we were kids," Colt added. "It was only later as Dad started drinking that life took a different turn, but we were still a family. Mom made sure of that."

Colt and Ace got up and each reached out a hand and pulled him to his feet.

"We're sorry you're hurting so much." Ace rubbed Tuf's shoulder. "Get some rest. You're dead on your feet. Tomorrow things will look a little better."

Colt threw an arm around Tuf. "Ace is right, and I don't say that often."

"Get some sleep," Ace said before the door closed.

Tuf fell across his bed fully clothed and with his boots on. He was so tired. He didn't have the energy to change. Sleep tugged at his eyes and he closed them, letting his mind take him wherever it wanted to go. Nothing mattered anymore.

Before the much-needed slumber claimed him, he saw Cheyenne's frightened face. It would be with him for the rest of his life.

CHAPTER SIXTEEN

THE NEXT MORNING, Tuf woke up still fully clothed and stiff. He hadn't moved all night and his shoulder was aching. He ripped off his clothes and took a hot shower.

He picked up his jeans to remove his wallet and loose change. He pulled out the small velvet pouch with Cheyenne's ring and his Silver Star. One was his past and the other he had hoped to be his future. He expelled a long breath. He placed the medal in the tray of buckles he'd won in his youth. The ring he slipped into his pocket, clinging to the last shred of hope he had.

To accept a future, he had to let the war go. He knew that as well as he knew his own name. And he prayed it was a possibility.

Over the next couple of days, Tuf's family gave him his space just as they had when he'd first come home. The first morning, his mom hugged him and told him she loved him, and that was it. No one pressured him. He spent that morning with his counselor going over every detail of the dream. With each dream, the details often changed, but his traumatic reaction when he reached the top of the hill was always the same.

They didn't have any breakthroughs, but at least he was talking about it. He threw himself back into rodeoing and helping out the family. They carried a load of stock for a rodeo in Great Falls, Montana, and Tuf,

Beau and Colt entered to ride. Tuf and Beau wanted to maintain their ranking. After unloading and checking in, Tuf walked around talking to some of the cowboys he'd met on the circuit.

A lot of vendors were setting up near the entrance. His eyes zeroed in on red hair. *Cheyenne.* He should walk away, but he couldn't move. His eyes were glued to her face. She looked tired, worried. He'd done that to her.

Angie had a booth next to her. Luke helped his mom put out her horse cookies, and the girls chatted to Cheyenne as she arranged her jewelry and a large mirror. Buddy stood some distance away talking to someone, but he glanced at Tuf. As much as Tuf knew he should leave, he couldn't make himself do that. He couldn't tear his eyes away from her face and the sadness he saw there.

At that moment Sadie noticed him. "Tuf!"

Cheyenne's head jerked up, and all her hurt was leveled at him. The bottom of his stomach gave way and he felt sick. Sick with himself. Sick at the pain he'd caused her. And sick at life's cruel blows.

He squatted to catch the girls and held them tight as they showered him with kisses.

"Mommy's here." Sammie pointed. "She's selling jewelry and we gonna watch the rodeo." He walked them back to Cheyenne.

Angie saw them coming. "Luke, take the girls to Buddy so y'all can find a seat before the rodeo starts."

"Okay, Mom." Luke took their hands and led them toward Buddy.

Angie busied herself talking to a lady who had questions about her horse cookies. They left him and Cheyenne staring at each other with a gulf as wide as Montana between them.

She wore a short-sleeved blue blouse, and he noticed a dark bruise at the hem of a sleeve—where he'd hit her. Tugging the sleeve lower, she tried to cover it. But it didn't work. How many times had she tried to cover bruises when she was married to Ryan? Nausea roiled in his stomach.

He fought the feeling. "How are you?"

She didn't answer. Her hand shook slightly as she rearranged her jewelry.

"I'm sor..."

"Don't say you're sorry." Her green eyes flared. "That doesn't even begin to solve anything. You want to know how I feel? I'll tell you. I feel betrayed by a man I love more than life itself. You didn't trust me enough to handle the situation. You gave up on *us*."

"I didn't give up on us. I will never do that. But you have to understand that the dreams will probably get worse and I could really hurt you. I couldn't live with that. I refuse to live with that. I have to get my head straight before I have a future to offer you. I'm not doing this intentionally. It's hurting me just as much as it's hurting you." He turned and strolled toward the chutes, feeling about as low as any man could get.

Colt met him. "What are you doing?"

"Nothing."

His brother fell in step beside him. "You hit her. It was an accident. You got to stop fighting that war in your head and let Cheyenne help you."

He stopped and faced Colt. "If I hurt her more than I already have, it would kill me. Don't you understand that?"

Colt sighed. "Aren't you already dead inside without her?"

Tuf stormed off to the chutes, but his brother was right. There was no life without Cheyenne.

CHEYENNE SHOOK SO badly she had to sit down.

Angie was immediately at her side. "Are you okay?"

"No," she replied. "He's hurting and I can't help him. That hurts even more."

"I'm sorry." Angie handed her a bottle of cold water.

She gulped a swallow and held on to the bottle as if it could save her. From what? She wasn't sure. Maybe from the pain.

After the encounter, Cheyenne tried to see Tuf's point of view. But all she could see was that he didn't love her enough to trust her. Luckily, she was busy and didn't have time to dwell on her shattered heart. The nights were bad. All she could think about was him.

August was big with rodeos in Montana, and she and Angie tried to make every one. She would now have two kids in school, and she would need every penny. Sometimes she would see Tuf at the rodeos, but they made no move to talk to each other. There was nothing left to say.

The next week, Cheyenne and the girls went to meet their new teacher. She thought the girls would cling to her, but they surprised her by being talkative. They sat in small chairs in Miss Huddleston's classroom. She was young and full of energy, and Cheyenne's daughters took to her immediately.

"What do you like to do?" Miss Huddleston asked them.

"We like to ride our horses," Sadie replied.

"Tuf taught us," Sammie added.

"Who's Tuf?"

Sammie was quick to answer. "He's gonna be our daddy."

"Oh."

"Our real daddy died," Sadie informed her. "We love Tuf." They both nodded their heads. Cheyenne sat in shock. She had no idea her daughters thought this. But why not? They all loved him.

It didn't stop there, though. On and on they talked about Tuf until Cheyenne wanted to tape their mouths shut. The teacher seemed dazed because Cheyenne had told her the girls were shy and Sammie rarely talked. One of the reasons she wanted the girls to stay together instead of in different classes. They made a liar out of their mother in true fashion. She had a feeling that was going to happen a lot now that they were more outgoing and unafraid.

In September, the girls had their fifth birthday. Cheyenne had a small party at the house with Jill, Davey and Luke. Dinah and Austin came, too, with Bre. The girls showed off on their horses at the stable. As they were returning to the house, Tuf drove into the driveway.

"Tuf!" the girls screamed and raced to meet him.

"I knew you'd come," Sadie said. He pulled two large packages out of the backseat and handed them to the girls. They sat on the steps and ripped into them.

"O-oh." Sadie's mouth formed a big O. "It's beau-ti-ful. What is it?"

Cheyenne looked down at the items. "It's a horse blanket." The main color of one was purple interwoven with yellow, orange, green and brown colors. The other was pink with the same motif. On a corner their names were stitched. Cheyenne had never seen horse blankets like that. Tuf must have had them specially made and ordered months ago.

"I'm putting it on my bed," Sadie announced.

"Baby, it's for your horse." Cheyenne tried to explain it to her.

"I don't care. It's mine, not Toughie's."

"I'm keeping mine, too. It has my name on it." Sammie mimicked her sister, and they went into the house to put them on their beds.

An awkward silence stretched. No one knew what to do.

"Say hi to your niece," Dinah finally said to Tuf.

Tuf lifted the baby from his sister's arms, and Cheyenne noticed how comfortable he seemed holding four-month-old Aubrey. He would make a wonderful father if only he'd allow himself that honor.

Tuf left soon after and they hadn't even spoken. They were at least twelve feet apart at all times. She wanted to reach out and touch him, feel the heat of his skin against hers. She wanted it so badly she hurt.

Life would be easier if they didn't see each other all the time, but they were connected by family and that wasn't possible. Back in July when it was clear Tuf and Beau were going to make it to the finals in Vegas, Sarah had booked a block of rooms for the family and Cheyenne, the girls and Buddy.

She couldn't change her plans now because it would hurt Sarah's feelings, and Cheyenne had wanted to sell her jewelry at the Western-themed Cowboy Christmas Gift Show at Las Vegas Convention Center for years. Over four hundred vendors from the U.S. and Canada would be there to sell their wares from jewelry to Western apparel. It was a great opportunity for her. She and Angie had already booked spaces.

Angie wasn't a fan of rodeos, but Duke wanted to see Tuf and Beau ride in Vegas, so she'd agreed to go. Everyone supported each other. That's what families did. But Cheyenne didn't feel like a part of the Hart family, and she and Tuf would always be twelve feet apart.

TUF RODEOED IN MONTANA, his region, and stayed close to home to help carry stock to rodeos. His points in the standings changed with each rodeo, and he ended up in fourth place behind Kinney, Watson and Hobbs. The odds of him beating them in Vegas were very slim, but he kept in shape, preparing for the biggest rodeo of his life.

In October, the Hart family received the news they'd been praying for. The Midnight Express had been voted by the cowboys as the PRCA Bareback Bronc of the Year. Ace bought a case of champagne, and the family held a party at the house. After years of struggle, his mother's dream had come to fruition. Her decision to diversify into raising rodeo stock had been risky, but she saw it as a way to save the ranch she loved, and her instincts had been right. The Harts were in the rodeo contracting business—big-time.

Colt raised his glass. "C'mon, Ace. Say it one more time. Colt was right."

Ace clinked his glass against Colt's. "Hell, yeah. Colt was right."

Leah stood by Tuf watching her husband. "In about ten minutes, my husband is going to be drunk on his ass with happiness."

"He's done an amazing job with Midnight this year."

"Yeah. Everyone has done an amazing job to pull this ranch out of debt, including you." She kissed his cheek. "Don't forget to be happy." He felt she wanted to say much more, but stopped herself.

After everyone had left, Tuf stood in the kitchen with his mom.

"I didn't see you drink a thing."

"My mind's already messed up. I don't need liquor."

"Tomas, I would rather be in debt for the rest of my life than to see you so unhappy."

"I know, Mom." He kissed her forehead. "Night."

He went upstairs to his room and stood at his window, looking toward the Wright property.

And dreamed of Cheyenne. All he had now were his dreams...and his nightmares. Which one would win the battle in his head?

In November, the Harts were busy trying to finalize plans for Vegas—not only for the family, but for the animals. Besides Midnight, Bushwhacker, Back Bender, Asteroid, Bossy Lady and True Grit had been invited to the big show.

After going over details many times, a final plan emerged. Tuf, Duke, Colt and Leah would transport the animals. The rest of the family would fly out. Because of Dinah's job, she and Austin didn't make the trip. Jill and Davey didn't, either. They stayed with Leah's mother. Leah decided to go with the stock to share the experience with Colt and to take care of the paperwork once they arrived.

Over Thanksgiving, they went over the plans again. Tuf wondered if they'd ever leave. With the cattle carrier, the drive would take from seventeen to nineteen hours depending on stops to water the stocks, and bathroom and eat stops for them. They would drive through the night. Tuf followed the carrier in his truck in case they broke down and so they'd have a vehicle in Vegas.

They left Thunder Ranch about noon and arrived in Las Vegas at six the next morning. Midnight was in the TV pen, which contained champion horses that were fun to watch, and he would buck on nights five and ten of the ten-day event. His breeding fee was now a hot commodity.

While Colt and Leah dealt with paperwork, Tuf and Duke drove the small distance to the Thomas and Mack Center on the University of Nevada Las Vegas campus. The football-like stadium was awesome.

"Are you nervous?" Duke asked.

"Hell, yeah." Even though he was numb inside, he felt a flicker of nerves.

Duke slapped him on the back. "You'll do fine."

They joined Colt and Leah. The animals had made the trip without a problem. Midnight, on the other hand, was restlessly circling the pen, wanting out.

Later the family arrived, and after settling in, they had dinner together. Cheyenne, Angie, Duke and Luke were taking the cookies and jewelry they'd had shipped over to the convention center to find their spaces and figure out what else they had to do. He should be helping Cheyenne. But he sat missing her and wondering if his pain would ever end.

The girls and Buddy joined them. Sadie and Sammie squeezed in next to him, and after picking at their food, they crawled into his lap. He held them tight, drawing strength from their warm little bodies.

I have to let the war go drummed through his head.

For a life with Cheyenne and the girls, he had to let the war go. He just wasn't sure how to do that. God knew he'd tried so many times, but the bad stuff was still there inside him like a festering sore that would not heal.

Maybe he was always going to be trapped between good and evil.

THE NIGHT BEFORE the rodeo started, his mom, Ace and Colt attended an awards banquet to receive the PRCA World Champion Award for Midnight.

The National Finals Rodeo started with a big fanfare. The stadium was packed and the tension level high as the cowboys readied for the biggest night of their lives. The crowd stood as Reba McEntire sang the national anthem. Tuf and Beau sat on their horses, loaned to them by a rodeo friend, with their hands over their hearts. Whooping and hollering, the cowboys and cowgirls charged out into the arena in their Wrangler National Finals jackets and took off their hats to the crowd. The roar was deafening.

Sadie and Sammie stood at a rail, waving. Buddy had a hand on each one. "Tuf!" they screamed, and he tipped his hat to them. They went back to their seats with the rest of the family.

Bareback riding was first. In the locker room, Tuf donned his protective vest, chaps and spurs and made his way to a platform where the cowboys could watch the action.

"This is it, Tuf," Cory Kinney said. "Good luck." They shook hands as friends who wanted the same thing, but only one could win.

Chad Canter from Stillwater, Oklahoma, was up first. All eyes were on the chutes as Chad burst out on Foxy

Lady. He made the ride to the roar of the crowd and scored an 87. That set the bar high and the next ten cowboys didn't beat it. Neither did Jesse Hobbs. Tuf was up next. He settled onto Fire and Ice, his draw, a chestnut-colored mare.

"Just stay calm," Colt said as he helped Tuf adjust his rigging. The owner of the horse attached the flank strap, and the horse moved restlessly, ready to buck.

"She bucks hot and cold," the owner said. "Just be ready for the hot, 'cause she'll bust your ass."

"Thanks," Tuf said, fitting his hand into the handle.

The announcer's voice came on. "Up next is Tuf Hart out of Roundup, Montana. He's the youngest of the Hart rodeo family. His father rodeoed, as do his brothers, Ace and Colt, and his cousins Beau and Duke Adams. This is Tuf's first full year on the circuit and it's been a banner year for him. A former marine, you might notice his red, white and blue garb. This guy is cowboy tough. Let's see what he can do here tonight on Fire and Ice, owned by Barker Rodeo Company of Denver, Colorado."

Tuf raised his left arm, leaned slightly back and stretched out his legs, ready to mark the horse before her front hooves hit the ground. He took a deep breath and shut out everything but him and the horse. He nodded to the gate handler to signal he was ready. The gate swung open with a bang, and Fire and Ice bolted out bucking with a powerful force. Tuf held on, keeping his rhythm marking the horse. Four. Five. The horse kicked high with her back legs, trying to dislodge him. He managed to stay on. Seven. Eight. The buzzer shrilled and Tuf let go, sailing to the ground and losing his hat. The congratulation whoops and clapping were deafening, and the bright lights blinded him for a moment. Picking up his hat, he stared at the JumboTron. Waiting and waiting.

The ride was good, he assured himself. Seemed like forever before 88.5 popped up. He started to throw his hat into the air when he heard his favorite squeaky little voices shout, "Tuf!"

He tipped his hat to his munchkins and they stopped screaming. Buddy had a death grip on them and guided them back to their seats. Tuf walked out of the arena and joined the other cowboys to watch the last two riders. Beau joined him.

"Good ride," Beau said.

"Yeah. Let's see if it holds up."

It did. No one bested his score in the first round.

Winning the first round gave him a boost. He'd earned money for Thunder Ranch, but his arm and his heart ached, and he wondered if he could withstand nine more grueling nights without seeing Cheyenne.

CHAPTER SEVENTEEN

CHEYENNE DIDN'T HAVE time to think about Tuf, but she got updates from the family, her dad and the girls. She'd wanted to share this experience with him. Once again, though, they were so far apart.

She and Angie had been over almost every inch of the 300,000 square feet of the North Halls Las Vegas Convention Center. The place was jam-packed with every Western item imaginable from furniture to art to handcrafted items. They had fun browsing through the treasures.

Most of the time they were at their booths selling their wares. Her leather-and-turquoise cuff was the most popular item. She feared she'd run out before the show ended. Angie was busy, too. People had a lot of questions about her cookies and what was in them. They passed out tons of business cards.

But her thoughts were over at the Thomas and Mack Center. Tuf had won the first round and she wondered how he felt about that. He had to be happy about it.

The girls and Luke sat on the floor behind them playing with a deck of cards.

A lady tried on a silver necklace with a horseshoe pendant. "I like this. It's very simple. I'll take it."

Cheyenne swiped the woman's card and put the necklace in one of her trademark brown boxes with an orange *C* on top.

Josh Adams, Earl McKinley and Buddy walked up, and the kids ran to them. Earl pushed Emma in a stroller and the girls kissed her cheeks. "Bye," the kids shouted and followed their grandfathers through the mill of people to the door.

Angie stared at her.

"What?"

"Go over and watch Tuf ride. He wants you there."

"No, he doesn't."

"Cheyenne…"

Her words were cut off as Leah, Flynn, Sierra, Jordan and Sarah strolled over.

"How's business?" Leah asked.

"Good."

They checked out the jewelry and talked for a minute.

"We better go." Jordan spoke up. "Joshua is waiting at the entrance."

"Yes. I don't want to miss Tomas ride." Sarah glanced at her watch.

"Why don't you come for a little while?" Sierra suggested to Cheyenne.

"Thanks, but no."

"It's fast-paced and exciting until someone you love gets on a two-thousand-pound angry bull. I don't have any fingernails left and it's just the beginning."

"You'll survive," Flynn said. "I better find my daughter."

Her friends left, but Leah lingered. "Please go to the arena and watch Tuf ride."

"Thanks, Leah, but I can't."

"You two take stubborn to a whole new level."

"It's Tuf… I…"

"I know. He's so sad. I just want to hug and slap him at the same time."

"That's the problem. He's shutting everyone out, even me. If he'd just let me help him, I'd be over there cheering him on."

"If you change your mind, just call me."

"I won't. I can handle a lot of things, but I can't handle Tuf not trusting me enough to understand and share his pain."

A group of women came up, and Leah waved and left. As the women tried on pieces, she wondered why Tuf couldn't love her enough.

THE SECOND NIGHT, Cory won on Black Widow. Trey Watson won the third round. It was going to be a dogfight to the bitter end. Adrenaline surged through Tuf's veins and he settled in to compete for the next seven nights.

The fourth night, Jesse Hobbs won. The fifth night, Tuf scored an 88.5 on Wild Deuce. Cory drew Midnight.

"Ladies and gentlemen, next up is Cory Kinney out of Hutto, Texas. He's number one in the standings and he's riding The Midnight Express. This stallion's lineage dates back to Five Minutes to Midnight, a hall-of-fame bucking bronc a lot of old-timers will remember. The stud has made it to the NFR five times and was chosen the NFR bucking bronc two times. He disappeared from the rodeo scene for a while until the Hart family purchased him at auction. He's had a great year winning the PRCA bucking bronc of the year in October. This is Midnight's sixth appearance at the NFR. Let's see what he and Cory Kinney can do tonight."

Midnight kicked and bucked but Cory stayed on. Tuf held his breath, waiting for the score.

When 89 came up, Beau muttered under his breath, "Shit."

Midnight was magnificent, though. Every bareback rider there wanted a chance at the stallion because they knew the stud had the power to garnish a top score that could lead them to the world title.

Cory won again on the sixth night with an 88.5 ride on Razzle-Dazzle. Tuf placed second again.

Beau suited up for his ride. He was feeling the frustration, too. He'd garnered second and third spots but hadn't won a round yet.

"I want to win a round, Tuf," Beau said as he put on his helmet. "That's where the money is."

"You have a good chance since only one out of eleven cowboys have managed a ride this round."

"I drew Hellacious Sam and he's a mean bastard. He'll trample you if he gets a chance."

"Show him who's boss, coz. Good luck." Tuf ran back to the rail to watch. Duke joined him.

"He can win this round," Duke said.

"Yep. Let's watch."

The chute gate flew open, and Sam fired out like a bullet bucking with a surge of power. Beau held on. The bull went into a spin. Still Beau held on. The buzzer blared and Beau jumped off, landing on his backside.

"He did it," Duke shouted and they high-fived.

But Sam wasn't through. He turned and charged before Beau could get out of the way. With one thrust of his powerful head, Sam threw Beau into the air, and Beau landed on his back with a thud. Sam stood over him, stomping around, daring anyone to take his prize.

The clowns and cowboys on horseback tried to get Sam away from Beau to no avail. Sam swung snot six ways from Sunday and was ready to take them on.

"Shit." Tuf jumped over the rail, followed by Duke. Their appearance startled Sam, and the clowns were able to get in and distract him. The bull charged the clowns, and the handlers had Sam headed toward the open chute in a split second.

Tuf fell down by Beau in the dirt. "Beau!"

"It hurts," Beau moaned.

A flashback from Afghanistan hit Tuf like a sledge-hammer. No! He would not keep fighting that war. That was in the past. This was the present. And Beau was not Frank.

"Where?" Duke asked as Tuf checked Beau's dust-covered body.

"My...my left arm. I can't move it."

Damn. It was probably broken. Tuf realized there was complete quiet in the large stadium. The announcer wasn't even talking as they waited for news on Beau's condition.

"What do you think?" Duke asked.

"Probably best to get a stretcher," Tuf replied.

"No." Beau vetoed that. "Sierra has to see me get up. Just help me."

"Don't be stupid." Duke wasn't having any of it. "That bull gave you a tromping."

Beau turned to Tuf. "Help me up."

"C'mon, Duke, it's what he wants. Support his arm while I help him."

Beau bent his knees, and Tuf put his hands beneath Beau's shoulders and lifted while Duke raised Beau's arm and held it against his chest.

"Shit. It hurts. What's my score?" Beau said all in one breath.

"Look up," Tuf told him.

Beau glanced at the JumboTron. "Hot damn. Eighty-nine."

A cowboy retrieved Beau's hat, and Tuf stuffed it on Beau's head as they made their way out of the arena through the cowboys to a ramp to the locker room. The crowd erupted with loud applause. Colt and Ace met them there, as did the rodeo doctor.

While Beau was being x-rayed, Tuf hurried to get his truck because he feared Beau's forearm was broken. It had an S shape. The bull had obviously stepped on it. And he knew Beau was going to fight getting an ambulance every step of the way.

Tuf's fears were confirmed, and they got him to the hospital as quickly as possible. Sierra, Uncle Josh and Jordan were meeting them there. Beau was quiet on the ride to the hospital. Everyone was.

They took Beau in right away and prepped him to get the bone set. Sierra arrived in time to see him before they whisked him away. The rest of the family trickled in and they waited. Sierra came out with tears in her eyes.

"I'm so sad for him. He knew the cowboys here were good and he's placed every night, but he wanted to win at least one round."

Everyone seemed to reach for his or her phone at the same time. They'd been so worried about Beau they hadn't checked to see how the bull riding had come out.

Colt was fastest on the draw. He gave a thumbs-up sign as he talked. "He won," Colt shouted. "Only two cowboys made their rides, so Beau's gonna get a big payout on this one."

"Oh, that's good news," Sierra cried. "I can't wait to tell him."

The doctor decided to keep Beau until morning and Sierra stayed with him. Tuf promised to pick them up in the morning.

At ten the next morning, Tuf's cell woke him. In less than five minutes, he was dressed and headed for the door.

Ace met him in the hall. "Give me your keys. I can collect Sierra and Beau. You need your rest. You have to ride tonight."

"I gave my word and I'm going."

"You got a thing about giving your word, and it's nice to be so honorable, but I didn't see any of that when you ditched Cheyenne."

Tuf frowned at his brother, who was usually so calm and rational. Was he goading him? "I didn't ditch her. I broke up with her to protect her."

"Mmm." Ace nodded. "Or are you protecting yourself?"

"What?"

"Cheyenne's been through her own kind of hell with an abusive husband. She knows what being hit for real feels like. Yet, when you had the nightmare, she was willing to accept you warts and all, but you're the one who backed out of the relationship. Why? Because you have one foot in that war at all times. It controls you. During the day you're good at protecting yourself from all those memories. At night there is no protection and the memories torture you. You have to stop protecting whatever bad stuff's in your head. Let it out, please, and start to live again."

Tuf stared at Ace as if he'd grown two heads. Was he that transparent?

TUF HAD BEAU and Sierra back at the hotel in no time. Beau looked a little pale, but he seemed okay. He lay in bed and Sierra propped pillows behind his back.

Their affection for one another got to Tuf. Cheyenne would be upset if he was hurt, too. *Because she loves me.* He closed his eyes briefly to let that sink in. Was Ace right? Was he protecting himself? Protecting the awful memories? And how did he stop? He didn't know how to stop.

He couldn't think about this now. He pulled up a chair to sit by the bed. "How are you?" he asked.

"Sore and mad," Beau replied.

"I'm sorry your NFR experience ended like this."

"Yeah. This broken arm sucks, and I wish I could have walked out of the arena under my own steam after the win, but, man, I'm going home with over sixty thousand dollars. I'm happy about that." Beau scooted up in bed. "The damn bull stunk and he peed on me."

"He marked his territory," Tuf quipped.

They laughed and Tuf got to his feet. "I'll catch y'all later. Right now I'm going to crash for a few hours."

When Tuf reached his room, he stripped out of his clothes and fell across his bed. But visions of Cheyenne tortured him. He'd crushed something valuable—her love. And he had to make it right. This wasn't the time or the place, though. Now he had to concentrate on the rodeo and his commitment to his family.

That night Tuf won the round on Magic Realm, and Trey won the eighth round. That left two nights, and Tuf would have to win both to win the title. The pressure was on, and it was the buzz around the cowboys. Could Tuf come from behind to win? Or could Trey? Could Cory maintain his lead? Who was going to win?

On the ninth night, Cory made his ride with an 88.5. Tuf had to beat that to stay in contention. He drew Scarlet Lady, a horse known to buck hard and wild. As he slid onto the reddish-colored mare, the horse immediately tried to jump out of the chute, banging against the pipe. Tuf got off and a man from Pioneer Rodeo who owned the horse tried to calm her.

Tuf eased onto Scarlet one more time.

The announcer's voice came on. "Let's turn our attention to chute number three. Tuf Hart is ready to ride."

Tuf took a deep breath and shut out everything but himself and the spirited horse beneath him. He nodded and the gate swung open. Scarlet leaped out of the gate. Bucking, leaping and kicking, Scarlet showed no mercy. Tuf settled into a hard, rocking rhythm. Five, six. Tuf held on. A wild kick from Scarlet's back legs almost unseated him, but Tuf managed to stay on. Seven. Eight.

At the buzzer, Tuf jumped off, lost his balance and staggered backward. And backward until his head hit something and the arena went black.

Home to Thunder Ranch in a coffin. He saw the coffin clearly draped in an American flag. Saw his mother crying. Saw Cheyenne…Cheyenne! No! He forced his eyes open and saw the people in the stadium, waiting.

"Tuf!" he heard his munchkins scream.

Colt and Ace ran toward him, and Tuf lumbered to his feet. The arena swayed as thunderous applause erupted. He blinked, trying to focus, and waved to the girls to let them know he was fine.

"Are you okay?" Ace asked as he reached him.

"Yeah. Just lost my balance."

"Look at the score," Colt shouted, handing him his hat.

Tuf looked up to see 89 stuck on the JumboTron as

if it was waiting for him to notice it. He lifted a fist in
the air in acknowledgment and walked out of the arena
with his brothers flanking him.

"The cowboy marine is walking away," the announcer said. "He's tough. Congratulations! Tuf Hart
wins the round on Scarlet Lady. This sets the stage for
a showdown between Tuf and Cory Kinney. It'll be a
nail-biter, so don't miss bareback riding tomorrow night
when we crown a champion. Now get ready for more
excitement..."

The voice faded away as they walked up the ramp to
the locker room. Tuf sank onto a bench and took off his
spurs. Ace felt Tuf's head, his neck and his shoulders.

Tuf pulled away. "Will you stop? I'm not a horse you
can practice your vet skills on."

"There's a knot on the back of your head where you
hit the advertisement sign. You might have a concus-
sion."

"I can handle it."

"Yeah, you're a tough-ass," Ace snapped. "You can
handle everything by yourself."

Cowboys walked in and out. Several shouted, "Way
to go, Tuf. Good ride." He lifted a hand in response.

Colt knelt in front of him. "Why are you so down?
You've worked all year for this and broke into the top fifteen cowboys in the country. You're standing toe-to-toe
with the best riders in the world and you have a chance to
win it all. Every cowboy here wants to be in your boots.
Why aren't you two-stepping across this room in joy?"

"Because I made a mistake with Cheyenne and I keep
making them."

"Tuf, we all make mistakes. Why do you think I didn't
see my son until a year ago? I wanted to, but I thought

he was better off without me. Big mistake. Give Cheyenne a chance. It won't be a mistake."

Tuf stood, as did Colt. He removed his chaps and protective vest and placed them in his locker. "I need some time alone."

"Tuf...."

He walked away. He was good at that.

CHEYENNE SANK ONTO the bed as she and Angie returned from another day at the convention center.

"Why does love hurt so much?"

Angie sat by her. "I don't know. Sometimes it just does. Life's about changes, accepting, forgiving and moving on. I feel your situation with Tuf can be resolved with a simple 'I'm sorry' from Tuf."

Cheyenne shook her head. "No, it can't. Tuf doesn't trust me enough to handle his nightmares. That's not going to change. He said he's been having them for over two years and they could get more violent. There's no way around that."

"Unless Tuf lets you into his thoughts."

Cheyenne looked at her friend. "That's not going to happen and..."

The buzz of her cell interrupted Cheyenne. She rummaged in her purse for it. "It's a text from Leah."

"What does it say?" Angie asked.

Cheyenne couldn't speak. She kept staring at the words.

"Cheyenne...?"

She read the text word for word because she couldn't form any of her own. "'Tuf got hurt. He hit his head on a sign, but he's okay. Just thought you'd want to know.'"

Tuf is hurt.

CHAPTER EIGHTEEN

CHEYENNE'S FIRST INSTINCT was to run to the arena, but Tuf had made it very clear he didn't need her comfort or anything else. She hated the ache inside that she couldn't control.

"Cheyenne?"

She turned to her friend. "What?"

"Are you going to the arena?"

"No. He hasn't asked for me."

Angie rolled her eyes. "You need an invitation?"

"Oh, no. The girls are there, and they probably saw what happened." She called her dad and he answered promptly. "How are the girls?"

"Fine. Why?"

"Leah said Tuf got hurt."

"Yeah, but they just thought it was part of the rodeo. They were screaming 'Tuf, get up' so loud they put them on the large JumboTron. They saw themselves and waved and screamed louder. Tuf waved to them and they were fine. They're waiting for barrel racing. That's their favorite next to Tuf riding. Since Beau was injured, they don't want to watch those mean old bulls, so we'll be back after barrel racing."

"Okay. Thanks, Dad."

She dropped her phone into her purse. Tuf was fine. That was all that mattered.

TUF MADE HIS way out of the arena and started walking. Then he broke into a run like he always did when the walls closed in and he tried to escape the pain inside himself. Through the pounding of his heart, he realized he had to stop running. With extreme effort, he made himself stop, and then he just kept walking. He had no destination in mind, but he wound up back at the hotel. He took the elevator up to his room.

Cheyenne's room was next to his, and he paused outside her door. He had to see her. He didn't care about anything else. For the first time in his life, he needed someone. He couldn't handle life without Cheyenne. After admitting that, he felt better. They could talk and work this out—if only she'd forgive him.

He knocked and waited, but there was no response. She had to be out. That was no problem. He'd wait in his room until he heard her come in. All the days they'd been in Vegas, not once had they run into each other. When he woke up, she was already at the convention center. When he came in from the rodeo, she and the girls were asleep.

Sitting in his room, he listened for a noise next door. He had acute hearing. Something he'd mastered in Afghanistan. The hallway was relatively quiet, though. He could call Cheyenne, but he needed to see her.

His cell beeped with a text message. It was from Michael Dobbins. Good luck, buddy. Rooting for you all the way. M

Tuf sat staring at his phone and realized the war was always going to be a part of him. He'd made lifelong friends, and he and Michael had a special connection— a bond that could never be broken. All along he'd been thinking if he could get rid of the bad memories, he could live life again. But it wasn't like that at all. He had to find a way to live with the memories, and he could only do that with Cheyenne. It was so clear now. He couldn't fight the memories alone.

A tap at the door had him on his feet. Maybe it was Cheyenne. His mother stood outside. "Hi, son. How do you feel?"

"I'm fine." He opened the door and she came inside. Her hands went immediately to his head. "Oh, you do have a knot. Does it hurt?"

"Nah," he lied.

"We've decided to take in a Reba McEntire show and then have dinner. Would you like to come?"

"Who's 'we'?"

"Earl, Buddy and me. Everyone else is spending this last evening with their spouses, and we thought we'd have some fun, too. Tomorrow night we'll be busy packing, getting ready to catch a flight home."

"No, but have a good time."

"I plan to. Now I'm going to change and put on some sparkly earrings I bought from Cheyenne." She paused. "You do know her room is next door."

"Yes, Mom."

She hugged him. "I'm so proud of you. Win or lose tomorrow, you're our hero."

The word didn't bother him like it usually did. "Thanks, Mom. Have a fun evening."

After she left, he took off his boots, planning to stay in and order dinner. He didn't want to leave the room in case he missed Cheyenne.

His right arm ached so he took two Advil and lay across the bed. Listening. Waiting.

Thirty minutes later, he felt drowsy and he fought it, but soon sleep claimed him.

THE NEXT MORNING, IT WAS almost noon when he woke up. Damn it! He jumped up, slipped into jeans and yanked a T-shirt over his head. He hurried to the hallway and knocked on Cheyenne's door, but he knew she was already gone. Slowly, he went back to his room. Sitting on the bed, he slipped on his boots. He had to find Cheyenne.

Thirty minutes later, he found her. A group of women gathered around her booth trying on earrings, bracelets and necklaces. She was busy and he couldn't talk to her in front of a crowd. But he watched her for a moment to get himself through the day. Her hair was up like he'd seen so many times. He'd take it down just to run his fingers through the silky strands and to kiss the warmth of her neck. The taste of her skin was strong on his lips. He turned and walked away. A habit he was beginning to hate.

Back at the hotel, he took a hot shower to ease his aching muscles. The knot on his head had gone down, so that was good. Before long, he headed over to the arena. He was anxious to get his draw for the night. The horse he'd have to ride would play a big part in his chance for a title.

He stood with the other fourteen cowboys to get their draw. Tuf was stunned, hardly believing that his year had come down to this.

"Who'd you draw?" Cory asked.

"Midnight."

"Well, now, my odds just got a little better."

"Maybe."

"I hope we can still be friends after this," Cory said.

"I don't see why not. We'll buddy up anytime we can." Tuf walked off to where his brothers stood.

"Who'd you get?" Colt asked.

"Midnight."

"You're shitting me."

"Nope. I got the black stallion."

"Damn," Ace said. "What a finale. Just stay focused. You can ride him."

"Yeah. You've been a little distracted, but now you really have to rein in your emotions," Colt added.

"I gotta go. It's time to ride in." Reining in his emotions might be the hardest thing he'd ever have to do, and that included riding Midnight.

In the locker room, Tuf strapped on his chaps and grabbed his Wrangler NFR jacket out of his bag. As he slipped it on, Beau walked in, his arm in a sling.

"You riding in?" Tuf asked.

"You bet. This is the last night and I'm not gonna miss it." He held up his arm in a cast. "I'm not putting on my jacket. Do you think anyone will mind?"

"Nah. Let's saddle up." They headed toward the pens where two horses were waiting. Because of the brace, Beau had to mount from the right side. The horse didn't seem to mind. They got in line behind other cowboys waiting to ride into the arena. A cowgirl carrying the U.S. flag rode in on a beautiful golden palomino. The lights dimmed and a spotlight shone on the girl as a starlet from Vegas sang the national anthem. He bowed his head and placed his hand over his heart. When the last note died away, the bright lights came on, and the cowboys and cowgirls charged into the arena single file for the last night of the rodeo.

The pace was fast as they circled the arena and then lined up side by side. The crowd roared with applause. Tuf and Beau came to a stop in front of where the Hart family sat. Sadie and Sammie were at the rail waving. Tuf nudged his horse forward and tipped his hat to them.

"Tuf!" they screamed.

He backed his horse into the lineup and saw they were captured on the big screen.

"Show-off." Beau laughed.

Soon they charged out of the arena whooping and hollering. A sense of excitement filled the air. Nine long days, and tonight world champions would be awarded in each event. Time to rodeo. Time to find out who those champions would be.

TUF SAT IN the locker room attaching his spurs, mentally preparing himself.

"This is it," Beau said. "This is what we've worked for all year, sleeping in the truck, eating crappy food. It's all come down to a hell of a ride."

Was this what he'd worked for? In his mind that didn't seem right. And he knew what it was. All year he'd worked to regain his freedom. Freedom from the nightmares. Freedom to live again—with Cheyenne. But he hadn't accomplished that. He took a long breath and suddenly realized that freedom was a state of mind. And his mind was locked in combat.

The past nine nights hadn't been the thrilling experience he'd expected and he knew why. Cheyenne wasn't here. But for his family, he would do his best.

He placed his hand over his jeans pocket and felt the ring he carried. Cheyenne's engagement ring. Then it hit him. He couldn't ride tonight without her here. It was that simple. He jumped to his feet.

"Where you going?" Beau asked.

"I have to see Cheyenne."

"What? Bareback riding is fixing to start. Are you nuts?"

"I have to see her."

Beau shook his head.

"Cover for me with Colt and Ace. I'll be back."

"You better be."

Tuf made his way out of the cowboy-ready area and then broke into a run. His spurs jangled, but he didn't have time to take them off. A shuttle was outside letting people off to see the rodeo. He jumped on and did something his pride wouldn't let him do last night.

He called Cheyenne.

CHEYENNE AND ANGIE WAITED for the elevator.

"It's over. After ten long days, I sold out of horse cookies and I'm ready to go home."

"Me, too," Cheyenne said. "Although I do have a few earrings left, but I plan to give those to some of the ladies here in the hotel."

"That's nice."

Cheyenne's cell buzzed and she fished it out of her purse. *Tuf.* Her heart raced as she read the name.

"Where are you?" he asked quickly.

"Uh…at the elevator in the hotel. Why?"

"I need to see you. Can you meet me at the entrance?"

"Why?"

"Please, Cheyenne. Just for a minute."

The *please* got her. "O-okay."

"Who was it?" Angie asked.

"Tuf. He wants me to meet him outside."

"What are you waiting for?"

"You're coming with me. I'm not standing out there alone. There are a lot of strange people here."

"Like my one-hundred-and-ten-pound frame is going to deter anyone."

"You know what I mean." Cheyenne's hand shook as she dropped her phone into her purse. *What does Tuf want?*

"Yeah. Let's go." They walked toward the entrance. "Bareback riding is first, isn't it?"

"Yes, and I don't know what Tuf is doing coming here. He should be getting ready to ride."

They went through the glass doors and into the cool evening. People were milling around, laughing and talking.

A man puffing on a cigarette sidled up to them. "Hey, ladies, need a little company?"

"No, thanks," Cheyenne replied.

"You sure?" The cigarette bobbed on his lip. "I could show you gals a good time."

"Will you get that smoke out of our faces?" Angie said in a voice Cheyenne had never heard her use before. As the man turned tail and went back into the hotel, Angie laughed. "Hey, guess I'm tougher than I thought."

Cars and cabs dropped off people, but she didn't see any sign of Tuf. Then a shuttle bus roared up and Tuf jumped out dressed in his red, white and blue rodeo garb, including the spurs that jangled as he rushed toward her. At the sight of him, her heart knocked wildly.

"Hey, cowboy, lost your horse?" a guy shouted at him, but Tuf ignored him, running straight to her.

"Listen, Cheyenne, I screwed up. I know that now. I'm

sorry, but please come to the rodeo and watch me ride. If you love me, if you think we have a future, you'll be there. I need you to be there."

Hurt feelings and love warred inside her. "But you don't need me. You've proven that in the last few months. You shut me out and refused to trust me. And 'I'm sorry' doesn't even start to erase all that pain."

He cupped her face, and she felt the calluses on his hands. "If you love me, none of that will matter. Be there—for us. I've got to go." He ran and leaped on the shuttle that was waiting for him, and it roared away. For some reason, she felt as if he'd stomped on her heart, and she couldn't get past that feeling.

"Why didn't you go with him?" Angie asked.

"What?"

"You should have gone with him on the shuttle."

"I can't."

"Cheyenne."

"I just can't."

"Then why are you crying?"

"I'm not crying." She brushed away tears with the back of her hand, belying her statement.

"Your face is leaking, then."

"Angie, it's not that easy. We still have the same problem. He doesn't trust me."

"This whole week you kept saying he hasn't asked you. Now he has. It's time to go."

"It's not that simple."

"Oh, but it is. I'm getting a cab. I'll even go with you, and you know I don't like rodeos." Angie turned toward the curb.

"No, don't."

"Cheyenne." Angie stomped her foot.

"Please understand I can't do this. I'll talk to him later when we have more time."

"By then it will be too late. The rodeo will be over and you'll regret your decision."

Cheyenne drew a heavy breath and looked at the sparkling lights of Vegas that rivaled a thousand Christmas trees. People passed by her as if she didn't exist, and in a way she felt all alone battling the pain inside herself.

"Don't do this to yourself." Angie kept up her pleas.

"I can't seem to do anything else."

Angie hugged her. "I'm sorry."

"Me, too."

TUF MADE IT back into the cowboy-ready area amid a few startled stares. Luckily none of them were Colt's, Ace's or Duke's. He thought he was home free until Ace stalked up to him.

"Where in the hell have you been? I've looked all over. Beau said you were in the bathroom. Are you sick?"

"No. I…"

"You're not a kid anymore, Tuf. What…"

Suddenly, without warning, the part of his brain he'd kept vaulted tight opened and he could see what was on the top of that hill—the horror. The unthinkable horror he'd protected for years. He staggered backward with the force of the truth. Ace caught him and he struggled to regain his composure.

"Damn, you are sick," Ace said. "I'm sorry. I shouldn't have yelled at you."

"I'm fine." He sucked in puffs of air and stood on his own two feet.

"You don't look fine. You're pale and shaky."

Before Tuf could reply, Duke ran to them. "Kinney just scored a 90 on Tempting Fate."

"Shit." Ace shook his head.

"Colt has Midnight in the chute, Tuf. You ready?" Duke asked.

Two sets of eyes stared at him. A year of riding the circuit had come down to this moment. His stomach was raw, his back tight and his nerves frayed, but he ignored all that and said, "Yes."

He walked to the chute, but before climbing it, he put his hand over his right pocket and felt the ring. *She'll come. She'll come.* Climbing the chute, he kept repeating that.

He carefully slid onto Midnight's back, and the stallion flung his head in protest. Beneath him, Tuf felt the raw power of the animal. It was like sticking his finger in an electrical socket and knowing he was going to get knocked for a loop. Strong muscles rippled, and Midnight banged restlessly against the chute, ready to buck.

The announcer's voice came on. "Ladies and gents, Cory Kinney just made an outstanding ride. Tuf Hart is getting ready and he has to be feeling the pressure. Everyone is. Bareback riding has come down to this last ride. This is as exciting as it gets."

Ace and Duke helped with his rigging, and Colt worked with Midnight's flank strap. He was the only one who did that on Midnight. As soon as Colt tightened it, Midnight jerked his head.

Tuf slipped his gloved right hand into the handle on the rigging and worked his hand to get a secure grip.

"You about ready?" Ace asked.

"Is Cheyenne sitting with the family?"

"What?"

"Look and see if Cheyenne is with the family."

"Tuf, forget about Cheyenne for a minute."

"Look, damn it."

Ace raised his head. "No, she's not there, but the twins are waiting."

The bottom dropped out of his stomach, and he fought to regain his focus. For his family, he had to focus.

He got into his groove.

"Good luck," Ace and Duke shouted.

Then Colt was there. "You know how Midnight bucks. Just be prepared for the power."

The announcer's voice pushed through. "In chute number two, Tuf Hart is on The Midnight Express, owned by the Hart family. This horse has the power to get the job done, and Tuf Hart knows it. As does everyone here. For Tuf the trick will be to stay on the horse for eight seconds. What do you think, Bob?"

The other announcer chimed in. "Cory Kinney had an impressive ride and it's going to be hard to beat that. But anything can happen here. Tuf Hart's got the talent, though. Let's see what happens."

Everything faded away, and it was just him and Midnight. And eight seconds. He raised his left arm and nodded. The gate banged open, and Midnight reared up on his hind legs out of the chute, almost unseating Tuf, but he kept his balance and his grip. And the show was on. The power of the bucks jarred his kidneys, strained his back and his arm, and pounding waves of pain shot through his head, but he got into a rhythm and kept it. He lost track of the count and thought the damn buzzer must be broken. It felt as if the black stallion had jarred his body for at least ten minutes. Then he heard it and let go. The power catapulted him into the dirt and he landed on his back. Pain radiated through his body. He thought he was dead, but if he was, he wouldn't be able to feel the agony.

He stared up into the bright lights and thought he should get up, but he couldn't move a muscle.

The announcer's voice penetrated the fog. "Cory Kinney is waiting for the score to pop up. Everyone is. I'm glad I don't have to judge this, Hal. That was an astounding ride. Man, what an ending to bareback riding."

"Wait, Bob. Tuf Hart is not getting up. Is he hurt?"

"Ace and Colt Hart and Duke Adams are racing to his side. Big Ben, the clown, is there, too. Everyone is waiting for this tough cowboy marine to get to his feet. I'm sure the Hart family is holding their breath."

Tuf stared at a big red nose.

Then there was Ace's, Colt's and Duke's anxious faces. "Tuf, you okay?" Ace asked.

"I might need a hand up."

With a smile, Ace and Duke lifted him to his feet.

"What's my score?" Tuf asked.

"It hasn't come up yet," Colt replied. "I don't know what's taking so damn long."

The crowd erupted into applause and shouts. "There it is," Duke pointed.

"Hey, hoss, look at that," Colt shouted. "Congratulations, bro. I have to check on Midnight."

Tuf glanced up and saw 91. He'd done it. He'd won the title. But where was his joy?

"C'mon, Tuf, show some reaction." Ace slapped him on the back. "The crowd expects it."

"You might have to lift my arms."

Ace laughed, and there in front of eighteen thousand

people, his big brother hugged him. "I'm proud of you. Dad would be, too."

"Thanks." Tuf picked up his hat.

"Tuf Hart seems a little dazed," Hal said. "I don't think he realizes he just won the title."

"Tuf!" The little voices drew Tuf's attention. He lifted his hat in acknowledgment, trying not to flinch, and froze. Cheyenne stood with them, her hands over her mouth in worry.

She's here.

Renewed adrenaline pumped through his veins, re-charging his tired and sore body.

"Tuf, where you going?" Ace shouted.

"Where's he going, Hal?"

"He's climbing into the stands where those little red-haired girls have been cheering for him all week. And now there's a young red-haired woman there."

Tuf swung over the rail at Cheyenne's feet. "I love you," he said to her startled face. He pulled the ring out of his pocket. "Will you marry me? Nightmares and all."

"Tuf." Her eyes glistened with tears.

"Yes or no?"

"Y-yes." She hiccuped.

He slipped the ring onto her finger and kissed her, and suddenly he was at peace for the first time in a long, long time.

"Tuf," she whispered against his lips, "people are clapping and staring at us."

He drew back and saw all eyes were on them. "Let's get out of here." But he couldn't move for the two munch-kins wrapped around his legs. He knelt down. "Stay with Grandpa. I love you."

"I love you, too," they called as Cheyenne and Tuf made their getaway to the roar of the crowd.

The announcer's voice followed them. "Congratulations to Tuf and his special lady."

"Tuf Hart is our bareback-riding champion. This cowboy marine has had a big night."

TUF PULLED CHEYENNE into a corner away from the bathrooms and people milling in and out of the stadium.

"You came. You came," he said, stroking her hair and kissing her briefly.

"I didn't want to," she admitted. "I fully intended not to. I was hurt and 'I'm sorry' just didn't cut it, but in the elevator I couldn't stop crying and realized that no matter how much you hurt me I still loved you. The next thing I knew, Angie and I were in a cab coming here." She sighed and leaned her head against his chest. "We still have the same problem, Tuf. This hasn't solved anything."

He lifted her chin from his chest. "Everything's changed. I now know I can't handle the nightmares alone. I need you. I need your love and support."

"Oh, Tuf…"

"And there's more. When I snuck back into the cowboy-ready area after seeing you, Ace was livid and said something like I wasn't a kid anymore. Suddenly the steel curtain across my brain lifted and I could see what happened on the top of that hill in Afghanistan. The scene that was too horrible to recall."

"What was it?"

He cupped her face so he could look into her green eyes. "When we got to the top, six insurgents were coming out of a cave with high-powered weapons. We took them out, as ordered. Only after we shot them did we realize they were just boys. Maybe fourteen, fifteen years old. We killed kids."

"Oh, Tuf." She wrapped her arms around his neck and held him. "It was either you or them and it was war."

"I know, but I have such a hard time with that—so hard that I blocked it from my mind for over two years. It has controlled my life, my thoughts and my dreams, but not anymore. I'm ready to live again, to love and be happy with you and the girls. I'm not saying the nightmares are over. They will probably always be a part of me, but I give you my word as a marine, as a cowboy, I will never shut you out again. And you know if I'm known for anything, it's keeping my word. We'll work through it together."

She kissed the side of his face. "That's all I ever wanted." She drew back and looked at the ring on her finger. "I love the Yogo sapphire. It's gorgeous. I've never seen one quite this color. Look how it catches the light."

"I told the jeweler I wanted it as close to green as possible to match your eyes."

"It's perfect." She raised her eyes to his. "I love you."

He gathered her into his arms again and held her. "I love you, too, and that's never going to change."

"Congratulations, cowboy. I'm so proud of you," she whispered into his neck. "Don't you have to go back to the rodeo?"

"Probably." He stepped back and held out his arms. "Look at me. I'm happy. I'm free."

She burrowed against him. "Yes, you are. I am, too."

He reached for her hand. "Later, we'll get reacquainted."

She laughed softly and his heart soared. Amid all the pain, he truly had found happiness. Arm in arm, they made their way back into the stadium so Tuf could be awarded his gold buckle. But he'd already won what he'd really wanted.

Cheyenne.

EPILOGUE

Christmas morning

"ARE THEY AWAKE?" Sammie asked.

"I don't know," Sadie replied. "I can't see. It's dark."

"Mommy said not to get up early. We're gonna get in trouble."

"Nobody gets in trouble on Christmas."

Tuf ran his hand across his wife's bare stomach. "The munchkins are awake."

"I hear them," Cheyenne replied, kissing his shoulder. "I guess we better get up."

"Yep." He reached for his robe.

The early moonlight spilled through the window, and Tuf glanced around his horseshoe bedroom. Never in a million years did he ever think he'd have Cheyenne Wright in his bed, much less make love to her until after midnight. It seemed surreal at times, but wondrous and uplifting, too.

So much had happened since Vegas. They were married that last night of the rodeo in a small chapel surrounded by the whole family.

Once the ceremony was over, Sadie had asked the minister, "Are they married?"

The man looked a little confused, but answered, "Yes."

"Is Tuf our daddy now?" Sadie had quizzed Cheyenne.

"Yes, baby." They did the twin-talk whispering thing, and from that moment on they called him Daddy. It sounded right and it felt right. In the New Year, he planned to hire a lawyer to adopt them. He and Cheyenne had talked about it. They would keep Sundell as their middle names.

When they'd returned from Vegas, they'd stayed at the Wright house, but it was crowded. There was no place for his clothes in Cheyenne's jewelry-supply-cluttered room. He slept there and ate there but showered and changed at his mom's until Cheyenne could make room. He even looked at mobile homes to solve the problem, then his mother had stepped in. She wanted them to move into the house. She said they could have the upstairs because she never went up there unless she was forced to.

Tuf wasn't sure how the family would feel about that, so he called a family meeting. Ace said he and Flynn were happy at the McKinley place and he had no problem with the arrangement. Neither did Colt and Leah, who had house plans already drawn up and were starting construction soon. Beau had plans to fix up the foreman's house for him and Sierra, and Duke and Angie had their own place. That left Dinah. She surprised them by saying she had no desire to live in her childhood home. She and Austin wanted to build a home one day either on the Wright property or at Thunder Ranch. Because of his mother's heart condition, they all felt better that someone would be in the house with Sarah. No one had enough nerve to tell her that, though.

So he, Cheyenne and the girls had moved in for now,

but Tuf laid down some rules. His mother was not to be their maid. She would not cook for them, clean or pick up after them. So far it was working out.

They had left the girls' furniture at Buddy's for when they visited. Cheyenne wanted the twins to have separate rooms, but so far that wasn't working. They slept in Dinah's old room. Cheyenne planned to do some redecorating after the first of the year, but now they intended to enjoy the holiday with the family.

He flipped on the light and yanked the door wider. "What are you two doing?"

The girls jumped back, their green eyes wide. "You scared us, Daddy," Sammie said, and they flew into his arms. "It's Christmas. It's Christmas!"

Cheyenne joined them in her green robe, yawning with a video camera in her hand. "What time is it?"

"Five."

"Let's go, Mommy. We have to see if Santa's been here." The girls darted down the stairs.

"Wait a minute," Cheyenne called. "We don't want to wake Grandma Sarah."

They crept down the stairs through the foyer and started toward the great room when his mom and Buddy appeared from the kitchen.

"Grandma Sarah's awake," Sadie shouted. "And Grandpa's here, too."

"I wouldn't miss my girls' Christmas." Buddy hugged his granddaughters.

Tuf turned on the light, and the girls' mouths formed big O's at the brightly colored packages under the ten-foot spruce tree. Scents of pine, vanilla and cinnamon filled the room. A roaring fire in the fireplace enclosed them in cozy warmth. Snow silently fell outside the French doors.

They sat on the sofa and watched as the girls tore into their gifts. Cheyenne filmed away, and they laughed at the girls' excitement.

Tuf scooted closer to his wife. "Happy?"

"Yes."

He brushed her hair from her face. "I love you."

She nuzzled into him, resting her head on his shoulder. "Mmm. I've never been this happy. Ever."

"Me, neither." Whatever they had to face down the road, he knew they could handle it. Cheyenne now went with him to see the counselor so she could learn more about helping him. He didn't have a problem with that. Admitting he needed help was his first step in healing. He hadn't had any more nightmares, but if he did, he was prepared to handle that, too—with Cheyenne. He wasn't afraid to go to sleep, either. Finally, he had found his peace with the woman of his dreams.

It wasn't long before the family started arriving. Joshua and Jordan arrived first, quickly followed by Dinah, Austin and Bre. The others slowly trickled in. Colt and Leah were last because they had to pick up Evan. Sarah and Cheyenne had made enough food to feed an army, and everyone thoroughly enjoyed it. They did the white-elephant gift exchange, which caused a lot of laughter and family rivalry. The kids exchanged gifts, and the adults sat back and enjoyed Sarah's spicy cider.

After they sang Christmas carols, Sarah got to her feet. "I don't want to give a long speech, but I have to say how proud I am of all of you. We accomplished an awful lot this year, not because of one person, but because we worked together as a team, as a family. There were times we all wanted to kill that black stallion, but he came through for us. We have the PRCA horse of the year and NFR horse of the year. Midnight's breeder fee has gone up. Not only that, Bushwhacker placed second at the NFR. Another great accomplishment. Our breeder program continues to improve with great stock that will become champions, especially Midnight Heir. Our program is now recognized by everyone in the country. The Harts of the rodeo are in business and out of debt." She reached for some papers on the coffee table. "Thanks to everyone's effort, our note is now paid in full."

"Hot damn," Colt said. "A happy ending."

"It's not an ending, son," his mother told him. "As Tuf once said, it's the beginning. We're almost booked solid for next year, and we have a long list of owners wanting to breed their mares to Midnight."

"It's all good news, Mom," Ace said.

"And the lease on the three thousand acres is up for renewal next year. I've decided to take our land back and to continue to build our bucking program. We will have plenty of room to do that." She turned and tossed the papers into the fireplace. Everyone clapped.

"I just want to say one more thing. I'm so happy my youngest is home safe. For eight years I went to bed every night wondering if I'd ever see my son again." Her voice cracked.

No, Mom. Don't do this.

He got to his feet but she waved him back. "Of all the accomplishments this year, Tuf's happiness has been at the forefront of my mind. I'm so grateful he and Cheyenne have found each other. My heart is full. I love you all." She reached for her glass on the coffee table. "Let's make a toast."

Duke and Beau got to their feet. "I..." they said together and then stopped when they realized the other was speaking.

"Go ahead," Duke said.

"No. You go ahead," Beau replied.

"We'll have to flip a coin." Colt intervened, digging in his pocket. "Man, this is reminiscent of our childhood. You two doing everything at the same time." He flipped a quarter in the air. "Call it."

"Heads," Duke said before Beau could.

Colt looked at the coin on the floor. "Heads it is. Duke, what do you have to say?"

"Can I tell, Daddy?" Luke asked.

"Sure, son." Angie curved into Duke's side, and Duke had a hand on Luke's shoulder.

"I'm gonna get a little baby brother or sister," Luke said, his little chest puffed out.

Everyone jumped up in joy.

"Wait a minute," Beau said. "I didn't get my chance."

Everyone sat down again.

"Sierra and I are expecting, too."

"You're kidding." Colt started laughing loudly. "You guys synchronize everything."

"Behave," Leah said.

"Wait. Wait. Duke, when's the baby due?" Colt asked.

"August tenth."

"Beau?"

"August eighth."

"This is hilarious." Leah gave Colt a narrow-eyed glance and he added quickly, "But great."

Everyone hugged and added their congratulations to the two couples.

"Jordan, we're going to have two more grandbabies in August," Uncle Josh declared, beaming from ear to ear.

"Yes, and Sierra didn't mention a word."

Sierra hugged her aunt. "We wanted to surprise you."

"You certainly did that."

"What a wonderful Christmas," his mom said. "Any more exciting news?" She glanced around the room.

"Don't look at us, Mom," Colt said. "We have four kids, and one of them has four legs."

"You're hopeless." Leah kissed Colt's cheek.

"Same goes for us." Ace put his arm around Flynn. "We have one and that's enough for now."

Dinah sat in Austin's lap. "Our baby is finally sleeping through the night, so don't even think of looking our way."

"And we just got married." Tuf made that clear, but he couldn't imagine anything making him happier than having a child with Cheyenne.

"Get your glasses," his mom said. "I want to make another toast."

When everyone had a glass, Sarah raised hers. "To wise decisions, Midnight and the rodeo. May the Harts and the Adamses continue to prosper and grow—as a family in Roundup, Montana."

Tuf wrapped his arm around Cheyenne and whispered, "Merry Christmas."

"Merry Christmas."

At the love in her eyes, he knew he had what he'd been fighting for—freedom to live again with a girl he'd loved since he was a boy.

He was finally home.

* * * * *

THE WORLD IS BETTER WITH
WITH
Romance

Harlequin has everything from contemporary, passionate and heartwarming to suspenseful and inspirational stories.

Whatever your mood,
we have a romance just for you!

Connect with us to find your next great read,
special offers and more.

Available May 19, 2015

#1569 TO HONOR AND TO PROTECT
The Specialists: Heroes Next Door
by Debra Webb & Regan Black
Addison Collins will do anything to protect her son. But can she protect her heart from former Army special forces operative Andrew Bryant, the man who left her at the altar—and the only one she can trust to safeguard their son?

#1570 NAVY SEAL NEWLYWED
Covert Cowboys, Inc. • by Elle James
Posing as newlyweds, Navy SEAL "Rip" Cord Schafer and Covert Cowboy operative Tracie Kosart work together to catch the traitors supplying guns to terrorists. But when Tracie's cover is blown, can Rip save his "wife"?

#1571 CORNERED
Corcoran Team: Bulletproof Bachelors
by HelenKay Dimon
Former Navy pilot Cameron Roth has no plans to settle down. When drug runners set their sights on Julia White, it is up to Cam to get them both out alive...

#1572 THE GUARDIAN
The Ranger Brigade • by Cindi Myers
Veteran Abby Stewart has no memory of Rangers lieutenant Michael Dance, who saved her life in Afghanistan. But when she stumbles into his investigation, can he save her from the smugglers stalking them?

#1573 UNTRACEABLE
Omega Sector • by Janie Crouch
After a brutal attack leaves her traumatized, a powerful crime boss forces Omega Sector agent Juliet Branson undercover again. Now, Evan Karcz must neutralize the terrorist threat and use his cover as Juliet's husband to rehabilitate her.

#1574 SECURITY BREACH
Bayou Bonne Chance • by Mallory Kane
Undercover Homeland Security agent Tristan DuChaud faked his death to protect his pregnant wife, Sandy, from terrorists. But when her life is threatened, Tristan is forced to tell her the truth—or risk both their deaths becoming reality...

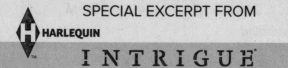

SPECIAL EXCERPT FROM

HARLEQUIN

INTRIGUE

Navy SEAL "Rip" Cord Schafer's mission is not a one-man operation, but never in his wildest dreams did he imagine teaming up with a woman: Covert Cowboy operative Tracie Kosart.

Read on for a sneak peek of
NAVY SEAL NEWLYWED,
the newest installment from Elle James's
COVERT COWBOYS, INC.

"How do I know you really work for Hank?"

"You don't. But has anyone else shown up and told you he's your contact?" She raised her eyebrows, the saucy expression doing funny things to his insides. "So, do you trust me, or not?"

His lips curled upward on the ends. "I'll go with not."

"Oh, come on, sweetheart." She batted her pretty green eyes and gave him a sexy smile. "What's not to trust?"

His gaze scraped over her form. "I expected a cowboy, not a…"

"Cow*girl?*" Her smile sank and she slipped into the driver's seat. Her lips firmed into a straight line. "Are you coming or not? If you're dead set on a cowboy, I'll contact Hank and tell him to send a male replacement. But then he'd have to come up with another plan."

"I'm interested in how you and Hank plan to help. Frankly, I'd rather my SEAL team had my six."

"Yeah, but you're deceased. Using your SEAL team

HIEXP0515

would only alert your assassin that you aren't as dead as the navy claims you are. How long do you think you'll last once that bit of news leaks out?"

His lips pressed together. "I'd survive."

"By going undercover? Then you still won't have the backing of your team, and we're back to the original plan." She grinned. "Me."

Rip sighed. "Fine. I want to head back to Honduras and trace the weapons back to where they're coming from. What's Hank's plan?"

"For me to work with you." She pulled a large envelope from between her seat and the console and handed it across to him. "Everything we need is in that packet."

Rip riffled through the contents of the packet, glancing at a passport with his picture on it as well as a name he'd never seen. "Chuck Gideon?"

"Better get used to it."

"Speaking of names…we've already kissed and you haven't told me who you are." Rip glanced her way briefly. "Is it a secret? Do you have a shady past or are you related to someone important?"

"For this mission, I'm related to someone important." She twisted her lips and sent a crooked grin his way. "You. For the purpose of this operation, you can call me Phyllis. Phyllis Gideon. I'll be your wife."

Don't miss
NAVY SEAL NEWLYWED
available June 2015 wherever
Harlequin Intrigue® books and ebooks are sold.

www.Harlequin.com

COMING NEXT MONTH FROM

H HARLEQUIN®

™

American Romance®

Available June 2, 2015

#1549 LONE STAR DADDY
McCabe Multiples
by Cathy Gillen Thacker

Rose McCabe wants to use Clint McCulloch's newly acquired ranch for blackberry farming, but the sexy cowboy wants it for pastureland for his herd. Can the two come to a temporary agreement...that eventually leads to love?

#1550 THE SEAL'S MIRACLE BABY
Cowboy SEALs
by Laura Marie Altom

Navy SEAL Grady Matthews and Jessie Long—the woman who broke his heart—are thrown together after a twister devastates their hometown. Can a baby girl found in the wreckage help them forget their painful past?

#1551 A COWBOY'S REDEMPTION
Cowboys of the Rio Grande
by Marin Thomas

Cruz Rivera is just looking to get his life and rodeo career back on track. But when he meets pretty widow and single mom Sara Mendez, he's tempted to change his plans...

#1552 THE SURGEON AND THE COWGIRL
by Heidi Hormel

Pediatric surgeon Payson MacCormack knows his way around a corral, so certifying a riding therapy program should be easy. But the complicated past he shares with rodeo-riding director Jessie makes that easier said than done.

**YOU CAN FIND MORE INFORMATION ON UPCOMING HARLEQUIN® TITLES,
FREE EXCERPTS AND MORE AT WWW.HARLEQUIN.COM.**

HARCNM0515

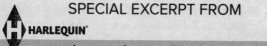
"You can ignore me as long as you want. I am not going
away." Rose McCabe followed Clint McCulloch around the
big farm tractor.

Wrench in one hand, a grimy cloth in another, the rodeo
cowboy turned rancher paused to give her a hostile glare.
"Suit yourself," he muttered beneath his breath. Then went
right back to working on the engine that had clearly seen
better days.

Aware she was taking a tiger by the tail, Rose stomped
closer. "Sooner or later you're going to have to hear me out."

"Actually, I won't." Sweat glistened on the suntanned
skin of his broad shoulders and muscular back, dripped
down the strip of dark hair that covered his chest, and
arrowed down into the fly of his faded jeans.

Still ignoring her, he moved around the wheel to turn the
key in the ignition.

It clicked. But did not catch.

He strode back to the engine once more, giving Rose
a good view of his ruggedly handsome face and the thick

chestnut hair that fell onto his brow and curled damply against the nape of his neck. At six foot four, there was no doubt Clint was every bit as much as stubborn—and breathtakingly masculine—as he had been when they were growing up.

"The point is—" he said "—I'm not interested in being a berry farmer. I'm a rancher. I want to restore the Double Creek Ranch to the way it was when my dad was alive. Run cattle and breed and train cutting horses here." He pointed to the blackberry patch up for debate. "And those thorn- and weed-infested bushes are sitting on the most fertile land on the entire ranch."

Rose's expression turned pleading. "Just let me help you out."

"No." He refused to be swayed by a sweet-talking woman, no matter how persuasive and beguiling. He had gone down that road once before, with a heartbreaking result.

A silence fell and Rose blinked. "No?" she repeated, as if she were sure she had heard wrong.

"No," he reiterated flatly. His days of being seduced or pressured into anything were long over. Then he picked up his wrench. "And now, if you don't mind, I really need to get back to work…"

Don't miss LONE STAR DADDY
by Cathy Gillen Thacker,
available June 2015 wherever
Harlequin® American Romance®
books and ebooks are sold.

www.Harlequin.com